Reach to the Wounded Healer

Reach to the Wounded Healer

Ernest de l'Autin

www.ivyhousebooks.com

PUBLISHED BY IVY HOUSE PUBLISHING GROUP
5122 Bur Oak Circle, Raleigh, NC 27612
United States of America
919-782-0281
www.ivyhousebooks.com

ISBN: 1-57197-399-0
Library of Congress Control Number: 2003095719

Printed in the United States of America

To the memory of my father, Ernest, and my grandparents, Samson and Elida.

To the Men of Manresa and the Jesuit Fathers who serve us.

And to the children of South Africa . . . our present Holocaust.

A.M.D.G.

Acknowledgments

Lucky is the man who in spite of himself has loving family and friends.

In the words of Sir Isaac Newton, "If I have seen further than others, it is because I have stood on the shoulders of giants." I have had mammoth, gentle hands supporting me; faith capable of moving mountains reflected to me from others; kind words and reassuring touches from hearts as magnificent and large as any; and the blessing through grace to be able to serve. I would add that if this work proves of value, it is truly because of many men and women who loved me into excellence. And while I acknowledge that I am far less the man than I desire to be, I am a far better man than I would have been were it not for this.

There are so many "thank yous" to be given. Certainly in my limited space I am destined to miss someone. Yet, I beg your forbearance of my weakness.

To Andrei Dokukin and Oleana for their patience and support in working with the Russian and Ukrainian translations and culture.

To Jane Nuffer and Dea-Adele Arabie for assisiting me in completing the art work for the dust jacket.

To my editor and friend, author of *Drowning and Secret*, Roger Leslie, my humble thanks for the hours of coaching that guided me through many chasms of capability.

To my friend, Brian Moreland, author of *Shadows in the Mist*, what a great blessing to create with you, to write with you, to talk with you, and to laugh with you.

To Eric, Aaron, and Marc, your fraternal love lives through me.

To my fellow scholastic and friend, soon to be Dr. Christopher Benjamin Soileau, thank you for believing in me.

To my brother Mike de la Garza, successful businessman, for backing me, finding the resources when I could not, and never waiting for me to ask.

To my family, Debbie, Daniel, Tess, and Beau, for the long nights, weekends alone, calls during meals, endless rewrites, bad moods, and oh so much more, and

To those of you who read this book, thank you for tolerating so much of what I am not, for looking beyond the messenger into the message, and for your willingness to journey with me for a little while.

Perhaps, I am telling this story in an attempt to heal myself, to confront what I do not know, to create a path for myself with the idea that 'memory is the only way home.'

—*Terry Tempest Williams*

One

The plantation bell clanged. Judging by the shadow of the oak, it was only 4 P.M. But men ran from the fields towards the main house. My best friend, Andre, grabbed my arm. "We betta go, Paul."

"No. Let's finish the game. Where are Phillip and Jean?"

"Look back to'ards da ditch. They ran dat'a way." Andre and I raced through the tall, thick leaves of the sugarcane rows.

A hand slapped my back. "Tag." Before I could grab Jean, he galloped towards the only tree in the middle of the field, a big oak with branches that nearly touched the ground.

"Andre, get him. He's running to base." A tire swing hanging from a tugboat rope was the ideal place for base. If Jean got there before me, he would declare safety from the chase and win.

Andre burst through the sugarcane patch. "I se'em, Paul." Even though Andre was eight years old like me, he could outrun any boy on the plantation, probably any boy on the bayou. But, before he could get to Jean, he stopped. The bell rang again.

The tailgate of Tomas' pick-up rattled down the field road. A cloud of dust caught up with him just as he honked his horn. "Boys, y'all best get y'all behin's on home before y'all folks come after ya," he shouted through the open window of the cab.

"Yez, sir. Paul, we gotta go."

"I'm gonna come over after while. I've got some new baseball cards for you."

"Okay." Andre dashed toward a corner of the plantation called the Quarters. He lived there along with Jean and Phillip. It wasn't too bad because the main house where I lived wasn't that far away.

The plantation bell rang again. With my arms flailing, I charged towards the shell road leading to the back of the house. I froze. Six wagons pulled by tractors and filled with men zipped by me.

I chased the tractors. The bell clanged continuously. The overseer directed the wagons behind the main house.

Mim paced on the back porch. "Paul de la Moret, ya betta git ya'se'f here, naw! Didn't ya hear dat plantation bell ring?"

"Yes, ma'am. But—"

"Child, where have ya been? Look at ya. Yo head is soakin' wet." The screen door slammed shut behind us. Mim's broad shoulders and tall stature filled the threshold.

"I was playing in the fields with Andre, Jean, and Phillip."

"Did dey get demselves home?"

"Yes, ma'am."

"Good. Naw git ya'se'f upstairs and clean up." She guided me towards the main staircase in the center foyer. "Yo mamma an' daddy are gonna be home soon an' dey gonna be expectin' everyt'in' in order."

"Auntie Gladys!" Georgia rushed down the stairs. "I moved dat statue outta dat trunk. But, I need help wit'—"

Mim frowned at her. "Hush naw. We're gonna talk about dat later."

"What statue, Mim? Can I help?"

"Child, I already told ya ta git ya'se'f upstairs and git yo bat'."

"Yes, ma'am."

Pictures of all the generations that lived at Oak Grove lined the walls of the staircase. One of my favorites was Mother in her white-hooped Southern belle wedding gown. She and Father were cousins, promised to each other when they were children themselves. Mother said it was proper to marry family in the South. And I was given my father's first name, Paul.

"Mim?" I shouted from the top of the stairs. "How about my chores?"

"We don't have time for dat. Git ya bat' an' wash behin' dem ears and unda' ya neck."

"Yes, ma'am."

Everyone had jobs at Oak Grove. Most of the men worked in the fields. I was in charge of catching bullfrogs in Grandmother's lily pond and finding snakes in the chicken coup. With the "smell of boyhood play reeking from my body" as Mother put it, I had to wash the ring of dirt around my neck every night.

Today was different, though. School was dismissed at 1 P.M. because of a hurricane watch along all the Eastern Louisiana coastal parishes. It didn't look like a hurricane was coming. When Hilda came, it rained all day. But today, the skies were blue with just a cool breeze blowing from the north.

Even so, I looked out of the French doors of my bedroom. Men rushed about, picking up the lawn furniture and all the ferns and hanging baskets from the porches.

"Paul . . . Paul." Mother's voice rang through the hallway over banging hammers. "Suga'?" She knocked and then opened my door. "I need you to clean up and get your pillows, a couple of blankets, and a few toys to entertain yourself."

"Is a storm coming?"

"Well, sweetie, we're not quite sure, but the weathermen are saying it may not turn."

"What's Grandfather saying?"

"Not much, at least not yet." Mother's voice softened. Her eyes glazed over like she was in deep thought.

"Mother?" I touched her hand. "Is Father coming home?"

She snapped out of her trance. "He's picking up your grandmother at the airport and they should be here in a few hours. Get your bath and then get your dirty clothes in the laundry chute. We've got a lot of work to do to get ready." Even though Mother hurried to my door, there was a saunter to her walk. Father always said watching her was like seeing a swan floating across a pond.

My door rattled shut. Mother's high-heeled shoes clacked on the wooden boards as she rushed off. Preparing for a hurricane kept folks pretty busy, even though Audrey, Hilda, and even some storms without names had called upon Oak Grove over the years. Maybe Betsy was going to be the next one.

The steam lifted from the tub. Hammers pounded the cypress planks just outside my room. I bathed as fast as I could, dressing still half wet. With my clean clothes sticking to my body, I dashed to see what was happening.

Shutters squeaked shut. Workers latched them closed and then nailed boards across the windows above the French doors. My room darkened.

"Paul," Mim charged into the bathroom.

"Mim, I'm naked.!"

"Child, I've seen ya since ya were born. You my third generation in dis house so hush." She eyed me. "Naw, fill the tub wit' some wata'."

"Yes, ma'am."

Water was real important when storms came. With power lines snapped and broken, fresh water could not be pumped to the house. Water for washing, drinking, and cooking had to be gathered in bathtubs, buckets, jugs—almost any container available.

The water drizzled from the faucet. I guess lots of folks along the bayou were storing water. As the bathtub filled, I gathered my baseball card collection and my favorite marbles and stored them in a cigar box Grandfather had given me. It still smelled like his tobacco.

I ran downstairs to the kitchen. Grandfather chewed on an unlit cigar butt. "Renee, I think we should prepare for the worst." Without interrupting Grandfather's conversation, Mother pointed me towards a group of jugs that needed filling. "I was outside just a few minutes ago, and I don't like the way the birds are flying. I checked the cattle and they're mighty restless, too. I think we're in for a rough night."

"Okay, Daddy. I've got the house and grounds staff picking up and boarding." Mother twiddled her handkerchief. "Have you spoken to the overseer?"

"I just left him. They're preparing the fields and barns."

As I filled the jugs, a southwesterly wind rocked the trees beyond the kitchen window. Even so, sunshine still brightened the oak grove.

A candy wrapper crinkled. Grandfather propped his cigar butt in an ashtray and then popped a fireball jawbreaker into his mouth. "Paul, how's your job coming?" He offered a piece of candy to me, then cracked a smile. His baby blue eyes always widened and his rosey cheeks plushed when he smiled.

"Fine, Grandfather."

"You're a big help. By the way, did you have fun in the fields this—"

"Da weather's comin' on," Mim called out. Everyone gathered around the kitchen television set. Nash Roberts' live broadcast suspended the regular programming. He predicted storms every time they came into the Gulf. You could find pictures of Nash fishing on Lake Bouef in many restaurants and filling stations along the bayou.

"Folks, we've got ourselves a serious situation. Earlier forecasts suggested that a cold front was coming from the north to steer this storm away from us. We're not seeing any evidence of this and I think we're in for it by nightfall.

"The National Weather Service has moved hurricane warnings to the west. They now extend from Pascagoula, Mississippi to Vermillion Bay,

Louisiana. They're also telling us that the storm is still growing in intensity and has slowed down just a bit. It's time to evacuate from low lying areas and to make your final preparations."

Stress lines wrinkled across Grandfather's face. "Well, that does it. Let's get the preparations completed and have everyone move to the main house. Gladys—"

"I'm already on top of it." Mim started organizing food.

"Renee, I could use Paul's help getting everyone out of the Quarters."

"Just be safe."

He winked at Mother with his left eye and then at me with his right. I hugged Mother, and then quickly followed Grandfather through the kitchen and onto the back porch. He always parked his International pick-up just behind the kitchen near the porte cochere. Its big round hood and shiny sky blue paint job made it stand out against the oaks. Andre and I usually flipped a coin to see who would get to sit by the door. Today I got the prized seat.

"Paul, you look worried." His hand swallowed my shoulder. "Don't you fret. Oak Grove is a strong house. We'll be just fine." The gears ground as he let up the clutch.

A dust cloud floated in the air behind us as we bounced down the shell road. Grounds workers and field hands scurried about. The farm equipment, usually outside of the barns, was locked away. The horses were boarded, except for the few being used to round up the milk cows.

"When we get to the Quarters, I want you to tell folks to pack up and get to the main house just as quick as they can. You think you can help me do that?"

"Yes, sir. I sure can." We drove past the orchards. "Why are they picking all the pears?"

"We wouldn't want them to become projectiles if the storm comes, would we?"

"No, sir."

6

Lines of barren pear trees yielded to several hundred bright green citrus trees. Two rows of weatherboard houses emerged on each side of the road. Grandfather pulled into the grass behind a string of pick-ups.

"Go tell everybody over on the right side of the road. I'm going to handle the left. Make sure you tell them to move to the main house now."

"Yes, sir." I slammed the truck door, and then raced from door to door. With windows to their homes already boarded, many of our workers waited with their meager belongings already bundled in sheets and blankets, or whatever they could find. An exodus followed behind me, with many of the older and younger family members crowding into waiting trucks.

Finally I got to Andre's house. His family had worked for ours for five generations—they were more like family than employees. That's just how it was at Oak Grove.

"Paul, I'll meet you at Andre's." Grandfather called from the left side of the road.

"Yes, sir." I ran to his porch. "Andre, Andre." The rocking chair that usually sat in front of the single window was missing, making the weatherboard look all the grayer.

The screen door squealed open. Andre smiled from ear to ear. "Hey, Paul." His overalls were unbuttoned and flapped over on one side.

"You get to stay with me tonight."

"Evenin', Mista Sam." My faced dropped as Andre's father, T'Bram, walked out from behind him. I wasn't sure if he liked me, or the fact that Andre and I were best friends.

Grandfather tipped his hat. "Good evening, T'Bram. There's a storm coming and we're moving everyone to the main house."

"Ain't no need fo' dat. We gonna be fine rit' hea'."

"Now, T'Bram, this is no time to be stubborn. Nash doesn't think the storm's going to turn and it's strengthening as we speak."

"Mista' Sam, I 'preciate ya comin' out hea', bu' me an' da boy gonna be fine."

7

"Look, you old mule, if you want to stay out here and risk your life, that's one thing, but, why don't you at least let me take the boy—" A clap of thunder shook the ground. It seemed to come from nowhere. We turned to darkened Southern skies. "I don't have time to argue with you. Are you going to let me take the boy or not?"

T'Bram and Grandfather stared at each other like two prize bulls in a pen, even though the skies stirred into an eerie, turbulent gray. Even though grandfather was a foot taller, T'Bram stood his ground like a banty rooster. For a petite man, T'Bram was strong as an ox. Andre was already taller than him, and very strong.

"Boy, git yo t'ings an' go on wit' Mista Sam."

Andre and I dashed into the house. We didn't dare waste a minute. Neither of us wanted to give T'Bram a chance to change his mind.

"I've got plenty of clothes, Andre. Just get your toothbrush and we can get on."

"Don't wanna forget 'dese. He placed another set of overalls and a shirt with the baseball cards I gave him into an old carpetbag. Andre and his dad didn't have much. No matter what Grandfather offered them, T-Bram would never take it.

The screen door slammed shut behind us. Grandfather stood by the truck still trying to convince T'Bram. "I'm going to ask you one more time to come with us to the main house."

"Boy," T'Bram growled like an old dog. "Ya min' Mista Sam."

"Yes, sir, Pa."

With all three of us scrunched into the front seat, Grandfather started the engine. He paused only for a few moments so that several folks from the Quarters could jump into the back. Lightening flashed and thunder roared. The wind whipped, shaking the cab. Huge raindrops splattered against the windshield. I thought they were going to break it.

The truck bounced through water-filled potholes dotting the shell road along already flooded fields. We arrived at the main house to see it stripped and boarded. It was like the War of Northern Aggression when the "damn Yankees invaded and took everything that wasn't rooted into the ground or nailed to a structure." Mother always said Oak Grove was a "beautiful lady, white with formality, her green shutters completing her wide porches and long white columns." Now she looked like just a house, battened down to protect her from another invader.

"Boys, I'll get you under the porte cochere." Just as Grandfather drove under the roof, the rain and wind stopped. "Well, that squall's over."

Thunder rumbled to the south. Workers filed from the back of the truck into the main house. But, everything else grew quiet. Birds no longer sang. None were flying. Locusts, so common to late summer afternoons, were silent. Only the Spanish moss drooped like any other lazy late summer day.

"Paul, you and Andre get into the house. The weather could come up anytime. And let your mother know you're back."

"Yes, sir." Andre and I entered the kitchen to food spread everywhere. Bread, jarred vegetables and fruits, and boxes of crackers filled the counters. Water jugs littered the floor.

"Boys, y'all best git out da way. Dere's lots a work ta be done in dis ki'chen."

"Yes, ma'am. Mim, where's Mother?"

"She's upstairs talkin' ta yo daddy."

I elbowed Andre. "Race you." We dashed out of the kitchen into the center hallway, but halted to blankets and pillows sprawled across the floor. Upright mattresses lined the walls. As I tiptoed through the sea of folks, I imagined that when our Southern boys fought the "damn Yankees" it looked just the same.

I tapped Andre's back. "Tag!" Our feet thundered against the wooden rungs of the main staircase. Even with a head start, Andre beat me. "Why don't you go on to my room while I say hello to Father. I've got some new baseball cards on my desk for you."

Andre turned to the right towards my bedroom while I approached the door to the upstairs master suite. I could hear Mother and Father talking, but couldn't make out what they were saying. Mother said to listen in on folks was rude, and a Southern gentleman was never that way. I knocked on the door and waited for an invitation to enter.

"Who is it?"

"It's me, Mother."

She opened the door. Father stopped unpacking his luggage. "Come here, pal." I wrapped my arms around him. He swung me around. Since returning from Vietnam, he spent most of his time in Washington. "He's grown ten inches." He squeezed my muscles. "I tell you what, you're growing into a fine young man. I don't know what makes you more handsome, those dark brownish-green eyes or that dark-brown hair."

"Mother, Andre is here, but his daddy wouldn't come."

"Hand me my brush on the counter, sweetie." She removed the silver hair clips Father gave her when they were first married. Her dark hair looked so soft when she wore it down. "Don't you worry, son. I 'm going to send your—"

Father lifted her hair, and then kissed her on the back of the neck. "T'Bram's being stubborn again, Renee?" He towered over her by at least a foot.

"I guess so. But, at least the boy is safe."

"I'll go after him." He grabbed his hat and started towards the bedroom door.

"Paul, be quick. I don't have a good feeling about this storm."

Father returned to kiss her on the cheek and then swatted her behind.

"Paul, the boy!" She eyed him even though a devilish grin swiped across her face.

"He's no boy. He's a man!" Father shook his head once in affirmation as he walked to the door. It rattled as it shut closed. Father's broad chest and narrow waist reflected years of military training. His hands were so big, he could almost wrap them around my whole body.

"Paul," Mother brushed her hair once again, "you and Andre can stay in your room. But if the weather gets bad, I want you downstairs with everyone else. Understand me?"

"Yes, ma'am. May I be excused?"

"Sure, sweetie."

I walked into my room finding Andre sitting on the corner of my bed. "Found the cards?"

He thumbed through the stack. "Sho' did. Are dese all fo me?"

"Sure are. By the way, my father's going after your dad. Come on. Let's find my binoculars." We tore into boxes of toys sorted in my closet.

Andre lifted two sets. "Got dem."

"Great. Let's go. We've got to find a place on the porch to watch the weather."

"We bes' clean up dis closet befo' Mim Gladys fuss."

"I'll do it later. Race you down."

Our mission was clear. As centurions stationed at our posts, we would be the first to see the next wave of weather. That way we could issue the warning.

We took post on the upper southern balcony. "Hey, Andre. Stand over there and give me our whistle if you see anything coming." Tomas, a part-Choctaw field hand, had taught us to whistle. He told us that his grandparents used bird whistles to warn each other of danger.

"Da sun comin' out." Andre pointed to a cloud breaking open to blue skies.

"Grandfather says that's how storms work. You get a little rain and wind and then it clears up. Then you get some more until it gets real bad."

We stood behind opposing columns. I watched the southeastern sky while Andre looked to the southwest. Mother and Father would be so proud of us for our warning.

"Andre, do you think your dad would let you come to New York with Father and me to see the Yankees play?"

"I don't know, Paul. Pa don't like me to travel away from him too much."

"Maybe I can get Grandfather to talk him into it."

"No kiddin'? You'd do that fo' me?"

"You're my best friend. It's not the same when you're not with me."

"I know what ya mean. Sometimes I can't sleep at night, and I wanna sneak on over to talk to ya, but I don't wanna make ma pa fuss."

"I could ask you over more often."

"I don't know, Paul. I wanna come over, but I worry about pa being all alone an' somethin' happenin' to him when I'm not around."

A boom, and then another, jolted the porch. Andre jumped. "What's dat?"

"I don't know. Sounded like an explosion."

A strong wind blasted through the trees. Lightning streaked across the blackened skies. Another clap of thunder, followed by another, rattled the hinges of the storm shutters. Raindrops splattered against the columns and the ground. I just knew our mission was about to be complete. But a wind burst nearly pushed us off the porch.

"Paul and Andre?" Mother called out in a high-pitched "you're in trouble" voice.

"Up here, Mother. On the front balcony."

Blowing rain soaked Andre and I to the bone. Mother peeked her head out from the lower porch. "Young man, you and Andre get down here and in this house. The last thing I need is for you to be sick or for lightning to strike you."

The gusting wind pushed us. We grabbed the rails to the outer staircase.

Andre shielded his head with his hands. "Ough! Dem rain drops sting."

Mother crossed her arms and patted her foot. "You're both soaked. Get upstairs this very minute and dry off. I don't want either of you outside again. Do you understand?"

"Yes, ma'am."

"Miz Renee, did Mista Paul git ma daddy?"

Mim wrapped Mother in a dry towel, then Andre, and then me. "Dat ole fool should have known betta wit' such a evil wind blowin'. Come on, naw. Let's git inside." Mim led us to the base of the foyer staircase. "Boys, git ya'se'f upstairs an' dry off. I'm gonna check on y'all in a minute."

"Yes, ma'am."

Stripping out of our wet clothes at the foot of my bed, we quickly dried off. As we dressed, the house shook to the crack of a lightning strike followed immediately by thunder. The lights flickered. The wind whistled and howled. A loud pop followed a small explosion. The room went dark.

I tried to pull the plug out of a peephole in a storm shutter covering my doors, but it was wedged in there too tightly. I tried another.

"Paul and Andre," Mim shouted. Her tone was identical to Mother's at times. "Git some pillas and blankets and git ya'se'f down here naw."

With pillow and blankets in hand, we headed into the upstairs hallway. Shadows from downstairs danced on the darkened walls. The hallway was eerie from the quiet of the absence of televisions and radios. Only the whispers of folks competed with the howling wind.

We descended the staircase. Families gathered around mattresses propped against the walls. Hurricane lanterns with an orange glow brightened the room. Black smoke smelling of kerosene and burning candle wax wafted into the air.

The wind whistled through openings in the shuttered French doors and windows. Grandfather said this prevented the house from exploding, something to do with the pressure. The heavy, damp air chilled me, even though I felt sticky and clammy. With so many people bunched together, the room smelled stale.

"Paul, you and Andre get over here with me right now." Mother pulled us under the staircase of the main foyer.

"Miz Renee, di' ma daddy make it ova?"

"Oh, sweetie, he wouldn't come."

The candles flickered. Andre's charcoal eyes saddened as he crawled up near Mother. Father stood by us. People were holding on to each other. Some folded their hands, grasping to rosary beads.

"Mother, where's Grandmother and Grandfather?"

"In the chapel praying."

It was hard to see through all the men standing in the center hallway. Finally, one of them moved. The door to the small chapel across from the kitchen was closed. Grandmother was surely kneeling in prayer and lighting candles in offering.

The hallway clock chimed eight times. Murmurs and prayers of those gathered around us competed with the snarl of a wind sounding like a hungry beast.

With the stroke of 9 P.M. and then 10 P.M., the wind pushed the walls of Oak Grove. Thuds and bangs sounded against the cypress planks outdoors. Mother grabbed a bottle housing Holy Water. She walked to a corner of the house and began to pray, "St. Michael the Archangel, defend us in battle, be our protection against the wickedness and snares of the devil; restrain him O God, we humbly pray; and do thou, O prince of heavenly host, by the power of God, cast into hell Satan and all evil spirits who roam about the world seeking the ruin of souls. Amen."

"Amen." The word rang through the rooms and hallways of Oak Grove. Goose flesh ran up my spine and tingled all over my body. Four times she did this, once in each of the corners, each time was followed by a chorus of "Amens."

The wind eased. The thuds and bangs on the outside walls slowed. Maybe it was over. But another thunderclap rocked the house followed by another and then another. It sounded like cannon fire. Wind pelted rain against the walls with ever increasing intensity. Wood cracked. A thud on the eastern porch shook the floors of the house.

Women started screaming. "Wha's dat! Jesus save us! He'p us, Laud!"

Father jumped up. "Renee, stay here. I'll check." Moving to one of the French doors, he opened a peek hole. He stared for a while. He went to several other shutters to see what had happened. "It's all right every-one. It's just a branch that fell on the porch. Everything's okay."

Sighs filled the room. Shoulders once pinched high lowered in relief. Those who had grabbed onto one another relaxed their grip.

"Renee, turn on the radio so we can get an update." With no power, maybe now for days, anything with a battery was used sparingly. Father strained to hear the AM station. "Hurricane Betsy . . . landfall with one hundred and twenty-five mile an hour . . . eye expected to reach central Lafourche Parish by . . ." Static replaced the broadcast. Father dialed the radio to a faint Coast Guard signal. We were on our own—cut off from the world. Stress lines and wide eyes replaced hopeful smiles.

The winds grew more deafening. My ears popped. Beyond the shutters came loud booms. Snapping and crashing filled the air.

"Oh ma God, da walls. Dey bucklin'!"

"It be soundin' like a train!"

"Everybody, pull da mattresses ova ya. Do it naw!"

Screams filled the house. The few men standing hit the floor. Father pushed the mattress over us. It pounced on top of me, taking my breath away. I wiggled to the edge to see what was happening.

"Cover your heads!"

The wind growled like a monster eating its way through the creaking walls of Oak Grove. It sounded like spears were pelting the wooden slats. Glass shattered. The wind blasted through the house, flinging pictures onto the floor. I could feel the gusts sucking my skin off of me.

"Oh ma God, we's gonna die."

"Renee, hold onto the boys! I need to see what's going on!" Covering his face, Father strained against the force of the wind. He grabbed hold of the rail and began to pull himself up. It looked like he was going to be blown away, but Big John jumped up to help him.

"Hol' on, sir. I's right behin' ya."

The hurricane lanterns flickered. The room darkened. Mother squeezed me so tight it hurt. She grabbed her rosary. "I believe in God, the Father almighty—" she all but yelled.

The door from the chapel slammed open. Grandmother stood defiantly against the wind. Signing herself with her right hand, she lifted a statue of Mary with her left. She shouted, "Purest virgin mother of the Russian land, with angels and saints we magnify you. You ease the suffering of sinners with your hand. Do not let us perish. Keep us safe today. Amen."

The wind stopped. In the snap of a finger, everything went calm.

Father roused the men to action. "It's the eye! Hurry! We've got to check damage and make repairs. I'm not sure how much time we've got." Mattresses flew back against the walls.

I searched for Grandmother, but could not find her with all the men charging towards the door. Andre and I started to join them, but Mother pulled us back.

"Where do you boys think you're going?"

"We need to help the men."

"Yes, I'm certain they could use all the help they could get, but for now, you two are going to remain right here by me."

"But Mother . . ."

"Paul de la Moret, don't make me discuss this with your father."

"Yes, ma'am." I sat back, antsy to see what waited outside.

"Suga', we need ta check da ki'chen." Mim lifted the mattress near us. Mother followed her and quickly disappeared in the crowd.

"Let's go, Andre." We bolted to the only open door. "Whoa!" A huge branch from one of the oaks blocked much of the porch. We climbed over it.

Branches and leaves littered the yard. Moonlight easily filtered through the barren trees. Wooden boards, tin sheets, and even a small *bateau* was scattered about. It looked like someone had just dropped all this stuff on the lawn.

"Paul, ma daddy. I gotta go afta' him."

"No way, Andre. The storm's not over yet. Let me get Father. Wait here."

"I's gonna be right back." Andre's voice faded as he dodged the debris littering the yard. I strained to see him and started to follow, but a faint glow in the trees stopped me at the edge of the porch. A figure shimmered in blue and white light. I drew back towards the kitchen.

"Child."

I jumped.

"Wha's wrong wit' ya? Ya look like you seen a ghost."

"No, Mim, I mean, can you see it?"

"See what, child?"

I turned back towards the trees. Whatever the faint glow was, it had disappeared.

"Child, where's Andre?"

"He went after his dad."

"Dat ole fool. Go fine yo daddy. He's upstairs, busy takin' care of repairs. Go tell 'im wha's goin' on."

I ran upstairs. Hammers pounded. Father overlooked a group of workers. "Let's get a board over that window. The shutter's been stripped loose."

I tiptoed through broken glass scattered on the floor. "Father!" He did not hear me. "Father!"

"What do you need, son? I'm real busy right now."

"It's Andre. He's gone after his daddy."

"Who went with him?"

"Nobody. He went by himself."

"Damn! Son, you stay here. Find your Mother and tell her I went after them. You understand me?"

"Yes, sir."

"Big John. Come with me. Paul, you do what I told you. Rest of you men get this window boarded."

17

He and Big John rushed out of the room. I ran down the stairs and then through the mass of women and children scattered in the foyer. I pushed the kitchen door open.

"Mother, Father's gone after Andre."

"What?"

"Yes, ma'am. Andre was worried about his dad and went after him."

Mother grabbed my wrist and dragged me to the door of the rear porch. "Paul, you do not move off of this porch."

"Yes, ma'am."

Mim wrapped Mother in a shawl. "Suga, are ya okay?"

"Mister Paul and Big John went after Andre and T'Bram."

"Dat stubbo'n ole fool. He shou'da got himse'f here when Mista Sam went fo 'im."

Mother searched the darkness. She twiddled her handkerchief and bit her upper lip. Mim and I stood by her side. With the winds temporarily calm, stars sparkled and even the moon made an appearance in the clear skies of the eye.

"I hate waiting."

"What's that, Mother?"

"Nothing. I was just thinking out loud." She sighed and then stepped to the side porch. "Sweet Mother of Jesus!"

"Wha's wrong, Suga?" Mim rushed to join Mother.

"Look over the field, across the bayou."

"Laudy, Laud. It's gonna git 'em if dey don't git here soon."

"Mother, they're coming!"

"Where?"

"Look into the oaks behind the third tree."

"Paul, do you need help?" The shrill of Mother's voice chilled me. She ran back to the rear porch. Father and Big John were carrying something, but I couldn't see Andre. Finally, a lightning flash revealed him holding to Father. A faint growl intensified as the eye wall approached. The stars were still out, and not one leaf on a tree moved.

"Andre, run ahead, son," Father yelled. "We've got your daddy. Get to the house." Another bolt of lightning struck the ground with an immediate clap of thunder.

"Mother, look!"

She gasped for breath. "Paul, hurry!" The monstrous eye-wall barreled in from the south. Gray and black clouds reached from the ground to the heavens, visible only when the lightning flashed and illuminated the beast. The distant grumble had turned into a mighty roar. The leaves on the trees trembled again.

The winds blew horizontal rain from the front of the house. From the porch, we watched the eye wall grind toward us. Like spears thrown by ancient warriors, stalk after stalk of flattened cane snapped at the root and shot through the air.

Father shoved Andre to run ahead, but they were too far from the house to reach it safely.

Leaves swirled about them. The wind threw all of them to the ground. I searched for Andre, then for Father. Branches cracked. Shingles stripped from the roof flew to the ground and blocked my view. The wind howled. Debris was flying everywhere.

"Paul!" Mother screamed.

"Where's Father?"

"I don't know. Let's get to the rear porch and take cover."

"I'm going after him."

"No!" She jerked my arm just as I started to bolt, pulling me to a sheltered side of the wrap-around porch. "You can't go out in that. It's too dangerous."

"But, Mother, he needs help." I searched in desperation. The wind and rain, cane and leaves, flying metal, and snapped branches made it impossible to see anything.

"Paul." Grandfather grabbed my back pocket as I struggled to free myself from Mother's grasp. "We're going to help your father. Getting yourself hurt or killed wouldn't be what he wanted." He nodded towards

Mother. "We need volunteers. Get some rope, pillows, bed linens, tape, and whatever we need to wrap ourselves. Gladys—"

"I'm already on it." Mim rushed to the kitchen. Tomas roused the men.

Mim returned with a bundle of stuff. The men stood on the porch as the wind continued to whip. Gladys and Georgia wrapped the men in makeshift armor, circling each man with tape to hold the blankets and pillows in place.

Grandfather grabbed the end of the rope. "We're going to make a human chain and tie rope around each of us. We want about twenty feet or so between each man. That way we can search the area. If any one falls, we'll pull back to safety."

"I see them!" Mother screamed from the back porch.

"Let's go, men." Grandfather led the biggest men into the torrent. As soon as they stepped off the back porch the wind moved them like toy soldiers. "Hold on!" Grandfather shouted.

I stood there wrapped in Mother's arms. My heart pounded.

"Paul," Mother screamed into the dark fury, "hold on!" Father clung to a large tree.

Grandfather slipped, but Tomas helped him up. They crawled towards Father. The wind lifted them as they struggled to find something to grab hold of. Locked arm and arm, they inched their way along—a new man added to the chain every few seconds.

The wind bellowed. We froze to a slow cracking sound, like something being ripped from the earth. We jumped back towards the wall of the house. More branches crashed onto the porch.

I strained to see Father through the rain. "Please, God, save him."

"He's got 'em! Look out dere." Mim pointed, but I could not see until they got closer. The chain recoiled as each man re-entered the porch.

Mother squeezed my arm. I could feel her heart pounding. Big John climbed from under the blanket followed by Grandfather.

My throat tightened into a strangle. I struggled to free myself. Breaking from Mother's grasp, I looked down. Finally, Father's shoes appeared from under the blanket. I leapt to him.

"I'm fine. It's okay. Let's get back in the house."

My heart throbbed in my head.

"Let's go. Dey gotta be out dere somewhere!" Big John stepped off the porch.

"Big John, no!" Father looked at Mother. "Renee, take Paul inside."

"But, Father. I've—"

"There's nothing you can do, son."

My knees buckled. "Where is he?"

Father's silence said it. Andre was not there. My best friend was gone.

Through the night, the wind raged. None of us slept. While some feared for their lives, I feared for what I would find, and maybe not find, in the morning.

By first light, the storm subsided. We walked outside to what remained of Oak Grove. It reminded me of my uncle's pictures of Hiroshima. Intact rooftops lay where cane once stood. Even the white paint of Oak Grove's walls had been stripped away, leaving only bare wood.

Snakes slithered in search of dry ground. White egrets plucked crawfish and small frogs washed in from the swamps. Vultures circled over cows rolled on their bellies and already smelling of rot.

A search party gathered, but it did not look long or far. Andre was pinned under a large branch while T'Bram's mangled and twisted body lay among flattened sugarcane. I bolted towards the fields.

"Come back, son." Father started after me.

I ran through the muddy rows of flattened sugarcane until my legs burned. My shoes were heavy with mud. My side ached. I didn't know where to go.

I dropped into a puddle of water. Looking up, I found the tree where just yesterday we played tag. It looked dead and barren with no leaves to shade or cool the ground anymore.

My feet sloshed across the washed out rows. The sun perched on the horizon like a big fireball resting on the earth. Low clouds hanging on as a reminder of Betsy's wrath cast the sky in hues of violet, pink, and yellow, darkening to blue-gray towards the north. Grandmother called this the "peace sky."

I climbed the tree as high as I could. I arched my back towards heaven and screamed. "Why? Why?" Only the sound of cleaning crews sawing fallen branches answered me.

Tattered from the wrath of another invader named Betsy, Oak Grove was ugly now. She had lost the fight. Though the house remained, I had lost my best friend.

ʗwo

"Today is the 'Feast of the Presentation of the Lord.' Let us greet our celebrant, Father Cecile Boudreaux as we rise to sing, 'Praise to the Lord,' found on page sixty-three of your hymnals." The organ piped the opening notes. The congregation rose in mass. The smell of burning incense reminded me of Andre's funeral. I couldn't get the image of the black-draped coffin in the center aisle of the church out of my head.

My buddy, Kevin, led the procession down the center aisle of the church. Because he was a few years older than me, he got to be an altar boy. Today, Father Boudreaux even let him handle the incense.

"Paul, face forward," Mother whispered sternly. With her chapel veil covering her head, she reminded me of President Kennedy's wife, kind of tall and thin and with black hair. She even walked like Mrs. Kennedy. We met her when we visited Washington with Father. That was before they shot the president.

A puff of smoke smelling of incense floated by me. I finally got a view of Kevin out of the corner of my eye. He kept swinging the chain of the metal chalice housing the incense back and forth. The sweet scent sickened my stomach.

The procession reached the Communion rail. Because my father read for Sunday mass, he got to walk in with Father Boudreaux and then sit near the altar until it was time for him to read. Father had to place the big red book he carried on a stand in the crow's nest; well, that's what I called it. Father Boudreaux read the Gospel from there after all the opening prayers.

"In the name of the Father, and of the Son, and of the Holy Spirit."

I signed myself in the cross like everybody else standing around me.

As Father Boudreaux lifted his outstretched arms, he prayed, "The Lord be with you."

"And also with you," the congregation replied. The echo bounced off the high ceilings and brick walls until the words muffled into silence.

"Lord, have mercy." Father Boudreaux pressed his fingers together into praying hands.

We use to say all these prayers in Latin. Mother made me memorize them even though I didn't know what I was saying. I guess they thought God only understood Latin or something. I even helped Andre learn them just in case. Maybe Andre died because I stopped praying in Latin.

"Glory to God in the highest—"

"And peace to his people on earth. Lord God, heavenly King—"

I looked back to where all the colored folks sat. Even though they never let Andre and me sit with each other, we always walked in together. It was neat having him come to church with me. We could talk about things after mass. But not anymore.

". . . you alone are the Holy One, you alone are the Lord, you alone are the Most High, Jesus Christ, with the Holy Spirit, in the glory of God the Father. Amen."

"Let us pray."

"All-powerful Father, Christ your son became man for us and was presented in the temple. May he free our hearts from sin and bring us into your presence. We ask this through our Lord Jesus Christ, your Son, who lives and reigns with you and the Holy Spirit, one God, for ever and ever."

"Amen."

People dropped back into the wooden pews. The thud filled the church. For a place that was supposed to be quiet, it sure was noisy.

My father straightened his tie. He opened another red book like the one he carried, but this one was on a lectern instead of the crow's nest. "The Epistle is taken from the Book of Isaiah.

"Who would believe what we have heard? To whom has the arm of the Lord been revealed? He grew up like a sapling before him, like a shoot from the parched earth. There was in him no . . ."

Sometimes Andre and I talked about why we couldn't sit with each other even though God didn't seem to mind. I guess they had some reason for it.

"Yet, it was our infirmities that he bore, our sufferings that he endured, while we thought of him as of stricken, as one smitten by God and afflicted. But he was pierced for our offenses, crushed for our sins, upon him . . ."

The stain glass window showed several men beating Jesus. Another windowpane had a soldier stabbing him with a sword. With Jesus already hanging on that cross, I bet that had to hurt. I hope Andre didn't hurt like that when he died.

"He was silent and opened not his mouth. Oppressed and condemned he was taken away, and who would have thought anymore of his . . ."

Father finished the reading and returned to his seat. Father Boudreaux waved the incense filled chalice towards the crow's nest. The smoke drifted toward the painted ceilings. He climbed the circular staircase, and then positioned himself at the podium. There he flipped open the big red book, using the red ribbon to find the correct page.

"The Lord be with you."

"And also with you." Kneelers pelted the wooden spools as the congregation stood. Somebody coughed. I turned to search for Andre. We had a secret code to let each other know that we were thinking about each other. I would cough once and he would cough twice. Sometimes we would do it three or four times during mass.

"Paul, face forward," whispered my mother.

Father Boudreaux scanned the crowd. "A reading from the holy Gospel according to Luke."

"Glory to You, oh Lord.

"And when eight days were completed for the circumcision of the Child, his name was called Jesus, the name given by the angel before he was conceived . . ."

Andre's birthday was just a few weeks off. Father bought me a new set of baseball cards. I didn't have anybody to share with anymore.

"There was a man in Jerusalem, named Simeon. He was just and devout . . ."

I'm sure Andre would have grown up to be like Simeon. He never did anything mean to anyone, even when some of the white boys from off the plantation called him mean names. He would just walk away, even though I knew it had to hurt his feelings. Why did people say ugly things? They had to know it hurt.

". . . and took him up in his arm. He blessed God, saying: 'Now, though doth dismiss thy servant oh Lord in peace, for my eyes have seen Your salvation which You have prepared before the face of all peoples, a light to bring revelations to the Gentiles and the glory of Your people Israel.'

"Joseph and Mary marveled at this. Then Simeon blessed them, 'Behold, this child is destined for the fall and rising of many in Israel, and for a sign which will be spoken against.'

"Then turning to Mary, Simeon said, 'And you, a sword will pierce through your own heart, that the secrets of many souls will be revealed.'

"Mary stored these things deep in her heart, saying nothing of this to anyone."

Father Boudreaux lifted the book. "The Gospel of the Lord."

"Praise to You Lord, Jesus Christ."

"In the name of the Father, and the Son, and the Holy Ghost. In today's Epistle we hear from the Prophet Isaiah of the death to be endured by our Savior."

Pictures of Mary covered the painted ceilings. One scene showed her holding Jesus after the Romans killed him. Mary's lily-white hands were covered with blood. No wonder she looked so sad.

"And Mary, the Mother of God. She knew these things, but kept them hidden deep in her heart. Can you imagine knowing that a loved one is going to die, but not saying a word to anyone about it? That's what Mary carried. She revealed very little of the things she knew, just like Bernadette Soubirous who saw our Lady in a grotto in Lourdes.

"We are fortunate to have Sister Claire Thomas visiting with us today. At the invitation of the archbishop, Sister Claire agreed to make a rare appearance. She was one of the small children who received a healing at the hands of our Lady of Lourdes. She traveled from her convent just outside of Lourdes to be with us this week.

"I ask that you join her in prayer as we pray for the strength to keep what God reveals to us as a gift. We should pray that if God pierces our soul, we only seek His will. Let us pray."

Mother told me the story of Bernadette. After seeing Mary, police officers harassed her. Even her priest didn't believe her at first. Bernadette suffered much in her life because of what she knew. I guess she, like Mary, knew what I felt like when Andre died.

"Stand up, sweetie." Mother lifted me up by the arms.

"We believe in God, the Father almighty, maker of the heaven and the earth, of all that is seen and unseen. We believe in one Lord, Jesus Christ . . ."

One night, Mother and Father watched a movie on television about Bernadette. I remember her rubbing mud on her face and people making fun of her. They thought she was crazy.

". . . he was born of the Virgin Mary, and became man. For our sake he was crucified under Pontius Pilate; he suffered, died, and was buried. On the third day . . ."

One man in the movie had Bernadette arrested, even though she was a young girl who had done nothing wrong. But he had to let her go. At the end of the movie, she kept saying she was weak and hadn't been a very good girl and that's why the lady didn't appear to her any more.

Maybe Andre died because I didn't pray enough. What if he died because I did something wrong? Was it my fault?

". . . the forgiveness of sin . . ."

I dropped back into the pew. I was kind of dizzy, like I had lived this before or maybe dreamed it.

"Paul, sweetie, what is it?"

The ceiling of the church spun wildly. The images blurred even though I tried to focus on them. A wave of heat rushed through me. A bright white light blinded me.

Ꮳhree

The fish wiggled to free itself. Blood rushed to my head. "I've got him, Father."

"Reel him in, pal. Don't give him any slack."

"Look at him pullin' on the line." I shifted my weight. The small flat-bottomed boat dipped to the right and then to the left. Like inky-raised lines on a glassy surface, ripples flowed across the water.

"You're doing fine, son. Just keep the tip of your pole up and the line tight."

The fish jerked as I reeled it towards the boat. The glare off the clear, black pool made it hard to see. "Father, can you see him?"

"Not yet. But he'll be up soon. The way he's pulling, I bet he's pretty big."

The reel squeaked as I cranked it. My arms ached from reeling so fast. The prize catch of the day was going to be my claim to fame.

"Nice and slow now while I get the net under him." Father yanked the net out of the water. "Got him!" The *sac a lait's* thick scales flushed its green skin milky white. Folks on the bayou called a fish like this "sack of milk."

"That's one really nice fish, pal. You did a great job reeling it in."

A tingle seized me. I drew a deep breath of the fresh lake smell. *Thank you, God,* I thought.

Father laid the fish in the ice chest. He took a hard look at our catch, and then nodded. "Nice, very nice. What say we get things stowed and get home so we can show off our catch, especially your fish?"

"I'll get the anchor." The boat rocked as I tugged on the rope. Mud percolating from the bottom clouded the water. I swished the anchor rope to loosen the "Black Jack" clay from the metal teeth until I was able to lift it.

"Bundle up, son. The blue skies of early March make for warm days, but chilly nights." Father started the boat engine. He slid over. "Why don't you bring us in? Go ahead."

I leapt into his seat. As I pushed the throttle, the small *bateau* trudged through the shallows. With each chug, we pierced through the *gren a volait,* lilies with big yellow flowers that matured into edible seeds.

Several white egrets lifted into full flight, squawking with their bellies full of crawfish. Their massive wings blocked the sun and almost darkened the sky.

This was the first time I had been on the lake since Hurricane Betsy. Catching a record size fish with this rod and reel was pretty cool. Father had bought it for Andre just before he died.

We emerged from the lily-thicket into the channel. Continuous boat traffic deepened the twenty or so foot wide path, clearing it of the *gren a volait.*

"You want to open her up, pal?"

The bow of the narrow-beamed cypress hull lifted out the water. Even though the channel appeared jet black, the wake of the boat shone crystal clear.

The chatter of the boat engine drowned out all sounds with the exception of the wind rushing by me. A pair of summer mallards furiously paddled to take off before we reached them. I could imagine their webbed feet swishing the water. They flapped their wings to draw air beneath them. One, two, three, four—off they went to a quieter side of the lake.

The sun tucked behind the approaching tree line. Not one cloud filled the air. Only a dim cast of the new moon broke the sea of blue above us.

The channel narrowed as we approached the marsh. A big log drifted right at the entrance to the *tranos*. Narrower than the channel, by more than half in some places, the *tranos* connected the lake to a small bayou that drained Oak Grove.

I slowed the engine, steering the boat's bow to the submerged portion of the log. The keel lifted the boat a few inches as it guided us right over it.

"Good job, pal."

"Father, look ahead. Is that another—" The boat chugged towards an obstacle floating in our path. "Man, that's one big alligator."

"Sure is. Looks like that big bull your grandfather's been talking about."

Without so much as causing a single ripple, the alligator floated with its head and spiny back and tail out of the water. I aimed the boat towards him. We inched closer.

"You've got that steering wheel gripped pretty tightly, don't you think?" Father whispered as we paralleled the fifteen-foot creature. Its head must have been three feet long and over a foot wide. Its eyes were brown with that typical black iris that looked like hell's soul.

Thud!

"Oh, shit!" I jumped. With the flick of his tail, the bull alligator slapped the side of the boat and drenched us in a watery spray.

Father chucked. "Startled you, did he?"

"I'm sorry—"

"No. 'Oh shit' sums it up nicely. You look a little pale. Want me to take over?"

"No, sir. I'm fine." I pushed the throttle forward, steering us through the winding path. Thin reeds of marsh grass anchored into the bog, a floating island pushed against the banks of the swamp, enveloped us on both sides.

The *tranos* opened into a bayou lined with rows of barren cypress trees. Spanish moss, draped across rust colored branches, and birds, mostly white egrets, dotted the wooded swamp.

"Paul, I've got to cut several cypress knees. Some of my friends in Washington want them. How about you giving me a hand?"

"Yes, sir." I slowed the boat.

Brown-barked cypress knees littered the banks like spines of that alligator. The low water levels of early March exposed more of the bark than usual.

"Don't you just love the shape of some of those knees?" Father pointed to a cluster of twenty, maybe thirty protruding from the water. They lined the entrance, giving the appearance of centurions guarding the bayou. "It amazes me how the roots of the tree emerge from this muddy water to form a new tree."

"Grandfather says they look like the severed leg of an old man, cut just at the knee. Then they start to look like people as they grow, just like that one." I pointed to one looking like a Greek statue.

"I bet when Jean Lafitte floated this bayou, he cut his fair share for trade."

"Jean Lafitte came here?"

"It's pretty easy to get to here from Barataria."

"Isn't that a long way for someone to travel by boat?"

"Not if you're Jean Lafitte."

Suddenly, birds stirred from their perch. Turtles resting on logs dove into the water. The wind rushed through the trees, whispering to us like a forgone ghost revisiting its playground.

"You see? He's here even now."

My hair stood up on the back of my neck. Father's serious countenance changed to a devilish grin. Was he yanking my chain or was the Jean Lafitte legend real? Either way, it was eerie.

"Father, do you want to cut those?"

"No. They're just to be admired."

The boat drifted deeper into the bayou. We huddled together in search of the perfect knee. Swamp irises, adorned in purple and yellow, swayed in the wake of our passage. Alligators gathering the last of the day's light retreated into the murky waters.

"Father, how about those three knees over to our left?"

"Good eye, son. They're perfect."

I eased the boat towards the bank, and then shut off the engine. "Should I throw out an anchor?"

"On three." Father paddled the boat into the cluster as I readied the steel teeth. "One, two, three." The boat rocked. The weight of the metal nearly dragged me into the bayou. As it settled into the mud, a milky white cloud bubbled from the bottom.

"Easy, pal. That water's still chilly for a swim. Let's get situated and then you can help me." Father jabbed the paddle into the soft, muddy bank. "That should keep us fairly stable. Hey pal, hand me the saw and the wood wedge."

The metal toolbox squeaked as I opened it. The shiny, sharpened tip glistened against the other tools. I handed it to Father.

"This has been in the family for as long as I can remember." The hammer pinged against the blunt edge as Father drove it into the cypress knee just at the water line. Small fish skirted away, rippling the water. "Now the two man saw. Grab that end. Remember, the art of sawing is nice, long, smooth strokes. Let the saw do the work and let your partner help."

He set the teeth into the notch. With the boat leaned to one side I grabbed the wooden handle and braced myself. Father pulled the saw forward. The teeth grabbed the wet cypress bark. I pulled it back towards me. We repeated the action, slowly establishing a rhythm.

The blade sang as it chewed through the bark. It vibrated my hand. Saw dust sprinkled the surface of the water as we inched through the bark bit by bit.

"Let's slow down so we make a nice even cut to free it." Father steadied the knee with one hand while he held the saw with the other. With one final stroke the cap separated from the main root. It dipped into the water and floated while Father placed the saw back into the boat.

Lifting the pointed stump out of the water, Father carefully inspected it from several angles. He ran his fingers across the cut. "That's as good of a cut as I've seen. Come here and feel it. Nice and even. Just the way men are supposed to be. Watch how well it stands up on its own." When he placed it on the seat, it stood straight and tall. "Feel the rest of it."

"It's so light."

"That's why folks want the wood."

I took a deep breath.

"There's nothing like freshly cut cypress. I think that's why Oak Grove is the way she is. She's made from this wood. It's tough and lasts forever—good stock, as they say. Just like you, Paul." Father squeezed my shoulder. "Let's get a couple more and then we can head on home to show off that fish of yours."

Fresh cut cypress, a limit of fresh fish, and a record size big one—what incredible trophies to show for our day. This was the best day of my life.

Locating two additional knees, we repeated our work. Five three-foot monoliths soon filled the boat, leaving us with little room to sit.

"Get the anchor in and I'll stow our gear."

The anchor was so caked with mud that I could barley swish it in the water. But after bobbing it three or four times, the clay washed off.

I settled into the driver's seat.

"Hold on a minute, son." Father's tone softened.

"Is something wrong?"

"No, pal. I just want to talk." Father smiled warmly. He looked into my eyes as never before. It was like he was searching for the words to speak. "I spoke to Kevin. He said you didn't want to go to New Orleans to spend the week."

"Tomas needs help in the orchard, and I've got a lot of things to do before going back to school."

"You miss, Andre, don't you?"

I nodded yes.

"You know, having another friend doesn't deny the love you had for Andre."

My stomach sickened.

"Hey, pal. Look up. It's okay if talking about Andre still hurts. I just want you to know that I'm concerned. But more importantly, I'm proud of you."

"Sir?"

"Yeah, pal. You've done well. Your grades are good. Everyone reports what a polite and caring gentleman you are. I was just wondering if you've found a roommate."

The image of Andre pinned under that tree flashed into my head. I shuddered at the lifeless gaze gripping his face. It was like his very breath had been crushed out of him.

"I know you and Andre were best friends—"

"I'll never have another friend like Andre."

"Maybe, but you've got a lot of life yet to live. Who knows what the future holds? Remember the saying, "And the friends of thy boyhood—that boyhood of wonder and hope, present promise and wealth of the future beyond the eye's scope.""

"'Saul'."

"That's right, pal. Robert Browning. But he said 'friends of thy boyhood'."

My eyes pulled away from Father. Something glowed in the trees behind him.

"What is it, son?"

"I—" The words just wouldn't come out. "Umm . . . umm . . . that—" A white egret lifted out of the tree. I searched for the image I thought I saw, but only Spanish moss swaying from the cypress branches remained.

"Oh. Kind of looks like a ghost, huh? The legend of Jean Lafitte doesn't have you spooked, does it?"

"No, sir."

The setting sun cast shadows where light once brightened the trees. The lone egret soared above us, searching the waterway for a stray fish or turtle for dinner. Yet, my eyes drew to the perch where the egret once stood. The ghostly image of a lady blazed in my head.

"Son—"

I jumped.

"Are you okay?"

"Yes, sir."

Father looked deeper into my eyes. I didn't dare look to the tree behind him. "Let's head home, pal."

I searched the tree once more to the chant of a bullfrog inviting twilight.

As I steered through the watery path, the waves from our wake folded into each other covering our passage. The tree line, dashed with white-feathered egrets, opened in front of us, while collapsing from behind. Like the image, or illusion, I had seen, these too faded into obscurity.

Andre and I learned to swim in this bayou. We had spent many days skinny-dipping, only to rest in the warm summer sun. Sometimes I wondered how long I would have to sit in the sun to be dark like him. Maybe then he and I wouldn't have had to sit apart from each other at ball games and at mass and at other places. Now we would never sit with each other again.

"Hey, pal. Where're you heading?"

Almost missing the narrow cut to our boat landing, I steered the boat under the railroad tracks. We arrived at the boat sheds to Grandfather standing near his truck. "I was about to come looking for you two."

"Sorry, Sam. The fishing was great and we couldn't help cutting a few knees."

"Some real beauties, I see. Let me give you a hand."

The boat rocked even though we were only in inches of water. We packed the knees into the back of Grandfather's truck, and then loaded our tackle.

"How'd you do, Paul?"

I almost tripped getting to my fish. "Look here, Grandfather." The slime made it difficult to hold.

"It's bigger than my hand. Looks like a record. We'll measure it the minute we get home." Grandfather started towards his truck. He waved me over to the driver's side.

"Father—"

"Go ahead. I'll take care of the rest."

I dashed towards Grandfather.

"Can you reach the pedals?"

"Yes, sir." I slid under the steering wheel. Stretching my legs as far as I could, I barely touched the accelerator and the brake.

With a turn of the key, the engine purred. I let up the clutch and we bobbed forward. The gears ground as I shifted into second and then third.

"I guess we'll have to work on that," Grandfather chuckled.

A dust cloud floated up behind us as we drove down the shell road. The headlamps reflected off a sea of yellow ragweed and dandelions blanketing the fields. The cane had not yet budded from the sandy soil covering the rhizomes.

The truck rattled across the cattle guard of the road back to the main house. As we pulled into Grandfather's parking spot, Grandmother, Mother, and Mim paced on the rear porch.

"Paul, they're going to fuss. Just say you're sorry, then we can show them your fish."

The door squeaked open. We stepped out to Mim's tapping foot. "Where have y'all been? Next time y'all leave dis house it's gonna be wit' some food!"

Grandmother eyed us through her reading glasses. "We were worried sick!"

"You smell like fish." Mother's nose wrinkled. "Where's your father?"

Just then, a second set of lights blinded us. Before he even turned the engine off, Mother preached at him. "Paul de la Moret, you had me—"

"Hello, beautiful. You should see the fish the boy caught." He bent Mother over and planted a big kiss on her.

"If you think you can waltz in here and sweep me off my feet—"

He kissed her again. She tried to talk, but he didn't let up until she yielded.

I perched under Grandfather's arm as Grandmother eyed him and Mim eyed me. We were in big trouble.

"Old woman, stop eyin' the boy and grab these fish. They need cleaning."

"Who ya callin' ole woman." Mim strutted over to the truck. "I can keep up wit' any man on dis plantation an' dat includes you."

"Well, then take these fish inside and fry them for the boy." Grandfather grimaced. "And leave the big one so we can measure it."

"If y'all ain't measurin' one thing, y'all measurin' anotha. Well, y'all bes' git ya'se'f cleaned up so y'all can eat, cause ya ain't sitting at my table smellin' like dat." With fish in hand Mim headed towards the outdoor kitchen where fish and game were prepared for either eating or showing off. "Well, y'all gonna measure dat fish or are we gonna have ta do dat fo' ya too?"

The screen door to the outdoor kitchen squeaked open. Tomas lowered his head to see over his reading glasses. "Good evenin'. What we got here?"

38

"A record, I think." Grandfather reached for the official Oak Grove measuring stick. Laying my fish on top of it, he carefully arranged the fins.

Tomas drew closer. "I don't know, Sam. May be a bit smaller than the one we caught last year." Tomas pointed to a mounted *sac a lait* hanging on the trophy wall.

"I think you're right. We need another opinion. Big Paul, come take a look."

With the verdict hanging, Father walked over and examined the fish. "Like Tomas said, looks mighty close."

The three of them hovered over it while I paced the floor. Finally, Grandfather looked up. "Well, I think its official. It's an Oak Grove record."

"Dat's a big fish, boy." Tomas nodded. "I'll git yo name, da date, and da size burned inta a plank befo' I mount it." Tomas carefully wrapped the fish in paper. "Judgin' by dat smile, I think dat makes ya kind a happy."

The wall, filled with prizes of past fishing and hunting trips, would soon have my trophy added to it.

"Naw, are y'all done wit' all dat measurin'?" Mim peeked up from cleaning the fish. "I'm gonna have dese fish fried in fifteen minutes. I expect y'all ta be washed up and ready ta eat. Ya bes' hurry cause Miz Elida and Suga' are waitin'." Mim pushed us along.

Grandfather popped a fireball jawbreaker in his mouth. "Before you start, old woman—"

"I've told ya about dat ole woman stuff. An' don't go eatin' a bunch a junk ta mess wit' yo appetite." If a woman could throw daggers with her eyes, Mim would have been a champion. I had learned long ago not to rowel her. She could pluck a fly's eyes off of its head with a dishrag from twenty paces, and a boy's britches from his bottom at forty.

"We best get to the house."

I guess Grandfather knew better than to argue with her.

Gas lamps flickering on the porch softly lit our path. The aroma of crawfish in a muddy brown roux and a slight hint of tomato, an *étoufée* as it was called, filled the main house kitchen. The cover of a pot jiggled against the steam of boiling rice.

"Get cleaned up, son, and we'll meet you downstairs."

"Yes, sir."

The portraits lining the walls seemed to come to life as I climbed the stairs. I could almost hear their voices congratulating me for setting an Oak Grove record and adding to the legacy of this house.

I glided my finger along the chair rail of the upstairs hallway. As I approached my room, a crack in one of the boards of the beaded walls splintered my hand. It appeared pried open.

I pulled the board. A door I never saw before popped into the wall. An empty staircase stood nestled inside. I looked to see if anyone was around. Other than the tick tock of the grandfather clock, the upstairs was quiet.

I climbed through a narrow passage, using a wall to guide me. Something tickled my forehead. Reaching up in the darkness, I grabbed a string. A single light bulb dangling from the rafters snapped on.

An old oak trunk sat alone in the middle of the floor. The hinges squeaked as I lifted the heavy top.

Papers and other things filled the chest. Light reflected off a book wrapped in ornate gold foil with buckled leather straps holding it shut. It sat atop a brightly decorated and embroidered vest.

Dark Night of the Soul. St. John of the Cross. I loosened the strap to the smell of raw leather. A letter slipped from the cover. The parchment was dry and brittle. I unfolded it to see words written in French.

J'aime ma famille—

I love my family and always will. But, to the Virgin, I have consecrated my life. Even though they choose to leave France, I will not follow. Rather, I with my wife will travel to Spain. There I will reside faithful to the vow once made.

Pierre Paul Guidry
11 November 1611

What a strange letter this was. Guidry was Grandmother's maiden name, though she rarely spoke of her family, telling us that she knew little of them. But here in this chest was a book and letter. Why?

I dug deeper. A velvet cloth covered a statue or something. I started to pull it out.

"Paul, are you up there?" Mother's muffled voice echoed up the passageway.

My heart raced. I placed the statue and the books as they were and closed the trunk. "Paul, did you hear me?"

"Yes, ma'am." I called down to Mother as I entered the upstairs hallway.

"Hurry up. Mim's holding dinner."

"Yes, ma'am." I bolted to my room and slipped off my clothes. With a little cologne sprayed on my body, I hurriedly dressed. But I couldn't help wondering, *Why is that chest up here? What is someone hiding?*

Four

Oak Grove Plantation, September 1969

A lady with lily-white hands folded in prayer and black beads weaved through her fingers hovered above me. "I choose you."

"What do you mean?"

"Look around you. Many are in pain. Reach to them."

"And what of my father? Can you help him?"

"Who is your Father?"

"Paul. His name is Paul, just like mine."

"I know. But, who is your Father?"

The light brightening my space weaned. My body drifted into a darkening chasm. I grasped for the lady's hand, but she was no longer present. The faint sounds of weeping women rippled the silence.

"Paul?"

"Kevin, where are you?" I reached for him, but my arms flailed as if no longer in my control.

"Paul, your father . . ."

An icy wind blasted me into a whirlwind. I spun around and around.

"Help me. Please help me." A myriad of voices shrieked through the gale.

"Kevin, are you safe?"

A fierce wind roared. Lightening flashed about me. The crackle of thunder vibrated my chest. Warm air, sucked from my lungs, made it impossible for me to speak further. Was I dying?

■

My palms were sweaty. I was breathing hard. With my sheets and blankets tossed on the floor, I must have twisted and turned for quite awhile before finally waking from the dream.

The grandfather clock in the upstairs hallway tolled 3 A.M. Through the French doors, darkness veiled the balcony of Oak Grove. Silence filled the hallways.

Vivid images of a lady raged in my head. Once more she visited me. With lily-white hands folded in prayer, the black beads weaving through her fingers were as clear as ever. "I choose you." Her words once again made no sense—this ghost that haunted me.

In it, I remembered my buddy, Kevin. As I lay in bed, I thought about the dream, hoping that something would trigger what he told me. Tossing and turning, I attempted to sort through the details. Nothing came to me.

I opened a book given to my by my father. It contained the writings of Marcus Aurelius.

How quickly all things disappear, bodies into the universe, memories of them in time. What is the nature of sense objects, and particularly of those, which attract with the bait of pleasure or terrify by pain, or are known everywhere for their vapory fame; how worthless, and contemptible, and sordid, and perishable, and dead they are—all this it is the part of the intellect to observe. To observe too what people they are whose opinions and voices create a reputation; what death is, and how, if a man looks at it in itself, and by the abstract the features of it which strike the imagination, he who fears the course of nature is a child. Death, however, is not only a work of nature, but it is also a thing that fulfills the purposes of nature. Observe, too, how man comes near to the Deity, and by what part of him, and when this part of him is so disposed.

The grandfather clock sounded 4 A.M. and then 5 A.M. Finally, my eyes grew heavy.

■

A soft knock woke me. "Mista Paul, breakfast is gonna be served soon," Georgia called through my bedroom door. "Auntie Gladys is gonna fuss if ya don't git up and git ready."

"I'm up, Georgia. Please tell Mim I'll be down soon."

"Ya betta hurry. She's expectin' ya in a few minutes."

Light streamed through the French doors. A rooster crowed. I was tired, yet not. With only two days remaining before I returned to school, I had a great deal to do, especially with Father in the hospital again.

I flipped on the television. "Unrest continues to escalate in Washington as the death toll in Vietnam rises. This morning, protesters clashed with police—" I turned it off. It was more than I wanted to hear with the dream still seducing me.

I wrenched the shower valve open. Hot water cascaded over my body. The crust of my night's sleep seemed to melt away with each drop. I just stood there. But thoughts of Mim impatiently tapping her foot prevented me from doing so for long. I hastily dressed and got downstairs.

"Child, I was wonderin' if I waz gonna have ta go up dere an' git ya ma'se'f."

"Sorry, Mim. I was—"

"Git ya'se'f in dere and eat. I neva' liked da idea of sendin' ya up dere ta dem Yankees. Dere isn't any good cookin' up dere like dere is down here."

"Yes, ma'am. But, nobody cooks like you, Mim. Why, I've heard people as far away as Baton Rouge talk about your cooking."

45

"Don't trifle wit' me, child. I guess ya gonna fill dat belly a yo's wit' dem grits, eggs, fresh ham, and biscuits I just cooked."

"Yes, ma'am. Two servings."

"We'll see. I'm gonna check on ya in just a few minutes." Mim cocked one eye. As Grandfather said, she was "spyin'" on me.

I joined Grandmother and Grandfather in the dining room. While Grandfather read the morning newspaper, Grandmother prayed from her St. Joseph's missal.

"Good morning, Grandmother."

"Why, good morning, Paul."

The paper ruffled as Grandfather placed it in on the table. "Morning, rascal. What's your plan for the day?"

"I'd like to spend some time with Tomas, if that's okay?"

"We're working the south orchard this morning. Why don't you come out with me?"

"Yes, sir!"

"Miz Elida, I've got breakfast. Paul's gonna eat two servin's of every-t'in'. We're gonna make sure he eats up befo' he goes back ta dat school. I don' wanna send 'im back lookin' thin. Mista Sam, do ya wan' me ta serve ya plate?"

"Please, Gladys."

"And you too, Paul. Just keep yo seat while I serve up dis food." With the sterling clanging against the china, Mim heaped food onto the plates. Like mountains created before the coming of man, mounds of grits, eggs, ham, and biscuits lapped over the sides.

Grandfather surveyed his plate. "That sure is a healthy serving."

"Yeah, sir. Nobody's goin' outta dis house lookin' frail while I'm still here."

Grandmother crossed herself, then bowed her head. "In the name of the Father and of the Son and of the Holy Ghost. Amen. Bless us, oh Lord, for these thy gifts, which we are prepared to receive, through the bounty of Christ, our Lord. Amen."

We lifted morsels of food to our mouths. Mim hovered over us like an eagle on high as she inspected our plates. My belly puffed as I stuffed the food down my throat. What was I thinking when I told her I would eat two servings?

"You look like you're ready to pop, rascal." Grandfather rolled his eyes. "Well, old woman, you've outdone yourself again." With his thanks to Mim complete, he walked over to kiss Grandmother good-bye. "Paul, time to wrap up so we can help Tomas in that orchard."

"Yes, sir." I bolted up from my seat right behind him.

"Child, ya haven't quite finished cleanin' dat plate."

"Got to go, Mim. Grandfather's waiting on me. But, whoa, was it good. I can't wait until lunch. Love you, Grandmother."

"Ya hardly ate." Mim's voice faded into a hum as I bolted out of the dining room, through the kitchen, and then to the back porch.

Grandfather was already sitting in his truck with the motor running. "You're ready?"

I nodded yes. He shifted the truck in gear. But just as we started to move, Grandmother raced out of the house and waved us down.

"We've got a phone call that's urgent."

"I'll be right in." Grandfather parked the truck. "Can you get the fungicide in the back of the truck to Tomas? I'll join you as soon as I'm done with this call."

As I sat behind the wheel, the warmth from where his body had been permeated my back.

"Just take your time. Give it a little gas, release the clutch, and you'll be off in a flash."

"Yes, sir." Pressing the accelerator pedal, I lifted my foot off the clutch. The truck glided forward. As I drove my first few yards, Grandfather stood with a "thumbs-up" and a broad smile across his face. I looked back in the rear view mirror several times as I drove around the oak grove. He waited there until I turned towards the orchard.

47

I honked the horn at several field hands on their way to the plantation store and returned their waves. With the windows rolled down, a cool wind blew through the cab. I drove past the storage barns and then past the Quarters. The orchard entrance was just beyond the house where Andre and T-Bram once lived.

As I arrived at the orchard, Tomas paced. "Where's yo grandpa?"

"He had to take a call."

"Ya drove out here by ya'se'f."

"Yes, sir."

"Well hop outta dat cab and give me a hand wit' dis fungicide." Tomas said very little when work in the orchard remained unfinished. I grabbed the fungicide and paced large steps to keep up with him. "Grab dat bucket ova dere and then unroll that wata' hose."

I wasted no time. As I pulled on the water hose, it snarled in one of the satsuma trees.

"Go easy there, boy. Ya don't wanna damage any of dem trees or bruise dat fruit. Yo grandpa would be mighty upset wit' dat."

Dropping the hose, I walked over to unsnarl it. Green oranges filled the trees with the scent of fresh citrus. We were lucky that Hurricane Camille missed us just weeks earlier.

"Beautiful, ain't it? There's nothin' like da orchard when da oranges start ripenin'. In a few weeks, dese satsumas are gonna be bright orange. They're gonna be so juicy dat its gonna make yo mouth wata'. Ya miss it, don't ya?"

"At times, especially fall. But . . ." My head dipped.

"But what? Ya miss Andre. There's not a thing in da world wrong wit' missin' yo friend."

"Not only that. I mean—"

"Yo daddy told me ya still rooming alone. Ya know sulkin' ain't gonna bring Andre back. Y'all were two of da happiest boys I ever saw. Ya think he would want ya livin' like dere was nothin' ta live for?"

"No, sir. But—"

"But, what?"

"Father thinks I should find another roommate, too."

"So what's stoppin' ya?" I lifted my head. Tomas' jet black eyes locked into my own. "When ya gonna realize ya don't have nothin' ta prove except ta ya'se'f? Nobody can do that fo' ya. That's gotta come from inside ya." Tomas wiped the sweat from his brow. "Ya been sleepin'?"

"A little."

"That's not what I hear. Mim tells me ya been havin' nightmares again."

"A few."

"Uh huh. Like every night."

"Yes, sir."

"So when are ya gonna talk ta somebody about what's goin' on in dat head of yo's?" Tomas eyed me.

Maybe I should talk to him, I thought, *but even if I did, what could he do about any of it? Most of it doesn't make sense to me.*

Tomas drew a deep breath and then looked around the orchard. "Let's git back ta work."

I spent the day working with Tomas, even having lunch with him. We paused only for short breaks to catch our breaths or get a quick drink of water.

The sun crossed the orchard. Shade appeared where light once brightened it. The day had passed quickly.

"I wonda what happened ta ya grandpa."

"I don't know. Guess he got tied up with business."

"Musta been mighty impo'tant ta keep him away from da orchard." Tomas poured cool water over his head and then over mine. With summer still raging on, we had built up quite a sweat. "Ya ready fo' school?"

"Still have some packing to do."

"Maybe ya should git back ta the house and git packed up."

"How about what's left in the orchard?"

"I'm jus' about done. Why don't ya git on home?"

49

"Yes, sir. See you tomorrow."

"If da good Laud says so."

With my shirt sticking to me from sweat, I tried to dry off before getting into Grandfather's truck, but the heat made it impossible to stay dry. The ride back to the house provided the only reprieve. As I arrived there, Mim waited by the kitchen door.

"Child, where have ya been?"

"Helping Tomas."

"Git ya'se'f upstairs and showa off befo' ya git the death-a-cold."

"Yes, ma'am."

She followed me through the kitchen and into the main foyer. Just as I started up the stairs, the phone rang.

"Oak Grove Plantation. Gladys speakin'. How may I help ya?" Mim stood silently with the phone in hand. "Hol' da line please. Paul, close dat do' and git ya'se'f ova here. You got a phone call."

"Yes, ma'am. Hello."

"Paul?"

"Kevin! I had a dream about you just last night."

"Listen up. Your father's not doing well. You need to—"

"Hello? Kevin?"

"Child, wha's wrong?"

"The phone line is dead."

Mim wiped her hands on her apron and took the receiver from me. "Sho' is. I'll have Francis ride inta town ta let da phone company know."

I couldn't move. The images of the dream raced in my head.

"Child?" The embroidered lace of Mim's apron brushed against my arm freeing me from my trance. "I think ya best go lay down fo' a spell. I'm gonna bring some food up ta yo' room." Mim led me to my bedroom. "I gonna come back an' check on ya in a bit."

Kevin's call sent shivers down my spine. His family lived in New Orleans and had been helping Mother with Father. If only I could remember more of the dream.

My mattress springs whined as I sat on the corner of the bed. Struggling to unknot my shoes, I crawled on the floor. An old cigar box stashed under my bed caught my attention. I had forgotten about it.

Reaching under the bed, I grabbed it. The scent of Grandfather's cigars remained as strong as ever inside, even with the lid held shut by two large rubber bands crisscrossed to secure it tightly. The first band snapped against my finger as I lifted it off. Careful to avoid the sting of the second band, I rolled it to the corner.

A locust shell, a katydid as they called it, several old marbles, two-hundred-plus baseball cards tied in string (Roger Maris on top), and other various items were entombed in this old box. Andre and I had spent hours collecting the things inside. Pretending to find treasure left behind by Jean Lafitte, we placed our goods in this "chest." Sometimes we would even hide in forts made of clumped mud to fight bandits who sought to steal our booty.

"Child, come open da door fo' me. I've got yo food," Mim said softly as she knocked on my door.

I stuffed the items back into the box, then carefully stretched the rubber bands to secure the tattered lid. With a gentle shove, it slid across the wooden floor back under the bed.

"Child, are ya comin'? Dis tray is startin' ta git heavy."

"Coming, Mim." I leapt up to open the door. Mim stood there holding the tray against her belly. "I'm not real hungry."

"I t'ink ya should eat so it can make ya stronga. Naw eat up befo' it gits cold."

"Yes, ma'am." I knew better than to argue.

As Mim stood watch, she wiped her hands on her apron, wringing it like a wet dishrag. With enough starch in it to stand on its own, the white embroidery on the edges added extra stiffness. Grandmother often embroidered lace on aprons and handkerchiefs, giving these as gifts to members of the staff. Mim always got the most beautiful pieces.

"Mim, are Mother and Father coming home tonight?"

"Oh, child, I don't t'ink so. Yo daddy is still in da hospital and yo mamma's surely gonna stay wit' him. She's been at dat hospital fo' almos' two mont's naw." Mim's sad voice matched her melancholy eyes. "I've got ta go finish ma dinna. Naw, ya eat up."

"Yes, ma'am."

Father had been in the hospital for most of the summer. With the exception of our fishing trip in early spring, I had seen little of him since returning from school.

I crawled into bed. The food in my full belly sloshed around as I rolled onto my side. From the floor, the white edge of my Roger Maris baseball card shimmered. I reached for it and then the cigar box.

Sorting through the cards reminded me of times at baseball parks when Father took us, even though Andre and I couldn't sit together. I loved to sneak Cracker Jack boxes to him so that we could compare the secret surprises we found in each. The drive home always gave us plenty of time to swap.

We collected everything, even locust shells. Finding hundreds on the rails of the balcony, barks of trees, and on almost any stationary object, we pretended these were monsters from another planet, seeking humans to experiment on. We gathered them so that the menace did not spread.

A breeze whisked the shear covering the open French doors to my bedroom. Several cars drove up to the house. Doors slammed shut. More cars followed.

I strolled onto the upper balcony and peered through the rails. Hiding behind a large white column, I watched as family members streamed in. Had it not been early September, I would have sworn Christmas Eve celebrations were underway.

My uncle's black Ford Continental was already parked near Grandfather's truck. I always thought its square hood and trunk made it look like a tank. You could almost house a family in it. As a matter of fact, I had seen a family living in a car once when going through the lower end of the French Quarter with Father.

"Paul, are you there?" The sullen tone of my uncle's voice startled me as he called from the threshold of the French doors. "I'd like you to clean up and then come downstairs."

"Is something wrong?" I asked as I turned around.

"We'll talk about it once you're dressed. Be quick." I followed him back into my bedroom. He closed the door behind him. With shaking hands I stowed the cigar box back under my bed.

"Paul, your father—" Kevin's voice echoed in my head. I climbed into the shower, allowing the water to wash over me. But, the words repeated. "Paul, your father—" Not since Andre's death had I felt this way.

My heart pounded in my throat. I slipped my coat on. I reached for the doorknob, then backed away. "Please, God, make whatever is going on happy. Please, God—" The door rattled from a brisk knock.

"Paul, are you dressed?"

"Yes, sir." I opened the door.

"Let's go over to the chairs and talk for a moment."

My heart sank even further. We walked to two armchairs grouped near the upstairs railing. The house was very quiet. The grandfather clock had even stopped ticking. As Father's closest brother, he spent as much time with him as anybody.

"Paul, your mother is downstairs in the parlor—"

I jumped up and started towards the stairs.

"Hold on, son. In just a few moments, I'm going to walk with you downstairs to your mother. I want you to collect yourself and be strong. Understand?"

I nodded yes. My throat tightened. As he lifted from the chair, he motioned for me to stand with him. His huge frame cast a shadow around me.

"Let's go, son." We descended the staircase together. Folks mulled about in the foyer. As they caught sight of me a path cleared. Some shook their heads. Others looked away.

My uncle whispered to me. "Just keep moving." With his hand on my shoulder, he steered me through the crowd. I searched for Mother. Grandmother, Mim, and several others hovered over her. Ice shot through my veins. I began to tremble.

The sun pierced through the French doors. Beams of hazy light encased Mother. It was almost blinding. A chasm separated us. It felt like something wouldn't let me reach her.

I searched the room, hoping that something would give me strength. An image of something hovered in the light. Unsure as to what it was, I stopped. The blue veil that draped her head was the only thing I could see—at least I thought I was seeing it.

"What is it, Paul?" My uncle's inquisition distracted me. A hush of whispers rippled through the room. I looked to find Mother, then turned back to the image in the light. Squeezing my eyes shut, I reopened them to Mother, who was crying. Dressed in black, she sat in the Queen Anne chair often occupied by Grandmother.

"Go to her, Paul." My uncle nudged me forward.

I inched towards her. Everything around me—every sound, every thought—slowed. Wanting to be strong as my uncle suggested, I walked deliberately, but with each step I fought not to cry. I knew then what had happened. My dream was now clear.

I stood before her. She grabbed my trembling hands. "Son, your father died this morning." Even with each word spoken softly, her declaration struck me like an apology delivered for wrongdoing, like there was no other way to make it easier.

Her brown eyes shimmered from the tears that filled her pain-filled face. My head started to spin. She reached to hug me. But I turned away, bolting from the room.

"Paul! Wait! Sweetie, come back!"

The crowd parted as I pushed my way through. With one destination in mind, I forged forward. First Andre, now Father . . . Oak Grove was cursed!

"Paul, get back to you mother!" my uncle shouted.

"No! Let him go." Mother's voice was the last I heard as I ran through the front door. It slammed shut behind me. I ran as fast as I could through the oak grove.

"Mista Paul, is sometin' wrong?" A field hand called to me as I ran by. With my tie and jacket flapping in the wind, I galloped towards the fields. Nothing could stop me.

I heaved for breath. The branches of the lone oak loomed towards the ground. Like a squirrel chased up a tree, I climbed to the highest limb within my reach. Perched like a bird and nestled among the leaves, I sat and wept. Crying until no more tears could be shed, I looked to the sky and then screamed, "Why?" Over and over, the word just seemed to form on my tongue.

With the sun fading, locusts began their nightly chant. Numb—no part of my body moved, with the exception of my chest expanding with each breath.

Acorns crunched beneath me. Mim was searching the tree for me. "Child, where are ya? Answer yo ole Mim."

I just sat there wishing she would go away, yet relieved that she was there.

The plantation bell sounded. The Angelus echoed in my mind. I shimmied down the tree. There, Mim waited with outstretched arms.

"I know. It hurts somethin' fierce. If I could hug it outta ya, I would." She wrapped her arms around me. I felt drained, like my very life had been sucked out of me. "Yo mamma's worried sick ova ya. Let's git back ta da house. She needs ya naw more dan ever. Come on naw."

Hand in hand, we walked through the field and then into the oak grove. Lights beamed from the porches and balconies. Lamps glowed through the French doors. Our feet shuffled across snapping twigs and crumpling oak leaves.

The cars had thinned. The porches once filled with people were now empty. Only the shadows of people inside were visible.

As we drew closer to the house, a lone person walked towards us with a light in hand. "Auntie Gladys, is dat you?"

"Yeah, baby. I got Paul wit' me. Go ahead an' tell Suga' he's comin' home."

"Yes, ma'am. She's gonna be real happy ta hear dat." Georgia ran ahead.

"Child, when we git ya home, ya go spen' some time wit' yo mamma. I'm gonna fix ya somethin' ta eat and bring it ta ya. Nobody's gonna botha ya. Ya hear me?"

"Yes, ma'am." My voice cracked. The thought of seeing Mother sickened my stomach. I ran away when she needed me. How could I face her?

"Child, wha' ya freten' about? Tell me. What's goin' on in dat head a yo's."

I feared telling her.

"Honey child, nobody can say dey know what ya t'inkin' or feelin'. Laud knows I've seen a lot ma'se'f. But I know dis much. Yo mamma loves ya and ya love her. Y'all've got each otha'. Go ta her, child. Go ta her right naw." She patted my behind as she pushed me forward.

I resisted for a few moments. Suddenly, a burst of energy filled me. With my arms flaying, I bolted with all my might.

In the scant lighting, I barely made out Mother's silhouette. She paced on the lawn just off the back porch. I ran all the harder to reach her.

I leapt into her arms. She welcomed me with hugs and kisses. "I love you, sweetie." She repeated the words as she wept with me. Holding each other, we stood on the porch until Mim joined us.

"Suga', I think we should go on inside befo' da mosquitoes eat us alive."

Arm in arm, we walked slowly to the porch. Mother rested her head on Mim's bosom. Tears dropped from Mother's eyes.

Grandfather greeted us on the back porch. "Gladys, would you take Renee inside while I talk to Paul for a bit. Miss Elida is in the parlor."

"Sho' will, Mista Sam."

Grandfather rested his hand on my shoulder. "Paul, let's swing out here for a minute. We'll give the ladies a chance to manage the affairs of the house without getting in their way." He guided me towards a large, green cypress swing on the rear veranda.

The grandfather clock in the parlor chimed the stroke of seven. The wooden frame holding the cypress lats strained under Grandfather's weight. The swing swayed to the whine of the chain as I hopped on.

"My stars, Paul. This old swing used to never do this when you sat with me. I guess you're really growing up." Digging into his jacket, he lifted a fireball jawbreaker from his pocket. "Your grandmother says I'm addicted to these damn things." He handed one to me. The big round ball bulged from my cheeks as the first tinges peppered my mouth. "Clears the sinuses real quick, doesn't it?"

"Yes, sir."

"I'll tell you, there's nothin' like a warm summer night and a good old fashion fireball—just a sucking on it while rockin' on an old swing to clear a man's head." He nudged me with his elbow. "Tough day, huh?"

My lips pressed tight as I nodded.

"Want to talk about it?"

My head dipped.

"That's fine. No need to. Just want you to know that if you want to talk, I'm here." He placed his arms around me. We rocked back and forth on the swing. Every now and then, a tree frog serenaded us.

"Is that your stomach growling?"

"Yes, sir."

"You must be starved. How about we get ourselves inside and go get something to eat? I'm not sure what Gladys prepared for dinner, but I'm sure it's good."

The swing strained in relief as we lifted off. Grandfather stretched. We walked around the porch to the kitchen door to the aroma of shrimp creole.

57

"I was wonderin' if y'all were gonna come inside ta eat. I went ahead and reheated da food. Y'all go clean up an' I'm gonna git it out dere in jus' a few minutes. Go ahead naw."

"Come on, Paul. We best do as the old woman says before she busts a gut."

"Ole woman?" She picked back at Grandfather.

Grandfather pushed me along. "Let's get cleaned up." The kitchen door swung open from Grandfather's push. It squeaked as it swayed back and forth. "I'm gonna have to oil that door."

We walked down the hallway connecting the kitchen to the foyer. The staircase stood there sandwiched between the parlor and dining room.

"Paul, is that you?" Grandmother's voice echoed through the hallway.

"Yes, dear. I've got him with me." Grandfather answered for me.

"Renee would like to see him for a minute."

We entered to lamps glowing softly. Mother sat in the red velvet Queen Anne chair.

"Go hug your mother, son." Grandfather nudged me forward.

Mother opened her arms. As I hugged her, she sighed. "Are you okay, sweetheart?"

"Yes, ma'am."

"I love you," she whispered. The words echoed against the walls.

"Miz Elida—" Mim's voice resonated through the room. "Oh, I'm sorry. Didn' know y'all were in here tagetha'."

"It's fine, Gladys."

"I'm almos' done heatin' dat shrimp creole. I know dis is Paul's favorite, so I dished out some earlier so dere's gonna be lots of shrimp in it. But, Mr. Sam an' Paul need ta wash up real quick."

Mim stroked my cheek. Her smooth, soft hands smelled of Jasmine, probably hand lotion given to her by Grandmother.

"Ladies, if y'all will excuse us." Grandfather led me out the parlor. "You're quite the young gentleman." He followed me up the stairs. "See you in a few minutes."

"Yes, sir."

I entered to my bed turned down and Georgia drawing the drapes.

"Oh, Mista Paul, I didn't hear ya comin'."

"Excuse me, Georgia. I didn't mean to startle you."

"Oh, no. I'm just turnin' down da beds fo' da evenin'. I'll be out yo way in jus' a second. I know Auntie Gladys is heatin' up dinna, an' I'm sho' ya need ta git down dere quick."

"If you'll excuse me, I'll step into the bathroom to freshen up." I closed the bathroom door. In the mirror, a reflection startled me. *Father?* I squeezed my eyes shut. "Please be real. Please, God." I held them closed, hoping that I was waking from a bad dream. Reopening them, nothing more than the reflection of my brown and green eyes, my father's eyes, stared back.

My knees weakened. The room spun. I grabbed the counter and held on to it tightly. The appeal of dinner waned as my stomach soured. Perspiration glistened from my lip and my brow. I couldn't breathe.

My father was dead. Another life had been stolen from me. I didn't know what I was going to do.

Five

The Confederate rifles making up the rails of the Huey P. Long Bridge zipped by us. Mother and I swung in the back seat as Francis, our driver, swerved to miss the infamous kink on the eastbound descending lane. There, the bridge joined, not quite fitting together, the joke being that Aggie engineers were hired to build it like a crooked Louisiana politician.

"Miz Renee, beggin' yo pardon, ma'am. Are we goin' straight ta da airport?"

"Yes, Francis. We'll get Paul checked in and then grab something to eat." Mother twiddled her white-laced handkerchief. "Sweetie, are you sure you're ready to leave for school this soon? The headmaster said you could wait another week."

"Yes, ma'am. Classes start in two days and I don't want to fall behind."

"Promise me if it gets rough or if you need something you'll call me."

"I promise. But I want you to promise me the same."

Mother kissed me, quickly wiping her red lip marks off my cheek. "I'll call you everyday if you'd like."

"That won't, I mean . . . if you need, you can call me ten times a day."

"Your father would be so proud of you. I . . ." Her upper lip quivered.

"Mother, if you need me to, I'll stay. I don't want—"

"Oh, no sweetie. It's not that. I'm just concerned."

"I promise, if anything comes up I'll call you and come home." I held my hand on her shoulder until she turned towards me.

"You're so handsome in that uniform. It always made your father proud to see you dressed so crisply. I know he's smiling from heaven." She folded her handkerchief into a neat triangle, then patted a tear from the corner of her eye.

The traffic along Jefferson Highway crawled. With large swampy areas between Thibodaux and the airport, and only one bridge and a couple of ferries to cross the river, this was the quickest route.

"Paul, your allowance will be deposited into First National Bank of Boston every Monday. They're authorized to release additional funds to you if you need them. Here's two hundred dollars in Travelers Cheques. You sure that's going to be enough?"

"Plenty. Seriously, Mother, I'm fine."

"You think I'm a mother hen, this being your fourth year at Ridgefield. I'm sure by now this is routine to you. But, I'll tell you, I don't think I'll ever get used to you leaving home."

The traffic blurred. Soon the roar of a jet engine drew our attention to the palm tree lined entrance of New Orleans International Airport. Cars paced slowly to the passenger drop off of the upper deck of the green-domed main terminal.

"My stars, this place gets busier every time we come. I can't imagine where all these people are heading to."

"Dey mus' be goin' somewhere mighty impo'tant wit' all dis rushin'." Francis steered the car to the curb. "Miz Renee, I'm gonna git da luggage ta da Sky Cab. Go on ahead an' I'll meet ya inside."

"I can help."

"Ya know betta. I got it unda' control."

Mother lifted several dollars from her purse. "For the Sky Cabs. We'll meet you at the TWA ticket counter."

"Yez, ma'am."

Mother and I negotiated our way through the crowd as it swarmed around us. "I wonder what's going on?"

"Go Green Wave!" A young man robed in green and blue regalia led hundreds of similar creatures through the doorway and into the terminal.

She turned to a lone voice yelling through the crowd. "I guess Tulane's got a ball game this weekend."

As a matter of fact, ma'am, they play the Aggies of Texas A&M on Saturday," a young gentleman wearing a uniform with the gold Ridgefield academic crest interjected. "Beggin' yo pardon, I heard there was another man from Louisiana going to Ridgefield and I wanted to introduce ma'se'f. I'm John Cheramie."

"My, my, Mr. Cheramie, you sure are a big fella."

"Yes, ma'am. Six foot five and just under two-hundred and twenty-five pounds."

"My stars, you could be one of those Tulane football players."

"Maybe some day."

"Well, it's a pleasure to meet you. This is my son, Paul."

"Paul, I'm John." My hand disappeared in his as he shook it. His deep voice vibrated my chest. "My dad's been assigned overseas and, well, here I am off to boardin' school."

Making eye contact with him was difficult. I pulled my head back just to see his jaw. He must have thought I was an idiot since I just stood there saying nothing.

"Mr. Cheramie, are your parents here with you?"

"No, ma'am. I flew in from the Netherlands yesterday to wrap up my packin'."

"You must be a fine young man for your parents to trust you so."

"Yes, ma'am. I'll be a sophomore this year and well, our driver brought me out."

"A sophomore. My stars! You look like you're ready to graduate."

"Not for a few years, ma'am. How about you, Paul?"

"I'll be a sophomore as well."

"Man." John's head popped back in surprise. "Ya don't look that old."

My head dipped as I compared my small frame to the giant standing near me.

"Well, he is. Go ahead, sweetheart. You can tell him. It's nothing to be embarrassed about." Mother drew closer to me. "Go on."

"Well, I'll be thirteen . . . I'm a . . . I'm actually a couple of years ahead of my class."

"Cool. I mean, that's incredible. Ya must have a lot of brain power in that little head."

"I guess so."

The crowds thickened around us as we stood just outside the doors. Green and blue banners filled the air in every direction. "Go Wave!" rang out from time to time.

Mother coddled my arm. "Gentlemen, what say we take this meeting inside?"

"I'll lead the way, ma'am." John pushed through the crowd. "Excuse us. May we slip by?" Maybe it was his size, or possibly his voice. Whatever it was, the crowd parted, allowing us to easily move through them.

"Mother, I believe the TWA counter is over to the left."

"Why I think you're correct, sweetie. How about you, Mr. Cheramie? Are you flying TWA?"

"Yes, ma'am, as matter of fact I am."

"That's wonderful. That will give you two quite a bit of time to get to know each other."

John grabbed my shoulder. "Hey, pal. Where ya sittin'?"

"I'm in 14A."

"Oh."

"Is there a problem, Mr. Cheramie?"

64

"Well, I'm in first class."

"Now, Paul, you see. Other boys at Ridgefield are traveling in first class. Why didn't—"

"Mother, please. Not here."

"Oh, I know. You don't want me embarrassing you in front of your new friend."

"My tickets are fine. The plane is empty at this time, and I've got plenty of room."

"Ya know, that's true." John joined us in the ticket line. "How about I turn these tickets in and join you?"

"There's no need. I wouldn't want to—"

"No problem, pal. It bein' my first year at Ridgefield, it'll be kinda cool to get the inside scoop." He briskly tugged on his jacket, straightening the lapels and aligning the buttons. With his shoulders pulled back and chest extended forward, he looked like a recruiting poster Marine on his way to Vietnam. "Do you have a roommate?"

"Um, no. I, um, I mean, I roomed alone for the last couple of years."

"Bad breath, huh!" John slapped me on my back. My body jerked forward and I almost fell over. "So, why don't we talk about roomin' together on the plane?"

Mother smiled. "I think that's a wonderful idea, don't you, Paul?"

"Yes, ma'am."

"May we help the next person in line?" We moved forward in unison to the ticket agent greeting us. It was Mrs. Boudreaux, a friend of ours.

"Ma'am, I'd like to cash these in for a coach seat." John winked at her.

"Why certainly, sir. Is there a problem?"

"No, ma'am. I'm travelin' with this young gentleman. He's booked in coach and doesn't wanna impose on his parents for the expense. You know boardin' school tuition and—"

"I see. So is he your friend?"

"Yes, ma'am. We've been friends for years. I'm the big, dumb jock and he's the quiet, unassumin' scholar. If it wouldn't be for him, I'd not be returnin' to school. As a matter of fact—"

"Young man, that's one of the best lines of bull I've been fed in some time." Mrs. Boudreaux peered through her reading glasses. She turned from John, then faced Mother. "Good morning, Mrs. de la Moret. How are you doing?"

"We're doing fine, Faith. It so very kind of you to ask."

"I see young Mr. de la Moret is traveling with us today."

I approached the counter. "Yes, ma'am."

"If I recall, your folks flew out about this time last year to see you for your birthday. How about a complimentary ride in first class? Let's say 3A for you and 3B for your best friend. The stewardess can watch him that way." Mrs. Boudreaux sneered at John.

"Busted." John's fair complexion caused his face to glow all the redder.

I gave her my ticket. "Thank you, Mrs. Boudreaux. It's very kind of you to do so."

"It's always a pleasure to have you aboard. And, Mrs. de la Moret, if there's anything we can do, please let us know."

Mother stiffened her upper lip. Her eyes welled with tears, as did Mrs. Boudreaux's. They touched hands. With a deep sigh, Mother bid a silent farewell. She took several deep breaths and with a shake of her head, poised herself.

"Mother, I see Francis coming. Would you like to join him for something to eat?"

"Sure, sweetie." She targeted a po' boy stand just across from our concourse.

"Mother, what would you like?"

"The usual, sweetie."

"How about you, Francis?"

"I'll take an oysta' po' boy."

"John—"

"Let me give ya a hand, pal." He joined me. "This is one of the best things about New Orleans."

"What's that?"

"The food! There can't be any place on the planet with food as good as home, especially French bread baked at Dufrene's. Man, those big holes in the bread and that light, flaky crust. I love how it crunches when you smash it to get your mouth around it."

I had no argument. Even Mim, for all of her culinary excellence, struggled to bake bread with holes as large and crust as light and flaky as Dufrene's. She could fry shrimp and oysters with the best of them. But the bread was yet to be mastered by anyone I knew other than those who baked it at Dufrene's.

"So, what's your favorite, pal?"

"I prefer a shrimp and oyster combo."

"Never had one, but today's gonna be the day to try." John's lips smacked.

"May I he'p ya, sir?"

"Yes, ma'am. I would like two oyster po' boys, two shrimp and oyster combos, two Cokes, a Dr. Pepper, and a . . ."

"Dr. Pepper," John added.

"Dat comes to twelve dollars and t'irty-two cents, sir."

"Hold on, Paul. I've got money."

"Mr. Cheramie," Mother called to John from the small cafe table, "put your money away this very instant. Paul will take care of it."

"Yes, ma'am. But—"

"Don't 'but' me, young man. Just do as I say."

John leaned over. "Your mamma's a beautiful lady, but mighty tough."

With sandwiches and soft drinks in hand, we joined Mother and Francis at the small table. Gulps replaced any form of conversation between us.

"Why Mr. Cheramie, you practically inhaled that po' boy."

"Yes, ma'am. I was pretty hungry and these po' boys are the best in the city."

"You know dats right. Dey sho' are finga' lickin' good." Savoring the last of the drippings from his sandwich, Francis loudly popped each finger out of his mouth after he sucked it clean.

"My, my, Francis. Is that a smirk on your face?"

"Yez, ma'am, sho' is." He bobbed his head.

"You make finishing a po' boy sound like a p-i-g whalin' in the mud with its belly full and singin' in a symphony orchestra." Dipping deeply into her drawl, Mother fluttered her eyelashes. "Mr. Cheramie, y'all must consida ma comments humorous, I see."

"Yes, ma'am. I mean, no, ma'am." With a smile broadening across his face, John struggled to get the words out. "How do you keep a straight face with her?"

"You boys talkin' 'bout little ole me again? Cause y'all betta watch what y'all sayin'."

"Oh, yes siree. I know dats a fac'. Why, when she gits a goin' wit' her hominy grits all stirred up, well, hell hath no wrath—"

"Why Francis, whatever do you mean? I declare, young Mista Paul. Yo selection of friends might come unda' considerable scrutiny, sir."

Several passengers turned their chairs and were now chuckling at us.

"Ladies and gentlemen, announcing the arrival of TWA Flight 26 from St. Louis. Passengers can be met momentarily at Gate 4 on Concourse C."

"Is dat yo plane, Mista Paul?"

"I believe so. I'll check if you'll excuse me."

"Wait up, pal. I'll come with you." John leapt up to join me. "It's pretty cool that we're both from New Orleans and headin' off to boardin' school."

"Yes. It's quite nice."

"You don't say a lot, do you? Are you always this serious?"

"There isn't a great deal that warrants discussion, and yes, I'm always serious."

"Man, I've got to lighten you up." John lagged behind as we walked to the ticket counter.

Mrs. Boudreaux smiled. "Can I help you, Paul?"

"Yes, ma'am. Is the St. Louis flight our plane to Boston?"

"As a matter of fact it is. By the way, you look mighty handsome in that uniform."

"Man, you're blushin'." John whispered from behind me.

Mrs. Boudreaux cocked her head. "I bet you don't blush at anything, do you, Mr. Cheramie?"

John's face flushed beet red.

"Thank you, Mrs. Boudreaux."

John blocked my path. "Do ya always talk like that?"

"Like what?"

"Like so formal and stuff?"

"Let's just get to our gate." We joined Mother and Francis.

"Mista Paul, I've got yo and Mista John's bags right here."

"Thank you, Francis. I'll take it."

"Oh, no sir. I'm gonna carry it ta da plane." Francis tucked the bags behind him.

"Francis, I can carry my own bag."

"Yez, sir. I've seen ya do it, and ya mighty good at dat. But, when I'm around, ya ain't gonna carry no bag, no how, no way. Understood."

"Yes, sir." I knew better than to argue with him. "Mother, after you."

"Why thank you, sweetheart." I extended my arm. Mother sashayed past John to join me. We looked like toy soldiers standing guard over her. "If you gentlemen would excuse me, I'd like to speak with Paul in private for a minute."

We walked ahead of John and Francis toward the gate. Mother rested her hand on my arm. Looking up at her I realized why Father stared at her so often. Even now I could hear him saying to her, "My love, you are so beautiful." I missed him.

"Paul, what is it, sweetie? You look like you're a million miles away." Light reflected off the silver comb in her hair.

"No, ma'am. I was, um . . . I was just thinking."

"About what, sweetheart?"

"Just . . ." A strangle hold of emotion gripped my throat.

"You were thinking about your father, weren't you?"

I nodded.

"There's nothing to be embarrassed about. You look up, now." She lifted my chin. Her eyes greeted me. In her smile, she attempted to assure me that all was okay.

"Ladies and gentlemen, in just a few moments we will begin boarding TWA Flight 26 to Boston's Logan International Airport. If you would—" The gate agent's voice faded.

I looked deeply into Mother's eyes. Father would have never left her under these circumstances. We held on to each other tightly. Seeing her reminded me of all the times Father embraced her.

"Miz Renee, Mista Paul, beggin' yo pardon, but dey callin' fo' Mista Paul ta board."

"There's so little time and so much to say. You remember, Paul de la Moret, I love you."

"Yes, ma'am."

"You remember yourself up there with all those Yankees."

"Yes, ma'am. Southern born, Southern bred, Southern alive, Southern dead." The last word faded as it barely made it out of my mouth.

I embraced her once more. Her heart pounded. My throat tightened. I could hardly breathe. Releasing her, I walked towards the gate. I turned to gather one last look. "I love you." She lipped the words, then patted her handkerchief to her eyes.

With a sigh, I turned and entered the jet way. Hot, humid air hit me. I dared not look back.

"Hey, pal. Wait up." Even with the thud of John's steps shaking the walkway, I pushed forward.

I boarded the jet and moved to stow my bag in the overhead compartment.

"What's the rush?"

I struggled to reach the overhead compartment, but John pushed my bag inside. I tucked my head away so that he would not see the tear on my cheek. The window provided an excellent escape from any further conversation.

I opened my father's copy of Marcus Aurelius.

> In my father I observed mildness of temper, and unchangeable resolution in the things which he had determined on after due deliberation; and no vainglory in those things which men call honors; and a love of labor and perseverance and a readiness to listen to whoever had anything to propose for the common weal; and undeviating firmness in giving to every man his deserts; and a knowledge derived from experience of the right times for vigorous action and for relaxation.

My seat jolted as John dropped into his. He pulled my book forward. "Heavy reading for a flight back to school, don't ya think?"

I peered out of the plane window in search of Mother.

"It's okay, pal. It's hard to leave our folks behind. But we're gonna have a great time. Man, I can't wait. Just think about it—"

"Think about what? You think you can just pop in and all of sudden we're best friends or something? That I need some big guy like you to watch over me? That I look so pathetic, like some little kid in a uniform—"

"Whoa, man, I'm just tryin' to be nice."

"Do me a favor."

"What's that?"

"Leave me alone."

John's face dropped. For over a week, I had dealt with people telling me what I felt or what I should feel. The last thing I needed was some big, dumb jock joining in.

"Excuse me, gentlemen. Care for anything to drink?" The stewardess smiled.

John forced a smile. "Orange juice, please ma'am."

"And for your, brother?"

"Brother?" John's voice boomed through the cabin.

"Yes, aren't y'all brothers?"

"No, ma'am. Why? Do we look alike?"

"No, you were fussing with each other. I've got two boys about your ages and they fuss with each other all the time." The stewardess returned to the galley. Thuds of cargo doors beneath us shook the plane. A steady stream of passengers filed past us.

"I don't have a brother," John muttered. "At least I don't think I do."

"What are you talking about?"

"You seem close to your mom."

"Yes. Very."

"I wish I knew my mom."

"But you said your parents are in the Netherlands."

"My adoptive parents."

"Oh, I'm—"

"No. Don't. They're wonderful parents. It's just that they told me while I was in the Netherlands with them. I mean, I've kinda suspected it for years. I'm almost a foot taller than my dad and don't look like any of the family, what little there is."

"Here you go, gentlemen, two orange juices, fresh squeezed—that is, several months ago. Drink up. We'll be departing shortly."

John sipped his orange juice. "I don't mean to pry, pal, but are your parents divorced?"

"No."

"So where's your dad?"

I clinched my jaw.

"Hey, man. What's wrong?"

"My father's dead!"

"I'm—"

"Please don't say anything. Just . . ." The blue leather upholstery of the seat in front of me blurred. Nausea overtook me. "If you'll excuse me . . ." I bolted up from my seat to the lavatory. I tripped over John and the flight attendant. Slamming the door shut, I locked myself inside.

As I splashed cool water on my face, I peered into the mirror. "Dear God, please help me." Sweat beaded on my forehead and upper lip. The wall of the lavatory seemed to squeeze in.

The door rattled from a knock. "Sir—"

"He's fine, ma'am. Just gets a little queasy when he flies, that's all." John's muffled voice carried through the door. "Hey, Paul. I've got your Dramamine if ya need it. We'll be takin' off in a few minutes and whenever you're feelin' better, they need you to take your seat. Okay?"

"I'll be out in a moment."

"See, he's fine. I'll take care of it and get him situated."

"All righty. Just have him take his seat as soon as possible."

"You heard that, pal. You've got just a few minutes." The door pressed inward as John leaned against it. "Hey, pal, take slow deep breaths. Everything's gonna be cool. We've got plenty of time."

"How's he doing?"

"Better, ma'am. He'll be out in a minute."

I slid the latch. The bulge from John's weight against the door eased. With one hand folded over the other, John grimaced. "Now, didn't I tell ya to take the Dramamine before we boarded? Man, I can dress you up, but can't take you anywhere. Let's take our seats before we get this nice lady in trouble."

The stewardess shook her head. "Buckle up, gentlemen."

"Yes, ma'am. The moment I get him situated I'm gonna strap 'im in good." John whispered in my ear, "Just keep walkin'. I've got ya covered."

Warmth rushed over me. With my seat in clear view, I walked with John's support.

The stewardess placed a glass on my console. "I've brought some club soda over. Sometimes it helps settle the stomach."

"Thank you, ma'am." John sat next to me. The seat rocked. "Are ya alright, pal?"

I nodded.

"Ladies and gentlemen, with the cabin door now closed, please give your attention to the stewardesses as we prepare for departure. We have—" The engines rocked the plane back from the gate. The jet bridge cleared from my view. I peered out of the porthole in search of Mother. Her silver hair-comb shimmered through the plate-glass window of the terminal.

Constraining my wave to her, I slouched into the seat. "I hope I made the right choice." The words spilled softly off my lips.

"What's that, pal?"

"Nothing." If I could just get a glimmer, a brief connection to tell me all was okay. "Please wave," I prayed quietly to myself.

"She's standin' there, isn't she?"

"I beg your pardon?"

"Relax, man. It's cool. There's nothin' wrong with lovin' your mom."

Just then, I caught sight of her handkerchief fluttering back and forth. "She sees me."

"Yeah, pal. I bet every wakin' moment of the day."

The jet engines ceased to roar. The plane turned. Her image faded, and with one final bob, it was gone. As the wheels rolled down the runway, I turned to John. "I'm—"

"No, don't. Ma mom says you never apologize for lovin' someone."

With one great blast, the engines lifted the jet off the runway. A white egret floated over the green duckweed filling the cypress swamps of the Bonne Carre spillway. With Lake Pontchartrain to our right, sugarcane fields bordered the river to our left. The view faded as we lifted through puffy white clouds.

"Would you mind grabbing my bag for me?"

"Yeah." John opened the overhead bin without leaving the seat. He pulled my bag out and handed it to me.

I unzipped my bag to the cigar box carefully positioned at the very top.

"What's that, pal?"

"Nothing. Just my baseball cards and stuff."

"You collect baseball cards?"

"Yes. Why?"

"Let me show ya somethin'." John opened his bag. "Have you ever seen one of these?"

I sat stunned. The Roger Maris card on the top of his stack was identical to the card that I had. Andre was the only other person I knew who had one.

Six

"On a dark night . . ." The lamp light reflected off the writings of St. John of the Cross. While I quietly studied at my desk by the window, John had propped a chair in the hallway just outside of our dorm room. From the bell tower, the clock struck 10 P.M. Darkness masked the beauty of Ridgefield's snow covered Commons.

"Hey, is Paul sleeping?" William's voice carried through the closed door. The twenty-foot ceilings of the dorm exaggerated every sound.

John snorted. "You're kiddin', right?"

"How many nights with no sleep?"

"Can't count that high."

"More dreams?"

"Yeah."

"Has he talked to you about them?"

"Just one. His mother remarryin' or something."

"Heavy shit." A fist hammered on my door. "Hey, Paul." The door flew open, banging against the wall. William sailed across the room and rolled across the floor, a victim to another of John's pranks.

I lifted my eyes off the page. "Go easy, fellas. If Father Chandler catches you—"

"Yeah, I can hear him now." John bowed his chest as he stood in oration. "Gentlemen, these hallowed walls have seen to the education and edification of hundreds of this country's greatest leaders. Why the very hinges and fixtures of the doors themselves were designed and assembled by famous local artisans, many of whom carry historical prominence. Let us preserve their memory in the manner in which we open and close each and every door."

William lifted a note from his blazer. "Paul, as much as I dig this ritual, you've got a phone call. Father Chandler said you could take it in his office."

"Who is it from?"

John snatched it out of William's hand.

"I don't have time to mess with you, John. Give me the damn note."

"Note. What note? Do you see a note, my gentle sir?"

William shrugged his shoulders to John's silly British accent.

"Dammit, John. I'm not playing. Just give it to me!"

"Oh yes you are." John yanked my chair.

I struggled to reach him, but the momentum from my flying across the room was too great. I wanted to whack the smirk off his face as he peeled the note open with his pinkie extended.

"Now dats what I call cultua'." John dove across the room. "I think it's time you shut that book and come," slapping my book shut as he flew by, he landed with a thud in his bed, "play!"

"Damn, John. I was—"

"Let me guess. Readin' St. John of the Cross, reviewin' the writings of Aristotle for Father Chandler's exam, and sittin' in that chair far too long."

"The note! Read it or give it to me."

"Oh, yes. The summons from the headmaster. Let's see. Please have Mr. de la Moret report to my office A.S.A.P. His mommy requests that he call her when possible."

William rustled my hair. "Oh, Paul, your mommy wants you."

"Shut up, William."

John spun my chair back across the room. "Paul's in trouble, nanna, nanna, boo, boo."

"Would you stop, already! I swear, I'm going to request another roommate."

"I'm the only senior who'll room with a sixteen-year-old and ya know you worship the quicksand I walk on."

I started towards the door. "Yes, especially the quicksand. By the way, I might only be sixteen, but you behave like you're six."

"Your coat and hat." John stopped me halfway out the door. "Remember, white, snow, cold, freeze, demerits for bein' outta uniform on school grounds. I'll come with ya." He pushed me into the hallway. It was unusually quiet for this time of night.

Our suitemate, Ted, peeked out of his room. "Where're you heading, Paul?"

"The headmaster." John head-locked me as he dragged me down the hallway.

Ted pursed his lips. "Woe, man. Make sure you pucker pretty for him."

I smacked John. "You've got a big mouth."

"Almost as big—"

"Grow up."

"Never!" He thundered down the stairs. "Tag!" John almost knocked me over. He bolted through the doorway and sprinted across the Commons.

"I'm not doing this." The cold stung. It was hard to breathe. Steam streamed out of my mouth with each breath. Running seemed like a stupid idea.

"Come on, Paul. Don't be such a puss. Bet ya can't catch me."

"Okay. You win."

"Ya need to lighten up."

"You need—" I bumped Brother Michael.

"Good evening, Mr. de la Moret."

"Oh, good evening, sir."

"Heading to Father Chandler's office, I see."

"Yes, sir."

"And Mr. Cheramie?"

"Uhh—"

"Yes, I understand. Confucius said, 'To see what is right, and not to do it, is want of courage.' Let's not want for courage, shall we? Have a good evening, Mr. de la Moret."

"Same to you, sir." Snow crunched under my feet. "John, wait up." John's shadow stretched forty feet from the lighting near the flagpole. I picked up my pace. "You saw Brother Michael walking across the Commons and didn't say a word. Thanks for nothing."

"Hey, am I my brother's keeper?"

"No, you're a—"

"Look! Over there!" Pointing to the corner of the headmaster's office, John froze.

"What?"

"Nothin'. Just wanted to make ya look." He rubbed his hands together. "So, ya up for a visit to the headmaster? Enterin' into the hallowed halls of academia. Venturin' into classic tombs and tales of forgotten lore." He braced himself before pulling on the double doors. They weighed a ton. "Careful. Don't let it knock ya in the ass."

"Shh! This place is nothing more than an echo chamber."

"Man, you're so scared of the headmaster it's pitiful."

"Oh, and you're so brave."

"Good evening, gentlemen." Father Chandler's voice resonated off the wooden rafters of the cathedral ceilings.

"Good evening, sir."

"I take it you're here to return the call to your mother?"

"Call your mommy," John muttered.

"Did you have something to add, Mr. Cheramie?"

"No, sir. I was just—"

"Yes. I'm sure you were making some notable contribution to Mr. de la Moret's edification." Father Chandler signaled for us to move ahead. "Prize Bull" was the description he usually gave when John tried to talk his way out of trouble. "Inside my office, gentlemen."

Having the headmaster walk behind us was always eerie. The wood paneled walls and turn of the century overhead lighting cast his office in a dim glow, like something out of a Dracula movie, except for the life-size crucifix hanging on the wall.

Father Chandler pointed to the phone. "I'll wait outside, Mr. de la Moret."

"Thank you, sir."

"Call your mommy." John mumbled out of the corner of his mouth.

"Shut up!"

Father Chandler cleared his throat. "Is there a problem, gentlemen?"

"Oh, no, sir. Just helpin' Paul." The door vibrated against the shim as Father closed it behind him. "Call your mommy."

"Would you shut up while I dial the number!"

"Oak Grove Plantation."

"Mim?"

"Child, it's so good ta hear yo voice. Are ya eatin'? Ya stayin' warm and outta trouble?"

"Yes, ma'am."

"I'm gonna git yo mamma. She's been waitin' fo' yo call. Hol' da line."

"Be a good boy and talk sweet to your mommy," John purred.

I elbowed John in the ribs. "If you don't shut up, I'm going to—"

"Gonna what, suga'?"

"Mother!"

"Oh sweetie, it's so good to hear your voice."

"Is everything okay, I mean—"

"Everything's fine, sweetie. I wanted to hear your voice and, well, I've got wonderful news. You remember Jacques?"

"Yes, ma'am. How's he doing?"

"Wonderful. He asks about you every day."

"Every day?"

"Yes, sweetie. He's been spending quite a bit of time with me here at the plantation and well . . ." Mother sounded wonderful. The sadness that filled her voice since Father's death was gone. "Jacques has something to ask you. Hold on."

"Yes, ma'am."

John leaned into the receiver. "What's goin' on, pal?"

"Shh!" I pushed him away.

"Paul, how are you, buddy?"

"Doing very well, sir."

"Now what did I tell you about all that 'sir' stuff." His voice was already very deep, but his heavy Texas drawl deepened it even more. "Paul, I have something to ask you."

"Yes, sir."

"As the oldest man in the family, I thought I'd come to you first. I'd like to ask you for your mother's hand in marriage."

"I'll be dammed." John pushed the phone from my ear.

"Shh!" I pulled the receiver away from him.

"What's that, buddy?"

"I'm sorry. The lines must be crossed."

"So what do you think? If you need time to think about it—"

"No, sir. I mean, as long as Mother is happy."

"Buddy, I promise you I'll take good care of your mamma. So what do ya say?"

"I'm, I mean—"

"I have one other thing I'd like to ask you. Would you be my best man?"

"Me?"

82

"I can't think of a better man than you."

"I don't know what to say."

"How about yes?"

"Well, yes, sir. I mean, Jacques."

"Sounds great, buddy. I'm gonna give you back to your mother."

"Sweetie, we're planning a December wedding. Jacques and I are going to come to visit before then. Sweetie, are you okay with—"

"Oh, Mother. I'm very happy. I'm . . ."

"What is it, sweetie?"

"Well, I mean, it's just good to hear you laugh."

"Oh, sweetheart. You've been so brave, beyond anything I could expect. I'm happy, and I want you to be the same."

"Yes, ma'am." Don't cry. I repeated the words over and over to myself. It had been a long time since I heard Mother happy in this way. "Mother, I've got curfew coming up."

"Okay, sweetheart. I love you."

"I love you, too. Tell Jacques good-bye for me."

"I will, sweetie."

The phone line clicked off. The grandfather clock in the corner of the headmaster's office marked eleven o'clock.

"Your mom's gettin' married." John squinted. "Man, that's weird."

"Not really. Jacques is a good guy and they've been dating for almost a year. So—"

"No, Paul. Not them gettin' married . . . you dreamin' about it."

"Oh, that."

"You don't think it's weird that you had a dream and here she is not even three days later callin' to tell you?"

"I guess so."

"You guess so? You described this almost to the letter."

"We better hurry back to the dorm before we're late for curfew."

"Look, if you don't want to talk about it, just say so."

"Okay, I don't want to talk about it."

"That's bullshit. Why is it that every time this comes up you won't talk about it?" John squared his hat on his head and then tucked his hands into his gloves.

"Maybe because there's nothing to talk about."

"You can be so damned stubborn."

We pushed the wooden doors open. A cold wind smacked us in the face.

"Ya know, maybe if we talked about this stuff, you'd start sleepin' at night."

I was breathing too hard to reply. With the jog across the Commons complete and four flights of stairs yet to climb, commenting seemed stupid. The tower bell tolled 11:20 P.M. The ten-minute warning before lights out was now in play. "We better hurry."

"Yeah. But don't think I'm lettin' this drop."

We arrived on our dorm floor to the ritual chaos prior to lights out. Ted and William, our suite mates, scurried to get everything done before the trumpeter sounded "Taps."

"Did anybody see my toothbrush?"

"Yeah, I used it to clean the toilettes."

John pushed me aside. "I got the bathroom first."

"No way, John. You'll stink it up beyond—"

"Tough. I outrank ya. I'm a senior and you're—"

"A senior, too."

"Yeah, but you're two years younger than me."

"What does that have to do with getting the bathroom first?"

"I'm your elder and you can call me St. John of the toilette seat for the next few minutes. I shall return!"

"Just hurry and don't stink it up."

"A rigatoni puca meci. A dark night I sing about." Flinging the door shut, John serenaded us with words he made up. Even with music classes, he couldn't sing a note. Tonight's performance kind of sounded like Mozart, except this version had the makings of a large animal being processed live through a meat grinder, the primal scream of which would frighten any creature in the forest.

"Shut him up already!" William and Ted banged on the bathroom door from their side of the suite.

"Hurry up!" The door rattled as I whacked it.

"Don't rush me while I'm creatin'—"

"Just hurry!"

The door rattled open. John peeked out. "Ah, I do some of my best work in there."

"No. You've died and are rotting from the inside."

"That's nothin' more than the aroma of processed intelligence and creativity."

"Yes, I must admit it smells like pure bullshit to me." Quickly brushing my teeth, I gasped for each breath. The bell tower tolled 11:30 P.M. Silence quickly veiled the dormitory.

"Hey, Paul," John whispered. "Are you okay?"

"I'm fine. Go to sleep."

"You don't sound fine. I mean, this whole weddin' thing with your mom . . ."

"Taps" bellowed. The hallway darkened. With my blankets pulled up to my neck, I settled in for the night. But my mind raced.

"So, you're just gonna lay there and say nothin'."

"You're talking enough for both of us. Just go to sleep." I rolled onto my side. Light filtering through our windows reflected off the whites of John's open eyes.

I tossed and turned. The words of St. John of the Cross resounded in my head.

"On a dark night—" A thunderclap shook my bed.

"Kindled in love with yearnings
—oh, happy chance!
I went forth without being observed,
My house now being at rest.

In darkness and secure,
By the secret ladder, disguised
—oh, happy chance!
In darkness and in concealment,
My house being now at rest.

In the happy night,
In secret, when none saw me,
Nor I beheld aught,
Without light or guide,
Save that which burned in my heart.

This light guided me
More surely than the light of noonday
To the place where he
(Well I knew who!) was awaiting me
A place where none appeared.

Oh, night that guided me,
Oh, night more loved than the dawn,
Oh, night that joined
Beloved with lover,
Lover transformed in the Beloved!

Upon my flowery breast,
Kept wholly for himself alone,
There he stayed sleeping,
and I caressed him,
And the fanning of the cedars made a breeze.

The breeze blew from the turret
As I parted his locks;

With his gentle hand he wounded my neck
And caused all my senses to be suspended."

Maybe I over-studied.

The tower bell tolled 12:00 A.M., then 12:15 A.M., 12:30 A.M., and then 1:00 A.M. My eyes finally grew heavy.

∎

"Help him! Please help my son!"

A ring of blood surrounded a woman and her dying son. I stretched my arms, but could not reach them. Whaling and weeping women surrounded her. "Please, God, help my boy." She lifted her eyes to heaven.

"I can't reach them. Help me." I searched for the lady who visited my dream. A roaring wind swept me into the vortex of a tornado. I swirled around, helpless. Lightening flashed. Faces of people unknown to me drifted by. Their blood-drained countenance and blank stares smacked of death. "Help me, please! Help me!"

Something nicked my neck. I wiped blood away with my hand. A familiar face pierced through the maelstrom encasing me. "Kevin, is that you?"

"Yes! Help—"

"Kevin? Kevin—"

∎

"Paul, wake up!"

I jumped, but could not move. The overhead light blinded me.

"William, unravel his arms and legs. Ted, grab the blanket." John held me up as the blanket and then the sheets loosened around my body. "Take it easy, pal. We'll have ya unknotted in a moment. Ted, get a towel. He's soakin' wet."

"I'm okay. There's no need—"

"Bullshit! You were screamin'. Don't tell me you're okay."

Dripping sweat caused my eyes to sting. My head spun for a few seconds.

Ted handed me a towel. "Here you go, Paul." I lifted my shirt off to dry my chest. "Why don't you shower off real quick?"

My knees wobbled a bit.

"Here, I'll walk with ya." John held my arm. I closed the bathroom door, then slipped off my wet cloths. The shower snapped me out of my daze.

As I dried myself, the chill of the air raised my skin. John, William, and Ted whispered beyond the closed door. I pressed my ear against it to hear.

"Paul would have a fit if we talked to the headmaster."

"This is every night, John." William lowered his voice. "Who's Kevin, by the way?"

"Yeah, he kept screaming his name."

"A friend of his from Louisiana. The guy who got shot."

I rattled the doorknob. As I peeked out, all three of them stared at me in surprise.

"So, John, what do you think about the football game Friday?"

I stepped towards my bed. "Don't even try it, William. I heard the conversation."

"We didn't mean to talk behind your back and stuff. We're just kind of worried."

"It's okay, guys."

"No. It's not okay." John dropped down onto my bed. "You can't go on like this. You're not sleepin' and at times not eatin'. That's not okay."

My eyes traced the seams in the wooden planks of the floor.

"Lift your head, pal." John rested his hand on my shoulder. He pulled me to his chest. "I don't care who you talk to, but you gotta talk to somebody."

William and Ted joined us on the bed. "Yeah, man. That's right."

All three of them huddled around me. The bell tower tolled 3 A.M. "Guys, I'm really tired. Maybe we should just get some sleep."

Reluctantly, William and Ted returned to their room. John and I crawled into our beds once more. I resisted moving or even breathing too hard.

"Paul—"

"I don't want to talk about it. I just want it to leave me alone."

"Who, Paul? Who do you want to leave you alone?"

"Nobody. I mean the dream."

"No, pal, that's not true. You keep sayin', 'Who are you?' I hear you when you talk in your sleep. Then you toss and turn until you scream. Who is it? What is it sayin' to you?"

"I don't know."

"Think! Whatever's scarin' you might go away if you just tell it to."

Silence filled the room once more. I turned on my side, away from John. But my mind raced with the unspoken truth. As the tower clock tolled 4 A.M., I sighed.

"Paul?"

"Just go to sleep."

"No, man. Hear me out." The bed frame squeaked. "These dreams happen almost every night. Don't you think that maybe its time for us to find what's up with it?" The floor creaked. The room darkened. His frame cast a shadow against the wall.

I jerked as he sat on my bed. Slouching deeper under my covers, I closed my eyes, silently repeating the words, "Make it go away."

"Paul—"

I jumped to the touch of his hand. "I can't talk about it."

"Why?"

"You don't understand."

"Don't understand what? I live with you, man. I spend more time with you than anybody you know. If you can't trust me—"

"It's got nothing to do with whether or not I trust you."

"Then what?"

"Please don't make me say anything more."

"Is someone hurtin' you?"

"No! I just can't talk about it."

John retreated to his bed. Silence entreated again with the bell tolling 4:30 A.M. I felt myself slip away to the memory of my father reading the words of Aristotle to me.

> People are not terrified by the same things. Some things indeed we feel are far beyond the power of human endurance, and such things therefore are terrible to every intelligent person. But terrors that are not beyond the power of endurance vary in magnitude and degree; the same is true of things that inspire confidence. The brave man is unshakable as far as a man may be. Hence, though he will fear terrifying things, he will face them in the right way and in a rational spirit for honor's sake, since this is the end of his virtue.

■

Roosters crowing from a nearby farm woke me. If not for the 6 A.M. bell and the smell of bread baking from the cafeteria, I would have sworn I had been asleep for just a minute.

"Hey, Paul, you awake?"

"I am now."

"Let's go for a run."

"Are you nuts? It's freezing outside."

"Come on, it'll do ya good."

"I'd love to, but I've got to finish studying for my religion exam."

"Man, you need to give it a rest already. How many times are you gonna read *Dark Night of the Soul*? Hell, even I've got it memorized."

Ignoring him, I walked to the bathroom. My body ached from so little sleep.

"Come on, don't be such a wuss." John followed me in.

"Can't a guy at least pee in peace?"

"Not if he refuses to run with me." John handed me my shoes and pants. "Here you go. Ah, what a great mornin' for a short jog." He bobbed up and down doing his pushups while I tied my shoes. "Hurry it up. Mornin' light is just a few minutes off. Don't wanna miss it."

We tiptoed down the hallway and down the stairs. "Let's stretch." John pushed against the wall of the last rung of the stairs. "You ready?" A frozen blast greeted us through the open door.

"It's freezing!"

"Don't be such a wuss. Let's go." Hoarfrost shimmered off the trees. Even the ivory covered walls of the building in the Commons glistened. The frosty snow crunched under our feet. The cold air stung my lungs as steam-wisped, heavy breathing filled the air.

"Let's head toward the river." Even though his legs were longer than mine, I paced myself to John's lead. "Wow. Take a look at that."

Surrounded with lush vegetation, ash and cedar trees blended together along a rocky knoll bordering the river. The gray barren barks stood in contrast to the evergreens around them. Water rushed under the frozen surface of the streambed carved below us. The narrow footpath meandered through the woods unzipping the forest before us.

"Let's go down to the river." John descended a steep path. Large boulders protruded through the undergrowth, serving as stepping-stones at times, but obstacles at others. "Take it easy on the rocks. I wouldn't want you to break a nail or—"

"John!"

He slipped and rolled down, finally smashing through the thin layer of ice covering the river.

"Are you—"

He sprang up, laughing. With the robustness of Santa himself, his voice bellowed through the woods. I navigated down to him. "Are you okay?"

"Perfect. It's been some time since I busted my ass like that."

"You could have killed yourself."

"Ah, not on a little tumble like that. Anyway, you said I'd live forever 'cause God don't want me and the Devil's afraid."

"Yes, but—"

"Paul, you gotta lighten up."

I reached my hand to help him up, but he yanked me off the rock and I plunged into the ice-cold water. "Are you nuts!" My teeth chattered.

John held me in the water. "No. Just glad to have you join me."

"Oh, so that's how we're going to play."

"Wow, you do know how. So much for *Dark Night of the Soul*."

Splashing each other, we laughed. After a few minutes, the water didn't even feel cold. Nothing seemed to matter other than having fun with my best friend.

Seven

Thibodaux, Louisiana, September 1976

The class bell rang. "Wait one minute, ladies and gentlemen." Professor LeBlanc stepped from behind the podium into one of the rows. "Tomorrow we'll have our first quiz on Homer's *The Odyssey*. We'll begin with, 'Lo you now, how vainly mortal men do blame the gods! For of us they say comes evil, whereas they even of themselves, through the blindness of their own hearts, have sorrows beyond that which is ordained.' Class dismissed."

John pushed his way through the double doors to the Quadrangle. "Our last college semester at good old 'Harvard on the Bayou.' Here I was thinking, party, fun, and boom, we land in that class. It's gonna suck!"

"It won't be that bad." As John and I exited P.G.T. Beauregard Hall into the courtyard surrounding it, students streamed by. Puffy white clouds floated overhead with a light breeze blowing off the Gulf of Mexico. Even with summer lingering, squirrels scampered across the Nicholls Quad storing acorns for the winter.

"So what were you and Ivan talkin' about until five o'clock this mornin'?"

"Nothing really. I couldn't sleep so we stayed up and—"

"Talked about *Dark Night of the Soul,* then that whole thing with the statue?" John picked up an acorn and sailed it across the lawn.

I shrugged.

"Come on, let's see what's happenin' in the Union."

"I'm going to head back to the room. I have practice soon and I need to study."

"Your class rank is number one. It's too beautiful a day to waste it on studyin'."

"You get accepted to Tulane Med and all of a sudden there's no need to study."

"You know better than that. Come on. Remember, 'I will, to will, thy will.' Besides, we need to get our drinking legs under us with your nineteenth birthday comin' up." John blocked my turn. I pushed back on him, but I was like a gnat shoving a gorilla.

A mat of fallen Cypress needles blanketed the entrance to the Union. Knees sprouted where barren earth once stood, creating the illusion of sculptures placed there by artistic design.

"Gotta love the day. I'm ready to party."

"You're always ready to party. Hell, the sun comes up and the sun goes down. That's two reasons to party a day, not to mention if a cloud shows up or blows away."

"Paul, is that humor? Wow, I'm not sure if I should trust—"

"Are we done here. I need to get back to the room?" I hastened my pace across the brick floors of the Union.

"What's the big rush?"

"I told you I've got practice and—"

"Okay, what's up?" John nearly shouted as he competed with the myriad of conversations bouncing off the twenty-foot ceilings. "You've got that heavy feelin' about ya."

Pushing through the crowded hallway, I carved a path for us. Hundreds of students packed the Union. They were buying books, arranging mailboxes, renewing relationships, and doing all the things that go on when the fall semester kicks off. "It's a zoo in here. Let's go," I yelled.

The glass doors of the Union slammed shut behind us. Walking through the alley between Talbot Hall and the Union, we emerged on the backside of campus. Sparrows playfully chirped. Even for the noise inside the Union, calm pervaded the campus.

"So, I guess we're gonna go through the ritual. I talk. You don't. I pry. You resist."

"If you shut up, we don't have to talk."

We crossed Audubon Drive near the intramural fields. Guys were already gathering for flag football.

"Hey, John, come play ball," a blond guy named Craig sarcastically shouted at us.

"Can't. Gotta study then gotta practice."

"Ya shouldn't let classes and stuff get in the way of a college education. Trust me, I've been here for a long time."

"At the rate he's goin', he'll be here forever," John muttered.

"You've never liked him. What's up between you two?"

"Just know the type. All mouth, no brains. A walkin', eatin' machine. A testosterone container."

"Sorry I asked."

"What? You think I'm bein' too judgmental again? Can't you just accept that some people are rotten to the core?"

A breeze whispered through the pines near our fraternity house. The needles created just enough resistance to capture it for a moment, and then let it go.

"So, you're not gonna talk anymore?"

"Don't have anything to say. And from the sound of it, you're not going to talk any less."

"Somethin's up. I know it."

"Would you give it a rest already?"

The double doors to the fraternity house flew open to an exodus of thugs. A tall redheaded guy bounced me against the bricks. "What ya looking at butt-lick! See ya got your bodyguard with ya again. What a puss!" An endless parade of "assholes," as John put it, barraged us with flippant comments.

"What the hell are they doin' here?"

I stepped in front of John. "Easy, big boy. Just consider the source."

"Before it's all over, I'm gonna beat his ass."

"Is he really worth it?" I maintained my stance between them and John's stranglehold.

Just as the last of them exited the house, the door slammed shut, then slapped open against the wall again. A dozen brothers snorting like a lynch mob in pursuit of thieves filled the porch. "Did the MUs just come through here?"

John moved me aside. "Yeah. They just ran towards the Union. Why?"

"Those S.O.B.s trashed Ivan's room."

John smashed his fist into his hand. "Dammit. I should've—"

"Let's kick their asses." Like a thundering herd, our brothers raced towards the Union. And with a number of football players in our house, I was certain that if they caught the MUs, they would deliver vindication with perfection.

"John!"

He stopped mid-gate. "What?"

"Let them handle the MUs. Let's check on Ivan."

"But—"

"But, nothing. Remember, Ivan. Brother in need. Fraternal bond."

John's pinched shoulders relaxed. "You know, sometimes you can spoil a good ass whippin'. With the number of pranks those assholes have pulled on us—"

Pictures tossed off walls, chairs upside down, and scattered papers littered the floors. Several brothers congregated near Ivan's room. His belongings were strewn throughout the hallway. My mouth dropped as I read the words "Sand Nigger Go Home" spray-painted across the wall.

"Ivan?" I searched the tattered room.

With a pale face and sullen spirit, Ivan sat on the closet floor picking up small pieces of broken plaster. "They broke it." His lip quivered. "My statue. It is all I have of them."

Even though he was of Arab and Kazak descent, his family migrated to the Ukraine prior to the formation of the Iron Curtain. Captive to the U.S.S.R., he and his parents managed to escape when he was a boy. But they had left much of his family behind. In the small Ukrainian village where his grandparent's lived, a legend of the appearance of a lady many hundred years ago followed Ivan's statue, an icon of the Virgin Mary, given to him by his grandmother.

"Why did they do this?" His dark eyes searched my soul for an answer.

"I don't know, Ivan." I carefully placed several broken pieces into a towel, a chunk of her blue veil, then a fragment of rosary intertwined in a broken finger.

John leaned over to help. The veins bulged from his beet-red head and neck. "They're dead assholes when I get my hands on them."

"Easy, John. Ivan, my parents know art dealers that might be able to repair this. Let's put each of the pieces in a plastic bag. We'll minimize any further damage. John, grab that piece by your foot." Carefully wrapping each piece in tissue, we placed them in separate bags.

Ivan lifted a smashed picture frame from the floor. "It's my mother," he said sadly.

John sprung to his feet. "I've had it. I'm gonna take care of those assholes once and for all."

"Hold up, John. I think I have an idea. Ivan, we've got to take care of something. We'll check on you later."

Returning to our room, I carefully laid out the details. With a few preparations to make, all we had to do was wait for nightfall.

■

"Hurry, John. They're coming."

"If you don't shut up, I'm gonna kick your butt."

"If you don't hurry, they're going to do that for you." I swatted the mosquitoes away from my face. The warm day had yielded to a hot, sticky night with a southerly wind blowing from the marshes. "Damn! I'm about to be eaten alive."

"Would you quit complainin'! And hold the light so I can see. Okay, one more turn and . . . done. Let's get to those bushes." We hid behind a group of large azaleas. "Duck. I see them comin'. They're gonna crap when this one hits them."

I struggled to peek over the azaleas, but not John. He towered over them with the greatest of ease. Crouching down low was his challenge. "Paul, watch. One, two, three . . . bam! Look at that. They don't know what hit them."

We roared with laughter. The Sodium Dodecyl Sulfate bomb exploded just as they dove into their pool for a midnight swim. Concentrated soap powder packed into a sodium metal ball effervesced into a wall of foam, made worse by their movement. And then, balloons filled with every imaginable type of water-soluble paint splattered all over the MUs. Their attempts to rinse off mixed the soap with paint, creating a scene that looked like the sixties were back once more. An LSD trip had nothing on this.

It was art in motion, science in action, and the laws of nature suspending the laws of man, blending into a symphony of visual experience that satisfied the senses. That and the fact that we could not stand the little sons-of-bitches made the event one indelibly engrained in my mind, all of it delivered in a way that caught them completely off guard.

"Good evening, gentlemen." The voice behind us was oh-so-familiar. John and I slowly turned our heads. Feelings of adulation changed to a sick sensation right smack in my gut.

"Officer Blanchard. Amazin' what happens on college campuses these days."

"Yes, Mr. Cheramie, it certainly is." To our relief, he began to walk off, saying nothing more. John and I looked at each other, just knowing that we had escaped this time. "Gentlemen, I'm certain that Dr. LeBouef will be thrilled to speak to you . . . his office . . . 8:00 A.M. sharp. Now get on home and get some rest. You're going to need it."

"Yes, sir," we replied in unison as we shared an "Oh, Shit" glance.

"Damn, John. I swear, if my parents find out about this, they're going to kill me. I can't believe we're back in the dean's office tomorrow morning!"

"Not if ya can't catch me." John shoved me. I turned a complete summersault, then rolled several times.

I dusted the grass off my back. "John, if I get my hands on you!" I chased my Goliath friend across the open field back to our fraternity house. Dealing with big assholes like John had earned me the nickname "Spider Monkey" since I was the target of the playful affection of the brothers in the house. Guys would pick me up and toss me from jock to jock, like some play toy created for their amusement.

"Paul's coming." A fraternity brother opened the door. I raced up the stairs. John slammed the door to our room.

"Brad, is your bedroom unlocked?" I heaved.

"Yeah. Why?"

I sprang through the sash and shimmied along the small ledge. John's laughter rang from our open window. I leaped in and threw myself on him. John swirled around, but my grip was too tight for him to throw me off his back.

The door to the room flew open. A congregation of the brotherhood gathered to watch the ritual unfold. "Hey, ya'll. They're at it again." Footsteps thundered from the hallway.

Even as John tossed me about, I rebounded for wave after wave. The jousting continued until we both fell to the ground, exhausted, laughing so hard that it ached.

"You don't give up, do ya?"

"Never."

We chuckled in the after-glow of our prank, but a lightening bolt followed by a clap of thunder shook the room. The clock showed 1 A.M., reminding me of the reality we faced tomorrow morning.

"Paul? We're not gonna toss and turn all night over this visit to the dean thing, are we?"

I nodded halfheartedly, already ruminating over it. I could feel the anxiety building in my unsettled stomach.

"Paul, you didn't answer me."

"No, just shut up about it and let's get some sleep."

"Good, because I don't wanna have to come over and knock you out." John flicked the light off. I lay motionless as I tried not to keep John awake. But scene after scene filled my mind. This evening's prank seemed like such a wise idea when we planned it. Now I wasn't so sure.

The first drops of rain pelted the window. The wind howled. Lightening flashed, streaking momentary brightness into the room. A shadow of Andre's broken body pinned under the oak tree danced on our bedroom wall. The words "I choose you" rumbled with the thunder. I roiled in the memory of my hurtful past. Even avoiding a better friendship with Kevin had not helped. He was just as dead as the rest of them.

I sat frozen, yet wide-awake. John sighed as he rolled onto his side. Watching to ensure he was asleep, I slipped out of bed. I slowly turned the door handle to make my exit.

"So where do you think you're goin'?"

"I, um, I wanted some milk."

"You've got five minutes and then I'm comin' after you." With the door opened, light streamed in. John's wide-opened eyes fixed on me. "Paul. Five minutes."

I tiptoed down the hallway. Hoping John would go to sleep, yet frustrated by my own insomnia, I walked to the kitchen in search of a snack. Although I wasn't hungry, I needed something to do until I grew exhausted enough to rest.

Finding a left over peanut butter and jelly sandwich, I climbed into a big chair in the television room and began flipping channels. The long hours of no sleep had provided me with ample opportunity to perfect my technique over the years. It was one of those mindless activities that allowed me to do something while I attempted to sort through all the stuff in my head.

I turned the volume down. The television hummed. The storm raged outdoors. Memories raged within. I sighed, drawing in a heavy breath as my heart ached once more.

"Paul." John's hand touched my shoulder just as he spoke. I jumped. "Why don't you come up? We'll watch a movie or somethin'."

Brad popped up his head from the sofa. "Movie, did I hear movie?"

"Brad, where the hell did you come from?"

"I followed Paul to make sure he was okay."

Brad was one of many brothers in the house, shift workers covering the watch, one of them typically awake whenever I was. Sometimes I felt like such an imposition.

"I'll get some of the guys and see y'all upstairs." Brad jogged up the stairs.

"So, what's goin' on?"

"Nothing."

"Yeah, right. Like all the other nothin's that keep you up every night." John offered his hand. "Let's go up, pal."

A congregation of brothers greeted us. "Hey, what are we watchin'?" Fifteen, maybe twenty bunched into our room. Like ants crawling all over an anthill, bodies strung out from one end of the room to the other. "Hey, Paul, come crawl up over here. We need a pillow. You're about the perfect size."

Soon everyone settled into a comfortable position. With *In Harm's Way* playing, everyone grew quiet, except for the soft murmur of munching popcorn. Even the weather had subsided. Within minutes, my eyes grew heavy.

■

The sun shining through our bedroom window woke me. Our room was now empty. Somehow I had found my way into bed.

My heart felt like it was in my throat. I tightened the knot in my tie, completing my preparation for the somber affair awaiting us. The consequences of our actions were in motion—the choices we made yesterday now dictating a visit to the dean.

I reached for my jacket. Our fraternity crest stitched across the breast of the blazer created the illusion of recruiting poster students. Such was the dress for a formal occasion, a visit to Elkins Hall, to the corner office of the Dean of Student Affairs.

"You're lookin' mighty sharp." John escorted me through the door and then down the hallway. With only a few brothers stirring about, the early morning hour allowed us to slip out with little interruption. "I can't believe it's almost over. You ever think how lucky we are to have been able to go to college so close to home?"

"I guess so."

"What do you mean, 'I guess so'? Don't you love it here?"

"Of course. It's home."

"No, Paul. Not just because it's home. Look at this place."

We walked across the University Quadrangle towards Elkins Hall. Oak trees towered where saplings once stood. Squirrels scurried, gathering acorns for a morning treat. As a young boy, I often visited this spot with Grandfather, hanging on his coattails and every step he made.

"So, what's it like to walk on a campus with buildin's named after family?"

"Let's not start that again."

"Start what? You know it's okay—"

"Alright, already. There's no need for a lecture."

As we approached Elkins Hall, the tree line thickened. Twigs fallen from the passage of the frontal boundary snapped under our feet. With a gentle breeze blowing from the north, unusually crisp air and blue skies replaced the dampness brought from the Gulf, like the day Hurricane Betsy struck.

"You've got that heavy feelin' about you again. Your worried, aren't ya?"

"Aren't you?"

"Come on, Paul. We've been through this drill before. We'll get a few hours of campus service, a reprimand, and we'll be off."

"I guess so, but—"

"But, what?"

"What we did yesterday, I mean, we're seniors, John. In a few months you'll be off to med school and I'll be in grad school."

"Paul, we're seniors, not priests."

"I know. But what we did to those fellas . . . I know they're pricks, but two wrongs don't—"

"After all the crap they've done?"

"While we were doing it, it felt like the right thing to do. I can't say that I didn't enjoy getting back at them. But—" John opened the door to Elkins. The stark silence that typically filled the hall greeted us. With the same smell of a doctor's office, the floors sparkled from continuous cleaning.

Dean LeBouef's secretary showed us to his reception area. "Good morning, gentlemen. Had fun last night, I hear."

"Yes, ma'am." Our relationship with her had become almost intimate in some ways. Her fingers had typed the legacy that we had built there over the years.

"Gentlemen," Dean LeBouef snarled. "My office."

John and I snapped to attention. "Yes, sir." Our gate on the stone floor corridor echoed off the walls and ceilings. My pounding heart competed with each step.

"Have a seat, gentlemen. I trust you are both doing well." Walking around his desk, Dean LeBouef eyed us the entire time. He lowered himself into the high-backed, blue leather chair. He cleared his throat several times, giving an indication that he was prepared to speak. But each time he relaxed, just sorting through our files. He sipped his coffee and read more. Regal silence was Dean LeBouef's mechanism for making the guilty nervous.

"Gentleman, we're going to have to stop meeting this way. People are beginning to talk."

John and I snapped to attention.

"How is it that I have over four thousand students on this campus, but I spend a significant percentage of my time dealing with you? Don't get me wrong, I enjoy conversing with students and getting to know them, especially honor students such as you. But I must admit that in the time I've known you, I really have come to wonder what would happen if you two spent as much time in the library or in a laboratory in pursuit of scholarly endeavors as you do pulling off these moronic pranks. What were you thinking!"

"Well, sir, Paul here has been strugglin' with some of that research he's been doin' and so I just wanted to help him out, sir."

"By exploding a bomb?"

"Oh, no sir, that was just a field test that went amuck."

"I see. I'm sure this disappointed you greatly."

"Why, yes sir. You see, sir, Paul had this theory about this water-soluble membrane thing he's been workin' on. And, well, sir, with budgets bein' so tight, and research space bein' so limited, we felt in the interest of science, we should find a suitable place to test his theory, and—"

"Mr. Cheramie, forgive me for interrupting you, but I am originally from Texas."

"Yes, sir. I'm aware of that."

"Do you know what El Toro cookies are?"

"Why, no sir."

"They are the source of a smell that I get each time I encounter you and Mr. de la Moret."

"Beggin' your pardon, sir?"

"More plainly put, every time I deal with you boys, the air surrounding me becomes filled with the most pungent aroma of bullshit. El

Toro cookies, gentlemen!" John and I jumped as the dean slammed his fist against the desk. Even the hardware on it rattled. His voice vibrated inside my chest. But we did not dare look at him, nor each other. Rather, we remained at attention with our faces turned forward in a fixed and locked position.

"You're going to clean this campus until it shines! I almost sleep at night when I know where you two are and what you are doing. That way, I can occupy those busy little minds of yours and direct them to more productive and fulfilling activities."

John and I would once more rake leaves, wash dishes, and perform other cleaning tasks. Dean LeBouef suggested that when we were busy, little time remained in the day for us to pull another prank. Yet, it was such occasions that gave John and me ample opportunity to create whatever it was that we were going to do next, especially when a brother was threatened.

John loosened his tie as we walked back to the house. "Gettin' back at those S.O.B.s was worth it." He kicked a pine cone across the street.

"Feel better?"

"They're lucky that wasn't one of their heads."

"Okay."

"You don't think they deserved what happened?"

"I didn't say that."

"Yeah, but I know that tone."

I looked up to a lone Egret gliding towards the fields bordering campus. The wind brushed by me. The hair on my arms and the back of my neck lifted.

"Somethin's up."

"Let's not—"

"Bullshit. It started Sunday. It's been five days now. What gives?"

Looking away, I searched for the strength to tell him. Even for all the years of knowing him, I had said virtually nothing about it. Talking about it would lend it credence. That was the last thing I wanted.

Eight

With only minutes left before we were scheduled to depart for the airport, I stashed the remaining clothes I needed into my luggage. I couldn't help but look at that old cigar box stashed away in the corner of my closet. The innocence that had collected all those things seemed so far removed from me now. Yet I longed for it.

A soft knock rattled my propped open bedroom door. "Sweetie, may I come in?" Mother's sullen eyes spoke volumes to her thoughts on my decision to travel to South America for the summer. "You're all packed I see. Are you sure you want to do this?"

"Oh, yes, ma'am. Dean LeBouef—"

Mother peered through the top of her reading glasses. "Yes, I know. I spoke with him. With some of the pranks you and John pulled on that campus, it's amazing that he would even recommend you two for a mission." My face flushed.

Jacques winked at me. "Now, Renee, we've already talked about this, and as I've told you, those boys were just doing what red-blooded American boys do."

I breathed a sigh of relief for his support.

"But ten weeks is such a long time. He just got back from that graduation trip to Florida, and now he's off again for the rest of the summer."

"Why don't we let him pack and we can discuss this on the way to the airport." Jacques gently escorted Mother from my room.

"Mista Paul." Francis rapped gently at my door. "I don't mean ta be botherin' ya and what not, but it's about time we git ta da airport. I'll git yo luggage, when ya ready."

"I can manage, Francis."

"We have dis discussion every time. But—"

"I know. As long as you're in this house you'll carry the luggage."

"If you'll excuse me, I'm gonna git dese bags in da car."

With a final look through my closet, I closed the door. The plantation hummed with activity just beyond my French doors. The dry days of June would quickly yield to the wet tropical days of July and August. Another of life's cycles raced to completion.

Grandmother and Grandfather waited for me at the base of the staircase. "We're very proud of you. Take this." She pressed a St. Christopher's medal into my hand. "I had it blessed at mass this morning." We were the first to exchange a farewell hug.

Grandfather clacked his unlit pipe between his teeth as he piddled with a fireball wrapper in his coat jacket. "You're off again. Do be careful. We're going to miss you this summer. The crop looks like it's going to be a good one. And the citrus orchards just aren't the same when you're not around. Tomas said you saw him this morning."

"Yes, sir. I went out to the orchards early."

"I think he misses you when you're not around." I closed my eyes tightly to Grandfather's embrace. "No one to fetch water hoses and what not."

"I guess so."

"You take care of yourself, rascal," he whispered.

"Yes, sir." Releasing him, I looked around the room. "Mother, Dad, I'm ready."

Jacques led the way. "Let's get on the road, then."

Walking to the front door, we exited the house. I wondered where Mim was. With the car parked under the porte cochere, Francis stood waiting. Before I stepped into the car, the kitchen screen door screeched open. Mim raced to the car with a paper sack.

"Child, hol' up. Ya didn't eat enough breakfast, so I made ya a san'wich. Ya make sure ya eat dis befo' ya git on da plane. Ya here me?"

"Yes, ma'am."

"Naw, come ova here and give me a hug." She pulled me into her bosom, wrapping her arms around me. I felt warmth radiating from her body as she whispered though a tightening throat, "Ya take care of ya'se'f." With a swat on my behind, she pushed me towards the car.

I waved my final good-bye. As Francis navigated through the winding path carved through the oaks, I settled in for the ride to the airport.

"Son, when you get back, I'd be honored if you'd join me at Manresa. I got some information for you to read on the plane." Jacques handed me the folded pamphlet.

"Did you go recently?"

"Not since spring. We've got a retreat coming up in September. Why don't you come?"

"Once I know my fall schedule I'll let you know."

"Wonderful."

We traveled south along Highway 308 from Thibodaux to Raceland. The sugarcane undulated in a gentle breeze. Just beginning its growth, the stalks would be six to eight feet taller by the time I returned. The transformation from seedling to mature plant would be well on its way to completion, barring any hurricanes or such.

Mother snapped her compact shut. "What are you thinking about, sweetie? You seem a million miles away." She rolled her lipstick to brighten her lips."

"I was just thinking about the crop."

"I tell you, you and your grandfather. You two spend more time in those fields." Her face glowed through her broad smile.

"I guess I do. It's—"

"Oak Grove?"

Moss covered oaks, dashed with occasional magnolia blossoms, dotted rows of sugarcane lining the bayou. Egrets picked worms from freshly tilled soil. Cajun cottages with steep-slanted roofs, and nestled under puffy white clouds in the deep blue sky, reminded me of our Acadian ancestry.

Jacques fidgeted with his wedding band. "So, son. Are ya getting excited for your adventure in the wilds of South America?"

"Wilds of South America. I thought you were going to—"

"Now, Renee, you know I'm just messing with the boy."

"He's playing, Mother. I'll be near Mendoza. There's a small mission just outside the city in the Andes. We're going to work with a couple of families. One lady, Maria de la Rosa, and her son, Xavier, have been hit with so much. After we meet up with several Jesuits from the New Orleans Providence—"

"Yes, yes, I know. I've spoken to Father Gaspard. He—"

"Mother, tell me you didn't—"

"Hush. I've got a right to know where you are and what you're doing."

"But I'm nearly twenty and a college graduate."

"I don't care if you're fifty and the president of the United States. I'll do as I please."

"Yes, ma'am."

A devilish smirk swiped across Dad's face. "There are some mighty fine señioritas down there."

"Jacques!"

"Renee, the boy's got to live. Well, look at him, he's a man now!"

"I'll 'he's a man now' you. There'll be no sowing of wild oats in this car—" Mother ranted for several minutes. Even as the murky-watered bayou flowed to the gulf, the rows of sugarcane marked our passage to the airport. John waited there. Soon we would be off to Argentina.

■

"Gentlemen, a cocktail before we depart?" The flight attendant winked at John.

"Why, yes, ma'am. We'd like orange juice. And while you're pourin', ya might wanna cut that fifty-fifty with vodka. After all, it's almost eleven in the mornin'."

"Am I going to have to keep my eye on you during this flight?"

"I sure hope so, because you have one pretty set of eyes."

"You're such a flirt."

"No, ma'am. Just believe in callin' it like I see it." John's dimples blossomed through his boyish grin. With his head cocked to one side, he traced the flight attendant's steps back to the galley.

I nudged him with my elbow. "You know, sometimes you behave like a big slut."

"Yeah, and your point is what, specifically?"

"Just thought I would remind you."

"Speakin' of remindin' me, your latest dream. What gives?"

The flight attendant placed our drinks on the console between us. "Here you go, gentlemen."

"Thank you . . ." John leaned to read her nametag. "Meg is it?"

"You read very well."

"Hey, I'm a college graduate."

The flight attendant turned, then paused to give John one more look. "Congratulations. I'm sure you got out in record time."

I choked on my drink.

"Look ya little asshole. I got out just as fast as you. So, whacha grinnin' at?"

"Nothing. Just the fact I think you've met your match."

"Paul, Kiss my—."

The fasten seat belt sign flashed on with a bing. "Ladies and gentlemen, before we push back, we need to ensure that everyone is in their seat with their seatbelt securely fastened . . ."

Meg grabbed John's cup. "So, Mr. Cheramie, I take it that you're from New Orleans."

"Yes, ma'am. I sure am. And please, call me, John."

"John, huh. Nice name."

I handed Meg my cup. "You would never know it, but his mother named him after the disciple, you know, the one that Jesus loved."

"Wow. He doesn't look like a disciple. Well, maybe St. John of Pat O'Brien's."

I smiled. "May I call you Meg?"

"Sure."

"I don't know you, but I like you already. Nice."

John eyed me and muttered, "When I get you alone, I'm gonna wipe that smirk off your face with my fist."

"Gentlemen, check your seatbelts, please."

A sinister smile swept across John's face as he yanked my seatbelt strap. It squeezed me tightly against the seat, causing me to groan.

The plane bounced along the tarmac of New Orleans International. Déjà vu overtook me. I had lived this, or maybe dreamed this, before. I hated this feeling.

"Okay, what gives?"

"Nothing."

"Don't bullshit me. I know that silence better than my own farts."

The engines roared. We lifted off the runway.

Barges lined the banks of the Mississippi River along with large ships, moored into harbor, all receiving cargo from grain elevators. A flock of pelicans, looking like specs of white on a brown, muddy soup, drifted lazily on the waters. Soaring above them, a lone egret targeted a partially drained crawfish pond. The land of my family teemed with life below me. Many of them had never seen our world from this view.

"Have you ever wondered why things happen the way they do?" The words tripped off my lips before I even realized what I said.

"Sometimes. When I think about it late at night, it kinda bugs me."

"Bugs you?"

"Yeah, Paul. There are things that bug me."

"Like what?"

"Like the fact that you don't sleep. The food we throw away in restaurants that could feed thousands. The identity of my real parents."

"I'm sorry, John. My question was incredibly inconsiderate. I didn't mean to imply that you don't think about things. It's just that I've never met someone that can handle things so calmly."

"You."

"What do you mean?"

"You handle things very calmly, Paul."

"I wish I saw it that way."

"Yeah. I know. With what you've lived through, well it's amazin' that ya haven't gone nuts. Why are ya shakin' your head?"

"I don't know, John. There are a lot of folks who have lived through a hell of a lot more."

"Maybe. But pain's personal. Victor Frankel says that sufferin' fills the entire void of a container irrespective of how much or how little."

"I guess my container is pretty full then."

"I'd say. So tell me about the dream."

"I don't know where to start. Very little of it makes sense. That is, not until it happens. Then its almost like I'm filling in details to prove the dreams real."

"Maybe. But you've been dead on target more than once."

"Ladies and gentlemen, we ask that your remain in your seats until the captain turns off the fasten seat belt sign indicating that it is safe to move about the cabin. We would like to welcome . . ."

"But, what if I'm creating all this stuff. Kahlil Gibran suggests we choose our joys and sorrows long before we experience them."

"Well if you can do that kind of stuff, then we've really gotta talk. There are a few folks I'd like you to deal with for me." John chuckled. His eyes widened, exposing his piercing blue irises. But the gesture warmed me. He was my best friend.

I peered out of the plane's window. The mouth of the river pushed muddy water into the clear, blue seas of the Gulf of Mexico. The wilds of South America awaited us. An anxious knot tightened my stomach. I closed my eyes in a prayerful moment. *Please, please don't let anything happen to him. Please.*

■

A knock at the door woke me. I sprang out of bed and bolted into the hallway. "What's going on, John?"

"I don't know." John wrapped his robe around himself. He reached the door to another pounding knock.

The young boy, Pedro, grabbed John's hand. "Señor, please! Follow me! Please!"

"Slow down, Pedro. What's wrong?"

"Señor, please! Maria wants you."

I rushed down the stairs. "Maria?"

"Si. She need you come quick, you and Señor John."

"I'll get my things. John—"

"Let me grab my backpack."

We ran after Pedro down the street towards Maria's house. After several hilly blocks, we were breathing pretty heavy. A crowd gathered outside the fence of the dimly lit yard.

"Señor Paul, inside. Maria wants you." Broken glass littered the narrow entrance. I walked through a small, crowded hallway to the kitchen. There, Maria held onto Xavier's bullet-laden body.

"Pablo, my boy is—" Maria's lower lip quivered as she grabbed my hand.

I dropped to my knees and applied pressure to stop the bleeding. With no doctor in the small village we were his only hope.

"Hold on for me, Xavier."

His eyes rolled back into his head. His body jerked. He gasped for breath. With a shudder, his body went limp.

Those surrounding us signed themselves in the cross. "Dios te salve Maria . . ." a woman standing near me led them in prayer. Maria closed the eyes of her son. A tear dripped down her cheek. She looked at John. "Find a priest." John stood frozen.

"John, do as she asks."

He shook his head, as if to wake from a bad dream. "Pedro, find Father Barrios. Hurry!"

A small mantle clock struck 10 P.M. A woman standing near it stopped it from ticking. I grabbed Maria's bloody hand. She squeezed my fingers. Xavier's limp body rested in her arms like Mary holding Jesus in the *Pieta*. She stroked his long black hair. His lifeless frame grew pale.

As she wiped the blood from Xavier's face with the towel she had been holding, she calmly spoke, "Get water and linen." One of the ladies rushed off to do as she asked.

Maria cleaned the blood from his body, first his face, then his hands. Lifting one finger at a time, she wiped each until the red stains faded from his skin. She looked at me. The pain in her eyes tugged at my being. I hurt like I had so many times before.

"Where is she?" Father Barrios pierced through the crowded hallway to find Maria and me huddled over Xavier. "Madre de Dios." He signed himself in the cross. While placing a purple sash around his neck, he reached into a black bag. With Holy Water in hand, he prayed, "En el nombre del Padre, el Hijo, y el Espíritu Santo." He blessed Xavier's body first with Holy Water, then anointed him with chrism oil by drawing small crosses on his forehead and each of Xavier's hands.

Maria said nothing, cradling her child like a newborn placed into her care.

"Señora de la Rosa," a policeman spoke to her. "Hemos matado uno de los asesinos y el otro uno está en la cárcel."

I looked at John. "It sounds like they've killed one of the assailants and the other one is being held in jail."

"First we finish here, then we go to the jail." Maria wiped more blood from Xavier's chest. With it cleaned, she dressed him in a fresh shirt, then combed his hair. Several men lifted his body to lay him in bed. She rested his head on a small pillow. I wiped a tear from Maria's cheek with my thumb.

"I am ready," she said calmly.

John cleared his throat. "Paul, can I see you?"

"Maria, if you'll excuse me." I followed John outside.

"Do you think it's a good idea to go to the jail. I mean, she's been so calm. You're not worried she might come unglued when she sees her son's killer?"

"She'll be fine, John."

"Are you sure?"

"Yes. Let's get Maria and go."

A crowd of people followed us in a silent procession. We walked up the hill, then crossed the street to the small village jail. Two officers greeted us with silent repose.

Maria squared off to the officer. "I wish to see him."

The officer hesitated, then escorted her to a back room. She motioned for us to follow. Her son's murderer sat behind bars, bruised badly, and was bleeding. "Open the door," she firmly whispered.

The officer looked at me. I signaled him to do as she instructed. The hinges of the barred gate screeched open as she entered the dimly lit cell. Staring at the man, she lifted his chin. I started towards her, afraid that she was going to slap him, but stopped before I reached her.

Her eyes never left him. Silence filled the cell. She reached into her pocket and whispered in Spanish, "You took my son, the only one I had left." Opening his hand, she cradled her rosary in it. "You must now take his place." With that, Maria turned to the officer. "Get me fresh water and towels so I can tend to his wounds." She then placed her arms around her victim's victim, hugging him and holding him as they both wept.

I stood in awe. How could she be so strong? She was like Mary, constant in her watch, even after her son had died. If only I could find that kind of faith.

■

I woke in a pool of sweat. The sheets on my bed lay twisted around my ankles once more. It was the middle of the night, yet I had to see him. With John asleep in the next room, I slipped on my slacks ever so careful not to wake him. With what little light streamed in through my window, I laced my shoes. The house was so quiet that any noise might rouse someone.

Cracking my bedroom door open, I searched the halls to make sure my path was clear. Seeing no sign of anyone, I tiptoed across the wooden floor avoiding the jigsaw puzzle of planks that creaked.

Escaping without notice, I walked the darkened path to the rectory. Although I had been cautioned about the dangers of the streets, I desperately needed to speak to Father Barrios. I could bear the haunting no longer. I needed to understand what was going on.

The faint sound of another's footsteps seemed to pace with my stride. I stopped and listened. The sound ceased. I walked further to the resuming sound.

Frightened, I moved quicker. The thin air labored my breathing. The interloper behind me seemed to match my moves.

Turning the corner, I glimpsed at the outer gates of the rectory. The street appeared empty, so I crossed.

I rang the bell. A young novice rattled the iron lock. I jumped.

"My apologizes, Señor. I didn't mean to startle you." His English was good, although his Spanish dialect was heavy. "Can I help you?"

"I'm need to see Father Barrios."

"He's resting. Can I—"

"No. I need to see him. Please."

"Come in. I'll get him for you."

I searched the street once more to see if anyone had followed me. Seeing no one, I followed the novice through the courtyard. We entered the foyer of the rectory. The intricate tile work suggested Spanish missionary design.

The novice led me through an arched doorway into a parlor. "Won't you make yourself comfortable while I get Father Barrios?" Artifacts and paintings adorned the room. Placed on a pedestal all by itself, an icon of Mary sat atop a shelf. A gold crown, intricately inlayed with leafing, capped the veil draping her head. She stood on roses with a moon sculptured under her feet. The statue resembled Ivan's.

"Interesting piece, isn't it?"

"Father, I'm sorry. I didn't hear you come in."

"That's quite all right. I wondered when you would come." His statement puzzled me. Other than this night, we had had little interaction. Lifting the crystal top off a wine decanter, Father Barrios poured us each a glass of wine. "Here, drink up. This will warm you a bit. It's my favorite. You do drink?" He lifted the glass. "Avante Sante."

"Merci, Pere." The alcohol warmed my empty stomach.

"The wine here is wonderful. It has it origins from France."

"Does it?"

"Pureya Andina's vineyards are not far from here. This is their Malbec vintage."

"From Bordeaux."

"Very good. You know your wine." He swished the wine and swallowed as if to savor the taste. "The vines were brought from Bordeaux in the eighteen hundreds. The terroir proved to be a perfect match for the rootstock."

"Terroir. It's a complex word, meaning both land and love."

"You know of this, yes?"

I nodded.

Father motioned for us to sit in a pair of armchairs positioned near a fireplace. Even though it was summer back home, winter raged in the Southern Hemisphere. "Come, warm yourself and we'll chat." Pulling the chairs closer to the fire, we huddled to warm ourselves from the night air. I wasn't certain if I was cold from it or from the fact that I was somewhat frightened to be in Father Barrios' presence.

My hands trembled as I raised the wineglass to my lips. Other than a log crackling in the hearth and a mantle clock ticking, silence pervaded the room. I squirmed in the chair, hoping that he would open the conversation, yet fearful of his doing so. My eyes wandered aimlessly across the floor.

"Long night?"

I struggled to reply. With little sleep in several days, coupled with Xavier's death, my senses were blurring. "I . . ." In trepidation, I attempted to speak.

"Yes, my son. Go ahead."

The words rested on the tip of my tongue. With so much on my heart, I ached. Having faced in this very night the death of another that I loved, I wondered when this curse would leave me. Wanting desperately to speak to him about it, I feared revealing what I knew. It seemed almost insane to me. Certainly he would find it the same.

"You're troubled." His words flowed softly off his lips. "I wish to help."

Help. What a notion. I wondered if I was beyond any such thing.

"You're Paul de la Moret, correct? You're John's best friend. He mentions you often."

My heart raced from hearing John's name.

"He's been by to visit several times. A fine young man he is. Speaks very highly of you. He told me you've been best friends for over seven years now."

"He's like my brother," I muttered.

"What's that, my son?"

119

"Nothing, Father. Just thinking out loud."

"I've always been partial to the names Paul and John. The story of Paul's conversion to the faith inspires me. It reminds me that even as evil as we can be, there remains always the hope for our healing and our salvation. And John. He's the disciple that Jesus loved. 'Son, behold your mother. Woman, behold your son.' What an amazing notion, to be asked to care for the mother of God and to have her do the same for you."

Could he be toying with me? What does he know? I wondered.

"So, you were a friend of Maria's, yes? Is this the first loved one you've lost?"

"No, Father."

"I see. Brings back many memories, doesn't it?"

As I looked away, the icon of Mary came into view, and with it came the horror of the night's events. Father lifted from his chair to stoke the log in the fireplace. With the flame renewing itself, warmth permeated the chill in the room. "That statue seems to perplex you."

"A friend had a similar one."

"Did he? Tell me about it."

"There's not a lot to tell."

"I see. So, did you meet your friend in the Ukraine?"

"John?"

"No, the one with the statue."

"We were fraternity brothers. A rival fraternity got into his room and broke his statue."

"Oh, what a shame. Was it repairable?"

"Fortunately."

"Where is you friend now?"

"He's in Boston with his family. They're hoping to return someday."

"Family still in the Ukraine I take it." Father Barrios folded his hands, then intertwined his rosary beads between his fingers. The beads clacked. I wasn't sure if he was praying or just twiddling. "May I show something to you?" He walked to the icon. "You may find this interesting."

I joined him near the shelf housing the statue. He flipped it so that we could see the base. "Look here." He pointed to an inscription. "La Madre de Dios calma el huracán con Su mano. Do you speak Spanish?"

"A little."

"I'll translate. 'The Mother of God calms the evil wind with Her hand'."

Chills ran across my spine. My flesh raised. Breathless, I stood in silence.

"You know of the legend." Even though I did not respond, he continued. "Yes, I see. Your friend must have told you."

"Yes. I mean, no."

"Here, let's sit by the fire."

Nestled in the chair once more, I placed my hands to feel the warmth. The air seemed colder.

"Many hundreds of years ago a wealthy merchant named Pablo Pedro Guidry—"

"Pablo Pedro Guidry?"

"You know this name?"

"No. It's just odd hearing a Spanish forename with a French surname."

"Come to think of it, it is odd." Father sipped his wine. "Nevertheless, Pablo Pedro was a merchant. His wealth was born from trading goods on his many journeys from Europe to the Orient. On one such journey, he and his men became stranded in what is now Kazakhstan. A dust storm, a huracán as they call it, came from nowhere. Blinded by the whipping dust, Pablo Pedro and his men sought shelter in a ravine.

"Hours past. The storm worsened. Dust filled their lungs as it slowly buried them. Pablo Pedro thought they were going to die."

Father sniffed his wine, then rolled it in the glass. "Pablo Pedro had never been a very religious man. But his wife, Marguerite, insisted that he carry with him the Most Holy Rosary of our Lady. In desperation, thinking that he would never see her again, he grabbed the rosary and held it tightly.

"One of his men saw him holding the rosary, even through all of the sand and dust. Pablo Pedro began to pray the words, 'Ave, Maria, gratia plena.' Soon, others joined in. Even as the wind raged, they recited the prayer together, calling for help in their hour of desperation.

"For hours they did so. This became the only thing that they could hold onto. It seemed that their faithfulness did not go unrewarded."

"Unrewarded?"

"Yes. When all seemed darkest, Our Lady appeared to them. She calmed the evil wind, commanding that it cease. What was a blackened sky cleared. Stars sparkled. The moon glowed.

"Pablo Pedro and his men fell to their knees pledging their lives to her devotion. He erected a shrine in her honor on a site in the Ukraine. A local artisan created an icon in her honor. This is but one of a few still in existence."

"And the shrine?"

"Oh, destroyed many years ago. Some say Cossacks did it. Others claim the Communists. Some even suggest the Moors. Whatever, all that remains is the legend and these replicas. So, do you plan to go?"

Andre's mangled body. My father in his coffin. Xavier's breathless corpse. Image after image flashed through my head. "I'm sorry for bothering you so late. I think it's time for me to leave. If you'll excuse me."

"Wait, my son. Are you all right?"

"Yes—" I rushed to the door.

"Did I say something to upset you?"

"No. I'm just tired. It's, well—"

"At least allow Brother Miguel to walk you home. The streets can be dangerous at—"

"I'm sorry for the interruption." I pushed the door to the rectory open. I charged the gate. As I attempted to pull it open, the lock held it shut. I struggled to free myself.

Brother Miguel appeared with the key. "I'll let you out."

"Thanks." I bolted free the minute the gate opened.

"Wait up. I'll walk—"

Before he could follow, I dashed towards the street corner and slipped into the darkness. Steam spewed from my mouth. A dog barked at me as I jogged by.

Soon I was alone. The snap of a tree limb spooked me. In desperation, I departed from the rectory without paying close attention to where I was going. Now I seemed lost.

Searching for something familiar, I turned slowly in a circle. Wiping sweat from my brow and my lips, I took a deep breath to still myself. I stepped forward, but stopped. With my ear pressed against my cupped hand, I held my breath. Was someone following me?

Hearing nothing, I walked almost aimlessly. I sought some sign to gain my bearings.

"You must go." The wind whipped from nowhere as the voice spoke to me. Chills ran through my body as I hunted for the source. With darkness encircling me, I strained to discern if anyone or anything was nearby. Yet nothing appeared.

As I looked further down the street, light radiated from an alley. Moving cautiously, I remained watchful for any person that might mean me harm. Nothing moved except me.

I turned into the alley. Fear paralyzed me. Seeing her in clear view, I didn't know what to do. "You must go." The wind whistled by me as my flesh stood up. All I could think of was Andre and the many horrible things that happened every time this vision returned.

"Paul."

Hearing my name I dashed from the alley, running until I found my way home. There I hid until morning light, praying that it would all just go away.

Nine

Fall after Graduation, September 1977

    "Meg? Why? They've just met. They're in love!"
    Silence entreated me.
    "Please tell me. I've got to know. This doesn't make any sense."
    "She will marry John, then perish after finding she is with child."
    "From what? Tell me so I can help her. You can't show me these things and not tell me more. Tell me! Tell me!"
    "I choose you. I choose you." The words echoed in the torrent engulfing me. The wind roared. Once more I fell through the vortex of the storm, hopelessly out of control.
    "Who are you? What do you want from me?"
    Contorted faces flashed before me out of the dark, spinning wall. I reached for anything to hold on to. Even with debris circling me, I could find nothing to grab.

■

    Late summer had already arrived and our short visit home was nearly over. Our last day found me not sleeping for most of the night. I snuck through the French doors to the back porch, stepping into the alley. Spanish moss splattered gray against the lush green oak leaves.

"Wait up, pal."

"John, you scared the crap out of me."

"Couldn't sleep, huh?"

I nodded.

"What was the dream about this time?"

"It's nothing but a big blur." With the sick feeling in my stomach, I didn't know if I wanted to remember.

John wiped the sweat from his forehead. The heavy, damp dawn air made for one of those typical mornings in South Louisiana when the long awaited arrival of the first cool front was still weeks away. It was a perfect time to twiddle, to snap sticks and throw rocks, to do those things from boyhood that occupied time and allowed the mind time to think.

"Hey, Paul. Look over the trees and to the east at that thunderstorm."

The clouds striated the light into single rays like fingers stretching across the sky. Mim told me many years before that this was nothing more than the hand of God reaching down from heaven to touch us, cradling us in His care, surrounding us in His warmth. Like so many tales told to children, my adult perceptions caused me to doubt this.

"Sure is beautiful." The storm painted the sky in an array of color as it moved away from us. John stopped. "That's unusual. Listen."

The chant of a lone locust bellowed through the oak canopy. Louder than any I had heard before, it surrounded us with an incantation of lonliness unlike any I had ever heard. I searched the oaks towering above us.

"I wonder where it is." John hastened his pace. Both of us looked up and down the trees lining our path. We paused every now and then only to listen, hoping to get a fix on this creature.

"Don't you think looking for a bug is maybe a little asinine?"

"It's an insect, Paul!"

"I know, but we're grown men. Well, at least I am. Are you ever going to grow up?"

"Not if I don't have to. By the way, that's why you don't sleep at night."

"Searching for a bug will help me sleep?"

"It's the whole *Dark Night of the Soul* thing, Paul. All work. No play. The way I see it, you've gotta keep the kid in you alive."

"I guess that's why you sleep like a baby."

"Wow, was that humor?"

"No, just sarcasm." There was something to John's reasoning, however. I had all but forgotten what it was like to have curiosity in that simple way.

"Let's walk out farther. I think it's near your tree."

It had been quite some time since I had been there. As a small boy, I visited the old oak often. Very large even then, the oak had grown into what was now a sculptured mammoth that all but towered to the heavens. Its trunk, which would have required at least four people with outstretched arms to wrap around it, was made all the larger by cascading branches that enveloped the bark and reached like fingers to the ground in a show of support.

Our locust hushed. "Shh!" John lifted his finger over his lips. He looked up the tree like a hound dog searching for a squirrel. Sullenness replaced the gleam in his eye. "Don't move. Those leaves crunchin' might scare it off." Like two big kids, we stood there until the locust resumed its chant. John smiled. "It's definitely in this tree."

"I think it's higher." Pulling myself up as I had done as a boy, I felt a tinge of exhilaration. I forgot what a cool thing climbing a tree could be.

Yet as I grabbed the next branch, something crunched under the weight of my hand. I hoisted my weight, finding hundreds of locust shells covering the mossy perch. I felt the muscles of my face fall. The pleasant memories of the moment vanished to the memory of Andre and I collecting these shells.

"What's wrong, Paul?"

"Nothing." Compelled to find the locust, I scouted the area. I searched through the nooks and crannies of the tree. Branches and leaves extending every which way safely tucked the locust away from my view.

Climbing even farther, I found myself on a branch—the biggest on the tree. Mangled and twisted from the fury of many storms, it curved to the ground gracefully. It was my favorite of all—my branch, in my tree. For years it had been that way, a special place where few had been, a spot reserved just for me.

When I was just a boy, I had run here, trying to understand what had happened to me. I had slept on this branch, angry and confused, the world no longer making sense to me. It was here that I had swung on an old tire tied with rope, both coming from the plantation store, stealing away to dream, to think, and to wish the day away.

I roosted on the branch where I had sat so many times. As before, I attempted to sort through that which I did not understand, or wasn't quite ready for. This oak had been a home to me, just as it was to the locust, protecting and shielding it too.

"Paul, where are ya?"

"Up here, to your left."

"How the hell did you get so high so fast?"

"I climbed."

"Okay, smartass. What's goin' on?"

"Nothing. I'm just thinking."

"Well, duh. I know that. What about?"

"Stuff."

"Thanks. It is so much clearer now. Next time, and I'm just offerin' this as a suggestion, could you be a little more vague?"

I flipped him off.

"That was graceful." The branch shook as John made his way towards me. "As my mamma use to say, there's nothin' like a wet and soggy moss-covered branch to soften the seat and wet the ass first thing in the mornin'." John nudged me with his elbow.

From our perch, the murky waters of Bayou Lafourche flowed lazily to the Gulf of Mexico. The early morning storm had washed brown sandy soil from the fields.

"Sugarcane's pretty amazin' when you think about it. When we left, it was maybe a foot tall. Now—"

"Over nine feet and growing an inch a day. Grandfather says it's the biggest ever."

The sun peeked over the horizon. Sparkling dewdrops covered the sugarcane leaves. A lone rooster crowed to welcome the morning as field hands drifted to the barns.

"Paul, are you ever gonna sleep?"

"I don't like to sleep."

"I woulda never noticed. Let's see. I've known you eight years, right? And, in that time, you've never slept through the night."

"Bite me."

"Yeah, I would if it would solve the problem."

"Can we just sit up here and watch the sunrise?"

"You know, if I was convinced that was what you were doin', I wouldn't say a damn thing. But I know another nightmare woke you just after you fell asleep. I know that you didn't wanna wake anyone. You twisted and turned until you got up. And then you walked the hallways. Let's see. Have I left anythin' out?"

Again, I flipped him off. It was moronic, but ever so fitting. For what I was feeling, for what I had been through, it was all that I could offer. I had no words to describe the hurt.

"Just talk to me, pal."

My throat tightened and I took a deep breath. "My father died eight years ago today."

Chirping birds joined the morning. A lone rooster crowed once more. The locust resumed its chant, singing its song before its impending death at twilight.

"Where are you goin', Paul?"

"I've got to find that locust."

"I thought—"

"You thought what?"

"Nothin'."

"No, what?"

"I was gonna say somethin' stupid."

"Dammit, John. Why is it the minute I talk about Father's death people become afraid to say what they're thinking? It's like they think they can hurt me more or something."

"Wait a minute, Paul. I just didn't want, I mean—"

"Look, you're the best friend I've ever had. Never once have you treated me like I was in some kind of glass bubble. Don't start now."

"Okay. Let's find that damn bug."

"Insect!"

"Oh, you're the expert now."

We scanned branch by branch, leaf by leaf, turning them over. We crouched, we squatted—we did whatever it took to find it. It had possessed me and would not release me unless I found it.

The sunlight filtered through the tree. Something glimmered. I crept, balancing myself on the branch. A light breeze ruffled the leaves, allowing me to catch sight of a single drop of water reflecting the brilliant greens and browns of the locust's bright coat. I dropped down onto the branch almost falling off. It reminded me of my father's tears when he rested in his coffin.

"Paul!" John scurried to my rescue. "Are you okay?" He examined my bleeding arm.

"It was a September day, much like this one."

"What was, pal?"

"The day Father died."

John drew closer to me.

"Andre had been dead only four years. I was preparing to head back to school and had worked in the orchard with Tomas that morning. Mother was the one who told me. I knew even before she said anything."

John rested his hand on my shoulder. I stiffened my upper lip. I had never cried in front of him. But there were many lonely nights when tears rolled down my cheeks into my pillow.

"I don't want to ever put my family through that, John."

"Through what?"

"Promise me if anything ever happens to me, there will be no funeral —none of that bullshit."

"But, Paul—"

"You don't understand. You can't hurt people like that. Just promise me! Please!" I searched the ground for the strength to tell him. I lifted my eyes to the heavens. A lone egret soared above me.

I searched John's probing eyes. Certainly, little of what I told him made sense. How could it? Even I struggled to understand what was going on.

"Three days after Father died, we drove to the funeral home. I remember my feet dragging across the granite steps as I climbed to the front door. Mother grabbed onto a rail anchored into one of four white columns. Even from outside, I smelled burning wax and pine cleaner.

"The director escorted us inside. Candles surrounded Father's coffin. It took everything I had to walk to that casket. I had seen it on television, you know, with J. F. K. being shot and buried. But that kind of stuff didn't happen to our family. It wasn't real on television. But here—"

"We remember those kind of things for a long time."

"No, John. Not like this. When I looked inside that coffin, something sparkled from Father's cheek. He was crying, John. My father was in his coffin crying. At first I thought I was dreaming. The director saw what was going on and rushed over. He started apologizing to Mother, wiping the tear from Father's cheek. I could hardly breathe. I mean—"

The locust started singing right there before me. The sound pierced my horror. My head pounded like it was going to explode. I looked across the fields. "I could hear him even though he was whispering."

"Who, Paul?"

"The director. He was explaining to Mother that Father's illness caused swelling and this happened. It was embalming fluid leaking from his tear ducts. I would have sworn he was just sleeping, dreaming some dream, just like mine, one that haunted his spirit and frightened him, too.

"They draped a flag across the coffin. An Honor Guard stood watch. The funeral parlor filled with people. They just kept pouring in. Flowers were everywhere—so many that they had to stop bringing them. People kept touching me, telling me to be strong. Every hour, the Honor Guard would change. It was a nightmare. Three days of it. And it just got worse with every hour."

"All those nights you didn't sleep, this is what was eatin' you, wasn't it?"

The locust chanted louder. I wanted to scream at it so it would hush. But the memory of all this would still be there to obsess me.

"He was buried in Arlington. We drove there in a motorcade. Anti-war protesters lined the entrance to the cemetery. They kept screaming at us. 'Baby Killer! Baby Killer!' They wouldn't stop. They . . ." I collapsed into John's arms, releasing tears held back for years. John sat there, saying nothing, just present, offering support for me in possibly the only way he could. No words, no actions could have spoken any louder to me than this.

Against the shouts and screams, I jerked to the memory of gunfire offered in tribute to Father. The lone bugle sounding "Taps" was as real now as it was then. The doctors offered no cure, even in an era of man landing on the moon, for the leukemia Father developed from exposure to Agent Orange. We were still in the dark ages in our understanding of such a disease, much less in curing it. So too was the cure for what ailed me.

The sun hovered above the tree line. A gentle breeze rustled the sugarcane leaves. Field hands busied themselves with the day's chores. Children laughed through playful screams, celebrating the remaining days of summer before school.

The aroma of roux cooking in preparation for lunch settled across the plantation. Women rushed to complete their work, cackling to each other for assistance or maybe just the gossip of the morning.

The plantation was alive. Night had ended and the new day called. Even with the morning dew lingering on the grass and trees, life was in full motion. Before we would realize it, the day would dry, the afternoon thunderstorms would build, and nightfall would approach again.

The plantation bell clanged. "It's about time, pal."

"Why don't you go ahead?"

"Are you okay?"

"Yes, I just need a few more minutes."

"I'll let 'em know you're comin'." He started up. Pausing for just a moment, he looked down at me. It reminded me of our first meeting. I once again extended my neck back to look at his towering presence. "Paul, you're the best friend I've ever had. I just want you to know that."

For all that I had been through, for all the times he sat patiently watching as I dealt with all the crap, he was constant, never once leaving my side. But I had done so little for him. How could I possibly be the best friend he ever had?

The branch shook as he shimmied down the tree. I remained behind, gazing, thinking, taking in the view, and storing as much of a memory of it as I could. A white egret glided into the field. I knew then that it was time to move on.

Ten

New Year's Eve 1979

John straightened his bow tie. "My palms are sweatin'."

"You're not nervous?"

"Oh, and you're not?"

"Scared shitless, but I'm not the one sweating."

"You can be such a smug little turd."

"And you're still a big asshole, and a sweaty one if you don't relax."

The doorbell to our uptown apartment rang. "Get the door, would ya? I've got to put a dry shirt on."

"It won't help." I opened the glass door to find the driver of our limo waiting outside.

"De la Moret and Cheramie?"

"Yes. We'll be just a moment."

"Take your time, sir."

"John, the driver's here."

"I'm comin'. Wait for me in the car. You make me nervous."

"No, it's not me. It's just the fact that you're about to ask Meg to marry you."

"Paul, get your ass in that car before I toss you into it!"

"All right already. I'll meet you out there. But remember, we've got reservations at Commander's Palace and they don't wait for folks who are late, even ones as important as you."

"Fu—"

I slammed the door before he could finish the expletive. A wind blowing off the Mississippi River added a nip to the already chilly night air. I buttoned my overcoat, a rare event for New Orleans. With temperatures falling, the Big Easy was to experience frost and freeze by morning.

John emerged from the stoop, his white scarf flinging in the breeze. With a snap of his wrist, his top hat popped out. Securing it on his head, he strutted to the car with walking cane in hand, sure to be the "beau of the ball." For all the years of knowing him, he still fronted like a model carved from some Manhattan modeling studio.

John pulled the limo door opened. "Not one word from you or I'm gonna toss your little ass outta this limo onto the street."

"Got the ring?"

"Dammit!" He sprung out of the limo and sprinted back to the apartment.

"Aren't you glad I said that one word."

He flipped me off. It was deserved. Ever since he decided to ask Meg to marry him, I had been giving "shit" as he said. It was a rare opportunity to find John rattled. And I was taking full advantage of giving him hell about it.

"Let's go! And, now not a word." He eyed me.

The limo driver pulled out into the light stream of traffic cruising down St. Charles Avenue. Anne and Meg waited at the house of the mayor—Meg's father.

We arrived at the wrought-iron gates of the red-bricked colonial. The driver lowered his window and pushed the call button.

"May I help you," the voice requested.

"Yes. Limo service for Miss Anne and Miss Meg."

"Drive on through."

The gates opened to the semi-circular driveway of the gated front yard. White rockers lined the lower porch, sandwiched between large white columns. The driver pulled to the bricked steps.

A doorman opened the door. "Gentlemen, this way. The ladies are waiting for you in the parlor."

Servants and caterers rushed about in final preparation for the New Years Eve celebration. Hundreds of champagne glasses on brightly polished silver trays encased champagne fountains and ice sculptures. Finger foods, desserts, and other goodies filled white linens-covered tables.

"John, is that you?" Meg entered the room like a princess transported to the present from some ancient time.

John froze. His eyes locked on her like he was seeing her for the first time. "She's beautiful," he whispered.

I nudged him. "Give her a kiss."

He staggered forward in a trance, then affectionately embraced her.

"Uh, uhm," the mayor cleared his voice.

John snapped to attention. "Mr. Mayor. I'm sorry. I didn't hear you come in."

"Obviously."

"Good to see you, sir." John extended his hand as the mayor blew by him, not even giving him a second's notice. "He hates me," he mumbled.

Meg smiled as she turned his face back towards her. "No, he's just being daddy."

"Meg, where's Anne?"

"Hey, stud. I'm right here."

The hair on the back of my neck rose and my breath shallowed. She dazzled in the chandelier's light. The sequins of her dress shimmered and her eyes sparkled.

"What, not even a compliment?"

"Cat got your tongue, turd?"

"Umm . . . no . . . umm . . . you're beautiful."

John elbowed me. "The poet laureate finally speaks. Shall we, ladies?"

Anne and Meg led the way, giggling as they walked toward the door. Certainly they knew two puppies lagged behind them, even without leashes.

The limo driver opened the door as they climbed in. John and I followed. Our short drive to Commander's Palace was filled with idle conversation between Meg and Anne, while John and I gawked at them.

"Gentlemen, I'll pull you around to the main entrance." The driver navigated the limo around the crowds scurrying through the streets. With the Sugar Bowl in town, the city was filled to capacity.

The doors to the limo opened. "Ladies." With Meg and Anne on our arms, John and I proceeded to the maître d'.

"Mr. de la Moret, how's your mother?"

"Doing very well, Emile. Thank you for asking."

"If you would follow me. Your table is ready."

"Ladies."

The restaurant was packed full of partygoers and revelers. Every table showed signs of the feast before the real festivities.

"Sir, your table."

"Thank you, Emile."

Meg giggled. "Well, Mr. de la Moret, you've outdone yourself this time. How did you arrange the chef's table on New Years Eve."

"His mother," Anne chimed in. "All I have to do is mention something and before I know it, it's there. The woman is a saint."

John nodded. "I couldn't agree more."

The cork of a champagne bottle popped. The bubbly filled the fluted stemware.

John cleared his throat. "Ladies, Paul, if I may propose a toast." He stood. "To the best friend a man could ever have and to two of the most beautiful women this city has ever seen."

The glasses pinged. The room came alive. With Anne to my left, and Meg sitting next to her, I saw in them love and warmth, life and vitality.

Anne squeezed my hand. "It's wonderful."

Samples of food, all pre-arranged by the cook, graced our table. First, we tried shrimp cocktail with a special sauce, then fried soft-shell crab. Soup and salad followed and then the entrées were served. We seemed to soar through the seven-course meal, including dessert.

The pace around us slowed. Almost on cue, everyone vanished with the exception of Meg, Anne, John, and me.

John caressed Meg's hand. "I've got somethin' to ask you."

"Let me guess, you and Paul want to raise hell in the Quarter later."

"No, seriously."

Meg drew a deep breath.

"Megan Elizabeth Galatoire, would you marry me?" John slipped the Tiffany setting on Meg's slender finger. The diamond glistened in the candlelight.

Meg wrapped her arms around John. Sniffles from happy tears greeted us.

Anne squeezed my hand. "Oh my God, Paul."

"Feel slighted?"

"What?"

"Do you feel slighted? Because I want to know the same thing. Will you marry me?"

Now it was Anne's turn to sniffle. I guided the ring onto her finger.

"Oh, Paul, it's beautiful. It's too much."

"Mother insisted, and I happened to agree. She wanted you to have the best, and so did I. She loves you almost as much as I do. And, I love you for loving her, even for the pain in the butt she can be."

A round of champagne in toast to us was in order. I was happy. For once, I was truly happy.

Eleven

Mardi Gras 1980

"Would ya get with it! The limo is here and we've gotta pick up Anne and Meg. If we're late—" John paced by the door. The purple and green jester's hat on his head presented a fitting completion to the black tux he was wearing.

"Stand up straight and let me check you out."

"Why?"

"Well, we're sitting with the mayor's family and I want to make sure you're presentable."

"Hey, the mayor—"

"The mayor thinks you're an idiot and at times, I would have to agree."

"Since when have you become the cool, calm expert?"

I pointed to his head. "Since you put on that stupid hat."

"The hat. Damn, I forgot to take it off."

"My point exactly. I can dress you up, but still find it hard to take you anywhere. So let's get you 'lookin' propa' as they say, so you can be presentable when you arrive with the mayor's daughter."

"He really does hate me."

"He's just protecting his daughter like any man with a gun collection would."

"Thanks a lot. That really helped. You're eatin' this shit up, aren't ya? What a smug little turd you can be. But since you're gonna be the best man in my wedding, if he takes aim at me, you're goin' down with me."

"It would be my honor to take a bullet for you, sir."

Closing the door to our uptown apartment, John and I strolled down the steps to the limo. St. Charles Avenue buzzed with activity. The Crew of Endymion prepared itself to roll through the streets of New Orleans.

With only one year left before completing his M.D., John had met his match—a flight attendant named Meg. I was completing my graduate studies. It was to be our last year together as students. Even though I was only twenty-three, Anne and I were to be married at the St. Louis Cathedral in August.

John and Meg were following us with a Christmas wedding. Ever since he met her on our flight to South America, she was all he could think of.

"After you, Monsieur de la Moret."

"Why thank you, sir. You are a gentleman and a scholar."

The driver closed the door. A line of limos and other cars headed downtown. The city teemed with life. With the oaks in their spring green, revelers filled the streets, draped in costumes of purple, green, and gold. Like the wise men bearing gifts for the Christ child, men riding floats decked in brilliant colors would soon shower bystanders with beads, doubloons, and all sorts of trinkets.

The car slowed. We approached the uptown apartment of Miss Anne Marie LeBauve and Miss Megan Elizabeth Galatoire. With the sunroof opened, John and I stood up to gather our first view of our brides to be. Dressed in flowing white gowns, they stood on their balcony. The Mardi Gras crew awaited their arrival to complete the court.

"Shall I compare thee to a summer's day—" John launched into his recitation of Shakespeare, showering the royalty awaiting us with prose befitting their regal stature. The facade of Mardi Gras made such things common in an event not so common except to those of us from New Orleans.

"Why, Miss Anne, you sure do look mighty strikin' tonight."

"Why, Mr. Cheramie, while your flattery causes me to blush, I must remind you that I'm spoken for by that strappin' fine gentleman standin' next to you."

I elbowed John in the ribs in hearing Anne's comments. Even in John's tomfoolery, he had described her just as she was . . . "strikin'"! Certain to be the belle of the ball, her green eyes, olive skin, and long black hair radiated against the white chiffon evening gown. Her white elbow-length gloves and a white pearl necklace, given to her by Mother as an engagement gift, added those final touches of elegance befitting a lady of her character.

"Why, Mr. de la Moret, I was wonderin' if you were gonna come callin' tonight."

"Well, Miss Anne, I wouldn't think of doing anything but."

Laughter replaced our antics as we climbed into the limo and rejoined the procession heading down St. Charles to downtown.

John straightened his bow tie and checked his picture perfect hair. His all-American build filled the tuxedo like a model prepared for a photo shoot. "We'll drop you ladies off at the float and see to it that you're situated, and then we'll wait for you in the reviewin' stands."

"I'm sure Daddy will be quite pleased to have you there. After all, with four daughters in the family, you're going to be like his first son."

"A dead one if you remove her resolve before that wedding, if you know what I mean," I muttered under my breath.

Meg chuckled. "What's that, Paul?"

"Oh, nothing. I was just reminding John here of etiquette for such an occasion. I'm sure your father will be thrilled to see him."

Anne jabbed her nails into my side. "Paul de la Moret, you behave ya'se'f and quit picking on John. The mayor just adores him. Why, I heard him talking about taking John on a hunting trip just yesterday."

"And John's the big game he'll be hunting for."

"You hush now and leave poor John alone. You're just jealous, that's all."

With the official carnival flags of the crew attached to the front of the limo, police officers blocking the street waved us through to the Louisiana Superdome. The parade organized and started here, weaving through the streets of downtown, but returning to travel through the enclosed stadium. There, it delighted family members and invited guests of the crew.

"Ladies and gentlemen, we're here." With the limo pulled near the float, the driver raced around to open the door. John hopped out first. I followed. We extended our hands in an offer of assistance. Anne stretched her foot out of the car, her white satin shoe arching forward as it gracefully encased her foot.

"Why thank you, gentlemen." She grabbed hold of my hand and then John's. We easily lifted her light frame from the limo.

Meg followed. John's mouth dropped open as she emerged from the car. "You are the most beautiful woman in the world."

"He's really in love," Anne giddily whispered in my ear.

With their evening gowns fluttering in a light breeze, Anne and Meg stood near the float. I wondered if the city had ever seen such beauty.

The limo driver cleared his throat. "Gentlemen, I hate to interrupt, but we need to depart shortly if we're going to get to the reviewing stands before they block the streets."

With hugs and then waves, we bid our sweethearts farewell. Passage through the street slowed as the crowds thickened. Our limo paced behind a stream of vehicles and other limos as we crawled to the reviewing stand. We arrived to the mayor impatiently pacing the stands.

John extended his hand. "Mr. Mayor, it's an honor—"

"Yes. Right. Just find your places. The parade's ready to start."

Meg's younger sister pointed to our seats. "Don't mind him, John. Daddy is always that way when it comes to any of us dating."

"He hates me," John whispered.

"No, not you. Just the idea of his daughter getting married."

As the parade approached, sirens screamed through the street. Crowds once scattered pressed tightly together. The honor guard marched by with the first band playing the Mardi Gras Mambo directly behind it. Dancing broke out in the streets. The party had started.

The float carrying the royal court neared. The crowd stilled. The bands grew silent except for a lone trumpet salute. A drum rolled. The mayor raised his glass in tribute. "Your Royal Majesty, I offer the streets of our fair city in homage to your royal reign."

"Thank you, Mr. Mayor. We are grateful to accept your invitation and wish to introduce to you our royal court." Meg stood, followed by Anne. Other young women on the float joined them. The mayor lifted his glass once more. Guests in the reviewing stand stood in ovation. John and I were lucky to have already snagged two of New Orleans' finest young ladies.

The royal entourage moved down the street. The blare of horns from a marching band followed. Floats streamed by. Trinkets, toys, and doubloons showered the reviewing stand. One by one, costumed-riders tossed the treasures of Mardi Gras to those standing below.

In a flash of time, the final float approached. The crowd roared. The last of the trinkets rained upon us.

With work crews now cleaning the streets, John and I prepared for our entrance into the Louisiana Superdome. Our limo paced behind a caravan heading that way. People milled about littered streets. Beads dangled from overhead wires and trees along the parade route.

"I'm having a blast."

"Yeah. You've gotta love Mardi Gras."

"We're going to slip into the Quarter tonight, right?"

"Bet your sweet ass."

"Think the girls will let us?"

"Charm, my friend. We'll charm 'em."

Arriving at the Superdome, we followed the crowd inside. With the parade due to arrive in less than a half-hour, the party was already underway.

"De la Moret and Cheramie."

A big guy dressed in a tux stepped in front of us. "Your invitations, gentlemen."

"Here ya go."

"You're located at the Court Table number one. The concierge will seat you."

"Thank you."

"Let's party." John wiggled his hips pretending to dance down the corridor. The band blared as the crowd filled the dance floor. Ladies in formal evening gowns sashayed, followed by gentlemen in black tie attire.

"Ladies and gentlemen." The band stopped. The crowd turned towards the announcer. "It is my privilege as your master of ceremonies tonight to welcome the Crew of Endymion and our first marching band, the Purple Knights of St. Augustine High School."

The crowd roared in applause. They pressed against the steel barricades to gather a glimpse as the Purple Knights strutted into the Superdome. Floats streamed in as trinkets and all types of toys showered the crowds.

"Throw me something, mista." Heralding the sea of masked riders, bystanders shouted in hopes of receiving a prize. The long white beads tossed from the floats blanketed the air above us. Hands waved, grabbing onto whatever zipped by. Float after float ebbed through the crowd. The party reached a feverish pitch.

"Gentlemen, may we join you?" Anne and Meg slipped in front of us. Masked revelers aboard brightly decorated floats tossed a torrent of white beads towards them. The beauty of Anne and Meg attracted the attention, and in some cases the affection, of crew members riding by.

With the last float exiting the Superdome, the band kick up again. Crowds once pressed against the barricades returned to the dance floors.

"Let's dance." John led the way. Together we boogied until we could hardly stand it.

"My feet hurt." Anne peeled the sandals from her feet.

I cradled her leg into my lap. "Here, I'll rub them."

"John—" Meg followed Anne's lead.

"At your service, my dear."

"Paul, you've done good with him. He no longer drinks out of the toilet bowl and you've got him housebroken." Meg pegged him. "Shall we call it a night, gentlemen?"

John cleared his throat. "Well, if you ladies would allow us, we'd like to meet a few friends in the Quarter. We'd love to have ya—"

"Save it. We've heard it before." Meg slammed him. "We'll see you two at mass tomorrow."

Anne stared me down. "No bars with ladies, if you know what we mean."

"No, no. Just a quick trip to Pat O'Brien's."

They looked at each other. "There's no such thing as a quick trip for you two."

"Hey, the streets shut down at midnight. Lent, remember?" John's retort rolled off his tongue as if he had rehearsed it.

We walked Anne and Meg to the limo and bid them farewell. With only a couple of hours left to the celebration, we galloped down Poydras, then Barrone, onto Canal, slipping into the Quarter via Dauphine.

"Let's head to Lafitte. We'll get to Bourbon easier." The crowds thickened as we walked deeper on Dauphine. Occasional shouts from revelers, with a little more alcohol concentration than usual, filled the air.

"Through here, Paul." John led us through a back alley to Bourbon. We emerged amidst a mass of people. With bodies pressed together, he guided us towards St. Peter. "What are you doin'?" John screamed.

I turned onto Bourbon towards Canal Street. "Go on. I've got to take care of something."

"What now?"

"I'll meet you at Pat O'Brien's."

"Wait up. I'll come with ya." John tagged behind me as I turned. "Where's the fire?" Even John's banter did not slow me as I pierced through the crowd.

A young man staggered towards a doorway. He dropped to the ground, banging his head on the wall. I dashed to him. His head was bloodied by the fall. Yet, he held onto his Hurricane managing to barely spill a drop.

"Hey man, are you okay?"

"Ah re, ha, fu' man." He slurred his words speaking in a language unto himself.

"Do you remember where you're staying?"

More slurred words followed.

"Do you know where you are?"

"Paul, he's too damn drunk to talk."

"Give me a hand then." Grabbing hold of his side, we lifted him to his feet. Both of them towered me by at least six inches.

"Damn, he weighs a ton."

"Just shut up and help me."

"So what are we gonna do with him?"

"Let's get him to those cabs." Spying a group of cabs clustered off St. Peter, we pushed our way through the crowd. "Excuse me, sir. Yes, you." The cab driver looked puzzled. "You're Muslim, I take it."

"Yes. I am."

"This man is in need of help. I want you to take him to this address. Give them this card. They'll see to him. Take this for your trouble."

148

"Very good, sir. You honor Allah in your charity."

"And you obey the laws of the Qur'an in showing mercy to any in need of help." As the cab drove off I turned to face John. "What?"

"Save the whales, save the trees, save the drunks. If you aren't savin' somethin', I don't think you're happy." Just then, the bell from the Cathedral tolled 11 P.M. "Oh, it's *Dark Night of the Soul* time."

"Don't start that."

"Lighten up, Paul. Remember. 'On a dark night, Kindled in love with yearnings—'"

"You don't even know what it means."

"And you do? If we wanna get any time at P. O.'s we better hurry." John pressed his hands together like an arrow as we weaved through the crowd. Navigating our way through a maze of bodies pressed tightly together, we managed our way to Pat O'Brien's. "Is Tres workin'?"

The doorman smiled. "Oh, Mr. Cheramie. I didn't see ya. Tres's workin' inside. Follow me." Even with hundreds pressed against the walls, we glided to the entrance of the piano bar.

"I waz wonderin' if y'all were comin'." Tres stood watch at the doorway. "I gotta table dat jus' opened up."

"You know we wouldn't miss this for anything."

Our faces reflected off the brass sides of twin pianos situated on a small stage in front of us. Monique and Claude waved us in. "Hey, fellas."

"How's ya mamma and dem been doin'?" John threw a kiss to Monique.

"Doing good."

"Beginnin' to wonda if y'all were gonna make it." Claude pressed his mouth against the microphone. "Whacha wanna hear? Neva' mind, I already know. *Do you know what it means, to miss New Orleans—*" He led the way as he and Monique serenaded us. John and I lifted our Hurricane-filled glasses in toast.

One song followed another. As they banged out "Oh When the Saints," the crowd sang along. John and I kicked back watching drunk after drunk regaling himself in Southern pride. With Hurricanes mixed to perfection and consumed to excess, their singing prowess was far beyond high quality or good taste. Yet, they sang to fair maidens, unsuspecting debutantes visiting our fair city, hoping that their display of manhood would relax the resolve of some cute, jolie blonde.

Maybe this was why John and I loved the city so much, especially Pat O'Brien's. After all, the corner of Bourbon and St. Peter Streets signaled the turning point that led directly to Jackson Square and the St. Louis Cathedral. It was along this route where, on the way to confession, we generated interesting dialogue for whatever priest was awaiting, by stopping by Pat O'Brien's and making the effort of confession worth our while.

John looked up at the ceilings as the lights came on. "What's goin' on?"

"Ladies and gentlemen, it's midnight. Thank you for coming to Pat O'Brien's and the City of New Orleans. We hope you've had a wonderful Mardi Gras and wish you a safe trip home."

Throwing kisses to Monique and shaking Claude's hand, we exited the bar.

John turned right on St. Peters. "Beignets?" The Café Du Monde was only blocks away.

"I'm starved."

"It's a 'Dark Night.' Look, no moon."

"You're drunk."

"Yeah. That's the only time that damn poem makes sense."

"It makes sense!"

"You're full-a-shit."

"No, seriously. It's about surrender—letting go. It's about the relationship between Adam and God prior to the fall from grace."

"Bullshit. St. John was on dope when he wrote the damn thing and he was just jackin' with us for shits and giggles. Ya know, shankin' our chain."

"Seriously, John. It's the ultimate prayer of surrendering to love."

"Love?"

"Yes. Like the love Jesus displayed for John, his disciple. The courage that John showed by being the only discile to go to the foot of the cross. It's like our friendship, I mean . . ."

"Don't stop. Say it."

My eyes traced the littered streets. I searched for the courage to speak. As I lifted my head, John's pleading eyes greeted me. I could remain silent no more. "It's like how you stand by me even when I don't sleep. I think when St. John of the Cross wrote that poem, he either had a friend like you are to me, or he too had gone through what I've experienced."

John stopped. A tear dampened his eye. "You're serious, aren't ya?"

I nodded.

"Ya know I don't have brothers or sisters, that is with the exception of you and Anne. But I never feel alone when I'm around you. It's like my adoption and all the times I wondered why my natural parents gave me up—well it all makes sense to me. It was so I could meet you, and we'd be best friends. I think I'm livin' my destiny."

As John and I walked towards Jackson Square, we came to the corner of St. Peter and Chartres Streets. We cut across the backside of the square just in front of the St. Louis Cathedral. Musicians, fortunetellers, artists, and other creatures of the night packed up as police cleared the streets. But a Creole gentleman with a black beret blocked our path. He poised himself into a stance of oration and in a broadening smile revealing his bright, white teeth, he spoke:

> "Befriend me night, best patroness of grief,
> Over the pole thy thickest mantle throw,
> And work my flattened fancy to belief,
> That heaven and earth are colored with my woe;
> The leaves should all be black whereon I write,
> And letters where my tears have washed a wannish white."

The man approached me. "And you, my man, grieve over a pierced heart."

The bells of the cathedral tolled midnight as the words of Milton spooked me. A chill floated across my spine. I paused. Light filled Pirates' Alley from the backside of the cathedral. Lured by it, I turned to see what it was.

"Paul—" John's voice faded as I entered. Unlike daylight, a glow cast the darkness of the alley aside. Warmth replaced the chill once nipping me. Feeling safe and secure, I walked. But as I turned the corner, an image frightened me.

"You must go." Her words unsettled me.

"Who are you?"

The touch of John's hand freed me from my stance. "What is it, Paul? Talk to me."

In silence, I stood there. Wanting to speak of what I saw, my mouth wouldn't move.

"Snap out of it, pal." John reached around me, pulling me to his chest. I resisted as the image remained there before me.

"Why? Why me?"

She peered at me.

"Who are you talkin' to, Paul?" I turned away from the vision to face John. He looked confused. But I was drawn back to face the ghostly woman.

"Paul—" John gently shook me. Unable to speak, I stood there shivering. I gasped for breath. John pulled me into his arms. "Please talk to me, pal. I can't help if you don't tell me what's goin' on."

Once more I searched for her, but she was gone.

My legs grew weak as I took my first steps.

"I've got ya, pal." He sounded as though he was speaking to me through a tunnel. "Here. Let's sit on the bench." A life-sized statue of the Scared Heart of Jesus greeted me. Its fifty-foot shadow, cast by two large ground spotlights, soared against the back of the cathedral. The open arms spread across the plaster wall.

The bell tower tolled 1 A.M. I couldn't move. Soon, it was 3:30 A.M. and then 4 A.M. rolled around.

"We've got to go, John."

"Yeah, I'm sure the girls are worried."

"No. To the Ukraine."

The puzzled look on John's face bore the question, "Why?"

First light drew us to the river. With the spring waters rushing to the Gulf of Mexico, the river surged above flood stage. The Cathedral tolled 6:00 A.M. Church bells peeled throughout the city. The revelry of the night yielded to the Ursuline nuns chanting the Angelus. It filled the air.

"The angel of the Lord declared unto Mary and she conceived of the Holy Spirit."

"Hail Mary, full of grace. The Lord is with thee—"

"My being proclaims the greatness of the Lord. Be it done to me according to thy will."

"Hail Mary—"

Twelve

Spring 1981

A mockingbird chirped from a one hundred-year-old oak in Audubon Park. With spring in full glory, lawn mowers were working overtime to keep up with the sprouting lawns and the weeds that came with them.

Azaleas covered with pink flowers ushered Easter's arrival. The forty days of fasting and prayer were coming to an end. Holy Saturday, as it was called among the Roman Catholics of New Orleans, was the only day in the church calendar where no masses or services were offered. Yet, even while Meg, Anne, John, and I lounged in the park on a quilted blanket, the religious busily prepared for the Easter Vigil and those waiting for their initiation into the church.

The church bells at Loyola University tolled 12:00 noon. Like Mardi Gras night a year ago, the peel called for me to travel to the Ukraine. Yet, the image that I saw, or thought I saw, made little sense to me. The Ukraine—why?

Meg sheepishly smiled. "John, be a dear and grab a bottle of water for me."

"Sure, love. Anne, would you care for one as well?"

"Please."

The mockingbird resumed its song, chirping as to celebrate the resurrection of spring. Butterflies sporting a fresh coat of transformation from caterpillar flipped and floated about as carefree as a day as beautiful as this one should be.

Meg flipped the sandals off her feet.

"Where ya goin', love?" John asked lovingly.

"Fresh cut grass . . ." She jutted off like a schoolgirl on her way to her first prom. Anne followed close behind and the two of them tossed grass about with their feet.

John and I sat back on the blanket, tapping our bottles of beer together. With a smile drawn from ear to ear, he nudged his head towards the girls.

"Do you think we should join them?"

"And spoil their fun? No way. We'll sit right here and watch 'em until they've tired."

They continued with the frolic of the spring day, their floppy hats and sundresses blowing about in the scant breeze. Seeing Anne and Meg so happy warmed me. They were best friends ever since high school, like John and me, except they went to school here in the city . . . The Sacred Heart School for Girls. From some of the stories we heard about them, the school was anything but sacred when they left. It wasn't really anything serious—just two girls becoming women, and finding every way to leave their mark through that right of passage.

Meg grabbed her floppy hat as the wind gusted for a moment. "Hey, boys. Anne and I want to go see your relatives."

On command, John and I folded the quilt and stowed everything else into the picnic basket. We dropped our wares in the car, then joined Anne and Meg for a walk to the zoo.

Kids dashed about on swing sets and monkey bars, playing chase and flying kites. The excitement of pending Easter candy filled their strides with energy only to be matched by the sugar high to come.

John led us through the turnstiles. "Which way first?"

"Well, I know Anne likes the monkey exhibit because it reminds her of Paul, but I have a preference for the apes."

Arm and arm, they giddily walked ahead of John and me. Although we were the butts of their affectionate play, we had the better view. Their flower print sundresses, all but woven around their sleek frames, made for a vision truly desired by the male of our species.

"Come on, boys. You can stop staring at our asses now. Just because we're married doesn't mean you can act like dirty old men."

"Whacha mean, dirty old men? Look at these abs." He lifted his shirt to a washboard of muscle rarely seen except in muscle magazines.

Meg glanced back at John. "Don't be showing me your business out here if you have no plans to close the deal."

"My lady, I would close that deal for you at your discretion. I am your humble servant."

Meg slyly looked at him. A pregnant pause stretched to the call of a macaw. Other beasts of the wild kingdom seemed to chime in on cue. "Good answer. Very good. Now get those buns of steel over here and kiss me."

John all but floated to her, like a victim placed deeply in trance. To her, was his affection devoted and committed.

"Well, Mr. de la Moret, are you going to leave me just standing here?" Anne patted her feet on the concrete walk.

I joined her in an affectionate embrace and kiss. We were inseparable, all four of us. Maybe every thing I had lived though was for this moment—all the pain and loss a down payment for this. I felt alive again. The day was so beautiful. The air smelled great, especially with the subtle scent of Anne's perfume.

We walked hand in hand, as did John and Meg. The animals and vegetation of the zoo provided nothing more than a backdrop for a stroll of two couples in love. Yes, in love. Oh, how I hoped it would last. Yet, a tinge of fear pricked me. My dreams—what of my dreams? *Please. Please. Anything but one of them. Please don't harm them. Hail Mary,* I thought.

Thirteen

April 1986

"Come on, John." I wrapped my arms around him. Anne matched me on the other side. Rows of aboveground, whitewashed crypts with white-cross caps enveloped us. The sight of Meg's coffin tucked into one numbed me.

"You think she's at peace?"

"Yes," Anne whispered. She reached for my hand around John's back. Her eyes connected with mine. "How about I leave you two for a moment?" Anne stood on her toes to kiss John on his cheek. "I'll meet you at the car."

The scent of sweet olive and fresh cut grass filled the air. A flock of brown Eastern doves, probably stirred by the buzz of a lone lawn mower, soared past us.

"She loved to walk in fresh cut grass." John lifted his head to the clear blue sky. He stiffened his upper lip, then clenched his jaw. "I feel like a big hole has been blown wide open in me."

What could I say to him? When my father died, not one word spoken eased my pain. But I couldn't let him hurt like this—not now.

"How do you go on? It hurts to breathe." His voice cracked.

To hell with it! I couldn't even find a word to make his pain go away.

"I don't know if I can go on, pal. I just don't know."

I bit my lip so as to not to lose my cool. "I can't tell you I understand what you're going through, because I don't know if anyone can. But, I want you to know, I care, and I love you."

John wrapped me in a hug. His tears wet the side of my face. Even for all I had lived through, it felt like my heart was being ripped from my body.

■

September 1986

Anne bounced on my bed. "I love being here. Why do you ever want to leave?"

"Now, honey, you know that Dad's been after me for years to go on this retreat. And, at least I'm not going to the Ukraine."

"Not that. I'm talking about moving away from Oak Grove. It's so beautiful."

"That's a conversation for another day."

Anne fluttered her eyes at me. "Well, Mr. de la Moret, if you've got to go, and I'm sure that you do, then you behave yourself on that there retreat of yours."

"I promise, no wild parties, but we've got to have dancing girls for one night."

"Well, you just keep your paws off their silky drawers and we'll be fine."

Francis knocked gently on our open door. "Afternoon, Miss Anne, Mista Paul."

"I know. You're here for my luggage."

"I do declare. I've been wonderin' if ya were ever gonna git it. Yo stepdaddy is about to wear a hole in the downstairs rug. We bes' git goin'."

We followed Francis downstairs. Family photographs lined the staircase walls. The memory of family members long since past seemed present in my farewell.

Mother waited in the foyer, her knee length red dress made her look as striking as ever.

"Mother, tell Grandmother and Grandfather I'm sorry I missed them."

"I sure will. You enjoy yourself."

Mim walked down the hallway from the kitchen. "Is dat da boy leavin'?"

"Yes, Mim. It's me. What, no food?"

"Oh, I've already talked ta da cook at Manresa. She's gonna see dat ya eat."

"Mim, you didn't?"

A smile blanketed Mother's face. "You better get going before your dad bites what little finger nails he has left. I tell you, I've never seen a man so impatient when it comes to going somewhere. You'd swear we were fighting the Yankees all—"

I kissed Mother on the cheek. Anne walked with me onto the porte cochere. I wrapped my arms around her.

"Let's go, son," Dad called from inside the car.

Anne's green eyes pierced through me. My heart fluttered.

"I love you," she whispered.

"Always."

Before stepping into the car I threw her a final kiss.

"Let's go, Francis," Dad eagerly directed.

Francis steered us to the driveway. "Mista Jacques, ya still wanna go through Vacherie?"

"Yeah. Paul loves to cross the river on the ferry."

"It's been years since I've been back there."

Following the bayou north to Thibodaux, we turned east towards Chackbay. With fields yielding to cypress-filled lowlands, swamp replaced fertile soil. Green palmetto leaves dotted the water-bordered highway. John looked like a kid on his first trip away from home. "What's this swamp?"

"It's the northern shore of Lake Bouef. We're driving around it to get to the river."

Water hyacinth floated undisturbed in the canals, their purple and yellow flowers sprinkled among them. White egrets, standing among hundreds of cypress knees lining the swamp, picked crawfish from lime-green duckweed peppering the shallows. The journey was like so many I had taken before.

As we emerged north of the lake, sugarcane fields reappeared. Green grass-covered levees marked the east bank. We turned south on the snaking River Road. The car weaved with each bend and turn.

"Looks like were jus' in time." Francis steered the car up the mounded earth on a shell road. As the last car on the ferry, we drove right onto the metal deck.

The horn blared three times. Two deck hands slipped metal barriers to close off the railing while others gathered the ropes mooring us to the dock. With the engines thrusting, the ferry glided into the channel.

John leaned against the front rail of the boat. "Look at the size of that log. I didn't realize the current was so strong."

A sick sensation soured my belly. The knotted bark reminded me of the tree and snapped branch that pinned Andre's broken body to the ground.

John bumped me with his elbow. "What's up?"

I shook my head, making eye contact with him, pleading that we just let things unsaid remain that way.

I felt Dad's hand on my back. "Son, let's walk around to the rear." The span of a new bridge jutted across the river. "It's almost finished. Next year at this time we'll probably drive across it." Saddened by the news, I looked away to relish the moment of maybe my last ride on this boat.

The sun descended behind the trees of the West Bank. The ferry pierced through the waves. The spray moistened my face. Large ships strewn along the river waited for cargo to be delivered or unloaded.

I choose you. You must go. If only I could silence the voice in my head.

The hum of the diesel engines slowed. The vibration once droning across the boat settled into a soft groan. The ferry glided into port.

We joined Francis in the car. Dad beamed with excitement. "We're only minutes away."

Driving over the levee, we followed River Road north, this time on the opposite bank. With the levee to our left, rows of cane to the right once more bridged the villages and plantations sprinkled along the way.

The car swerved in a huge bend in the road. Francis slowed to twenty miles an hour. Navigating a broad turn to the right, we curved backed to the left. A whitewashed fence emerged along the road.

"Francis, drive past the main house so the boys can get a look." The fence yielded to a four-foot brick wall parallel to the road. Francis pulled the car over to an embankment. Sandwiched between two large white brick columns, an iron-railed gate marked the main entry.

"So, what do you think?"

We crossed River Road. I pressed my head against the gate and latched my hands onto the rails. Just inside, two white-bricked guardhouses flanked each other. As the field opened, a massive antebellum structure stood nestled in the oaks. At least thirty massive, round, bricked columns supported her pediment and two-story porches.

Dad placed his hand on my shoulder. "Told you it was beautiful. You can feel the tranquility already, can't you?"

I stood motionless. Even Scarlet in all of her opulence couldn't have construed something as magnificent as this. Yet, images of boys in gray uniforms with others in blue, bloodied by a battle, fogged my view. A miasma, thick smoke smelling of gunpowder, floated around them. Cannon's rumbled in the distance like thunder from an approaching storm. Even those shackled and oppressed trembled in horror to the cost brought to bear by the fight for their freedom.

"Let's head back to the car, son."

Francis followed the driveway along the south side of the retreat house and then across the backside. Majestic oaks created a path like an honor guard standing in formation. The Spanish moss waved like draped flags of welcome. "Is dis okay wit' ya, Mista Jacques."

"Perfect."

Exiting the car, I turned in a circle to gather the grandeur of the surroundings. The air was warm and moist, but smelled of Sweet Olive. Azaleas and other shrubs encased the walkway on each side. Squirrels scurried as if to rush off with some newfound treasure. If the Garden of Eden could have existed in present time on earth, this could have easily been it.

"Come on, gentlemen. Let's get registered."

"Mr. Jacques, I gonna git da luggage."

"Dad!"

"No, Francis, you're on the retreat with us. We'll manage our own bags."

"But sir—"

"Francis!"

"Yez, sir." Francis fell into formation. "So what ya smilin' at, Mista Paul?"

"Oh, nothing. Just enjoying the moment."

"Ya been waitin' yo whole life ta git at me."

"Let's go, gentlemen." Dad led us to a building with a porch covered by a colonnade.

"Jacques, welcome back." As we entered through a set of French doors, a gentleman greeted us. "Is this your boy?"

"This is my son, Paul, his best friend, John, and another member of our family, Francis."

"Men, welcome to Manresa. Paul, Jacques' been talking about you for years. He's some kind of proud of you. Let's get you registered." As he sorted through stacks of registration forms, I couldn't but help noticing the hundreds of shelved books, among them a leather-bound version of *Dark Night of the Soul*. "Fellas, would the two of you mind sharing a room?"

John stepped in front of me as the gentleman handed us our registration forms. "Not a problem. Paul and I will share."

"Gentlemen, here's your retreat guide. It has a schedule. We're in the library. All presentations are done in the chapel and I'm certain Jacques will tell you about the rest."

John strolled beside me. "Are you okay?" he muttered.

I nodded.

"That Ukrainian thing botherin' ya again?"

Dad joined us before I had to reply. "Gentlemen, what say we get situated, and then I can take you on a nickel tour."

With luggage in hand, we entered the main lobby and trekked up the three flights of stairs. John waved me over. "Come here and look at this view." Our corner room overlooked both the chapel and an oak alley. "It's awesome, Paul."

As I turned to unpack, my eyes hooked on a picture hanging on the wall. My knees buckled to the haunting image before me.

"Paul, what's—" He hushed. "It's Ivan's statue."

My flesh stood up on my arms and on the back of my neck. I gasped for breath.

A knock rattled the door. "Hey, boys, you ready for the nickel tour?"

"We'll be out in a moment, Mr. Jacques."

I splashed cold water on my face hoping to regain my composure. Holding on to the side of the basin waiting, I prayed for strength to return to my body.

"Let's go, pal." John turned my body towards the door.

"Y'all ready?" Dad asked as he paced. I forced a smile and winked.

165

We walked down a circular staircase and exited near the chapel. Crape myrtles dotted the lush green grounds. Crows grouped in an open field cawed as they lifted into flight. Even a lone humming bird zipped by.

"It's hot." John wiped sweat from his forehead.

Dad patted his face with a handkerchief. "Typical Indian Summer. But don't worry, a cool front's due in tomorrow." He led us towards another white-bricked building standing in contrast to the gray barked oaks. "The Jesuits reside here. Upstairs. The dining room's downstairs. Let's save some seats." As we entered through a twelve-foot green door, the boards of the floor creaked even with a carpet cover. The faint aroma of roux competed with the stale air inside. Dad propped four chairs around a table. "That should do it."

Guiding us out of the hall, Dad directed our attention to statues of religious figures, alleys of oaks, and rooms tucked away in various buildings that held memories for him. Each seemed to blend into the landscape of the grounds like it was always there. "Paul, you're mighty quiet all of a sudden."

"Just a little tired, sir."

"I forgot you flew in yesterday. I tell you what. Why don't you boys wrap up your unpacking and we'll meet down in the library for the reception at six o'clock."

"Reception?"

"Sure. It's one of our traditions. I've got some folks I want you to—" His words faded as images of the icon flashed through my mind. "See you then."

Dad met up with several old friends while John and I escaped to the sanctuary of our room. A musty smell struck me as we entered.

I crawled into bed hoping that a brief nap would rid me of my torment. As I turned toward the wall, the picture of the icon hung above me. I rolled to the other side and closed my eyes. Yet I roiled in the memory of those I had lost. How could I ever tell John what I dreamed about Meg?

"Paul." John touched my arm. My eyes opened to his smile. "It's time for that reception. We've got five minutes."

"Why don't you go ahead? I'll freshen up and meet you down there."

"I'll wait."

I pulled my head through a fresh t-shirt. Our eyes met. John looked away. An awkward silence enveloped the room.

"Ya ready, pal?"

"I guess so." We walked downstairs and then to the library.

As I entered, my dad's face lit up with a smile. "Come over here, buddy, and let me introduce you to Mr. Perrin."

"Welcome, son. Your dad's been telling us about ya for years now."

"It's a pleasure to meet you, sir."

"Paul, this is Mr. Rachel."

"Your dad tells me you graduated from Tulane Medical and you're doing research for some big company up north." Their faces blended as one introduction followed another. I longed for silence, yet prevailed in my duty as a Southern gentleman to be gracious and sociable.

The library lights flickered. Men drifted to the doors and marched out towards the dining hall in small clusters. As we walked, the conversations about old times continued. I lagged behind, listening to the hum created by the myriad of voices and accents blending together. In quiet supplication, the retreat grounds just seem to absorb it all.

Sons and fathers with old friends and acquaintances congregated into the dining hall. Carts rattled through the isles with mounds of food. "Where's Paul de la Moret at?"

A gentleman pointed in our direction. "He's sitting with his dad."

"Who's his daddy?"

"Jacques LeBlanc. Over by the wall clock."

At that, a stout Creole woman strutted towards us. "Where Paul at?" Dad pointed to me even though he was now laughing. "Mim called me. She says ya don't eat some time an' dat I'm suppose ta make sho' ya eat.

So I jus' wanna let ya know dat I'm watchin' an' I'm gonna give her a call if ya don't eat." Our table and every one nearby exploded in laughter.

"It's the 1980s by God." Heat jetted from my face. If only to find a hole to crawl into—that would have been a blessing. John laughed so hard that he could hardly breathe.

"Son, if I were you, I would hush my mouth and fill it with food because she may be watching you now."

"Gentlemen—" A spoon clanged against a glass. "Grace Before Meals." Everyone rose from their seats. "Blessed, oh Lord, for these thy gifts—" we prayed in unison.

Steams of succulence wafted from dishes filled with food. Serving spoons clanging against the china joined joyous laughter and warm conversations. Each man spoke as if determined to get his last word in before silence began.

But like a maestro waving his wand to the conclusion of an aria, the dinner meal ended. The glee of the dinner conversation yielded to final sentiments and well wishing. One hundred men from every walk of life and from different parts of the world filed out of the dining hall. Darkness had settled upon the opulence of the retreat house.

Dad led us out onto the grounds. "You've been mighty quiet tonight, Paul."

"Yes, sir. Just a little overwhelmed by it all."

"Just relax and enjoy yourself. John, you do the same. I'll talk to y'all later, okay?"

"Yes, sir." I hugged him and began walking to a set of oaks.

John's feet thundered behind me. "Hey, pal. Wait up." With the moon absent, the walk to the oaks was particularly dark, but sparse ground lighting marked the way. Leaves and acorns crunched under our feet. Nothing moved. Only an occasional tree frog sang out. "That icon—"

"Let's not."

"Someday we're gonna talk about all this stuff."

Snapping twigs and tossing rocks, we walked through an oak alley to the river. Climbing the levee, we emerged onto the batture, the natural banks. Driftwood littered concrete boulders lining the river's edge as waters rushed to the Gulf of Mexico carrying sand and dirt from lands far removed.

Tugs roared, managing barges in the current. Ships glided by, some floating high with empty hulls. Others trudged low in the water. Catfish scurried along the shallows while crawfish tucked into the mud holes in shelter.

"Paul, I was thinkin'. Maybe we should take a trip when this retreat's all over. It's been a couple of years since Meg—" John grew silent. Tears filled his eyes. I had only twice before seen him this way.

I ached in seeing grief fill his face. Maybe it was my fault. I should have told him about Meg. But, what if I would have been wrong? Yet, I wasn't. I knew she was going to die and said nothing to him.

Church bells peeled in the distance. Sounding as though in stereo, the different pitches filled the river from the north and the south. Vespers were recited as the aroma of Creole kitchens permeated the air.

"Let's head up river, pal." With blades of grass in our mouths, the adventure of Huck and Tom seemed alive within us. The faint sounds of a calliope droned as a paddle wheeler steamed up river. "I miss her, pal," he whispered as he sailed a clamshell skipping across the murky waters. "How do you go on?"

"Sometimes one breath at a time."

"Ya mind if I walk alone a bit?"

"No. I'll see you in chapel at eight o'clock. Hey, John—"

"I know. Me, too."

A lump formed in my throat. I started to tell him, but hesitated. Instead I turned toward the main house.

I walked the levee until it reached the oak alley. I looked back toward John over the vegetable gardens surrounding the oaks. His silhouette faded into lightning flashes of a distant thunderstorm.

The whitewashed bricks of the main house glowed yellow in the soft lighting of the balcony. My solitary walk across the front lawn with oaks towering on both sides of me reminded me of my walk with Mim the night Father died.

Returning to our room, I felt cold, musty air strike me. I grabbed a rocking chair and moved it to the corner near the window. The straw strained and wood creaked and cracked as I rocked. I resisted looking at the image, but it was like someone was breathing on the back of my neck.

I faced the picture of the icon. The semblance of what I had seen or thought I had seen flashed before me. For all I had done to ignore her, to make the dreams of her go away, here she was once more.

My head pressed into my trembling hands. Fear rushed through me. Andre's death, then Father's, Kevin's, Xavier's, Meg's—their faces, their funerals—the image blurred. Who would be next? The words "I choose you" repeated over and over.

I reached toward the picture. Maybe if I tossed it out of the window, it would leave me alone. But I couldn't do it.

I grabbed a pillow off the bed, then pressed it to my face. "I choose you. I choose you." Each word painted the portrait of a lost loved one. Gasping for breath, I shouted, "No more!"

"Paul—" The door banged the wall. "What's—" Before John could finish, the first bell rang, calling us to instruction in the chapel. He handed me wet, cold towels. My face burned. "I'll let your dad know—"

"No! Just give me a minute." I walked to the sink and splashed cold water on my red and swollen eyes. I searched for something to mask the event.

"Here, take a handkerchief. It'll look like it's just an allergy." John grabbed clean linen from his luggage.

I drew several deep breaths.

"Sure you're okay, pal?"

I nodded.

We hurried down the stairs. As we entered the chapel, Dad sat with two seats reserved in the very back. He looked at me with a questioning gaze. I gestured that my allergies were bothering me. He whispered, "I've got sinus medication if you need it." I motioned that I was okay and then he faced the front.

The second bell chimed. Men settled into their seats. Our retreat master entered. At first, I could only gather glimpses of him through the crowd.

"He looks old enough to have known Jesus personally," John whispered. "I guess we're gonna receive a firsthand account of the story."

"Good evening, gentlemen. I am Father Miguel Barrios." I gasped in horror. It was the priest from South America. "Would you pray with me?" Kneelers pelted the floor as men knelt. "Most Holy Father, we come to You in silence and in want. Guide us in these days of fast and prayer that we may come to know Your will. Amen."

I slouched behind the man in front of me, avoiding eye contact with Father Barrios. Standing near the altar, he peered into his captive audience. Silence settled upon us. He scanned the crowd, making direct and intimate contact with each man present. He opened his Bible.

"Ask, and you will receive. Seek, and you will find. Knock and it will be opened to you. For the one who asks, receives. The one who seeks, finds. The one who knocks, enters. Would one of you hand his son a stone when he asks for a loaf or a poisonous snake when he asks for a fish? If you, with all your sins, know how to give your children what is good, how much more will your heavenly Father give good things to anyone who asks him!"

Again, he silently stared at us, this frail old man looking like some Jedi master cloaked in religious garb. The hush in the chapel deepened. Deliberately turning the pages of his Bible, he looked up as if to pray. "When he came down from the mountain, great crowds followed him. Suddenly a leper came forward and did him homage, saying to him, 'Sir, if you will to do so, you can cure me.' Jesus stretched out his hand and touched him and said, 'I do will it. Be cured.' Immediately, the man's lep-rosy disappeared."

Not a soul moved as his ritual continued. Eluding his gaze, I tried to maintain my stealth. With the pages of his Bible crinkling, he looked down. I breathed in relief.

"Jesus was walking and the crowds pressed upon him. A voice broke through the noise exclaiming, 'Son of David, have pity on me!' With that, Jesus paused and searched for the man. Upon finding him, Jesus asked, 'What is it that you want me to do for you?' The man reached for Jesus and said, 'I want to see!' With that, Jesus said go forth, your sins are forgiven you. The man opened his eyes seeing Jesus and proclaimed the miracle, praising God for his restored sight."

Father Barrios hesitated again, this time surveying the crowd almost like a hawk looking for prey. The pause stretched longer than before. His silence grew deafening. Yet his gaze pierced through it. With a softened tone, he spoke once more. "What is it that you want Me to do for you? Brothers, God is asking." Closing his folder, he turned and bowed to the Blessed Sacrament and with that he departed.

"In the name of the Father—" Men stood for evening prayers.

Yet Father Barrios' words penetrated the din of their voices, echoing off the brick walls of the chapel and the wooden rafters of the high ceil-ings. As if to peel through the layers of my own despair, I felt certain that he was speaking to me.

"May the all merciful God grant us a restful night and a peaceful death. Amen." Men rose and departed from the chapel and retired for the evening.

I sat in the pew. Only the altar lights remained on. The backdrop of gold metal inlay, looking hand-brushed by some artisan of times gone by, consumed the entire wall behind the high altar. A crucifix dangled from the ceiling. My eyes fixed on it. "What is it that you want me to do for you? God is asking." In quiet, I searched for answers, hoping to hear— wanting to know.

I dropped my head into my hands. Sweat beaded from my forehead and lips. Father Barrios' image in the South American rectory along with the memory of the icon flashed before me.

I lifted my head to the blood stained hands, feet, and side of Jesus' body on the cross. I wrung my hands of the blood once covering them from Xavier's lifeless body. "What is it that you want me to do for you?"

"Leave me alone! Show me no more!" My scream bounced against the brick walls of the empty church.

I tossed the kneeler up. I bolted from the chapel. Inconspicuous lighting illuminated the grounds. Against the backdrop of darkness, under the canopy of one hundred-year-old trees, silhouettes formed against the Spanish moss draped from the branches above. The statues of saints and religious figures all but came to life in the darkness—their presence made known by their haunting and focused gaze.

"I choose you." The words echoed once more. Cast in light and shrouded by crape myrtles overhead, water drops trickled from the eyes of a white plaster statue of the Virgin.

"Please leave me alone." The image blazed even against my closed eyes. Not knowing what to do, I climbed the stairs of the Jesuit residence. It was late and part of me hoped Father Barrios was already asleep. Yet, I yearned to speak with him, just as I had in South America.

As I made my way down the hallway, my feet shuffled across the carpeted floor. My heart pounded. Thoughts raced.

"So we meet again." With an abrupt turn, I found him standing behind me. "I was wondering when you would visit. Would you like to come in?"

I nodded.

He opened his door. Pointing to a lounge chair next to his desk, he rolled his chair to join me. "Please have a seat."

We sat in silence. I could not make eye contact with him.

"It still haunts you, doesn't it?"

My body trembled.

"Follow me." He got up from his chair and motioned for me to follow. I joined him in front of a full-length mirror. "A magnificent piece, isn't it? See the perfection of its design, the carved wood and bevels on its sides." He stroked the cypress wood, inviting me to do the same. "Look into the mirror. What an interesting likeness it provides us."

My eyes peered into my reflection, the green and brown tint reminding me of my father.

"Don't turn away, my son. Look, see the man before you," he spoke slowly and distinctly, yet ever so softly. "You know Psalm 139?"

> "O Lord, you have probed me and you know me:
> you know when I sit and when I stand;
> you understand my thoughts from afar.
> My journeys and my rest you scrutinize,
> with all my ways you are familiar.
> Even before a word is on my tongue,
> behold, O Lord, you know the whole of it.
> Behind me and before,
> you hem me in and rest your hand upon me.
> Such knowledge is too wonderful for me;
> too lofty for me to attain.
> Where can I go from your spirit?
> from your presence where can I flee?
> If I go up to the heavens, You are there;
> if I sink to the nether world, you are there.
> If I take the wings of the dawn,
> if I settle at the farthest limits of the sea,
> Even there your hand shall guide me,
> and your right hand hold me fast.
> If I say, 'Surely the darkness shall hide me,
> and night shall be my light'—
> For you darkness itself is not dark,
> and night shines as the day.

[Darkness and light are the same.]
Truly you have formed my inmost being;
you knit me in my mother's womb.
I give you thanks that I am fearfully, wonderfully made;
wonderful are your works.
My soul also you knew full well;
nor was my frame made unknown to you
When I was made in secret,
when I was fashioned in the depths of the earth.
Your eyes have seen my actions;
in your book they are all written;
my days were limited before one of them existed.
How weighty are your designs, O God;
how vast the sum of them!
Were I to recount them,
they would outnumber the sands;
Did I reach the end of them,
I should still be with you."

"Quite a remarkable prayer, isn't it? For those who are called, life can be quite interesting."

My heart pounded on hearing his words. "Called?"

"Yes, my son. Called."

"To what? By whom?"

"Who do you think?"

"Then why? Explain to me why we see things and then—" My throat tightened. My hands trembled all the harder. I wanted to crawl out of my skin. I searched the mirror. There, staring at me, a picture of that damn icon hanging on his wall. Anger filled me as I blurted the words, "If God, if He knows bad things are going to happen, why doesn't He do something about it? Just explain it to me. I've got to know."

Father Barrios said nothing. His clock ticked away. I wanted to smash it. But it wouldn't help.

"It's okay to be confused, my son—even angry. Peter, Thomas, Jesus, himself. All grew angry. All questioned."

"I wish I didn't know."

"Know what, my son?"

"Things."

"Like what?" He touched my hands. "My son, what is it?"

The walls of the room squeezed in on me. Yet, I had to speak. "It was just a year after my friend Andre died." My voice lowered and my tone softened. "I had a dream. It was like the one I had before Andre died, but this time it was about my mother and father.

"They had gone out for the night, something they did almost every weekend when Father was home. I had fallen asleep on the couch, waiting for their return. I didn't like when they were both away. The house always felt empty and I felt unsettled.

"The screeching of tires and gunshots woke me. I bolted up, half-dazed. At first I thought it was something on television. But it wasn't. I ran to the back door and looked out. Mother and Father were on the ground.

"I screamed for help. I ran to their blood-covered, bullet-riddled bodies. Father was still breathing, but Mother was already dead. I kept screaming for help, but no one came.

"I didn't know what to do. I just kept screaming. That's when I—" My jaw clinched. I swallowed as my throat strangled me. I struggled to breathe. Sweat dripped from my forehead. "I did it! I looked to heaven, my back arched as I did so, and begged God, 'If you take one of them, please take him, not her!'

"It's my fault. I'm responsible. I wished him away. Why did God choose then to grant my request? I . . . I can't!" I sprinted towards his door.

"Wait, my son!"

The stairs thundered as I slid down them. Pushing the exit door open, I slipped on the concrete. "My son!" Father Barrios called out to me. But I bolted towards the river.

Heaving, I pushed up the levee. Thick river fog veiled my escape. Without missing another step, I galloped towards a steeple of a church piercing through the dense misty blanket hovering close to the ground. My side ached. My legs grew weary as I slowed my pace. St. Michael's Church now stood before me.

The fog engulfed me as I descended the levee towards the church. A single streetlight cast a grayish tint to the white statue of St. Michael the Archangel. Etched on its pedestal were the words, "St. Michael the Archangel, defend us in battle, be our protection against the wickedness and snares—" My skin crawled.

I entered the church. Racks of candles, prayers offered by the faithful, provided dim lighting. Dark wooden rafters and sandy colored walls housed ornate wooden pews. The floors creaked as I walked to the high altar. I genuflected below a twenty-foot crucifix hanging from a column.

Someone coughed. I stepped lightly around the altar. More racks of candles lit the way. Nestled in an alcove, a figure of a young woman stood perched among the rocks in a grotto. A woman veiled in blue floated above it.

"Paul—" A whisper startled me. "I knew you'd come." John sat in a corner. "Can ya smell it?"

"Roses?" I searched to find them, but none were there.

"Yeah." John's face glowed. "You were right. We've gotta go to the Ukraine." Stunned, I knelt with him. His rosary beads clacked against the wooden pew in front of us. I watched his lips as he prayed, "Hail Mary—"

Fourteen

December 5, 1986

The steam relief from the engine fogged my exit off the train. I stepped to the right into a clearing, surprised to see Russian guards sporting AK-47s and patrolling the dock. I searched for Ivan through a small crowd gathered in front of me.

"Paul!" Ivan dashed towards me. We hugged. "It's great to see you. Where's John?" The stationmaster and a group of baggage handlers mingled with the other passengers lining the dock.

"Well, I was drunk, the day my mamma, got outta prison—" Singing David Allen Coe, John's voice thundered from the car as he stepped down.

Ivan chuckled. "He hasn't changed one bit. Still can't sing a lick."

Struggling to get his arms through the sleeves of his overcoat, John juggled his backpack.

I pointed to the headphones over John's ears.

"What?"

"You're a little loud, don't you think?"

"Don't start with me." His carry-on bags hit the ground. The headphones slipped off his ears. His voice lowered as he wrapped Ivan in a bear hug. "It's awesome to see ya, man, especially after twenty hours of travelin' with him."

"I see you and Paul still worship the quicksand you walk on."

"Don't mind him, Ivan. He didn't get his beauty sleep and he's kinda cranky. We better go before he throws a tiff." John started whistling before I could respond. He popped his sunglasses from his head to his eyes and walked ahead as if he knew where he was going.

Ivan joined me. "Any trouble with customs, Paul?"

"We probably spent two hours getting through the form in Kiev."

"The *Deklaratsia*. In Russian no less."

"We declared everything, just like you suggested. The customs agent was actually pretty helpful. But I think that's because she had a crush on John."

John nodded. "Helga! My woman!"

"Put the emphasis on man."

"Hey," John snapped back, "she's just healthy, that's all."

Two soldiers approached us, both looking like kids. Yet the red insignia on their dark, olive green uniforms and their AK-47s suggested otherwise. "Kuda vi sleduite?"

"Welcomin' party?"

Ivan stepped in front of us. "Let me handle this. Teto moi Amerikanskiye druziya. Oni khotyat posetit' universitet."

John lifted his sunglasses. "What's he askin'?"

"He wants to know where we're going. I told him you're my friends and you and Paul are here to visit the university. I need your passports and letter of invitation."

John reached for his papers. I handed the guard my own. He flipped through them. "Kak vas zavout?"

"My name . . . I mean, menya zavout Paul."

His partner motioned to John. "Vi?"

"I'm John." He offered his hand. Ivan and I drew closer.

With frowns plastered on their faces, both guards squared off to him. "Vi govorite po-Russky?"

"Yah nyeh gavaryu mnogah po-Russky. Vi govorite po-Angliysky?"

"Da. Ve speak English."

The guards chuckled at hearing him. "You speak Russian, funny man."

"Have to be if you're travelin' with him." John pointed at me.

"Da. Da svidaniya, funny man." He walked off with his partner, shaking his head. We each took a deep breath.

"Man, that was intense. They need to lighten up, like you, Paul." John elbowed me. "So Ivan, what's up with all the guards?"

"There's been quite a bit of student protest at the university. A major push for Ukrainian independence." Ivan lowered his voice. "I don't think the Soviets care for it all that much. Let's get your bags and get to your hotel."`

"That explains the State Department warnin'."

A baggage handler rolled a rickety four-wheeled turn of the century cart with our luggage. With only a few wooden benches and an arrival board filling the sparse train depot, we exited with ease.

I winked at Ivan. "Hey John, make yourself useful and grab our bags."

"Oh, the big man always gets to carry the stuff. Is that the way it works?"

"Come on, guys. I've got a cab waiting outside." Huddled tightly behind Ivan, we walked past armed guards posted near framed glass doors encased in a framed glass archway. I wanted to get a better look at the architecture, but fixed my eyes forward to call no further attention to us.

Ivan searched the parking area. "There." He pointed ahead to a double-tiered water fountain centered in a traffic circle. A gentleman stood propped against a small red car. With three square boxes welded on four wheels, the cab jutted in the center to complete a short fat "T."

The cab driver slid his beret low across his forehead, then tossed the remainder of his cigarette on the ground. The tobacco had the same strong odor we had smelled on the train. "Kuda vi edete?" This time the inquiry was much friendlier. The cab driver opened the trunk.

John scratched his head. "There's no way he'll get our bags in that car."

I stepped out of the way. "I'm more worried about getting you in it. It looks like the cars I drew when I was in first grade, and it's just as little."

"And so are you!"

Ivan folded his arms. "Watch this, guys." The cab driver maneuvered the bags into the square trunk, then slammed it shut. Ivan smirked. "Told you. Let's go."

Ivan and I slipped into the back seat. As John climbed in front, the car tilted. His knees pressed against his chest. "Ugh."

"I wouldn't breathe too hard. You might pop out and we could lose you."

Ivan chuckled. "No way. He's wedged in too tightly." Turning to the driver, Ivan said, "Provezi nas po prospektu Svobody cherez Rynok." He directed the cabby as we departed the depot.

"Where are we headin'?"

"To Prospect Svobody, a street near the hotel. I told the driver to bring us to Ploscha Rynok, the old Market Square. I want to show you two L'vov." As we drove around the small traffic circle, I glanced back. A spire capped the green dome of the station's main entrance. Sandwiched between two smaller steeples, it looked more like the entrance to a church, especially with its beige wings stretching for nearly a block.

The cab driver navigated through a series of turns. Earthy green, watermelon, and beige-fronted buildings bordered the narrow streets. Black wrought-iron balconies peppered the three, four, and sometimes five-story structures. Rising above the skyline, green onion-like steeples peeked through intermittently.

"Welcome to Rynok." The tires of the cab rubbed against the cobblestones. Overhead wires paralleled cable car tracks weaved into the streets. Unlike American cities, the sidewalks were barely elevated and only a few cars cluttered the streets.

Even though there was a chill in the air, merchants peddled fruit, flowers, and other goods from wooden carts. Women sporting handkerchiefs on their heads placed their purchases in oversized straw and leather handbags.

As the cab turned to the right, John pointed to a statue positioned in front of what looked like a tongue rising from the ground. "Man, what's that?"

"The Taras Shevchenko Monument and this is Prospect Svobody."

"It's like Vienna before World War II." A row of buildings lined the boulevard with Gothic, Italian, Renaissance, Byzantine, German Baroque, and Rococo styles.

"L'vov was spared bombing even though it was occupied. It's been like this for generations. Even the Russians left this section alone."

An ornate cream-colored building with a massive red paved entrance and a beautiful pond emerged at the end of the square.

Almost on cue, the driver stopped the car. "Prekrasnaya u vas muzika."

"He said there's beautiful music here. It's the Opera House." Glass arches placed on balconies crowned the three wooden doors fronting the building. Angel capped mires soared to the heavens, flanked by steeples wrapped in colonnades and housing statues. Even the peak of the pediment had its own winged creature watching the entrance to the hall.

The driver turned left. Beautiful old buildings, with shops and cafes nestled inside, lined the avenue. Passing yet another monument we arrived at the hotel entrance.

"Gentlemen, your home for the next two weeks." Ivan turned to the driver. "Skol'ko ya vam dolzhen?" He reached for his wallet.

"Hold on, we've got money."

"I'll take care of it, Paul. Why don't you pry John out of the front seat?"

John flipped Ivan off. "Ha. Ha. Ha. Pry John out. John's so big. I'd like to—"

"Come on, big man. Let's get you out."

John emerged like a balloon blown up at the Macy's parade. The car seemed to balance from its tilt as he popped out.

A bellhop greeted us. "Dobriy vecher. Registriruites'? Ya pomogu s bagazhom." Using white gloves to cradle our luggage, he stacked each piece on a shiny brass cart, while asking if we were registering and had baggage.

John looked up. "Not bad, not bad at all. White-glove, curbside service—excellent European facade. It looks promisin'." The modest angled front of the hotel sported two large framed glass windows, softening the exterior of the faded apricot bricks. A few blocks down, a church steeple pierced barren trees. "Man, look at that."

"It's the Bernardine Church and that's Halytsky Square. Come on. Let's get inside. We'll talk about all this later." Following Ivan and the bellhop, we entered into what would be described by American standards as a modest lobby. Simple furnishings and sparsely scattered fixtures marked the path to the front desk.

"Dobry vecher. Chem mogu pomoch?" Without cracking a smile, the clerk welcomed us and requested our reservation.

I approached the front desk, prepared to find out whether he spoke English. "Vi govorite po-Angliysky?"

"Yes, I speak English. And you speak Russian?"

"Nemnogo."

"Vhat little you speak is wery good, sir. Your name?"

"Thank you. My name is de la Moret."

"We have a suite ready for you and Mr. Cheramie. Here are your keys."

"Spasibo." Even though my thank you was delivered with a smile, the front desk manager barely grinned.

"Pozhalusta." His dry "you're welcome" was followed by a snap of his fingers.

A bellhop approached us, then pulled the cart with our luggage.

"I can help with the bags."

"Net. Nickolay take good care you." The bellhop patted my back. He showed us towards a majestic twin staircase.

Ivan headed out the hotel. "Hey, guys. I've got an errand to run. I'll meet you here in the lobby in an hour for dinner."

"See ya then." John turned back to face the patiently waiting bellhop.

"Velcome Ukraine. You good wisit here." He struggled to get each word out through his thick accent. "I not speak good English. Still learn."

I winked at the bellhop. "I wish my Russian was as good as your English."

The bellhop led us to a twin marble-rung staircase with an ornate railing. The first flight of stairs yielded to a single staircase leading to the second floor.

"Room up here. Follow." The bellhop walked to a balcony adorned with triple porticos and bronze colored columns. He then turned left down the corridor, passing at least eight doorways. Finally, we reached a set of double doors.

He opened one and escorted us into our room.

John tossed his jacket on a small couch facing a white-mantled fireplace. "We've got our own bath." John called out as he walked into the bedroom.

The bellhop rushed to the door. "I come quick wiz more bag." He closed the door, leaving John and I alone.

"So, whacha ya think, pal?"

"I would like to get unpacked and find out what Ivan's discovered."

"No, butt-lick. The room?"

"Oh. It's fine." I pushed the window sheer aside from one of the two windows in the small living area. The heavy tied-back drapery added only a little light into the room.

"Paul." I did not answer at first. "Paul! This is important." I looked at him, questioning the seriousness of his tone. "You know I'm always up for a good time. But this thing we're after, let's not go rushin' off like prized bulls in the ring." John's comments surprised me. Never before had I heard caution from him like this. "You've gotta promise me we'll be careful. You'll let it—" A knock sounded at the door.

"The rest of our luggage." As I opened the door the bellhop popped up from behind a stack of bags.

"Please to come in? I get inside. Da?"

"Yes. Come in." With a bag tossed over his shoulder and one in each hand, the bellhop slid sideways through the door.

"Here. Let me give you a hand."

"Nickolay take bag room." He arranged each of the pieces carefully near the twin beds.

Handing him a twenty-dollar bill, I folded his hand shut. "My gift."

"This much plenty. Thank you. God blessing you." The young man continued to thank me even as he backed out the door.

"You're somethin' else, Paul de la Moret. Always givin' somethin' away."

"Let's get unpacked."

"You can't take a compliment can ya?" He threw himself on the first bed and then propped his head against a pillow.

"You know I prefer the bed near the door."

"We've got two beds. Use the other one."

"Come on, John. I'm tired and want to get a quick nap and shower before Ivan gets back, so move your big butt." I lifted my luggage.

"No. I've got the bed by the door. That way you can't slip out when you don't sleep."

"Then make yourself useful and hang my jacket and overcoat."

I slipped into the bathroom. Washing the dirt from my body was refreshing, even though the water was lukewarm at best. As I stepped back into the bedroom, sunlight faded through the single window.

"I thought you wanted to rest?"

My stomach growled. "Dinner is in about twenty minutes. Don't you think you should clean up?"

As John dressed, I peered out the window. Steeples protruded atop the rolling hills of L'vov, capping the landscape with more green-onioned domes. Like a scene carved out of the imagination of some wizard, it was as though a city from a storybook had been lifted from the page and nestled amongst these hills.

"That was quick."

John emerged from the bathroom. "Hey, I was born ready. Here's your coat."

"Think we'll need it?"

"If we go out for dinner." He pushed the suite door open. The stark hallway joined the opulent staircase. A red runner draped down the stairs softened our descent.

Ivan stood near the base with a gentleman. "Paul, John—over here. I want you guys to meet a friend of mine I've invited for dinner. This is Marc."

"Ivan's spoken very highly of you both." Marc grimaced as John seized his hand.

"Easy big boy. Marc, I'm Paul. You'll have to excuse Mr. Neanderthal. He forgets he's not on the gridiron and has to be reminded on occasion. Too many knocks—"

"Wise-ass!"

"Look, I even got him speaking compound words. To think, he's a doctor."

Marc looked intrigued. "That's right. Ivan mentioned you were a doctor. So am I. Where did you study?"

John sneered at me, then said to Marc, "Tulane Medical. And you?"

"John's Hopkins. Your specialty?"

"Orthopedics, sports medicine."

"Cardiology and vascular surgery. How about you, Paul?"

"Oh, nothing really. Just the odd degree."

John shook his head. "Don't let him bullshit ya, Marc. He's got more initials behind his name than Patton's got medals."

"A smart one, huh?"

"Yeah, you'd never know it lookin' at him."

Ivan pointed to a wood-paneled doorway to our left. "What say we head to the restaurant? I took the liberty of making reservations."

As we walked through the lobby to the dining room, my new friend, the bellhop, greeted me with a smile. Behind him two old men shivered in the street just outside the plate glass window of the lobby.

"Gentlemen, I need to excuse myself. Go ahead, I'll join you in a minute." I waited for Ivan to guide Marc and John into the restaurant. "Nickolay, can I trouble you go to my room and get the blue coat hanging in my closet for me?" I didn't want to loose sight of them.

"Da. I come back fast."

The two old men huddled together to warm themselves. Memories of Manresa filled my mind. "Let the one of you who has two coats give to those who have none." I could hear Father Barrios speaking. For all the nights I slept in comfort with my tummy full, people froze and starved. Why? Even though I had been told that we would always have the poor, I struggled to accept their condition in my presence. Grandfather always ensured that people were at least fed, even those who stopped in at Oak Grove. If nothing else, he provided them a day's work, a hot meal, and a place to rest.

"Sir, coat." As I reached for my pocket, the bellhop placed his hand over my own. "No. Zhis my pleasure."

"Tell no one."

Walking outside, I approached the elderly gentleman. His gray whiskers blanketed his wrinkled face. His eyes were pulled deeply into their sockets. He moved away as I approached. "Please stop . . . I mean, podozhdite pozhalusta." Hearing my plea, he paused. "Dlya vas . . . for you, please . . . pozhalutsa." I handed him the coat.

He lifted his mangled fingers and stroked my cheek. "Da. Spasibo." His eyes glistened his thank you.

I swallowed. As he turned the corner and walked away, the shadow of his arms lifting to place the coat on warmed me. I removed my overcoat and wrapped it around the other gentleman. Then I returned to the hotel. Only the bellhop stood there waiting for me.

"You good man." He patted my shoulder and returned to polishing the cart.

"Did you find the restrooms?" Marc startled me.

"Umm, yes. I'm a little turned around." I spun to locate a sign. "Yes, right there."

"You look cold."

"No. I'm fine. I'll see you in the dinning room."

I headed for the restaurant. The maître d' stood just outside, reviewing the seating chart. "Tovarich Ivan Sebastionovich." I asked for Ivan.

"Da. Suda pozhalusta." He led me through two rows of white-clothed tables lining each side of the dining hall.

Ivan stood as I joined them. "Perfect timing. I was just reviewing the menu with John. Did you see Marc?"

"We passed in the lobby."

"Great. We're thinking of starting the meal with soup, then stuffed cabbage with rice and meat, potato pancakes, and cherry dumplings for dessert. Any objections?"

"Not from me." Marc smiled as he approached the table.

"Perfect." Ivan turned to the waiter. "Mi voz'mem Borsch, Kholodets, Holubtsi, e Vareniki."

"Vam nalit' vina?"

"Da." Ivan handed the menu to the waiter. "I took the liberty to order a bottle of wine from one of the wineries south of here. I think you'll find their Cabernet quite interesting."

"Kherson or Novaya Kakhovka?"

"Kherson. Paul, you're still the connoisseur I see." Ivan whisked the cork, whiffing its aroma. "Here Paul, try this." The waiter poured the richly colored red wine. Ivan swirled the glass. The bouquet lifted, subtly complimenting the redolence of the cork. "Ah, wonderful. May I propose a toast?" We lifted our glasses. "To old friends, and new ones, to our journey, and our search. Vasha zdorovie!"

As we each made eye contact with the other, some silent dance resonated between us. John placed his glass on the table, then sighed. "So, Marc, how do you know Ivan?"

"I'm from Boston. Our parents are good friends."

"Through Holy Trinity?"

"Not exactly. I'm Jewish." Marc snickered. "Our dads work with each other and we were neighbors. If Ivan wouldn't have been such a baseball jock, he could have come to college with me. But baseball called."

"Yep. Marc and I have known each other our entire lives."

John snapped his finger. "The picture in your room from little league? That's Marc, isn't it? You know, I've seen that picture a hundred times. There's somethin' about ya that reminds me of Paul."

John was right. There was something about Marc that seemed familiar.

"So what brings you to the Ukraine, Marc?"

"Doing some research on my family."

Ivan tore the bread loaf, handing a piece to each of us. "Our dads came to America on the same boat. They've known each other for nearly fifty years now."

"That's incredible. How'd they meet?"

Distress lines wrinkled across Marc's face. "Actually, my father doesn't speak of it very much." Finishing his last spoonful of borsch, he reached for his wine. As he sipped, his eyes settled into a gaze, as if he was searching for what to say. "My grandparents and all my aunts and uncles were lost at Belzec."

John leaned forward. "I'm not sure how to respond to that. I've never personally known anyone who lost loved ones to the Holocaust."

"My entire family was destroyed, except my father and his sister." He swigged his wine. With our glasses empty, Ivan signaled our waiter for another bottle. Numbing the senses wouldn't make this go away, but it would take the edge off.

"I can't say that I know what you feel. I don't think anyone can. But, you're a friend of Ivan's. That makes you a friend of ours, and friends care. So, if you need somethin', Paul and I are right here behind you."

"Here, here." Ivan lifted his glass.

"Ivan said he'd never seen two friends take care of each other the way you guys do. I thought he was kidding. But—"

"Yeah, Paul and me, we're like two pigs in mud. But Paul, well let's just say sometimes he's about as useful as tits on a boarhog."

Marc choked on his wine. "Where do you get all this stuff?"

I patted his back. "It's my fault, Marc. I haven't been screening his reading."

The waiter lifted the cover from the plate. "Pozhalusta, holubtsi e vareniki."

"Damn, that smells good."

"Marc, when food is served, you want to keep your fingers and hands out of John's path." More laughter ensued. The waiter placed our next course before us. With our wineglasses refilled, the bouquet of the Cabernet accentuated the aroma of the cabbage and pork.

"Oh man, this looks good." John dragged his fork through his lips. As he chewed, the muscles of his face synchronized in a dramatic dance.

Marc raised an eyebrow. "John, if I didn't know better, I would swear you were having sex."

A playful grin swiped Ivan's face. "He is, Marc. That's how they do it down South. Shoot it, stuff it, make love to it, and then eat it. You've got to admit there are some strange customs down there."

"Not strange, just different."

John looked at me. "Y'all have to excuse Paul if he's a little uneasy. His mamma and daddy are related."

"Is he serious?" Marc's eyes widened. Fortunately, the mounds of food on our plates provided ample excuse not to talk. Smacking replaced talking until every morsel was consumed.

John mopped his plate with the last piece of bread. "That was great."

I eyed his plate. "For a moment, I thought you were going to lick the platter."

"If y'all see a short little shit tossed outta a window tonight, it's only Paul. By the way, Ivan, wonderful selection."

"We've still got dessert. The vareniki here is incredible."

"Good. I'm still a little hungry."

I patted John's belly to nothing but muscle. "With everything you ate?"

"Hey, it takes a lot of energy to eat this way."

"I forget with a mouth that size—"

"That ain't the only thing—"

I shook my head. "Spare me the details, I've heard them before. On a more serious note, I'm curious, Marc, as to your success in locating your family."

Marc swallowed the last bite of food before speaking. "Ivan's granddad took us to a town just northeast of here called Brody. It has one of the oldest Jewish cemeteries in Eastern Europe. I found records of my great-grandparents and great great grandparents, some great aunts and uncles, cousins—"

"And your grandparents?"

"Nothing. When I leave here I'm going to Belzec, that's if I can get a Visa."

"I'm sorry you didn't find what you came here for."

"I've gotten more from this trip than I could have dreamed."

"Really?"

"Meeting Ivan's grandparents, and visiting Brody, the folklore, the people. Finding the Babin family who helped my family escape. It was amazing."

"Babin?"

"It's a common name in Brody."

Their voices garbled. The room spun. I lifted out my chair. "If you'll excuse me."

Ivan reached his hand to me. "Is everything all right?"

"Just a little too much wine. Please, continue. I'll be right back." I walked towards the lobby. Dim lighting and dark walls greeted me inside the bathroom. Splashing cold water on my face, I took several deep breaths. The antique mirror contorted my reflection.

"Paul?" The door opened as John entered. "What's wrong, pal?"

"Nothing. Just a little nausea."

"Bullshit. I know better."

"Not now, John. Please. Give me a few minutes and I'll be out."

He hesitated. "I'll wait outside and watch the door." Reluctantly, he left me.

Peering into the mirror, I struggled to get a grip. Visions of the dream that brought me here flashed before me. Thinking of all those things that happened because of it raised my skin. And Babin, the maiden name of Pierre-Paul's wife, Marguerite. What next?

"Is he all right?" Ivan's voice was muddled through the door.

"Yeah. I think he's just got jet lag."

"They've got dessert ready. Do you want me to have them hold it?"

"No. We'll be there in a minute."

I closed my eyes tightly, then took several deep breaths. "Get a grip. You can do it. Just get a grip." I repeated the words over and over. Finally, I calmed downed and opened the door. John waited just outside.

"We'll cut it short."

As we rejoined Marc and Ivan, the waiter placed the dessert before us. Pouring Cognac into wide-rimmed glasses, he once again inspected the table.

Ivan looked on with concern. "Feeling better, Paul?"

"Yes. Thanks for asking."

"We should probably wrap up so you guys can get some rest."

"Marc, where are you staying?"

"With Ivan's grandparents. Their apartment is about fifteen blocks from here."

Ivan turned to the waiter. "Check pozhalusta." He then faced John. "How about we meet for breakfast at nine o'clock? You guys can rest and we can still get an early start. My babo is preparing sort of a brunch. Head on up and get some rest. I'll take care of dinner."

"No—"

"I insist."

John knitted his brow, but Ivan grabbed the bill before John could reach it. "Go on, guys. Get some rest and we'll see you in the morning."

John hesitated, then stood. "Marc, it's been a pleasure meetin' ya. And Ivan, it was a wonderful dinner."

"You're quite welcome, John."

John and I bid them goodnight, then made our way to the staircase.

"How ya doin', pal?"

"Just thinking."

"You don't sleep worth a damn when you do that."

"There's a lot on my mind."

"And, how is that different—"

"Not tonight, John. I need to sort this out. I don't—" I turned away.

"Finish it."

The key clicked the door open. A beautiful fruit basket sat on our table. John lifted the card and handed it to me. "Looks like somebody made an impression. It's an uncanny gift you have. You say very little, yet your actions speak volumes to people."

"What are you talking about?"

"You, Paul. You and the way people see you." He handed me the note signed by the bellhop.

"We better get some sleep. You're getting batty."

"For once, just listen." John grabbed my arm and pulled me to him. "For fifteen years I've watched you. Shit eats at you, but you don't say anythin' about it. You help people, but I'll be damned if you'd take so much as a penny from someone. Don't you get it?"

"Get what?"

The straw basket crinkled as John selected a piece of fruit. He tossed it into the air and then caught it. "I'm not goin' to sleep until we talk."

I looked up, as if the answers were on the ceiling or some other sublime place. "It's like things start to make sense, then they don't. You know. These dreams. All this stuff with Andre, my father, Kevin, Xavier."

"Is that what happened durin' dinner?"

"Kind of."

"Look at me, pal. You can tell me anything. Let me help."

"Can we please drop it?"

John hesitated. He eyed me as though he might prompt me to say more. "Okay. But no slippin' out and no doin' it on your own. Not here behind the Iron Curtain. I swear, Paul, if you pull that crap here, I'll leave, draggin' you with me."

The muffled toll of a clock tower chimed eleven. What could I tell him of images that made no sense to me? How could I tell him of the image that did?

Fifteen

December 6, 1986

"Mr. De la Moret."

Energy surged through my body in hearing Father Cavender call my name.

"Yes, Father?"

"If you would please? A quote, sir, from Mr. Milton's "On the Morning of Christ's Nativity.""

My knees knocked together. I forced my frame straight as Father Cavender expected.

"Mr. De la Moret, are we going to grow old waiting?"

"No, Father."

> "The oracles are dumb,
> No voice or hideous hum,
> Runs through the arched roofs in words deceiving.
> Apollo from his shrine
> Can no more divine,
> With hollow shriek the steep of Delphos leaving.

No nightly trance, or breathed spell,
Inspires the pale-eyed priest from the prophetic cell."

"Very good, sir. I see you've studied. Now, Mr. Cheramie. How about you?"

John stood, then dropped. A bullet pierced his body. Blood fanned across the wooden floors. I leapt to him. But a wind pushed me back.

Dark swirling clouds engulfed me.

"Andre!" His face popped from the wall cloud, then faded back into it. Debris swished by me. My weightless body free fell into a chasm.

■

A squeaking board woke me. I opened my eyes to John thrusting up from the floor. "Good mornin', sunshine. Get your little butt outta bed and give me fifty-five."

"Why are you always busting my ass first thing in the morning?"

"'Cause everybody loves somebody sometimes—" Singing off key, he drove his frame up once more.

"All right already. I'll start if you'll stop."

"Just drop down and give me seventy-five." With my body sprawled across the floor, I strained to lift it as John began the count. "One my little cutie, two my gentleman, three if ya really hurry, four I'll take your hand, five is for wimpy, six is for sex, seven when your stronger, eight for big ole pecks—"

"Shh! I can't concentrate with all that noise."

"You should be able to concentrate in a rock concert."

"That's different. I wouldn't have your big mouth moving at the time."

"Thirty. I'm twenty up on ya." This morning's push-ups became a contest of wills. "I'm gonna do a hundred." He pushed his body upward. "Look at this form. Poetry in motion." In many ways he was. His lean, chiseled shape came so natural to him. "One-hundred. I think I've got another fifty in me."

"I thought we were doing fifty-five." I stood.

"Yeah. Three sets worth. And where do ya think you're goin'?"

"Didn't you hear it?"

"Oh no ya don't. You still owe me twenty more." John snapped to his feet. "Finish!"

He opened the door. "Good morning, sir. Telephone wery important." Nickolay handed John the note, then looked over to smile at me. The paper crinkled open.

"What is it?"

"Ivan wants us to call him. I'll be right back."

"I'll come with you."

"No. Finish your push-ups." He followed the bellhop.

I counted out twenty more. Breathing hard from the exertion, I sat up to the faint sound of a bell tolling outside our window. "The angel of the Lord declared unto Mary—" The words tripped off my tongue. Just as I wrapped up my prayer, the door to our room opened. John entered; the stress once lining his face now relaxed to a grin.

"Ivan's on his way. He wants us to meet him in the lobby in five minutes."

"Did he say why?"

"No." John grabbed his bag. "Get some of that fruit and bottled water."

"Yes, sir, Mr. John, sir." I presented him with a one-finger salute.

"Just do what I said." He surveyed the contents of his backpack. "Where's north?" He tested his compass. "Paul, hand me those maps off the end table." They rustled as he folded them. "Let's see. Compass, maps, first aid kit, water, energy bars—"

"Kitchen sink?"

"Look, wise-ass. We're not goin' unprepared." He added a sweater. "Let's go."

"How about we get dressed first?"

"Damn!" He slipped wool pants and a shirt on.

I ducked as he swung his backpack over his shoulder. "Paul, I'm not up for any antics. We're gonna play this straight and we're gonna think before we act. This is no time to go rushin' like bulls in a china shop." We turned to the single staircase and made our way down.

As we reached the base, Ivan waved us closer. "I discovered something when I followed Babo to mass."

"Mass?"

"Yep. The Feast of St. Nicholas Myra. After mass, I noticed the statue, an exact replica of mine. Let's go. I'll show you." We crossed the street and circled a water fountain. Red banners draped a number of the buildings as Russian soldiers patrolled the streets. Among them, women bundled in jackets and sporting kerchiefs on their heads busied themselves with the affairs of the day. Another statue stood perched atop a column. "That's Adam Mytskevycha, the poet. They named the square after him. The Cathedral is down a few more blocks."

"You look cold, Paul. Where's your jacket?"

"Left it back at the hotel."

"I didn't see it in the closet when I grabbed mine."

"Must of left it on the chair or something."

"Yeah. Right."

With white puffy clouds floating in an otherwise clear blue sky, the slight nip seemed to melt away. The air was crisp.

John extended his head back as we approached the Latin looking church. "Wow. Is that the cathedral? We saw the green roof and steeple from Prospect Svobody yesterday."

"Sure did. Come on. Let's get inside." Ivan guided us through the vestibule and into the main chapel. Frescoes, icons, and stained-glassed windows of Mary blanketed the walls and ceilings. As we walked towards the sanctuary, her eyes seemed to follow us. Even a statue of her, placed atop the main altar, peered through the church.

"That's him." Ivan pointed to a little old priest walking from the confessionals towards a nave. His mangled body hunched over, causing the right side of his cassock to touch the floor. Even using a walking cane, he needed a novice to support him. "Otets." The word "Father" echoed through the Gothic structure. The little old priest stopped. He searched through the darkened sanctuary, straining to see us. We navigated through the pews to reach him. "Ya Ivan. Pomnite segodnya utrom na sluzhbe?" Ivan reminded him of their meeting earlier.

"Da, da." He patted Ivan's hand. "Suda. Follow," he said, slowing his pace and leading us to a chapel. As I joined him, he passed his cane to the novice and then grabbed my hand. Walking by my side, he lifted his head. "Vi priekhali iz daleka?"

"He asks if you come from far away."

"Da. America."

Nodding, he once again walked towards the chapel. As we entered, he pointed to a corner. There perched on the wall was the statue. I stammered forward. "Vi znayete chto eto?" He stroked my cheeks.

"Da. I know this statue." My eyes fixed on it.

"Ya bil rebenkom kogda prinyos yehyo suda. Moi otets dal mne yehyo pered smertiu. Eto vsyo chto u nas bilo kogda ya nachal sluzhit'. Krassiva, da?" The old priest reverently grabbed his rosary and began to finger the beads.

Chills ran up my spine. "Da. It is beautiful."

John placed his hand on my shoulder. "What's he sayin'?"

"He was still a boy when he brought the statue here. His father gave it to him before he died. It was all he had when he entered the order."

"Ivan," John lowered his voice to a whisper, "ask him how his father got it."

"Anya know story." The old priest coughed and then gasped for breath.

The novice patted his back. "Cough bad, but okay. He captured Russians. Placed Siberia many years." As the novice spoke, John checked the old priest's pulse.

"Why don't ya let me take a look at him? I'm a doctor."

"Net." The old priest snapped.

The novice grabbed his arm to help him up. "He no like attention."

I looked deeply into his blue eyes. "Bolshoe spasibo, Otets."

"Da. Pazhalusta." Struggling to get "you're welcome" out, he looked up at me. He stroked my cheek once more. As our eyes connected, my body filled with warmth. Wobbling, he leaned towards me. "Pover', dover'sya. Togda ona put' tebe ukazhet." He paused. His dark blue eyes glimmered against his rosy red cheeks. With the novice supporting him, he turned and walked off.

I faced the statue once more. Gooseflesh rose on the back of my neck and on my arms. I shook my spinning head to the old priest's words. "You search. Here you find. Look for her. She waits for you."

"Are you okay, Paul?" John asked.

"Yes. Can I have a few minutes?"

"We'll wait outside." The thud of their steps faded. I peered at the statue. The gold inlay sparked in sunlight streaming through a window above. Its reflection formed a small rainbow on the floor.

Something about it was familiar, far beyond my encounter with it through Ivan or the night I saw it again with Father Barrios. But what?

A door closed; the sound echoed through the cathedral. The young novice who had helped the old priest smiled as he walked by me. I followed him into the vestibule, then pushed the doors open to join Marc and John outside.

"Hey, Paul. You okay?" Ivan smiled.

I nodded.

John stepped towards the street. "Then let's go. I wanna pick up somethin' for Ivan's grandparents."

"There's no need, John."

"Hey, it's my money, I'm a big boy, and I think I can get a gift for someone if I wanna. So hush."

"Okay. We'll grab a tram. There's a government store near their apartment." Ivan pointed to the electric trolley approaching a neighboring street.

Buildings streamed by as we bumped along the metal tracks. The facades blended into one. As we slowed to turn a corner, the large columns of a building jutted right in front of us.

"Paul, what is it?"

I turned to John's probing smile.

"Umm, nothing."

"Come on, pal. I know that look."

"The columns of that building reminded me of Oak Grove."

"And?"

"Nothing. Just struck me as odd." I looked back at the building once more. The image of the trunk I discovered in that hidden attic at Oak Grove persisted.

As the tram slowed, Ivan stood. "Here we are." He pointed to a group of buildings lining the boulevard. "There, just down the street. The government store." We stepped off the tram, immediately joining the long line of people waiting for the store to open.

The door latch turned. The crowd pressed forward through the narrow entrance. Feet shuffled across the stones as we made our way inside. "Paul, you get the chocolate while I get the Cognac."

Ivan blocked his path. "John, that's way too expensive. Flowers and table wine—"

"Am I gonna have to make you go stand outside like I do with Paul sometimes? As Paul says, there's only one use for money—the good you can do for others."

I eyed him, but decided to leave him be. I turned down a narrow isle in search of chocolates as ordered. An old woman rifled through the limited selection of confections.

"Tak malo, a kak dorogho!" She muttered in a wiry voice as she lifted a box to inspect it. Her kerchief-covered head swayed right and left. The selection and the price troubled her. She backed into me. "Izvinite." As she pulled away from me, she excused herself.

I smiled at her. "Nichevo, ne toropites'."

She looked at me with a wrinkled frown. Her eyes spoke of distrust, even though my words to her were soft and gentle. She turned away and then walked off.

"Hey, buttlick, are ya gonna get that candy today or are we waitin' for the new arrival of sugarcane so they can make some fresh ones?" John filled the narrow aisle where once the old lady stood. I selected a box of candy and turned to join him.

"John, they prefer U.S. dollars. It'll bring the price down a bit. Let me handle paying it." Ivan grabbed the Cognac, candy, and money as we approached the counter. He nodded his head to a gentleman standing near it. "Skolko eto stoit?" He showed him two American twenty-dollar bills.

"Eto vsyo chto u vas iest'?" Money exchanged hands.

As we departed, the old man to whom I had given my coat approached me. He smiled. "Molodets!" His rough hands grated against my cheeks.

"You know him?"

I jumped. "Just a gentleman I met last night."

"Isn't that your coat?"

"Paul. John. Over here. My grandparents' apartment is just around the corner." Ivan interrupted before I had to answer John.

We entered an arched doorway nestled among a group of buildings. The unfinished wooden planks of a barren staircase led to a second, third, and then fourth flight of stairs. We arrived at a corridor with a small window and a single doorway.

"My grandparents are lucky. Grandfather had an important job here in L'vov. The government gave them this apartment." He knocked on the plain wooden brown door.

"Hey, Ivan. Do your grandparents speak Russian?"

"With me, yes. With friends from their village, Ukrainian."

The doorknob rattled as the door opened. "Zdravstvuyte. Velcome. Please to come in." A black eyed, olive skinned man greeted us. With a pipe tucked in the corner of his mouth, a smile broadened across his face.

"Grandfather, this is John."

Ivan's grandfather kissed John on both cheeks. "John, zhis strong name."

"Spasibo, sir." John nodded in agreement. "This is for you."

Accepting the bottle of Cognac, Ivan's grandfather nodded approvingly.

"And this is Paul." Ivan placed my hand in his grandfather's warm palm.

"Ah. At last ve meet, Pascha." He used my Russian name.

"Ochen' priyatno Tovarich Sebastianovich."

"You fix Ivan statue? You good boy to help. Please to call me Jan. Come. Meet Anya." He led us down a narrow hallway to a modest kitchen. There, Ivan's grandmother rushed to a small oven. She removed a pan of sweet smelling muffins from it. "Anya. Eto Pascha."

She wiped her hands on her apron and then pushed her long gray hair behind her ears. Her face glowed as she looked me over. "Dobro pozhalovat'." With arms extended, she pulled me to her. Hugging me tightly, she whispered, "Blagoslavi tebya Bogoroditsa!"

I looked to Ivan. "She asks for Mary to bless you."

"Ochen' priyatno poznakomitsya."

"Call me Babo."

John handed the candy to her. "This is for you."

She lifted the box to her nose and then sniffed it. "Ah, good."

Jan dragged chairs against the wooden planks of the floor. "Sit, please."

Anya rushed to gather our jackets. She stowed them in a small coat closet. Her feet quickly shuffled across the floor as she returned to the kitchen.

Cups pinged on saucers as she laid out china. Steam wafted as she served the tea. With a basket of warm muffins on the simple table, she handed us honey from the cupboard. "Eat! Eat! Plenty food. Put meat on bones. Drink, zhis varm you." Her shoulders rolled back as she proudly watched us taste the first bites.

John smacked his lips. "These are so good!"

"Spasibo. Learn cook from friend, Olga. You meet her. She come soon." Babo inspected the table.

A knock rattled the door. We continued to eat the muffins. With a little honey added to them, they were as moist and tasty as any I had eaten.

We stood as a little old woman entered the room.

Babo pointed to us. "Olha, tse miy onuk Ivan ta yoho druzi John i Paul." It sounded like she was introducing us in Ukrainian.

The old woman removed her jacket with Babo's help. Her wrinkled skin made it difficult to see her eyes.

Jan kissed her on each cheek, then pulled a chair for her. "Olha, ti dobre vihladesh. Bud laska, siday, priyednuysa."

She sat, yet never stopped looking at us. She warmed her hands on the cup of tea placed before her by Babo.

Babo warmly smiled at me. "Olga from my willage. Old friend." She turned to Olga. "Paul—tse tovarish Ivana, shcho vidremontuvaw pamyatnik."

"Vin?" Olga pointed to me. "You fix statue, da?"

I nodded.

"You good fortune, like husband. You Ivan America brother."

The horror on Ivan's face that day flashed into my mind once more. With it, the memory of Xavier's loss sent chills down my spine.

Ivan touched my arm. "Paul, are you okay? You look a million miles away."

The teacup rattled in my trembling hand.

Jan added a healthy splash of Cognac to each of our cups. "We drink to friendship."

As I breathed deeply, the sweet flavor filled my mouth. I swallowed. The warmth numbed my body. John nudged me with his foot under the table. As I looked at him, he winked. He took a deep breath then nodded. I followed his lead.

Jan patted my shoulder. "Better, da?"

"Yes. Please continue with your story."

"Olga Hutsul. Live small willage Carpathians. Viedka, her husband good man. He molfar. Ivan, how say English?"

"A healer," Ivan answered. "Paul, what's the word used in South Louisiana?"

"Treatuer?"

"Yep. That's it."

Jan added more Cognac to our cups. "Have zhis you home?"

"Yes. I mean da. My grandmother's family."

"Viedka, good healer, good friend. Know since boy. He give statue Olga brother."

"Who's Olga's brother?"

"Priest you meet in cathedral." Babo walked around the table, freshening our cups with hot tea. "Vhen Olga and me small girls, I wisit willage. Many people run and say Lady appear to them. Viedka see her. Olga brother priest. He see her."

"So did you see her too, Olga?"

"Net. I busy vork. Viedka and Andrei run to me and tell about Lady."

"Andrei?" Chills ran through my body.

"Da, Paul. Andrei my brother, priest, " Olga answered.

The wind roared in my memory. The image of my boyhood friend, Andre, and his mangled body pinned under the branch of the tree horrified me. My face pressed into my hands. Mother's voice echoed, "Nunc et in hora Mater Dei—now and at the hour of our death."

Jan stood. "He sick?"

John grabbed my shoulder. "No, sir. He lost a friend named Andre years ago."

Olga approached me. "You know hurt. Lady tell many year hardship. First vars. Den communism. Sewenty years now." She stroked my face.

As my eyes locked on hers, my sadness seemed to ease. It was as if she knew what I felt. "The Lady, where did she appear?"

"Hrushiv."

"And the statue?"

"Hoshiv," Jan added. "My home. I meet Anya there. She come to wisit monastery. Olga, Viedka come wiz her." Jan smiled at Anya. "She beautiful girl. I see her valk to monastery. Follow her. She look back at me and smile."

"Da." Anya rested her hand on Jan's arm. "Ve go every year to pilgrimage. Many people come to monastery. I was young voman zhis trip. I meet Jan zhere. He wery handsome." Jan blushed as Olga described him. "Many hundred years Lady appear after merchant return from Kazakhstan. His caravan survive sandstorm and come to Hoshiv. Zhey tell story how Wirgin save his life. After, Lady appear willagers and say to care about merchant. Merchant use fortune to build monastery. Story tell his vife come from Spain to meet him. But she die on journey. After merchant build shrine on mountain."

"The merchant's name?" I barely got the words out.

Jan's eyes widened. "Piotr Pavel. Ivan, kak eto skazat' po Ispansky?"

"His name in Spanish?" Ivan questioned.

Jan nodded.

"Pablo Pedro."

I gasped for breath.

"You know zhis name?"

"No. I mean, a priest in South America had a statue like Ivan's. He used that name."

Jan leaned over to me as if he was going to share a secret. "Eleven statues vas made because eleven time he see Lady. Viedka family know merchant and help build shrine in Carpathians. He give zhem statue. Viedka give Andrei, Andrei give me, zhen go to Siberia. I give to Ivan papa, zhen he leave Ukraine."

"And the shrine?"

"Cossacks destroy many years ago."

"And, the monastery in—"

"Hoshiv. Ve go zhere tomorrow. Da?"

"Da." I swallowed hard and then stood. The room spun. "Could you excuse me?"

Olga rubbed my hand. "Wery heavy heart. Lady know people like you."

John stood behind me. "If you'll excuse me. Thank you for the muffins, Babo."

"Pleasure mine. You get air. Pascha feel better. Need friend." Her smile broadened. "Good boys, da!" Babo turned to Olga's agreeing nod. "More tea?"

Their voices faded as we walked down the narrow hallway to the apartment door. I placed my trembling hands in my pockets. We descended the staircase onto the street.

"Ya wanna walk, pal?"

I nodded.

We strolled along the avenue as John and Ivan chatted. I couldn't stop thinking about the statue, Pablo Pedro, and that trunk at Oak Grove. For all these years, my family claimed fifteen generations of French decent. Could it be that this little part of our family history had been left out, or were these facts just coincidental?

Ivan led us down the street. "I want to show you guys something." The buildings were old and very plain in comparison to his grandparents' building. We turned the corner. A small flower cart blocked the entrance of a short alley.

"Follow me." Just ten or so yards inside, another alley emerged. "Interesting, isn't it. It's an abandoned Jewish housing area." The cobble-stone floor was neatly laid out. The walls of the surrounding buildings ascended four stories high. Stones stacked along one side of the alley looked like the original raw material. John pointed to a simple wrought-iron balcony lining one side of the alley. "Look at this place. It's like we've walked into a time capsule."

"Yep. This is what fills L'vov with so many legends. With so little written, stories pass the heritage on. Think about it, John. We've lost that in America."

"Yeah, but that's also how tall tales are born."

"Maybe. But the Cossacks, the Nazis, the Communists—they all tried in their own way to destroy such thoughts. But the beliefs prevail. Their political ideologies failed. I think some legends are stronger than the machine."

"That doesn't make them true."

"Maybe. The way I see it, John, Jesus or Mohammed could have walked on this very spot. Marco Polo and others like him traveled through here."

"True. But America's got similar legends. Paul Bunyan, Sasquatch, Marie LeDoux."

"Granted. But look at the churches and temples here. Russian Orthodox, Catholic, Jewish, and some even Muslim. You can find almost everything here. And much of it is still in tact, like this place, for hundreds and in some cases thousands of years."

"To my point. It makes fertile ground for legends and myths. Get a group of old people who long for better times and next ya know, they're upstagin' each other with tall tales."

As Ivan and John chatted, I continued to search the walls and the ground. The tan colored stones appeared gray, not dirty, just old.

"So, why hasn't the city converted this into useful housing?"

"Most folks live in apartments built by the Communists on the outskirts of the old city."

"And your grandparents?"

"They're happy where they are."

"Don't they want to come to America?"

"The Communists would never let them leave. Grandfather's involved with some kind of power plant north of Kiev in Chernobyl."

"I thought he was retired."

"He still lectures at the university from time to time and makes occasional trips to Kiev. He doesn't talk about it much. Even so, they'd never leave. This is home, this and their village."

"Why don't they return there?"

"Food's scarce, little electricity, few phone lines. It's medieval when you leave the city." Ivan looked at his watch. "We better go. Marc's due back soon."

A pair of primitive archways looking like angled "pi" signs protruded at the end of the alley. Ivan pointed upward to a Star of David nestled in the brickwork.

German shepherds barking and whistles blowing against the screams and yells of Nazi troops herding men and women, old and young, with their children too, echoed off the walls. Loved ones separated from each other, families torn apart, and even some shot for hiding from death and torture seemed to come alive once more. I fell to my knees.

"Paul!" John grabbed me and wrapped me in a hug. Even though the day had warmed, I was cold. "Your hands are like ice." As he rubbed warmth into them, I looked up once more at the star. How could we have allowed so many to be hurt by so few?

Sixteen

December 7, 1986

The mattress springs whined as I rose. Grabbing my clothes, I tip-toed to the door.

John snapped the lamp on. "Where do you think you're goin'?"

"I'm just going to sit in the living room."

"Then why the clothes at this hour of the mornin'? Hell, the sun isn't up yet." John grabbed his watch from the end table separating our beds. "It's only five o'clock. We don't meet Ivan until eight and our train to Hoshiv doesn't leave until nine."

"I just want to go for a short walk."

"No. You're headin' back to the cathedral to talk to that priest. Why don't we rest another couple hours, we'll call Ivan and—"

"I'm tired of waiting. That's what I've done my whole life. I want to . . ." I still couldn't say it.

"Okay. You win. Give me ten minutes and I'll be ready." With his feet already on the floor, he scratched himself and then yawned. "Dibs on the bathroom."

"Just don't stink it up."

"Me? Never!" He eyed me through the partly propped open door. Familiar sounds emerged from the bathroom. "Another work of art."

"Who did you kill this time?"

"I've told you a million times—it's just the aroma of creation." He slipped his jeans on and then his shirt. "Hey, toss me my backpack." The bag bounced on the bed. John surveyed the contents. "Okay, we need a change of clothes, a light blanket, a canteen, more energy bars, and let's see—"

"I offered to detach the lavatory yesterday. Do you want it?" I walked towards the bathroom to brush my teeth.

"Look, smartass, this place is occupied by Communists. You know, the Russian Military. It's not the most stable political situation in the world today, not to mention that we're Americans on a Visa limiting our access to the city. We're gonna be prepared."

"A Boy Scout to the end! Guess that's why you wear a prophylactic to bed."

"Paul, kiss—"

"Shh, I'm praying. The angel of the Lord declared unto Mary—"

"I'd like to 'Hail Mary' you." He muttered through gritted teeth. "Now, hurry up so you can pack!" My backpack sailed onto my bed. John eyed me.

I entered the bathroom door and splashed the rotten smelling water on my face.

"Don't use tap water." A bottle of carbonated water hit my back.

The carbonated water left a sticky film on my face. It felt worse than leaving it unwashed. Only the taste of it as I rinsed my brushed teeth was worse. "This stuff is nasty."

"Sometimes you whine like an ole mule. It's better than dysentery, so just brush." John continued to stuff my backpack. It bulged, looking like a safari pack.

"Who's going to carry this?"

"You are!" John pushed me over. I tumbled onto the bed only to find him towering over me smiling from ear to ear. "Just like I like you. Under control."

"Are you crazy?"

"No. Just remindin' you that I'm bigger. So when we get out there, what I say goes! Grab your backpack." John swung his backpack over his shoulder. "Where's your jacket?"

"Don't need it. I've got a sweater on."

"Bullshit. It's cold outside. Wait here."

"It's not there."

"What do ya mean? You unpacked it yesterday."

"I gave it away. Last night. Some old guy was freezing outside."

"That explains it. Don't you move while I get the extra I packed."

"Extra?"

"Yeah. Anne insisted. Now I know why." John grabbed the jacket from his closet. "Here, put this on and no givin' it away." He lifted the jacket as I slipped my arms through it. "You know mass isn't until seven o'clock. Nobody's gonna be up at this hour."

"Then we'll go for a walk."

The gold inlay of the staircase sparkled as we descended to the ground floor. It was the one thing in the hotel that suggested a time when things were lavish and beautiful here.

We stepped off the last rung into the lobby. John approached a young gentleman. "Izvinite. Vi govorite po Angliysky?"

"Da. I speak English." As the young man turned, a smile extended across his face.

"Nickolay. I'm sorry. I didn't recognize you without your uniform."

"Please no apologize. Nickolay just get vork. Dress soon."

"No problem, man. Can you tell us how to get to some of the local churches?"

"Da. Bernadine Monastery is short walk from hotel. I show. But not open until nine." John and I followed Nickolay out of the lobby. He pointed down the street to spires jutting up behind the square. "See light. Go Halytsky Square. You see monastery."

"Yeah. We saw those yesterday when we arrived. Very good."

215

"Guide meet you?"

"Yes. He'll be here in a few minutes. See ya." John and I turned down the darkened street. Only an occasional street lamp added light. As we clogged along the cobblestones, the sound echoed off the empty sidewalks.

Winter had long ago stripped all leaves from the trees, and with it any hope of blocking the stiff wind. No wonder birds typically welcoming the morning were absent.

As we approached the monastery, four spires protruded from the landscape. We passed the first, a three-story rectangle in the middle of an open square. Plain by comparison, its green steeple was capped by a simple cross. John pointed to a monument resting in front of what looked to be the back of a church. "Take a look at that. Can you translate?"

"Hold the flashlight on it. 'Pillar of St. John.'" A clock tower, taller than the steeple of the church, tolled. The sun tipped the cross atop its narrow peak. The clock showed 6:30 A.M.

"St. John, huh? Somethin' for ya to remember."

"You, a saint?"

"What's wrong with that? Think about it. St. Paul of Thibodaux and St. John . . ." John looked away. The memory of Meg and our playful dealings when we first met her surely riveted his soul.

"John, I'm—"

The wind cut through us as we turned back towards the hotel. In Mickevich Square, people now strolled among Russian soldiers posted on the street corners. As we turned right at the corner, the single spire of the Cathedral stood over the buildings. With each step, we drew closer to the sandstone colored steeple. My heart pulsed a little faster.

John pulled the door to the vestibule open. The young novice we had met yesterday dropped several candles on the floor in surprise. John reached down to help him. "Sorry." He lifted the candles. "Is Father Andrei here?"

"Net. He go uniwersity see old friend. To bashnya. How say English?" Searching for the word, he stretched his hands apart towards the floor and ceiling. "Follow." He led us outdoors and pointed to the steeple.

"Tower?"

"Da. Tower."

"Come on, Paul."

"Hold up, John. Father, before we leave, can I see the statue?"

"Please follow." Guiding us through the Cathedral, he genuflected to the Blessed Sacrament housed in the high altar. "Zhis way," he whispered as he showed us to the chapel. With rosaries in hand, a number of old men and women knelt in silent prayer. Reverence cloaked their wrinkled faces. As I knelt to join them, the church bell tolled 7 A.M.

The angel of the Lord declared unto Mary and she conceived by the Holy Spirit. The words flooded my mind. *Be it done to me according to Thy will.* Chills reeled down my spine.

Light streamed through a window and reflected off the gold inlay of the statue. The reflection striated the light into a rainbow on the floor once more. A chant filled the sanctuary of the cathedral as the religious joined each other for morning prayers. The faithful filed in from the streets, genuflecting and then entering pews for devotion.

A chain clanged. White smoke wafted towards the ceiling. Burning incense fanned about. We stood and then kneeled. The ancient right of Benediction was underway.

The celebrant lifted the monstrance with cloaked hands. Bells chimed in adoration. I bowed my head, offering my prayers in quiet supplication.

With the final prayer recited, I looked to John. The religious filed out of the sanctuary. Yet, many of the devout remained in their sojourn.

"Ready?" John whispered.

"Yes." I exited the pew. The young novice waved us farewell.

John pushed the wooden doors open. The sunlight blinded me. Across Prospect Svobody, old men sprawled chessboards on park benches. Their concentration on the challenge before them seemed to dull their awareness to the chilly air or the cars and trams that rolled about.

Pedestrians filled the sidewalks. Umbrellas covering small tables blossomed in clusters as sidewalk cafes opened for business. The smell of fresh bread teased me.

"Paul, I wanna make sure we're headin' in the right direction. Get coffee and a couple of muffins and I'll ask." While I ordered, John turned to a young lady sitting alone.

"Izvinite. Kak proiti, pazhaluysta."

"Vhere do you vant to go?"

"You speak English."

"You seem surprised."

"I'm sorry. I didn't mean to offend you."

"It's fine. So vhere do you vant to go?"

"The university."

"Are you a student?"

"Sort of. We're visiting from America, doin' research on the area."

"Good. I teach zhere. I vill take you."

"Awesome. Can we buy ya a cup of coffee?" Just as he asked, she lifted her cup. "Oh. Well, maybe a refill?"

"I am fine. Thank you. I am Kataina." She extended her hand.

"I'm John and this is my friend Paul."

I returned her firm handshake. "Rad s vamee poznakomit'sya."

Kataina smiled. "It's good to meet you, Pascha. Your Russian is quite good."

"Spasibo."

"So tell me, vhat are you studying?"

John pulled her chair for her. "Folklore, legends, religious history of the area."

"And you do zhis for a living?"

218

"No. I'm a medical doctor and Paul here, well, he's this wiz-kid research scientist, pseudo-psychologist."

"Well, Paul. Zhat is quite the combination. So vhat is the link vit your research."

"None, actually. It's just an amateur fascination."

"You travel a long vay for a fascination."

"Enough about him. Tell us about yourself, Kataina."

"Zhere is not much to tell. I live here in L'vov. I am originally from Kiev. I studied zhere and zhen Oxford. I returned to teach at uniwersity several years ago."

"What area?"

"Language. French, English, and Spanish."

"And your husband?"

"I'm not married."

"That's hard to imagine as beautiful as you are."

"Vhat if I told you I am a lesbian?"

John smirked. "Then I guess I'd have to be one too." Silence pervaded the conversation as we turned the block. "Well are ya?"

"You are somezhing else. And, no." She stopped. "My building is over zhere. Are you looking for somezhing in particular?"

"Yes. The tower."

"Go two blocks down and turn left. You'll see it from zhere."

I kissed her hand. "It was a pleasure meeting you, Katiana."

"You also, Paul." She kissed me on both cheeks.

John pushed me out of the way. "So, will you be hangin' around?"

"Maybe." She started to walk off.

"Maybe yes or maybe no?"

"It depends."

"On what?"

"Vhether you call me. Fourth floor, Humanities." Turning towards her building, she crossed the street and waved good-bye. With long legs and a sleek frame, she sashayed down the cobblestone street. Her heels added a pecking sound to the rumble of small cars racing down Prospect Svobody.

"That's some woman."

"Yes. And you've got some nerve."

Following Katiana's directions, we strolled down the street. As we drew closer, shouts sounded in the distance. We turned the corner. "Osvabadite nas!" Groups of students rallied en mass towards an open square. "Daite svobodi!" They shouted for freedom and liberation as they marched. Soldiers were congregating to confront them.

"John, Paul. Over here." Ivan yelled out to us. Pushing through the crowd, we joined him. "Marc, I've got them."

"How'd ya find us?"

"First the hotel, then the cathedral. What the hell were you two thinking?"

"I don't know. We better get the hell out of here." The crowd thickened around us.

"Let's get Marc." Just as Ivan shouted, the crowd pushed forward.

John grabbed my jacket and pulled me across the mob. "This way, Paul!"

"Where are Marc and Ivan?"

"I can't see them." Guns fired. The protestors froze. "Tear gas. Run!" The crowd dispersed as white clouds lifted between us.

"John, where are you?"

"Get to the alley!" We bolted.

John's voice faded. With hundreds running around me, all I could do was run with them. Screams blended with more shots as everyone pushed and shoved their way through.

"Syuda, za mnoi!" In the chaos, a man pulled me with him as he said, "In here." As we ran through the street, more shots rang out. I looked back, but could see nothing in the smoke. "Zdes'!" Pushing a door open to a building, he shoved me inside. My eyes were tearing from the gas. The closed door muffled gunfire amidst shouts and screams. "Ve safe here." Even though his accent was heavy, his English was good.

"Yes." I gasped to catch my breath.

"Come. Rest." Pointing to the corner of the room, he motioned me to sit. "You leave hotel, yes." Even with my vision blurred, his smile seemed familiar.

"Nickolay?"

"Da. Ve safe here. Come. Rest."

"I've got to get going."

"No. Streets wery dangerous. Ve vait dark." Rifling through his knapsack, he lifted a chunk of rye bread and small piece of salo. "Ve eat." Splitting both in half, he handed me the food.

"I couldn't. It's all you—"

"Eat. I get more. Please." He nudged the food towards me with his hand palm up. "Drink." He lifted a small bottle of horilka, rye whiskey much like bourbon. "Ah. Good food. Good drink. Good friend. Da?" Raising the bottle to me in toast, he took a swig. He wiped the bottle with his shirt-sleeve and then handed it to me. "Drink. Varm you." Cold air seeped through the leaky windows along with faint smells of tear gas. Shouts and gunshots continued to ring from outdoors.

I raised the bottle in toast to him. "Vasha zdorovie."

"Da. So, vhy you come here?"

"It's kind of a long story."

"Good. Make time pass." He lifted his knapsack behind him as he leaned against the wall. "Tell story."

"I came with a friend. We're studying folklore of the region."

"Da. Zhis good place to study. Wery rich history. My family from here. Ve live Siberia now. Exiled many years. Russian government do bad zhings to people."

"We hear of these things."

"Yet do nozhing."

My face warmed from the flush. "Our government is not always perfect either."

"I study Uniwersity. Many great scholars here. Many in Siberia now."

"L'vov is well known. Is that why your family was sent away?"

"My grandfather and grandmother come here from Belarus many years."

"Belarus? Wasn't that where mass graves were discovered?"

Nickolay nodded. "Once Jews, Muslims, Catholics, many live here. Some killed, others exiled Siberia, few get out. I come uniwersity study engineering. But, study family." As our conversation continued, I wondered whether John, Ivan, and Marc were safe. Certainly if they were captured, I would have little ability to help them. And, if they had escaped, how would we find each other?

"Nickolay, yesterday my friend took us to an alley about fifteen minutes from here. It's in the section where Jewish people once lived. Do you know this place?"

"Da."

"Is it close by? I need to go there to—"

Nickolay patted his chest. "Take you vhen dark. Da?"

Someone banged on the door to the room. "Obischite zdanie!" He shouted for his comrades to search the building.

"Shh." Nickolay snapped his finger over his lips. Pointing to the window, he signaled that he was going to take a look.

Fists pounded on the door. Several men screamed, "Open the door." Nickolay lunged for his knapsack. "Go now!"

Springing to my feet, I followed him down a darkened hallway. Boards snapped as the door was kicked in. We turned the corner into another room. The voices behind us faded. Positioned against a door, he waved me closer.

"You run fast, da?" Bolting out of the door, we ran down a smoke-filled alley.

"Stoy!" With the call to halt, shots rang out. Bullets ricocheted by us. More shouts followed. Screams echoed through the air. We ran harder. The haze thickened.

"Dammit!" I tumbled, smacking my ribs on a rock. It burned and stung at the same time. I lost Nickolay in the smoke.

"Prochesat' ulitsy!" A Russian soldier shouted for others to search the streets.

I froze. Their voices sounded right next to me. I held my breath.

"Chert! Slishkom mnogo dima!" Their gate grew louder as one of them commented on the thick smoke.

"Igor! Alex! Otkhodi, pocka on ne abasralsya!" One of the soldiers teased that they better do as ordered before their commander shit on himself. The strong smell of tobacco suggested they were smoking a cigarette and were near me. Finally, their footsteps faded. I released my breath to a burning sensation on my side.

I stood, but cringed from my wound. Smoke thickened into a miasma engulfing me. This strange land grew stranger by the moment. Civilization had left it behind in so many ways. I needed to find my way to the alley.

My feet moved across the cobblestones. Gunfire rang out. I stopped to determine if anyone approached. Only distant shouts and screams echoed through the street. I walked down one cobblestone street after another, searching for something familiar.

The day darkened. "Shit." My shin pulsed from smacking it against a stone. I looked down. I had seen this marker before.

I pressed on. The smoke thinned. The columns on the building were those we had passed on the tram to Ivan's grandparents.

Soldiers surprised me on the next corner. I tucked into a small doorway, praying I went unnoticed.

I waited. The murmur of their conversation remained steady. I backed away, hugging the side of the buildings. I turned the corner of another street, hoping to blend with the locals, but the streets were empty. Neither cars nor trams were operating.

I tried to rest, but feet pounding the cobblestone approached. I slipped into another doorway. A dozen Russian soldiers marched by, heading towards the university.

Gunfire crackled through the air. Shouts followed. The air chilled as a wind whipped through the narrow streets. I turned another corner.

The arched doorway to Ivan's grandparents' building stood guarded by soldiers.

A clock tower tolled 6 P.M. I waited, hoping to see Ivan or Marc. They were nowhere in sight.

With the toll of 7 P.M., I backtracked to a neighboring street, but guards were concentrated on it as well. I made my way several more blocks. Rain pelted my jacket. Thunder rumbled through the town. Smoke blew by, making it difficult to see. The bell tower tolled 8 P.M and then 9 P.M.

In desperation, I turned down another street. My side throbbed. My backpack grew heavy. I climbed over a small hill, finally locating the flower cart that marked the entrance to the alley. I prayed John waited there for me.

I ducked into a doorway and watched for guards. The streets were dark and empty. Gunfire continued to ring out. Lowering my head, I moved towards the entrance. My heart raced. I steadied my pace. Seeing no one, I ran into the alley.

The sting of the wind finally subsided. With only the sounds of my steps on the stone floors, I tucked myself into a small doorway in the corner. Secluded from sight, I dropped to the ground. Maybe I could rest for a few moments.

I shivered as the air chilled my wet clothes. I fluffed my backpack and propped my head against it. With little to keep me warm, I yearned to see Anne's picture. I reached for my backpack, but a muffled groan accompanied my failed attempt. My side stung. The memory of her image would have to do. For now, I would focus on the legend that brought us here, the "legend of the lady."

My eyes grew heavy. Finding it difficult to breathe, I struggled to lift myself. My right arm felt numb. I slouched against my bag.

I closed my eyes. The thud of more footsteps echoed against the alley walls. My heart pounded as an interloper advanced. Pulling tighter to the wall, I curled up and held my breath. Pain surged through me.

"Hey, asshole, you look like a drenched and shiverin' mutt."

"John!" I slurred. "Where's Marc and Ivan?" I tried to disguise my injuries.

"Didn't find them. Went to Ivan's grandparents, but guards were posted outside. By the way, you look like hell. What happened?"

"I . . . I busted my ass." I struggled to gather the air to speak.

"Yeah, there you go again, trippin' over someone. You're always the life of the party. I can dress ya up, but I just can't seem to take ya anywhere." I flinched as John attempted to pull me up. "Here, let me take a look. I'm gonna open your shirt and see what you did." The mere movement of the fabric sent sharp pains through my body. "Just relax while I take a better look at this."

"I can't breathe. I think I messed up something inside pretty bad."

"Shut up then and let me take a look." His cold hands stung as he examined my side.

"How bad is it?" I shivered from the cold and the pain.

"If you were a horse, I'd ride you until I was done, then I'd shoot and sell you. Glue, yeah, you'd make good glue. Take a deep breath and hold it."

"Ugh—" Inhaling was like being stabbed. I tried to ride through the pain, but I only managed to moan.

"That didn't work so well. I've seen better breathin' in emphysema patients. I'm glad we aren't runnin' a marathon."

I coughed up blood. "John—"

"Take it easy. I'm gonna find a place that's a little safer and more secluded. This will warm you." He covered me with his jacket. "I want ya to rest while I search the area."

I didn't want him to leave. The noise outside the alley was escalating. Staying here was too dangerous.

"I'm not gonna be long. I promise, I'll be right back." Darkness swallowed his shadow.

I tried to rest, but footsteps marching in the street frightened me. There was no movement in the alley, other than an occasional snowflake blown by a gust of wind.

Each beat of my heart taunted the pain in my side. I battled to breathe. I focused on the pain, hoping to relax. I persisted, struggling to work through it. But centering on it only intensified the hurt.

Pressing my eyes closed I prayed, "Hail Mary." I whispered it again. "Hail Mary." Where was she? "Hail Mary full of grace, the Lord is with you." The words floated off my lips.

■

Something touched me. My body warmed. I opened my eyes. A glow enveloped a corner of the alley. Blinded at first, I looked away. As I turned back, she stood over me.

The chill left my body. The pain subsided. I breathed easier. Rescued by her love, I ceased to be as I was. But sounds interrupted my calm. I drew back in fear. Voices grew louder and clearer. Whatever was happening beyond the alley terrified me.

Had the soldiers figured out where I was? What if John had been caught again? Certainly he would never give away my location.

"Hail Mary. Please help me. Please. Where are you?"

Darkness replaced the once brightened alley. Shouting echoed off the walls. I jolted to the crack of gunfire. Pain devoured me. My nightmare grew real as people raced into the alley, screaming for help.

Adrenaline coursed through me. If ever I needed to run and hide, now would be that time. I leaned forward. A hand pushed me down.

■

"Hey. Wake up." I struggled to get free. "Paul, it's me, John. It's just a dream."

"Voices. Gunfire."

"No, Paul. Let's go." He lifted me, but all I could do was groan. "I've got ya, pal. I've found a place. It's safe and warm. Come on. You gotta hang on for me," John whispered. I felt faint. My body pressed against his shoulders. I had no control.

As we walked, everything blurred. He seemed to hover close to the buildings. "Damn. Patrols seem to be everywhere." We hid in another alley. "Let's rest for a minute and warm up. Try to take it easy, okay?"

We waited there as John checked the streets. Every now and again we heard shouts followed by intermittent gunfire. He tried to warm me, rubbing his hands briskly along my jacket, but it was to no avail against the chilling wind.

"It's gotten quiet. I'm gonna see if the coast is clear." He got up, sneaking to the entrance of the alley. Quickly returning, he grunted as he helped me to my feet. I could do little to help him.

We rejoined the street. As we walked uphill, I stumbled. My feet were numb.

"We're almost there, pal." John's voice tinged on desperation. "We've gotta get up these steps. Just lean into me. I'll help." He gasped for breath as we climbed.

We slipped into another alley, walking quite a distance. "Here we are." We entered a room. John laid me down in a corner. "It'll take me just a few moments to join these sleepin' bags."

The room spun wildly. As he lifted me, I flinched again. I tried to help, to get up on my own strength, but I couldn't move. I felt sick to my stomach. I coughed. Blood dripped on John's arm. I grew lightheaded. I took one more breath and felt myself leave my body. Then, all went black.

Seventeen

Father Cavender stood behind me. I all but felt his breath on the back of my neck.

"Mr. de la Moret, if you would, please sir, share with us your thoughts on the writings of St. John of the Cross. Let's see. Shall we start with:

'On a dark night,
Kindled in love with yearnings
—oh, happy chance!
I went forth without being observed,
My house now being at rest.

In darkness and secure,
By the secret ladder, disguised
—oh, happy chance!
In darkness and in concealment,
My house being now at rest.
In the happy night,

In secret, when none saw me,
Nor I beheld aught,
Without light or guide,
Save that which burned in my heart.'

"I thought this was lit class, not Religion," John muttered.

"Something to add, Mr. Cheramie?"

"No, Father."

"Proceed, Mr. de la Moret."

I rose from my desk with my knees knocking. I looked to John for a reassuring nod. He smiled.

"Sometimes we see things and know things, but we are hesitant to tell those around us, even those who love us." I fidgeted.

John winked at me and then mouthed, "Go on. Tell him."

I cleared my throat, hoping the lump in it would go away. "Darkness can make us feel secure because it hides and protects us from the scrutiny of others. When we experience things not of this world, it can be hard to know whether what we are experiencing is real or not. If we feel secure enough to drop our guard, then the 'not of this world' phenomena seems freer to make itself known to us. It's as though this thing waits patiently for our readiness, just like a good friend."

John smiled at me. The twinkle in his eye warmed me. I was glad what I said made him feel good.

"An intriguing observation, Mr. de la Moret. Now that we have heard from the brain, let us delve into the realm of the brawn. Mr. Cheramie, would you care to further this commentary, perhaps with your thoughts on:

'This light guided me
More surely than the light of noonday
To the place where he
(Well I knew who!) was awaiting me
A place where none appeared.

230

Oh, night that guided me,
Oh, night more loved than the dawn,
Oh, night that joined
Beloved with lover,
Lover transformed in the Beloved!

Upon my flowery breast,
Kept wholly for himself alone,
There he stayed sleeping, and I caressed him,
And the fanning of the cedars made a breeze.

The breeze blew from the turret
As I parted his locks;
With his gentle hand he wounded my neck
And caused all my senses to be suspended.'"

John stood. With an air of confidence about him, he arched his shoulders and puffed his chest. "Sometimes things happen to us. We probably don't understand the reason at the moment. But, if we hold the course with courage and conviction, and we remain faithful to our destiny, then things have a way of working themselves out.

"So if you really love someone, sometimes you have to be very patient and very gentle with them, especially if they've been hurt. You've got to wait until the appointed place and time to reveal to them what you know. It becomes a quest, forcing you to wait for the time when you reach to someone who's wounded."

Father Cavender nodded. "Surprisingly insightful. I suggest you continue your studies with Mr. de la Moret. His intellect seems to be rubbing off."

John reached to me, but a wind gust blew him back, pinning him against the wall. I struggled to get to him, but the gale tossed me into a torrent of rain and lightning.

I dropped into a ravine. Thunder rumbled against the rocky walls. Bodies fell around me to the crackle of gunfire. Only the light of the lady brightened the darkening space.

I climbed the ledge only to find armed soldiers charging towards me. The wall cloud of a hurricane pressed close behind.

More shots rang out. Blood splattered over me from a lightning bolt striking the ground. The roar of the gale grew deafening. I couldn't hear myself speak. I searched for a place to hide, but could fine none.

■

"Gunfire, bleeding. Why? Why?"

"What is it, pal? Who ya talkin' to?"

"Ravine, mountains, lady—" Something cool dampened my forehead. "Help me."

"Open your eyes, Paul." John's voice was fuzzy. It was as though I was awake, yet still asleep. "Come on, pal. You can do it. I know you're woozy. If you want me to kiss you, you've gotta open your eyes. Here, I'm gonna lift you so you can sip somethin'. It'll reduce the fever."

"Ogh—" I tried to drink, but couldn't. My head hurt and something tugged on my side.

"Sorry, pal." Liquid dripped down my cheek as a bitter taste filled my mouth. I flinched as I swallowed. "Good. Rest now. You'll feel better in a bit." John's voice faded into a mere vibration resonating in my body.

■

Light filtered into the previously darkened room. Blinded by the brightness, my eyes adjusted slowly. The room was still somewhat blurred. Wind whistled through a broken windowpane. Barren walls, chipped in places, matched the grunge of the ceiling.

My throat was parched. It ached when I swallowed. Nothing came out when I tried to speak. With my arms and my legs weighted like lead, I couldn't move. I squeezed my fingers into my hands and then wiggled my toes. It stung.

Closing my eyes, I counted one, two, and three. With a thrust, I pushed up only to have a jabbing pain race through my body.

"Paul, stop!" Something thudded on the floor as John placed his hands on my shoulders. He helped me down. Lifting the covers, he peeled away what felt like bandages. "Lay still while I take a look at this." I winced as he probed my side. "Come on now. You're not gonna let this little flesh wound turn you into a pussy, are you?"

As he worked, I tried to see what he was doing. But my side hurt so bad my eyes teared, blurring my view. "I'm gonna get you some water, but I'm not gonna move a muscle until I'm certain that you're not gonna attempt somethin' stupid."

I nodded. Even so, he waited a few moments. Finally, he turned and reached for the water, turning to peek back at me several times.

"I'm gonna lift you. Let me do the work. No antics, no bullshit. Understand?" He cradled me. I grimaced as a wave of pain washed over me. "Man, I'm sorry. Just let it go." John backed me down. "I've dampened a cloth. I'll squeeze a few drops for you." The cool water wet my lips. My tongue felt stuck to my pallet and my mouth felt stuffed with cotton. I tried to swallow the drops, but choked.

"Easy, pal. I think we've done enough for a while. Why don't you close your eyes and get some rest?" As he gently grasped my hand, I looked towards him in terror. "I'm right here."

I closed my eyes, but my side throbbed relentlessly. Unable to find a comfortable position, I grew restless.

"Can't sleep?"

I shook my head.

"You know, I'm ready for some of Mim's cookin'. Think about it. Shrimp Creole by candlelight, gentle breezes blowin' through the Spanish moss, soakin' our feet in that ole bayou on a hot summer day. We're gonna get home and sit back on the upper porch with a Mint Julep. And later, we'll head to the city for a night on the town."

The room brightened as he talked. To be back home—what a thought. It seemed a million miles away and a lifetime since we had left. But just as I relaxed, John snapped up with a log in his hand. Standing pensively, he listened as someone stepped towards the door. It pushed opened. He bolted towards it. My body jerked and I wrenched.

With the intruder already inside, John lowered the log. "Nickolay." His face lit up. "How'd you find us?" The floorboards creaked as he walked towards me.

"Ivan send me. He tell me vhere find you."

"Man, you scared the shit outta me."

"Nickolay sorry."

"Did Ivan give you supplies?"

"Da."

As John opened the knapsack, Nickolay walked over to me.

"Paul hurt, da?"

"That's why I found Ivan this morning. We agreed to get out of the city and meet up with his grandparents in Hrushiv. Did he give you the map?"

"Da. Tell you meet him in willage. Soldiers vatch family. Wery dangerous. I come back in dark. Show vay out city."

"Any word on Marc?"

"Net."

John surveyed the supplies now spread on the floor. "There're a few things missin'—"

"Da. Ivan get zhem. I bring to you tonight. Late—maybe midnight. Must vait so streets clear. Ve go zhen."

"We'll be ready."

"Good." Nickolay patted my hand. "Take care friend. Ve get you safe soon." As he walked towards the door, my young friend stopped to peek back at me. His smile broadened across his face as he nodded, reassuring me that help was on its way.

"Be careful."

"Da. God care for you." Nickolay peered out of the door before slipping away. I could hear his feet against the stone floors. The city had otherwise grown quiet.

"How are you feelin', pal?" Dipping into his deep voiced drawl, he smirked. "By the way, you look like crap. But I've seen you in worse shape. Mardi Gras when you hurled. When we get back to Louisiana, I think we should take another trip. Someplace wild and exotic. Maybe Disney World. We could pretend we're doin' the whole adventure thing instead of doin' it for real. I could be Sinbad; you could be my wench. You could wait on me hand and foot, kinda like I'm doin' right now, except I'd be the one loungin' around. Sounds like a good idea, huh?"

As John teased, the pain eased somewhat and my eyes closed. But as I drifted off, visions of bloodied people screaming and walking aimless through a rocky ravine horrified me once more. I jolted up as my eyes opened wide.

"Easy there, fella." John placed me back down.

I coughed, spitting up more blood.

"Let's take a look." Once again, I wrenched as he lifted the bandages. "Just try to breathe. I know it's uncomfortable. Did I ever tell you the one about Sister Mary Agnes?"

I flinched.

"Well, Sister Mary Agnes was a good friend of my mom. She'd come over to visit every now and then. They'd sit out on the veranda to have Community Coffee and catch up with each other. Sister Mary Agnes was from the bayou and some years older than mom. As she got up in years, we'd visit her from time to time. She musta been ninety or so 'cause on one visit, I couldn't help but notice how old she'd gotten. I asked her how she was doin'. She looked at me, kinda peekin' through her glasses, and started talkin'. 'Well my breasts sag almost to the floor. I've got enough loose skin to house another person, maybe another family. I've got hemorrhoids so big that they could be served as grapefruits. My joints ache, my breath stinks, my teeth are gone. I'm half-blind, and haven't had sex ever. But you know me, I've never been one to complain.'

"Done." John replaced the bandages. Covering me with the blanket, he kissed me on the forehead. "We're gonna be fine. Tonight we'll get outta the city, find help, and then head home."

I struggled to speak.

"What is it, Paul? I can see it in your eyes. I gotta admit, I kinda like you in this position. I can finally control the conversation."

My stare remained resolute.

"Okay, enough already." He knelt beside me. "Your side is pretty swollen. You may have broken a rib, but I'm not sure what it's done inside."

I turned my head away.

"Look at me." John turned my head back towards him. "I've placed a tube in your side to remove fluids and relieve the pressure. If you punctured a lung, this'll manage it until we get help."

I tried once more to speak, but John placed his hand over my lips.

"Save your energy. If you rest, you'll have strength when we leave tonight. I've got things under control. Do you understand?"

I nodded. John seemed confident, but the tight feeling right smack in the middle of my gut told me otherwise. I wanted him to know this.

With renewed conviction, I stared at him once more, this time with greater intensity.

"What is it? You've got somethin' else on your mind. I know that look like I know the smell of my own farts."

For all those times that I had so carelessly used words to fill vacant space, I could not muster the strength to mutter a single sound.

"Whatever it is, let it go."

So much raced through my head that I found it difficult to do so. My thoughts and my dreams told me that something was going to happen to us. But what? There had to be some way out of this, some explanation or reason why this had happened. John and I had traveled together before, but none of our journeys had imperiled us so. Why was the lady allowing this to happen?

"Please rest, pal. Here, focus on this." John rubbed my forehead just above the bridge of my nose in a circular pattern. The little light filtering into the room waned. My eyes closed once more, but as I drifted into sleep, a foreboding awareness spoke to me.

Clearer than ever before, the voice I had grown familiar with over the years persisted. Suddenly, warmth enveloped my body. A love as profound as any I had felt permeated my being, all of it encompassed with the vision of the lady. There she stood in radiant light, her blue veil draping her head. Yet her presence confused me.

Was she real? I wasn't sure. She spread her arms apart reaching to me. I yearned to be near her, but didn't dare move. Frightened, I turned my head away from her.

"Paul." She gently called my name. "Paul." Once more I heard her. As I turned back to face her, the softness of her eyes greeted me. I so wanted to trust her. Yet, thoughts of those I had lost haunted me. As I lay there looking towards her, the light around her seemed to brighten even more. She reached her hand towards me. My heart raced. Her touch scared me so.

"Hey, pal. What are you pullin' back from?"

I opened my eyes, waking, or maybe not. I wasn't sure anymore. Maybe I was still dreaming.

"It's okay." John placed a cold towel on my forehead, providing some relief to the heat encircling me. I just wanted to be left alone, engulfed in the thoughts racing through my head. It would have been so easy to just let go.

"Come on. Open those big brownish-green eyes for a minute. I wanna check if you're still full of crap." The sound of his voice strengthened as his words grew more demanding in tone. "I'm gonna lift you. This won't taste so hot, but I thought it might be easier than swallowin' them whole."

I took small sips, trying to breathe, to manage the pain.

"Take your time. We're in no rush. You know I could have shoved these up your butt, but I thought people might talk when we get back home." With a smile on his face, he helped me back down and began sponging my head. Even the chills brought on by it were a relief to what I had been feeling.

"John—" Finally a word came out, although only in a whisper. The whites of his eyes pierced through the darkened room.

"I love ya!" His voice cracked. "You've been with me through thick and thin. Nothin's gonna harm you. I promised Anne. I swear I'll see you home, safe in her arms."

I found myself flooded with love. It was like the love Anne had tried to show me and the love that I felt from the lady when I dreamed about her. It resided in a darkened space within me.

The lady I dreamed was like Anne in some ways, but different in others. Her warmth and compassion exceeded what I had experienced. And, like Anne she was simple and beautiful, a spirit mature in nature. But at this moment, Anne was so far away, as was the lady.

"On a dark night—" John whispered the words. I could barley see him in what little light filtered into the room. "Say it with me, Paul."

My lips moved even though nothing came out.

> ". . . Kindled in love with yearnings
> —oh, happy chance!
> I went forth without being observed,
> My house now being at rest.
>
> In darkness and secure,
> By the secret ladder, disguised
> —oh, happy chance!
> In darkness and in concealment,
> My house being now at rest.

In the happy night,
In secret, when none saw me,
Nor I beheld aught,
Without light or guide,
Save that which burned in my heart.

This light guided me
More surely than the light of noonday
To the place where he
(Well I knew who!) was awaiting me
A place where none appeared.

Oh, night that guided me,
Oh, night more loved than the dawn,
Oh, night that joined
Beloved with lover,
Lover transformed in the Beloved!

Upon my flowery breast,
Kept wholly for himself alone,
There he stayed sleeping, and I caressed him,
And the fanning of the cedars made a breeze.

The breeze blew from the turret
As I parted his locks;
With his gentle hand he wounded my neck
And caused all my senses to be suspended.

I remained, lost in my oblivion;
My face I reclined on the Beloved.
All ceased and I abandoned myself,
Leaving my cares forgotten among the lilies."

"Again, Paul. Say it once more with me. On a dark night—" With his hand in mine. he spoke the words once more. Even now he looked at me with compassionate eyes. "I will, to will, Thy will. Remember. I will, to will, thy will. Say it, Paul."

"I will, to will, Thy will." Over and over I mouthed the words. I knew of nothing else to do but surrender to a will that I knew of, yet struggled to trust.

"On a dark night—" He recited the words once more. My thoughts stilled, save that which burned inside of me.

My eyes grew heavy. John held my hand. With him at my side, I drifted off.

■

A tolling bell tower woke me to John's vigilant watch. "Hey there. I'm gonna check your bandages. You're lookin' a lot better. Before, you looked like crap on a shingle. Now you just look like crap." He removed the dressing and examined my side.

"John, something's about—" Finally words came out, but they were very coarse. John placed his hand over my mouth. Voices and footsteps approached the door. John's once relaxed frame tensed like a cat intently observing the threat of predators. Three men were talking, maybe more.

A knock rattled the door. John looked at me. With another knock, this one much louder and more forceful, John motioned for me to be silent and lie still. The voices were loud, but muddled.

John slowly released my hand and grabbed the log. Carefully shifting his weight, he poised himself to defend us. John pulled the covers over my face.

The board from the door jam cracked. "Obiskat'!" The men from outside thundered in. The room filled with shouting voices.

A board snapped. Shouts followed loud thuds. A body hit the floor, then another. The racket sounded like a barroom brawl. With a snap sounding like breaking bones and a final thud, only the gasps of one remained.

The floor whined as the single survivor approached me. *Please let it be John. Please let it be John,* I prayed. I jumped to the thud of someone dropping to my side. The blanket slipped off of me. My heart pounded. "I beat," he gasped, "the crap outta them." John smiled, then wiped blood off his forehead.

"You're hurt."

"We've gotta get outta here. They're sure to come lookin' for their buddies." His reply was raspy.

He dragged the first body, then the second—the boots of the soldier rubbing against the floor. As he reached down for the third body, John paused to catch his breath.

I attempted to sit up. "Wait up, Paul." John rested his hand on my shoulder. "I've got it, pal. But man, they smell. Give me a minute to take care of the last one and then clean up." He drew a deep breath and then lifted the last body. He stacked him on top of the other two in the corner, and rustled an old tarp over them.

John removed his jacket and then ripped off his shirt. The gold chain and cross given to him by Maria jingled as he mopped up the blood. "I've gotta get rid of this." He stuffed the bloody shirt into his backpack along with the flashlight, the maps, and the first-aid kit.

"I'm gonna lift you, pal. Can you walk?" I forced my legs to the floor. I had grown stiff from lying still for so long. He placed my arm over his shoulder and grabbed my side with the other. My knees wobbled as I walked through the door.

He peered out the door. As we stepped from the protection of the den, an icy wind pierced through me. Sleet stung my face. The cold burned my lungs. We hugged the sides of the buildings and moved as quickly as my legs would allow.

Several sets of footsteps echoed through the dark and empty streets. "Obiskat' tu ulitsu!" A commander ordered the soldiers to search the next street.

John pulled us into a doorway. I held my breath as the voices grew louder.

"Chert, kholodeyet!" The soldier complained about how cold it was.

'Da. Tol'ko zamalchi, a to tovarich Smirnov uslishit." One of the soldiers walked right by us as he told his comrade to hush before the commander overheard them.

My heart slowed as their bodies faded down the street. Only the sound of our feet shuffling and the heaviness of our breathing sounded in my head. Another night had dawned. Once again, we were fugitives on the run.

Eighteen

December 9, 1986

"Ugh." I groaned from John pushing me into the tall grass.

A Russian soldier stood not even twenty feet from us. "Ne ugostish sigaretoy?"

"Da." His friend handed him a cigarette. The scent of strong tobacco blew by us.

This was the fourth platoon to pass us since following Ivan's directions out of the city. The soldiers' boots shuffled along the gravel road until they crossed the hill.

John lifted me. "Let's get goin'." With the exception of this last patrol, the night had grown still. We turned from the hilly road we had been following into a rolling meadow. Without the moon, the stars provided the only light. I lifted my feet and legs even though I could barely feel them. One thought occupied my mind—taking the next step from harm's way.

We reached the bottom of a hill. A large rock blocked a wind that howled with an ever-increasing relentlessness. "Let's rest for a while." John grabbed a canteen. "Here you go. Get a little water down." My mouth was so dry that I choked on the first sip. "Let it wet your throat a bit, pal."

I began to shiver. My head throbbed.

"Can you swallow this?" John pushed two white tablets into my mouth. Flicking them back in my throat, I forced them down. "Good. Let's cover up. I wanna take a look at the map." John draped the blanket over us and then tightly tucked it along the sides so no light would escape. Holding the flashlight in his mouth, he unfolded the map. "I think we're here. That small bluff a mile or so back had a stone marker on it. I'm certain that's the one Ivan drew here." He pointed to the map. "We're still a ways from Hrushiv, but we've turned more westward. We should get there by mornin'."

He folded the map and then stored it in his backpack. With the flashlight turned off, he lifted the blanket from us. The gusting wind chilled me once more. He wrapped me in the blanket and then moved to block the gale with his body. "Here, let's warm you before we get goin' again. Ivan's got a place for us in Hrushiv. When we get there, we'll get cleaned up, have somethin' warm to eat, and take care of you." He swigged water from the canteen and then wiped his mouth. His backpack rustled as he stowed the remainder of our gear. "You ready?"

I nodded.

"I'm gonna lift you." John wrapped his arms around me. I forced my feet under me. With our gear in tow, we trudged up the next hill. "Watch your step." The terrain grew more rugged. Large rocks intermixed in the grassy rolling meadow slowed our progress.

The heavens glowed as the horizon seemed to drift on, touching the earth in the distance. "Look at that, pal." A shooting star streaked across the sky, burning brightly for just a moment. I searched for whatever he pointed towards. "Can you see it? Damn, I'm good." Nothing but darkness was there. "Let's get goin'. We're in the right place. I knew it." He moved faster than before. "It's the forest. I'm certain. Ivan's instructions said there'd be grassy meadows and then rocks. If we traveled with the Big Dipper, we'd find these woods. And here we are."

Thank God rest and warmth were only a short distance away.

"Let's get into the trees. The canopy will give us some shelter from the wind, and the undergrowth will help cover our tracks." As we entered, the wind whistled above us. Our path turned treacherous, though. The rolling terrain of the fields with the occasional rocks shifted to rocky knolls and crannies. John's vigilance was all that separated us from catastrophe. We inched towards our destination, even as I raced to it in my heart.

"Dammit." John slipped. Fatigue was taking its toll. "Let's rest." We sat against a tree.

I wondered what Anne was doing tonight. I longed to be nestled in the warmth and comfort of her arms, smelling her sweet scent. But the howl of the wind stinging my face and the ache in my body shattered those thoughts, reminding me all too quickly of the reality we faced. To think of Anne was a momentary reprieve. To think of the lady, the legend we had come in search of, faded into nothing but a pipe dream.

"Let's get goin', pal." John helped me up. We walked, and then we walked some more. From time to time, we tripped and stumbled. The darkness protected us from one enemy, but offered us to another.

"Whoa!" John looked down. "Damn that was close." Rocks and dirt plummeted off a ledge. We backed away and then turned towards a boulder. He leaned me against it. "I'm gonna scout the area. I won't be long." The underbrush rustled as John left in search of shelter. I closed my eyes. My head started to spin. It was time for us to find a place to rest.

A bright light startled me. Fearing discovery, I slid to the ground. I opened my eyes, blinded at first. I gasped for breath. "Look under the ledge. There it awaits you." I thought I was dreaming. Lying against the boulder was such a relief from walking that I must have fallen asleep. I heard the voice again. "Look under the ledge. There it awaits you."

As my sight adjusted, the lady stood not more than ten feet in front of me. I squeezed my eyes tightly shut and reopened them. Her long black hair and lily-white skin were as distinct as ever.

"Paul, who's talkin' to you?" John's approach surprised me.

"Look under the ledge," I snapped as I looked back to see her. But only rocks and brush were there.

"Do what?"

"Under the ledge."

"What ledge?"

"The one we almost stepped off of."

"But—"

"But, nothing! Just look under the damn ledge."

"Okay, but you don't have to be an asshole about it." John walked to the ledge and got down on all fours. He peered over the rocky crest. "I'll be damned." He popped up. "Give me a minute while I climb down and check it out." He paused for just a minute. "How'd you know?"

"Know what?"

"About the cave."

"Lucky guess."

"Right." As he lifted himself over the edge, rocks clacked as they fell, hitting whatever was below. His body and then his head disappeared behind a couple of small boulders perched at the end. I stared into the darkness.

Had the lady just appeared or was I dreaming? Maybe knowing about the cave was just a lucky hunch. But this whole journey—the statue, its legend—these were more than mere hunches. Why would the lady go through so much trouble to make a point? Through the years, she came and went, never really helping me understand why things were the way they were. Whatever was going on, I hoped John would find a place for us to rest.

Rocks tumbled. John pulled his body up. His feet shuffled through the light brush. "It's a small, shallow cave just beneath the ledge. It ain't the Ritz, but it'll shield us from the wind and hide us for the night. I'll get our stuff down and then help you." He lifted our gear and then returned to the edge. His body disappeared.

Was there a rhyme or reason to all of this? Couldn't there be an easier way to show it? Maybe this lady had nothing to do with any of it.

Maybe, just maybe, all of this was nothing more than my own devices gone astray.

I jumped to John's touch. "Sorry, pal. Didn't mean to scare you." He lifted me. "Let's get you down. We'll take it nice and slow." John held my arms as we grappled with the steep descent. "There you go. Just ease one foot at a time. I'll have you sacked away and fast asleep before you know it." What would normally have been a simple stretch turned into a monumental effort.

"Place your foot on the floor. It's just beneath you." My right foot touched a smooth, solid surface. My left foot followed. John joined me as we entered the twelve-foot space. I was hurting from the strain and energy needed to get there. Propped against the rocky wall, John breathed heavily. He seemed exhausted.

"Let's get you settled. One more lift and we'll rest." I moaned as he placed me in the sleeping bag. "We'll get you warm in a second. I'm gonna crawl in with you. We've gotta preserve our body heat." He zipped us up.

We were wet from perspiring. As if caring for a newborn, he rubbed my arms, generating friction to warm me. "What a great story this'll make. You can tell folks how I convinced you to go to a war torn country on this silly ass quest, just so I could get you in the sack with me. Whacha think Anne will say about that?"

My teeth chattered.

"When we get home, I'm gonna buy us a first class meal, the biggest damn steak this side of the Rockies. We're gonna wipe that cow's ass, knock its horns off, and eat it."

I coughed, spitting up blood. I gasped for air. John jumped up. He opened my jacket. His hand dampened with blood. "Damn." He applied pressure to my side with one hand while reaching for his bag with the other. "The tube's slipped out. This is gonna sting a bit." The aroma of alcohol filled the air. I flinched as he poured it on my side. "Okay. Your gonna feel some pressure and it's gonna hurt like hell for a second, but you'll feel better when I'm done. Ready?"

I gritted my teeth. My side burned and throbbed so bad that nothing could make it any worse.

"Relax." John repeated the word several times as he shoved the tube into my side. It felt like my lung exploded. A cramp seized my body. I couldn't breathe. Now sick to my stomach, I felt faint, but as air rushed into my lung, it eased.

"Better, huh? I'll clean up and then get you warm again." As he placed the supplies into his backpack, he murmured, "Wish I could light a fire, but—"

"John," I whispered. "If something happens to me, tell Anne I—"

"Shh! Nothin's gonna happen to you! We're gonna get home, you're gonna see Anne, and that's that." John's whisper grew forceful. "You're the one person who reached out to me after Meg . . ." His voice cracked. "I've lost one of you. I'm not gonna lose another." John hugged me tightly.

The wind howled outside the crevasse. Pebbles trickled from above. Blackness pressed within the reach of a hand. I pretended to sleep. John's arm relaxed as he drifted off. His deep breath warmed the back of my neck.

My mind raced even though I was numb. The dull throb on my side persisted. *Hail Mary*, I prayed. Maybe she could help us. But thoughts of death—Andre, Father, Xavier, Meg, and Kevin—answered me. Maybe asking for her help was unwise.

A rock plummeted from the ledge above, this time a big one. Several more followed. John snapped up and glanced to see if I was all right.

He placed his finger over his mouth. Maybe it was a mountain goat scurrying for food or looking for a place to rest. Several more rocks rolled down. John tensed. He slowly unzipped the sleeping bag. He reached for a log that looked like an oversized baseball bat. More gravel trickled into the dark chasm below us.

John pulled our sleeping bag over me. I peeked through the overlap of the covers. He edged to the crevasse entrance. Someone's feet emerged on the stone floor.

John cocked the log into a batting stance. Rocks gave way. The intruder slid off the edge. "Ugh!" His groans carried above the tumbling rocks.

With the log in hand, John lunged forward. He looked over the edge. Our intruder had fallen to his death.

"Shit!" John dropped to his belly. He reached down with his hand, then grunted and strained as though he was lifting something. Rocks continued to tumble down the ragged and unstable ledge.

The intruder reached up to a stable area on the stone floor. As he made his way back to safety, the emerging form seemed familiar.

"That was stupid!" It was Marc, thank God.

John embraced him. "Man, you're a sight for sore eyes. Here, come closer. Warm yourself."

"Thanks, I thought I was going to freeze to death."

"So did we. How'd ya find us?"

"I was captured and held in the city. They blindfolded me. I wasn't sure where they took me. I was in a room when something exploded. I escaped through a big hole in the wall and then headed for Ivan's house. When I got there, he told me that he'd seen you."

"So Ivan's safe?"

"I'm not sure. He was reviewing the map and escape plans with me. We were getting ready to meet you when someone came to visit his grandparents. He didn't know who it was, so he showed me an exit through a passageway and told me to find you. I hid until things settled down and then slipped out.

"I finally got to the room where Ivan said you were. I was there for a minute or so and heard noise coming from outside. At first I thought it was you and Paul, but there were too many footsteps. I backed into a corner and tripped on something."

"An old tarp coverin' several bodies?"

"It was gross, but I crawled under the tarp and hid with them."

"Ugh, man."

"The room was dark, but I didn't want to risk it. They came inside and scurried around. I thought they were going to find me. One of them came so close I could see his boots through a small hole in the tarp. It sounded like they were looking for something, but couldn't find it.

"I waited to make sure they were gone, then got the bodies off of me. When Ivan didn't show up, I snuck out. People were everywhere. It was like they were milling around, trying to make sense of everything. I went back to Ivan's, but there were guards posted outside. Then tanks started rolling through the streets. That's when I got the hell out of the city."

"Ivan's gonna meet us in Hrushiv, right?"

"I doubt it. He said his grandfather was brought in for questioning. He told me we should stay away and that he'd meet us where you guys were hiding."

John slumped. "I guess that means we're on our own."

An eerie silence interrupted only by Marc's growling stomach entreated upon us. The wind gusted for a second, then subsided. We were lost in a land unfamiliar to us all.

John handed Marc an energy bar. "It's kinda smashed, but how about somethin' to eat?"

"Is this your last?"

"Yeah, but we'll find more in the mornin'."

"I'll wait." Marc hesitated.

"No, please, eat up. We've all gotta keep up our strength."

Marc devoured the bar. The big bags and dark circles under his eyes protruded even in the darkness. He looked tired and scared.

The crevasse spun. Their voices faded. That awful premonition tightened my gut. John's silhouette blurred. He grabbed me as I keeled over. "His side."

"Let me take a look at it." Marc unzipped my jacket and then lifted the dressings covering the wound. "Do you have a flashlight?"

John was already searching. "Got it. Let's drape this blanket over us." Holding the light in his mouth, he supported the roof of our newly created tent.

Marc stroked my arm. "Paul, just breathe nice and slow."

"Yeah, pal. We've got help now." I was so tired and felt so weak that I really didn't care. Even with my side throbbing, all I could think of was the comfortable slumber of my own bed, curled up beside Anne.

"That's good. I'm going to clean this up and then leave you alone." Marc replaced the bandage. "All done. Hey John, why don't we get some fresh air and let this guy rest." Marc removed the blankets covering us.

John kissed me on the forehead. "You know you're a little asshole, but I do love you."

Stepping towards the ledge, they mumbled just out of earshot. I strained to hear their conversation. What were they talking about and why were they excluding me?

"John!" No answer. "Dammit, John!"

"What is it?" He turned back. "Man, you're a work of art. You have the shortest fuse I've ever seen. You've even got little wisps of steam comin' outta those cute little ears." I wasn't amused. "What, not even a smile?" John moved closer.

Marc followed. "I want to do something that might help. It may be a bit—"

"Just do it!"

"Okay, Paul. Relax." Marc rifled through his supplies. "John, I've got a local."

"All I've got is a little cognac. I've been mixin' aspirin with it to ease the pain. I've also had him on an oral antibiotic to reduce the infection."

"Great. Give him a dose of the cognac and use the local. That will dull it to a minimum." As Marc organized the supplies, John prepared the cognac with what aspirin he had left.

John lifted the elixir to my mouth. "Relax. Breathe with me." He slowed his speech and his breathing. Marc lifted the bandages. The needle pricked. The medicine burned. John chanted the word "relax," saying it slower and breathing deeper. The pain eased. My side numbed.

Marc tugged, but I felt no real sensation beyond that. "Okay, Paul. I'm going to get started. Just—" His voice faded.

■

An old woman appeared. Even in her age, her skin was smooth and soft. She touched my hand. Her voice calmed me. "All is well." She repeated the words. I felt suspended in her care. Yet I felt a deep foreboding of something coming. A dark shape was moving along the horizon. I struggled to distinguish the details. I was dreaming again. I had to be.

■

I forced my eyes open. Marc knelt over me while John held the flashlight. The wind whipped dried leaves across the rocky floor. Pebbles trickled down the walls as they had before. My eyes started to close, but I forced them open. I had seen enough.

"You must be pretty tired. Looks like it's nearly morning. Are you almost done?"

Marc smiled confidently. "I've got a few more stitches and then I'll be wrapped up."

Their voices faded in and out. Soon, tape tearing echoed against the stone walls. "Paul, we're all done. You rest now." His voice sounded optimistic. He gently patted my hands. John rested his hands on me too. I closed my eyes and felt myself finally drift off to sleep to the thought, *Lay your hands gently upon me, let your spirit gently touch my soul.*

Nineteen

December 10, 1986

"Did you find water?" I woke to Marc helping John back into the crevasse.

"There's a stream at the bottom of the ravine, but I couldn't find a way down. Here, grab this." John handed Marc chunks of snow. "I'll get the rest."

Within a minute, the next bundle slid into the crevasse. "Damn, John. You got the whole forest?" Marc called up to him.

"I'm tired of bein' cold." His voice echoed against the rocky walls. "Grab the rocks." The bundle clacked. Marc pulled them to the crevasse floor.

John climbed down. His frame blocked the sunrays now filling the crevasse.

Marc looked puzzled. "Rocks?"

"Yeah. They hold heat. Watch." John organized the rocks into a circle. He propped twigs against each other. As the kindling lit, smoke filled the crevasse. But a breeze cleared it quickly.

Concern covered Marc's face. "You're sure it's safe?"

"The afternoon sun's shinin' this way. There's little chance of anyone spottin' us."

"Good! My rear's about to freeze off." Marc drew closer as the logs caught fire. Chilled from the night before, we experienced real warmth for the first time in days.

John opened several cans of fish and heated them on the fire. The aroma teased us. "It's not borsch or vareniki—"

Marc sniffed the open cans. "Ah, slimy . . . warm . . . fish. Yum!"

I felt much stronger and breathed easier. Whatever Marc did had relieved the pressure and the pain.

A crow cawed. I searched for it, but the rocky terrain surrounding the crevasse blocked my view. I pushed myself up to get a better angle.

John leaped towards me. "Are you nuts?" He carefully laid me down. "I want you to drink some water. Take it nice and slow."

I swallowed with ease.

"Why don't you try to eat somethin'?" John handed me a tin of fish. As I reached for it, my side tugged, sending a sharp pain through me. I flinched.

With a pluck of the syringe, Marc leaned towards me. "It's only a partial dose, but it will take the edge off." The medication stung as Marc injected it into my side. The burn of the medication faded as my side numbed. "I want to take a look. I'll be quick and gentle," Marc assured. "If it starts to hurt, just let me know."

"Yeah, pal. You can grab him by the balls."

"Just remember whose got his fingers in your side."

"Marc, you've gotta remember he's one of those high-bred Southern boys. If you want him to calm down, you've gotta stroke him like a show dog." John drew circles on my forehead. His shoulders lowered with a deep breath. "Ah, that's so relaxin'."

"Now, that wasn't so bad, was it?" Marc winked at me. "Rest. You'll feel better in a bit."

John continued to draw circles on my forehead. I closed my eyes, remaining still until he returned to his meal.

The rocks surrounding the fire radiated heat. Snuggled in the sleeping bag I spied on Marc and John.

"So, Marc, your trip to Brody went well?"

Marc's jaw clinched. "Ugh, I guess." Stress lines filled his forehead as the words tripped from his mouth. "Sort of. But I'm really interested in hearing about Ivan's statue."

John stoked the logs. A blank stare draped his face. "Sorry, Marc. You were sayin'?"

"Ivan's statue. There's some link to it and Paul's dream, right?"

"Yeah. I guess."

"And?"

"It's a kinda long story."

"We're not going anywhere until Paul's stronger. So have at it."

John added logs to the fire, then propped against his backpack. He chewed a splinter of wood peeled from one of the logs. In a contemplative gaze, he stared into the fire.

"One night, just this August, Paul came to visit. He'd start talkin' about goin' on this retreat with his dad, but would change subjects and ramble about other things. After several hours of bullshittin', we went out for a few drinks. Later that night, I dared him to call his step dad. We were three sheets to the wind by then. After that it was too late to back out.

"The day we left for retreat, Paul was nervous as a long-tailed cat in a room full of rockin' chairs. If he wouldn't have disappointed his dad, he'd have canceled in a heartbeat. But we went.

"We got to the retreat house early. After registering, we went to our room to unpack and well, a picture of that statue, the one Ivan has, was hangin' on the wall."

The logs crackled as John continued to poke. He was so immersed in telling the story that he didn't notice me watching.

"We attended a reception with his dad. Despite Paul's strange mood, he shook hands and greeted folks like everything was okay. But when we walked to the dining hall, he lagged behind, kinda in his own world.

"When dinner was over, we went out to the oaks. It was already dark. Paul hugged his stepfather. It's really amazin' how close they are. But even with that, Paul turned away pretty quick. I stepped in to check on him. The minute we made eye contact, he headed to the river. I caught up with him and we talked a little while.

"I thought he could use some time alone, so I asked to walk by myself. But I actually followed him back to the room. I didn't go in at first. It wasn't until he screamed that I dashed in. His head was buried in a pillow. In all my years of knowin' Paul, I'd seen him cry like that only once.

"The retreat bell rang. We put cold towels on his swollen eyes, but it didn't help much. We had to hustle to the chapel before the retreat master arrived. Just as we snuck into the back row, a short old man in a black robe entered. I had to stretch to get a better look at him. But the minute the priest started to talk, I realized I knew him."

"The priest?"

"Yeah. After college graduation we went to South America to do some volunteer work. Paul has this uncanny knack for meetin' people and makin' friends with them almost immediately. We were assigned to a local hospital. The very day we started, Paul met a young guy named Xavier. Needless to say, we grew close to him and his mother very quickly.

"Xavier's dad, his two brothers, his grandfather, and three uncles did seasonal work. Comin' home at the end of a harvest, their bus was hijacked in Nicaragua and they were killed. Makes you wonder how much shit can actually happen to one family.

"One night, Paul was particularly restless. For several nights, he'd been havin' dreams. We went to bed kinda early. I'd just fallen asleep when someone pounded on the door. When we opened it, a young boy we knew begged us to follow him. We took off with him.

"We got to Xavier's house. It was hard to figure out what was goin' on. Women were wailin'. Some of them grabbed us, others just pleaded. We walked through a small, crowded hallway and then into the kitchen. It was there . . ." John stroked his chin as he stared into the ravine.

I yearned to comfort him like he had done for me so many times. Wanting not to embarrass him, I remained silent.

Marc fidgeted. A gust whipped embers about. "John, I, um, I didn't mean to pry. We can talk about something else if you want."

John added more logs to the fire, but his eyes never left the ground. Twiddling in the ashes, he finally looked up. "We found Maria on the floor holdin' Xavier. He was bleeding and dying in her arms. Maria called us to her side. But I couldn't move. I couldn't believe my eyes.

"Paul dropped down to his knees and applied pressure to stop the bleeding. I drew closer to him. Xavier's body jerked. He took a deep breath, and then his body went limp.

"Maria closed his eyes. A tear dripped down her cheek. She looked and asked me to find a priest. I was so caught up in what was happening that it took a few moments for her request to sink in. I told the young boy who had brought us to go for one.

"It felt like a year, just waitin' for that priest. But Paul just sat by Maria, holdin' her hand while she held Xavier. The priest arrived. It was Father Barrios. He anointed Xavier's bullet-laden body. Until then, I had no idea of the hurt and emptiness that Paul had been livin' with. I felt so confused. I was in a stupor like I'd never felt before. It was more than I could bear.

"The police finally arrived. They told Paul that one of the assailants had been shot and killed, but the other had been captured and was being held in jail. Paul was so calm, speaking so softly as he told Maria, just helpin' her clean every drop of blood off of Xavier. I couldn't do it."

"Do what?"

"I'm trained to save lives, not prepare them for death and burial. I'm not wired that way. But Paul, he sat right there by her, never once flinchin', never once turnin' away. The police attempted to question Maria, and Paul just talked with her, gettin' her to answer. I wondered how he could be so still at a time like that. For someone who never sees himself as strong, my God, Marc, he just didn't stray.

"He and Maria prepared Xavier with the love of a mother welcomin' a newborn. And Paul cared for him like a brother. Maria spoke to Xavier as she and Paul dressed him. She never wept, although her tears streamed gently down her cheek. Paul would reach up every now and then and gently wipe the tears away with his thumb.

"When they finished, she looked at Paul and asked him to take her to the jail. I didn't think it was a good idea. She had been so calm through it all. I thought she was gonna come unglued when she saw her son's killer. But Paul insisted.

"We arrived at the jail to an eerie silence. Maria asked an officer to see the man who had killed her son. The officer escorted her to a back room. She motioned for us to follow. Behind bars, bruised badly, and bleedin', sat the small frame of a boy no older than Xavier himself. Maria's face flushed. She asked the officer to open the cell door. He looked to me. Even in my fear I signaled him to do it.

"She entered the cell. She looked at the boy and then lifted his chin. I thought she was gonna slap him, but she whispered in Spanish, 'You took my son, the only one I had left.' She placed her rosary in his hand. 'You must now take his place.'

"She firmly instructed us to get fresh water and towels so she could tend to his wounds. She then placed her arms around her son's killer, huggin' and holdin' him as they both wept.

"Maria appeared at his trial, not as his accuser, but as his advocate. She told the courts of the awful life this young man had lived, how being orphaned had victimized him, how he was forced to live on the streets. She even chastised the court and the government for allowing such things to happen to young people like this boy.

"They sent him to a prison many miles from Maria's home. Everyday after work she'd make the journey to see him. Her friends thought she was crazy. Some stopped speakin' to her, others had very little to do with her. What little money she made was invested in him.

"When we left South America a few weeks later, Maria gave Paul and me each a chain with a cross. I never take it off." He opened his jacket and cradled the cross from his shirt for Marc to see.

Marc leaned over to touch it. "Solid gold! It's beautiful."

"Belonged to one of her sons." The glowing red rocks surrounding the fire added warmth to the rapidly chilling air. Sunrays once streaming into the crevasse now cast shadows against the walls. John reached for his backpack. "Just before comin' here, we got this newspaper editorial from Maria." He lifted the article from his Bible and handed it to Marc.

"It's in Spanish."

"I forgot. I'll translate."

"In a time when few stories have happy endings, Juan Garcia was released from prison today. This one-time murderer walked hand in hand with the mother of his victim, Mrs. Maria Rosa. Just eight years ago, Mr. Garcia shot and killed Mrs. Rosa's son, Xavier, in a robbery.

"Having received a life sentence, Mrs. Rosa pleaded with prison officials to release Mr. Garcia, citing that he was a changed man who had paid enough for his crime. Mrs. Rosa's efforts received national attention and weeks ago Mr. Garcia's sentence was commuted on her behalf.

"Since the night of her son's murder, Mrs. Rosa has visited Mr. Garcia daily. When asked why, Mrs. Rosa simply stated, 'He is my son.' Mr. Garcia will take up residence with Mrs. Rosa.

"Mr. Garcia was questioned as to his feelings about Mrs. Rosa's generosity. He stated. 'I never knew my mother. She died when I was a baby. Maria treats me like her son. She has lavished love on me, even when I least deserved it. I can't even think about being that man, the one that killed her son—so lost, so helpless, so filled with self-pity and anger.

Today I am still far less the man I want to be, but so much more of the man I would have been were it not for Maria.'

"Though a mortal wound inflicted by this man killed her son, Mrs. Rosa never allowed herself to be victimized by it. Rather, she exhibited courage and strength beyond compare. Through it emerged compassion that healed her wound and that of Mr. Garcia. He has become truly her son. She is his mother. Mrs. Rosa is an example for us all. We would only be so lucky to have more people like her."

The paper crinkled as John carefully folded it along the creases. He stored it in his Bible. "If there were any doubts in my mind about goin' to medical school, they ended the day Xavier died. But I've wondered for years how and why God would let things like Xavier's murder occur.

"For some time, I thought this was about me tryin' to get some understandin' of what Paul feels. But after readin' this, I think it's more about me. Meg, my wife. She'd tell me all the time that Paul was the best thing that ever happened to me. I thought I understood what she meant until I lost her."

Even in the scant light, I watched as the blood drained from John's face, leaving him in horror and pain. His jaw clinched as he fiddled with the fire. The blank stare on his face suggested that memory was playing itself like a film reel in the movies.

John cleared his throat. "Meg and I hadn't been married long." The words floated softly off his lips. "We were only weeks from graduation, so we decided to start a family. She went in for a routine medical examination.

"It was a Wednesday mornin'. We walked out of our small uptown apartment on St. Charles. Meg heard a lawn mower buzzin' across the median. She loved the smell of fresh cut grass. She ran across the street, threw off her sandals, and was just wigglin' her toes in the grass.

"We climbed aboard a streetcar, with sandals in hand. Meg smiled at me and grabbed my hand the minute we sat. She loved streetcars, the clangin' bell, the rickety sound it made on the tracks. As we made our way downtown, she grabbed her big floppy straw hat. The breeze almost blew it off. She loved spring and had just bought a new flower print sundress. She'd pinch it between her legs to stop it from bein' blown up. She was every hippie's dream of a Southern belle flower child, and New Orleans was her city.

"We got to the clinic shortly after lunch. I had gotten a great residency at John's Hopkins. We'd already found a little house up there. All Meg could talk about were names and what color we'd paint the nursery. But everything changed that afternoon."

"Was it Cancer?"

"Words can't describe the cruelty of watchin' a loved one die. It aches in the bowels of your gut. Every hair hurts. Even your skin. You just try to breathe, but the next breath is all you can hope for. Nothin' makes sense. No one can make the hurt go away.

"Paul and Anne never left my side. After Meg, they were all I had left. He was there for me, insisting that I go on."

"He's an incredible friend."

"Like no other I've had. I couldn't have a blood brother and love him any more."

My gut tightened. Haunted by Meg's death and that of Andre, Father, Kevin, and Xavier, the images, the dreams of the lady terrified me. I had to tell him. "No. I'm not!"

"Paul, what is it? Wake up, pal. You're dreamin' again."

"No! I'm not dreaming! I heard every word. It's all my fault."

"Paul, look at me man. What's—"

"I knew." My voice faded. "I'm not your best friend. I wouldn't have let it happen."

"Let what happen?"

"You don't understand." I looked away to disguise the shame.

John placed his hand on my shoulder. "Paul, what is it?" It was like that day in the giant oak when I told him the story, at least part of it.

Finally his eyes caught mine. I couldn't deflect it. The energy was too strong, the desire too great.

"I've never admitted this, but when I went to Manresa I—"

"You talked to Father Barrios, didn't you?"

I searched John's eyes for the courage to go on.

"Paul, what did you tell him?"

"Every time I love someone, they die. It's like I'm a victim of some master plot to screw with my life. People tell me that what I've lived through is God's will, and I should just accept it. But if it's God's will, why is it so damn hard, so painful? I thought Jesus was sent to earth to help us, to ease our burden. I . . . I won't accept all this tragedy as God's will. He just can't be that much of a son of a bitch."

"Did that priest tell you that all the crap you've lived through is God's will? 'Cause its not! What could possibly motivate God to be that vicious? The God I believe in is too kind for that."

"Then why does God show us bad things and then not help us, I mean, not tell us how to stop them from happening?"

"Stop what from happenin'?" He locked into a stare, piercing through my silence. I tried to look away, but couldn't.

"Just a year before my father died, I dreamt about Andre's death. Then a year later, it was Father. Kevin and Xavier were next, and—" My voice cracked. "Meg."

John blanched. He turned away.

"I should have told you." Fear enveloped me. I bore the guilt of surviving, of knowing and saying nothing. I felt responsible for it all.

"You dreamed she died?"

"Yes. And, she was pregnant."

John's face greened. Sweat beaded on his forehead. "We never told anyone." His head dipped. He glared into the fire. "I've gotta stretch. Can ya—"

Marc stood with him. "Go ahead. I'll keep an eye on him."

"John—" The wind swirled dry leaves on the crevasse floor.

"I can't talk about it right now, pal. I'm sorry." John pulled himself out of the crevasse. Small rocks and pebbles tumbled down the side again.

Marc rested his hand on my shoulder. "Why don't you rest for a while, Paul?"

I had hurt John beyond repair. But what if I had told him and I was wrong? Or worse yet, what if I had told him and ruined the six months of happiness he and Meg had when they were unaware? Would revealing what I knew have changed the outcome?

I closed my eyes to the hurtful look of John's face. Since Meg's death I had not seen anguish in his eyes like that.

"Paul," Marc whispered, "I've got to check your dressings." He lifted the covers. I couldn't help cringing. "Try to relax." Marc bundled a clump of snow in a shirt. "It'll help get the swelling down. I'd sing to you to take your mind off of it, but Ivan told me I sing like two dying animals fighting in a barn."

My smile yielded to thoughts of John. For all the times he added humor to whatever was going on, now when he needed me most, I was unable to help.

Marc's eyes warmed as he held the snow to my side. "How's the pain?"

"Kind of a dull throb."

"I'll give you another small dose of the painkiller." I barley felt the stick this time from the snow numbing my side. "Why don't you just get a little rest?"

"Maybe you should go after John."

"I think he's fine. You've got to get better so we can get home. Rest will make the difference." Even though I knew Marc was right, my thoughts were absorbed with John, but the effect of the medication overcame my concern.

■

"Hey there, Sleepin' Beauty." I was relieved to hear John's voice. "You had one hell of a nap. I don't think you've slept four consecutive hours since I've known you." John warmed cans of food on the fire. The aroma caused my stomach to growl. "Are you hungry?"

"Yes."

"Good. We've got hash a la John. It's shitty, but the taste will only be surpassed by the texture." John scooped healthy servings back into the cans. "Boys, dinner is served."

I started to pull myself up.

Marc supported my back to lift me. "Let's ask for help, please."

"Man, you look a hell of a lot better." John handed me the hash. "Take your time. Let's get it down and keep it down."

Marc sniffed the hash. "So John, did you find anything interesting out there?"

"Rocks, trees, a couple of wild sheep."

Were we ever going to make it home? It seemed like a lifetime since we first arrived. Our reason for coming here blurred. This search for deeper meaning and truth had turned into a contest for survival. Why had we positioned ourselves this way? What were we thinking when we came here? Where was our sensibility?

The sun settled just over the peak of the neighboring cliff. A cluster of small clouds drifted, causing its rays to brush the sky in color.

Marc turned to John. "Beautiful, isn't it?"

"God streakin' his signature on the heavens. Paul's grandma calls it a 'peace sky'." A sunset breeze whisked through the crevasse. Distant clouds signaled the approach of another front. "Marc, what say we clean up? It's time to extinguish the fire."

"What do you want to do with the cans?"

"Let's pack 'em away. I'll find some place to bury them. Don't wanna leave a trace."

With the flames extinguished, the glow of the dying embers warmed us and brightened our den. We huddled into the sleeping bags. I pretended to fall asleep to the crackle of the remaining twigs. Marc cleared his throat and stirred like he was uneasy. "John, how long have you known Paul?"

"We met in high school. We've been friends ever since. Why?"

"I've never seen two friends care for each other the way that you do."

"Yeah, he's like my kid brother. I didn't have any brothers or sisters growin' up. My parents adopted me when I was a baby. Neither of them had brothers or sisters. Other than my parents, Paul's the only family I have. Don't get me wrong, my parents loved me better than anyone could've. But they were so old when they adopted me, and now they're both gone. When Meg died, I thought I lost everything. Paul didn't let that happen."

"He's pretty amazing, even though he still confuses me at times."

"I know. He takes a lot of folks by surprise. I think he's actually afraid of who he is. It's like he has all this capability, does wonderful things with it, and then runs when anyone notices what he's done."

"So, is that why you guys came here? This is a hell of a place to vacation."

"The last couple of years have been really hard on Paul. It's like everything he's dealt with, all the loss, finally took its toll. At times he's been so distant that even his wife, Anne, couldn't reach him. When we were on retreat, I experienced somethin'. I'm still not sure what to think about it. But, comin' here seemed like the right thing to do."

My lips started moving. "I'm so sorry. I'm so sorry." Regret rushed over me. My ears burned from the heat leaving my body. "I should have told you. It's my fault. I'm so—"

"Paul?"

"John, I'm so sorry. I should have—"

"Whoa, pal! You can't think you're responsible for Meg's death. You had a nightmare. You can't hold yourself responsible for that. It's not your fault, or mine, or anyone's for that matter. Sometimes bad things happen."

"I could have told you. When you left the crevasse—"

"I was disappointed with myself for not tellin' you about her bein' pregnant, for runnin' the risk of destroying our friendship. It's been almost two years. I could've said somethin' to you."

"Two years. That's like yesterday when you lose someone you love."

"Well, I've lost one of you. I'm not gonna lose another."

The wind howled. The very sound chilled me. I started to shiver. The day yielded to the desolation of the night. But Marc and John shielded me from the brunt of it. Marc huddled closer. John zipped our sleeping bags to the very top.

I was alone in my thoughts, but not alone to myself. Marc and John were nearby, so close that I could hear, almost feel, their breathing. In their protection, no harm could come to me. But, were they safe from whatever karma followed me?

As I drifted into the cloak of slumber, the words "I choose you" hexed me once more. With it, the images of Andre, Father, Kevin, Xavier, and Meg appeared. Yet it was the unknown visions of the future that haunted me most.

Twenty

December 11, 1986

The frost stung my face. In spite of sleeping on the ground with nothing more than a sleeping bag and the clothes on my body separating me from it, I felt stronger. The night produced many things, including snow. With a drift mounded at the entrance of the crevasse, a hush enveloped the morning. As the sun rose, light filled the crevasse. With its rays reflecting off the blanket of white, John stirred. "Good mornin', gents. It's amazing what snow-covered ground and blue skies does for a day."

Marc shivered. "Hey, John. You need help with the fire?"

"Is that a hint?" John lifted out of the sleeping bags. A chill raced down my spine.

Marc pulled the covers tightly over himself. "I changed my mind. It was warmer when you were in the bag."

"Get up, lie down. The big man has to do all the work."

"Light the fire already." Marc grimaced. "Does he always bitch this much?"

I nodded as my teeth chattered.

"Y'all wanna fire or should I just let y'all freeze." The dry logs crackled as the fire warmed us. I sat up even though my movements were stiff. "Easy, Paul." John nudged closer. "How about breakfast?"

Marc's brows knitted together. "We've still got food?"

"Nope. Life's been good, but it's time to get sustenance and find our way home. Didn't find much yesterday. There's gotta be a small village or somethin' nearby. Let's take care of Paul, then search the area." He loaded chunks of snow into our rain gear for water.

"This is looking much better." Marc cleaned my wound.

John added more logs to the fire, leaving several small ones in arm's reach. "Paul, we're gonna be as quick as possible. Promise me no heroics, no antics, no standing, no lifting, no moving—"

"I've got the general idea, John."

"But will you keep your little butt still while we're gone?" He raised an eyebrow. It was the "look," the one he gave me when he was in his parental mode. Oddly, it reassured me that they would be quick and more importantly careful.

"Go, already. I'm fine."

He and Marc climbed out of the crevasse. The new fallen snow, now covering once barren and darkened earth, cloaked winter's bleakness in a renewed sense of purity. The world hushed in quiet abandonment to it, reminding me of my days at Ridgefield when I first met John. Every year we joined Father Cavender as he marched into the commons on what he described as "the event of the first snowfall." Standing in salute to the art he loved—poetry—the entire student body gathered with him. In oration, he commemorated the day with a reading from Robert Frost, inviting all of us to join him in his discourse.

> "In the thick of teaming snowfall
> I saw my shadow on the snow.
> I turned and looked back up at the sky,
> Where we still look to ask why
> Of everything below.

If I shed such a darkness,
If the reason was in me,
That shadow of mine should show in form
Against the shapeless shadow of storm,
How swarthy I must be.

I turned and looked back upward.
The whole sky was blue;
And the thickest flakes floating at a pause
Were but frost knots on an airy gauze,
With the sun shining through."

With the words proclaimed, he would dismiss us for those rare moments of frolic.

Frolic? My childhood ended with Hurricane Betsy. And whatever innocence remained after that was shattered when my father died. Even so, every time I flipped on a television or radio, someone was being murdered, assassinated, or starved.

The Crusades, the Spanish Inquisition, the Holocaust, and even the fighting in Northern Ireland reflected a legacy of people dying at the hands of men all in the name of God. Then, added to that were earthquakes, floods, and other natural disasters. And what was so natural about it anyway? I wasn't sure who or what to trust.

Why would God create us in His likeness and image and then allow such cruel and seemingly senseless pain to overtake us? Could He be that way? Or, had we missed what He was truly about? My hope to find answers dwindled the moment I was injured.

As I waited for Marc and John, the sunlight drifted deeper into the crevasse. Water droplets trickled down the rocky embankment from melting snow. At last, warmth radiated off the rocky floors and walls. I closed my eyes. Hail Mary.

∎

"Mi znaydemo, de mozhna tut poisti?" My heart raced as voices carried through the woods above the crevasse. I hoped it was Marc and John. But from the sound of it, three, maybe four people approached.

"Dobre, ya zholodniw."

I slid deeper into the crevasse. As I rested, the cold wall chilled my back.

"Shozhe, bahato ludey zburaesta." More voices sounded from above. "Tak. Tse dobre. Moskali povinni zalishiti nam nashi i zaymatisa svoyimi." These were deeper voices than the first. If they were soldiers on patrol, they made no effort to be discreet, and they weren't speaking Russian.

Every few minutes, a group passed by. Without knowing where we were or who to trust, Marc and John might remain hidden until whoever was up there moved away.

But rocks tumbled from above. Marc's foot appeared at the crevasse edge. John followed. "I think we gotta go. I didn't see any police or soldiers. It's almost like the war is over."

I leaned forward. "So, what's happening up there?"

"It's the legend, Paul. We met a few pilgrims who spoke a little English. They've gotta statue like Ivan's. They're sayin' the lady will appear in a ravine nearby."

I started up. "Then let's go."

"Are you crazy? You'll pop every stitch Marc put in you. It's too risky. I'll—"

"Bullshit. I've come this far. I'm going with or—"

"Pound for pound, you're the most determined thing I've ever met." Our eyes met. I stared at him with as focused and determined of a gaze as I could muster. "All right. You win. But if we're gonna do this, we're gonna have to tape you up. Now can we sit?" John propped me against his backpack. "Marc."

"Paul, I'm going to tape your chest. You may find it a little hard to take full breaths, but it should hold the stitches. But remember, they're just stitches, so go easy."

I nodded.

Marc wrapped the tape around me. Even though my side hurt like hell, I didn't dare flinch.

"We're gonna take it nice and slow, pal." John instructed us. "Marc, I'm gonna hand our stuff up to you. Then we'll help Paul up."

Marc lifted up from the crevasse. More rocks pelted the ravine below us.

"Are you ready?" John shouted up to him.

"Send him up."

We moved to the crevasse edge. Marc dangled from above. "A little higher, John." Our hands clasped.

"I've got you, Paul. Let me do the work." John strained as he pushed me higher. My head rose above the ledge. A group of pilgrims smiled at us as they strolled by. It was the first time that I had seen the area surrounding us by day's light.

John emerged from below, gasping for breath. "Hold up for a moment. Let's rest against these rocks." More pilgrims strolled by. Bread poked out of their straw baskets. My stomach growled. "Well, gents, shall we join 'em?"

At first, my legs were wobbly. But as we followed the pilgrims down the slope along a stony path, I began to feel strength return. From time to time, we passed by small groups either resting or simply enjoying the crisp air and blue skies overhead.

We turned back into the woods. The sun pierced through the canopy lighting and warming our path. Marc pointed to the valley below. "Take a look at that view. The Psalm of David." With a snow-capped tree line cascading down the slope, large boulders protruded through the rocky knoll like statues carved in the natural landscape. Groups of wild goats waltzed about, grazing on spikes of patchy brown, dried grass. Only the brightly costumed pilgrims gathering towards a remote corner of the meadow seemed to bother these creatures.

"I wonder where all these people are coming from. The village only had thirty houses. You think they've walked from the city?"

"That's a long walk, Marc."

"Look. More coming from across that hill to the west." We followed a group, joining their procession as they moved towards a ravine. Carved into the hilly terrain, it meandered through a rocky shoal.

"The statue." John pointed towards the icon of Mary. Four men, wearing laced up knickers and blue vests with embroidered roses, carried the statue on a litter. An inlay of gold capped the aura surrounding her head. Pink roses crowned her blue veil. A tear trickled from her left eye down her cheek. She stood atop the moon with one foot stepping on a serpent. Goosebumps sprouted across my arms. The icon was an exact replica of Ivan's.

As we walked, the faint sounds of singing resounded through the narrowing rocky passage. "Ave, Ave, Ave, Maria. Ave, Ave, Ave, Maria." With the tenor of an angelic procession, they repeated the stanza "Hail, Mary." The walls continued to press upon us, drawing us closer to one another. Soon people around us joined the chorus of voices as we moved deeper into the ravine. "Ave, Ave, Ave Maria."

Suddenly, the migration stopped. An old woman approached us, using a cane to part the crowd. She stared at me as though she recognized me. Her blue eyes and broad smile, the blue veil over her head, her narrow cheeks were familiar. Somehow I knew her.

She motioned for us to move forward. I hesitated until the words "I will, to will, thy will" released me from my fear. We drew closer to a crevasse in a rocky shoal.

Marc froze. "It can't be, John."

"I'll be damned. It looks like the crevasse where we rested. We must have come down that ledge and turned back into the ravine. God only knows what's next."

A crystal clear stream flowed from a crack in the wall of the ravine, just to the right of the crevasse. Even though parts of it were frozen, water filled a small rocky bed. A few scraggly shrubs sprouted even in this desolate place. Some folks dipped their hands for a drink.

The men carrying the icon placed the litter below the entrance of the crevasse. The old woman grabbed my arm. "Follow." She pulled me forward. The crowd parted. John and Marc joined us.

"Can you smell it?"

Smell what? I thought.

"Look," Marc whispered.

The crowd gathered in very close. They knelt. The old woman leaned towards me. "They are praying to Her as She stands next to you."

Praying to whom? I saw no one near me except Marc, John, and her.

"Deep hurt closed your heart. You must open it to Her. She chooses you."

I looked into her sapphire blue eyes. "Chooses me. For what?"

The old woman drew closer. "Courage through fear. Open your heart to Her."

"Who?"

"The lady of your dreams."

Hair stood up on my arms and my neck. A rush of energy overtook me. "No. I can't, I . . . they die. Every time, they die."

"You fear being chosen. You think some who came before you have suffered much because of her, yes? Of earth this is true. But not of God."

"Why death? Why all the destruction and pestilence. There's so much despair, greed, hurt, disease, anger, war, famine. Why?"

"You haven't learned yet."

"Learned what? Tell me so that we might know."

"You see. She touches you. She avails Herself to you. She blesses you and all who have gathered."

"But " The crowd rose. In harmony and beauty as ever before heard on earth, they sang like a choir of angels. Marc and John stood mesmerized. They stared through me. For that matter, so were the masses gathered.

"What does she—" I turned to speak to the old woman, but she was gone. I searched the crowds. Where was this lady she was speaking of? Why couldn't I see her? Where was she? Dammit, where was she?

People reverently approached the icon. One by one, they kissed her feet. They sang, "Ave, Ave, Ave, Maria," as the crowd pressed in. People milled around me. Rosary beads rattled as those gathered nearest the crevasse began to pray. More knelt in adoration. I felt exposed, yet alone. I dropped to my knees. Marc and John rushed to me. I knew of no other place to go.

As the words "Hail Mary" tripped off my lips, John and even Marc knelt beside me. With our shoulders touching, we prayed. The memory of Andre, Father, Xavier, Kevin, and Meg flooded my senses with an overwhelming sense of loss. To feel the pain again was more than I wished to experience, especially here and now.

"Amen." The crowd rose. I wondered if our efforts were misguided. Yet, even in the midst of the chaos raging just miles from these walls, many of them calmly touched me. Some spoke to me, but I could not understand them. Why here and now?

We waited near the crevasse until they dispersed. The sun ushered late afternoon as it slipped behind the walls of the ravine.

We departed the crevasse with a few of the faithful remaining behind. A profound hush pervaded their prayer. Marc and John mirrored this reflective mood as we moved slowly through the widening path to the world outside.

We walked in silence, speaking volumes in it, yet saying nothing to each other. Our contemplative continence suggested thoughts reaching far beyond the events of the day. I was certain that Marc and John too were rationalizing what had happened to us. After all, the Mother of God did not appear to people like us. We had allowed ourselves through our fatigue to be caught up in nothing more than a deified form of hysteria.

Our footsteps dragged along the rocky path. Snow crunched under the weight of our bodies and the sound echoed against the stone walls.

We exited the ravine. Marc and John, both of whom had exercised such careful restraint over the past several days, appeared lost in the moment. Had it not dawned on them that we would soon be in an open field, with nothing protecting us except our wits? The crevasse and the event that had transpired were quickly fading into the reality we once left behind. War had in fact broken out here, and although we had participated in a welcome refrain from it, we needed to regain our caution.

We entered the field that had guided us to the ravine. The dazzling sun made me long for home. Yet I had no time to reminisce. In the open field, we were easy targets.

Marc's and John's continued lack of awareness perplexed me. We wandered across the field like the Jews aimlessly through the dessert. Judging against the sun setting, we walked for over an hour.

Finally John spoke. "What's that?" A small cottage and barn, nestled in a remote corner of the field, broached the forest. We stopped several hundred yards away. "It looks abandoned. I don't see any lights on. Wait here with Paul while I check it out." John crouched as he approached the barn. His frame blended into the landscape.

Marc helped me to a large rock. There we rested. A curtain of stars shimmered in the blackened sky. Marc stared into the firmament. Only his silhouette was visible.

There was no movement, no air, no animals, nothing. Stillness pervaded. Marc's head bowed. His lips moved. I slowly nudged closer, careful not to disturb him. In a whisper he spoke. "Sherma, Israel, Adonai, Elohainu, Adonai, Echod."

Chills ran up my spine as he recited the words, "Hear of Israel, the Lord thy God, the Lord is One." Marc's prayer was devout, his focus resolute. Like a bird perched on a windowsill quietly watching, I secretly communed with Marc. We gazed at the heavens, watching the constellations go by. The beauty of Marc's prayer burned deeply into my memory.

John joined me on the rock. In a whisper he said, "I've been observing you two for awhile. It's like artistry in motion. I want you to know you're the brother I never had and that I dreamed of havin' since I was a small boy. I always knew you were special, but until today I never knew how much. You're truly blessed. So much now makes sense."

"What do you mean?" I pulled away. My sudden movement startled Marc.

"Today in the ravine . . . the lady."

"It was incredible." Marc joined him. "I never entertained that God could manifest in this way. As we walked through the ravine, I initially thought I was insane. What was a Jewish boy doing among a group of Gentiles, especially in the environment surrounding us? Hell, I have to admit that when I thought about where we were, and then realized how bad Paul was injured, I thought we were all nuts.

"But, as we approached the crevasse, a sense of peace seized me. Everything we'd been through seemed inconsequential to what we were experiencing. It made absolutely no sense, yet I was clear about what we were doing. It's the most profound day in my life. What was it like to be near her?"

"Who are you speaking of?"

"The lady. You know, that beautiful lady with the blue veil standing near you today in the crevasse."

"Beautiful lady?"

"There was a beautiful lady guiding you. She spoke with you and touched you. In all my years I have never witnessed such beauty."

"You thought that the old woman was beautiful?"

"No, Paul. The young lady next to you!"

"There was no young lady next to me."

John stood. "Don't be coy. I saw her, too. She held your hand and spoke with you. First there was the smell of roses, then the clouds formed around the sun like doors openin' up."

"I don't know what the hell you two are talking about. When we were walking through the ravine and got near the crevasse, an old woman approached me. She told me to move to the front and I did as she instructed. We got to the front of the crowd, just below the crevasse, and she told me about some lady. But I never saw or heard her. You were both standing right there beside me. What part did you miss?"

"Are you tellin' me that today in the ravine you didn't smell the scent of roses?"

"No, John. Just our stench. By the way, we could all use a bath."

"You never saw the clouds form in the sky outta nowhere?"

"Nothing but the ravine, the stream, and the crevasse under clear blue skies. And, by the way, no rose bushes either. Hell, there were scarcely any plants growing there."

"So you're sayin' no roses, no clouds, no nothin'. And you didn't see the beautiful lady?"

"What beautiful lady? I'm sure that the old woman standing next to me could have been a real beauty once. And, quite candidly, she was still quite beautiful in a grandmotherly sort of way, her blue eyes and what not. But I wouldn't go chasing after her. I haven't been away from Anne that long!"

"You sacrilegious little shit. How can you even talk about today that way?"

"What the hell are you talking about? We went into a ravine with a crowd of people we didn't know. They sang and prayed, an old woman talked to me, the crowds seemed impressed, and then we left. What's so sacrilegious about my comments?"

"You really didn't see her?" Silence gripped us. With the day's breeze emerging into a staunch wind, I zipped my jacket. A meteor streaked across the sky, then another. In a shower of light, one cosmic rock after another ended its journey by burning in the earth's atmosphere.

"Boys, it's time to move this party inside. The barn's empty and warm. Looks like whoever lives here has left for the winter." John led the way. The grassy meadow opened into a clearing as we neared the barn. The logs shaping its walls blended into the night. A well, just at its entrance, sported a smooth tree bark as a lever to draw water.

The hinges of the barn door squeaked as we entered into darkness. John shut the door behind us. Pitch darkness engulfed us. "I'll take the lead. Just hold on to me." We felt our way toward what I thought to be a back corner. The smell of fresh, dry straw filled the air. Ah, finally a warm, soft place to rest for the night.

Starlight glowed through the single window of the barn. Our eyes adjusted, making shapes of hay bales and farm equipment noticeable. "Here we are. Home, sweet, home. It might not be the Ritz, but for tonight, it'll just have to do. Make yourselves comfy boys." Whoever constructed this barn must have been a master craftsman as the walls were sealed tightly together. The extra insulation would at least keep out the chill.

"Marc, give me a hand joinin' our sleepin' bags. It's gettin' cold pretty quick." He unloaded his backpack. With temperatures sure to fall well below the freezing mark, we had to preserve our body heat to prevent hypothermia.

Marc sniffed the air. "I smell something cooking."

"I have a little surprise for ya." John uncovered a hole in the earthen floors, with stones, nice and hot from a fire. "I took the liberty of preparin' dinner." The glow pierced the darkness. "We've got your basic rocks for warmth, a few potatoes bakin', and eggs boilin'."

"The food from the village."

"Yeah. We've got a bottle of wine, a loaf of bread, and cheese. Why don't you open the wine while I drain the water from the eggs."

Using John's Swiss Army knife, Marc popped the cork out of the bottle.

"Here you go, gents, the specialty of the house." With the embers crackling and the rocks glowing, we dined, first the potatoes, then the eggs. "How about some bread?"

We downed the food like starved men, chasing each bite with the wine's sweet nectar. There was little conversation. But Marc slowed his eating, dropping the bread he was holding in his hand. "Your cross."

John reached up and fingered the cross given to him by Maria. It sparkled even in the dim lighting of the kindling.

"The story about Maria, well, I mean, it—" Marc gazed into the darkness. He traced the walls with his eyes as if he was searching for something. Even his chest compressions shallowed.

John reached to him. "Marc—"

"I was eighteen when my father finally told me about my grandparents. I always knew something bugged him, but he's a very private man so I learned not to pry. We got drunk on my birthday. It was pretty late. We were waiting for a cab. All of a sudden he walked up to me and he blurted it out. 'I love you, son.'

"The cab didn't come. We started walking home. He got real quiet. I started to panic, thinking he was having a heart attack. But when we walked by Ivan's church, he went inside. Imagine two drunken Jewish men inside a Catholic church at two o'clock in the morning. He genuflected before he went into the pew and then knelt. I didn't even know he had ever been inside a Catholic church. He must have prayed for half an hour.

"When he finally sat back in the pew, he told me how he and my aunt were smuggled across the border to safety when the Nazis invaded L'vov. A Catholic priest took them in. A Jesuit. Father Andrei. Can you imagine that?"

"Father Andrei?"

"Yeh. He wanted to help the whole family escape. But my grandfather was a prominent man. He feared if he disappeared the Nazis would search for him, endangering our family's passage to safety. That's why he and my grandmother remained behind. That's when Father Andrei placed my father and my aunt into the care of Ivan's grandparents. They were sending their children to America and forged papers showing they had eight children, two more then they really had. They had lost a boy and a girl shortly after birth and had baptismal certificates for them. They slipped right through.

"My dad pointed to an icon in the church and told me about the statue. He told me how Ivan's father had it with him. When I saw it today and then had the experience in the crevasse, well I . . ." Horror gripped his face.

I wanted to reach out to Marc, but I could not.

"Is that why you ya went to Brody? To connect? To understand?"

"All those people. Some killed by the T'zars. Others by the Nazis. Still some by Cossacks. One whole family has an entire row of plots in the cemetery. And the survivors aren't even Jewish any longer. Can you imagine an entire family? Babin's, the merchant that Ivan's grandparents mentioned. His wife, she's a Babin. She has a marker in Brody, even though she's buried somewhere in these mountains."

Like a lightening flash striking the earth, all the hurt and rage I had buried stormed inside of me. My mind raced with renewed ferocity. Any number of rational thoughts could explain what I saw and experienced. But Marc and John appeared touched, moved by her. Their demeanor reflected it. Their tones echoed it. But when would the drama end?

Twenty-One

December 12, 1986

Light streamed through the dust particles floating in the air. With the single barn window only twenty or so feet away on the left I could almost see outdoors. I yearned to look outside and see the new land we had traversed by darkness. Marc and John sandwiched me, making my avenues of escape difficult. I lifted John's arm from across me and gently placed it by his side. I pushed forward, slithering out of the sleeping bag.

"Where do you think you're goin'?"

"To the window and shh! You'll wake Marc."

Marc sat up. "I'm already awake, and if you pop those stitches I put in you, I'm going to sew you up, including your legs, with a rusty needle."

"You're taking bossing lessons from John or something?"

"Yep. So just lay your butt down so I can take a look at your side." The tape pulled my raw skin even though Marc removed it carefully.

"Marc, you're gettin' pretty good at managing him." John strolled to the window. The light cast an aura around him. He blankly gazed out of the panes like he was searching for something.

With Marc's examination complete, I joined John.

"Let's get ready," he whispered.

"For what?"

"The crevasse." In a resolute tone and serious demeanor, he looked to Marc as if to demand his approval. "We're goin' back."

Marc patted his back. "That's right. When we talked to those women yesterday, they said there would be three days of visits by the lady."

"Then it's settled. Let's get packed and we'll be on our way." John moved to our campsite. He tossed dirt in the hole he had dug in the barn's earthen floors, then bundled our sleeping bags and picked up our gear. Why was John so hell-bent in going back there?

I remained at the window. The neatly hewed gray logs making up the other buildings matched the wooden shingles of the house. Wild sheep grazed on tall grass piercing the snow. Everything was just as it was supposed to be. Seeing the farmyard by day starkly contrasted feeling my way through it in the dark.

A plantation bell tolled in my head. Men paused in the sugarcane fields. Women stopped their morning chores. "The angel of the Lord—" Grandmother knelt with her rosary entwined in her fingers. She reached for Mim's hand and then Mother's. Anne joined them.

"Are you ready?" The warmth of John's breath brushed my ear.

"Just a few more minutes."

"We'll meet you outside." He pushed the barn door open and then joined Marc near the well. Stillness surrounded me. Maybe John was right. I really didn't get it. I was either incapable of letting go or just unwilling. After hiding behind the hurt for so long, I couldn't imagine living without it. What would I rage against then?

I looked over the barn one last time. The dust particles drifted, as if by design, searching for that ideal place to rest. In some ways they were lucky.

I joined Marc and John. We started walking towards the meadow. Ice crystals glistened against the blue skies like diamonds across a down blanket. Our feet crunched the snow. Steam spewed from our mouths as we hiked towards the ravine. John and Marc walked beside me. Fortunately, gentle, rolling meadow greeted us.

The sun continued to rise ahead. Rocks dotted the landscape. The hills became steeper and the grass sparser. Even the imprints of our feet shallowed as we stepped through the snow.

Soon, the walls of the ravine jutted at the end of the meadow. Marc pointed to a distant hill. "John, I see people over the ridge."

"Let's check them out." John crouched. Shielding his eyes, he carefully scanned the area. "There are more comin' from the north. They look like pilgrims on mules. We'll join them, but let's be careful."

Crossing another hill, we soon found ourselves just outside the ravine entrance. Chilled by the morning air, small groups huddled around campfires. Resting on large rocks and boulders, they dined from open baskets. Many of them watched us as we made our way through the crowd.

An elderly gentleman draped in a brown cloak motioned us to join him. "Sidayte, yizhte." His pants were tucked into his boots. White stripes and shoulder fringes decorated his cloak. A round sheepskin cap with flaps covered his ears. He lifted a cup towards us. "Priyednuytes do nas." He filled three cups and tore chunks of bread. "Yizhte."

John accepted the cup of coffee. "I guess he wants us to join him. Spasibo."

"I don't think he's speaking Russian. I'm pretty sure he's a Hutzul. They're the folks who live in this region of the Carpathians. Remember Olga?" I nodded at the old man.

A smile broadened across his weathered face as we ate. "Tse dobra yizha dla vas."

I nodded.

The crowds thickened around us. I searched for the old woman, hoping to ask her questions about the day before. But a young woman, looking somewhat like her, milled about. Where most of the women sported sheepskin jackets with cherry colored velvet or yellow wool, she had a blue cape draped over her head and body. She walked to the ravine. The crowds rose and moved as well. John and Marc followed.

We entered to many greeting us with smiles. Others gestured for us to move ahead in the ever-tightening space. A path cleared. "Ave. Ave. Ave, Maria," peeled forth in harmony from the crowds. It echoed off the stone walls.

We neared the crevasse. It stood above us, silhouetted by the sun. The crowds pressed tightly together. They waited, singing and praying.

A shadow fell upon us from clouds drifting in front of the sun. Suddenly, the crevasse glowed, sending rays of light piercing through the darkened sky. I looked towards the crowd. Many of them pointed to the heavens, while others fell to their knees. Even Marc and John fixated on the firmament.

The smell of roses overwhelmed me. But I could find no bush.

The crowd stilled to movement on the crevasse ledge above us. Many of them lifted their hands to shield their faces. The brilliance of the celestial creature had to blind them as it blinded me. Yet I could not remove my eyes from her.

The glow dimmed. The young lady who had led us into the ravine stood in the crevasse above me. Rose petals drizzled over her body-length blue veil, collecting at her feet. Her divinity shimmered through the gold inlayed robe while her blue eyes softly searched the masses gathered before her. Was she real?

"Paul."

Warmth engulfed me. "The angel of the Lord declared unto Mary and she conceived by the Holy Spirit." The words flowed off my lips. For years, I had heard her voice inviting me to see and hear of those events to come.

"Hail Mary full of grace the Lord is with you, blessed are you among woman and blessed is the fruit of your womb, Jesus. Holy Mary, Mother of God, pray for us sinners now and at the hour of our death.

"Behold the handmaiden of the Lord. Be it done to me according to your word." Fear enveloped me.

"Paul." She spoke again. "Heal my people. Touch them. They need you as you need them." My flesh prickled on the back of my neck. "I know. It frightens you. We all fear. Even I feared at one time. We are here for each other. Reach to them. Let them reach to you."

Pilgrims rose around me. I scanned the ravine. "Ave, Ave, Ave Maria" peeled against the rocks. Marc and John now stood. I looked back to the crevasse. But she was no longer there.

The crowds pressed even closer upon us. Many of them reached to touch me. Hesitantly, I reached back. They grabbed my hands and then my arms. I could not resist their pull. In the sea of humanity before me were so many in need, their ailing bodies wrenched in pain from injury or disease. Some were dying, surely searching for a stay from the destiny seeking them or some reassurance that the next life would be better.

A woman's pleading voice tugged my heart. Her rough hands and wiry hair suggested she had aged quicker than her years. "Os miy malenkiy hlopchik, vin strazhdaye." Our eyes met. There before me lay a little boy, his body mangled from life's fury. "Bud laska, dopomozhit yomu." Even in a language I did not understand, her supplication crooned through. Her conviction was simple, childlike in its nature. Clearly she had little other than that.

I fell to my knees. John lunged towards me. "Paul!"

"I'm fine." Seeing the boy was like seeing Andre. I could do little then, and even less now. Even in his mother's grief I could offer little to comfort her. Why would the lady ask me to heal him when I had no capability to do so? If she were God's messenger, certainly she knew this.

"Bod laska, vilikuyte yoho," his mother pleaded.

John moved in to help. "Let us take a look at him. Polio! In this age."

"Is there anything you guys can do?" I looked to Marc and John, but they said nothing.

We sat until shadows replaced the sunrays. *Please heal him,* I thought. The dark circles under the boy's eyes bulged against his pale complexion. Yet, he smiled. I closed my eyes. "Please heal him." I whispered this time. My heartfelt compassion was all I could offer.

The young man's family lifted the gurney holding him. I looked to his mother. Even for what I had seen and heard, little had come of it. As they carried him away, the young man lifted his head. Although I had done nothing to ease his pain, his eyes warmly greeted me. I stood until I could see him no more.

The crowds thinned. We walked slowly, at times visiting with the pilgrims, never really knowing what they were saying. Yet their eyes told their story. They too longed for miracles. Their maladies, their pain, their suffering were made worse by their country being at war. It just exacerbated the situation all the more. On this day, there were to be no such miracles though.

An old man touched my arm as if I were some long awaited prize for his faithfulness. He smiled at my presence with him. Was this what faith really meant? If so, I saw my hollowness for what it was. If only my presence, my touch, could do more.

The sun hovered just above the horizon as we exited the crevasse. Many now made their way back into the hills and forest surrounding the ravine. Their bodies dotted the meadow for just a moment and then disappeared into the tree line. John pointed to a large rock just outside the ravine. "Let's rest for a minute." Pilgrims streamed by us. Some smiled. Others made the sign of the cross. Still others paused to speak to us.

Why me? What was so important that She would ask me to do the things She did?

"Whacha thinkin' about, pal?"

"Nothing really."

"Yeah, like the nothin' that keeps you up all night." Coiling like a cobra, crown and sheath fully exposed, he warned of his impending strike. "You really don't get it, do you?"

"Get what?"

"I've worked with you, studied with you, and gotten drunk as a skunk with you. Hell, I've even prayed with you. There aren't many things I've seen, heard, or done that you weren't right there with me. Yet, through it all, I've never once seen you think about yourself."

"All I do is think about myself."

"Yeah, right. Like when Meg got sick. Or how about that drunk kid in New Orleans, you remember the one at Mardi Gras when you arranged the cab ride. Or maybe—"

"Maybe, what? What have I done? Look around us. Look at them! They're the ones we should think about. The things we should do or maybe not do! It's all about them. For all intended purposes I'm a twenty-four-seven, three-sixty-five piece of work, in need of full attention all around the clock. No wonder God doesn't have time for anybody else!"

"As you'd say, 'to my point.' You don't get it."

I stood.

"Stop!" He grabbed my arm. "Hear me out. When Meg got sick, you never once left my side. When all was said and done, and praise was handed out, you had already quietly slipped away. Of course you didn't leave until you were sure everything had been handled and was okay. Man, you've helped others when most would have given up. You've reached out when others would not have even thought to do so.

"I've read what folks write about you. For that fact I've read what they've written to you. Anne shows me. You'd never think of sharin' these with anyone. They're all too private and personal. But I know. So does she. We see you differently than you see yourself. But heaven would stop the spinnin' of the earth before we ever got you to see things that way."

"John, you don't really know me."

"Like hell I don't! You think I don't know how sad you feel? Maybe I've missed those times when you're in the middle of a crowd, yet a million miles away? You think for a moment I've missed the quiet tears you shed when you've witnessed an accident or seen an injustice?"

"But—"

"But, what? Do you think that you've been foolin' me, for even a moment? I've watched you deal with shit that would stagger the imagination of most. I've watched you reach out, helpin' others, even when you felt like crap. Do you really think that helpin' others because you hurt inside is a bad thing?"

Weren't we supposed to do good just because it was good?

John came closer to me. He lifted my head. His steely blue eyes locked onto my own. It felt like he was inside me. I wanted to look away, but I could not. "It's that very quality of givin', when you feel most incapable or most unwilling to give, that I and so many others admire in you. And just because you do that because you hurt inside, well, can't you see that makes it even that much more special?"

I lowered my head. My suffering paled in comparison to what I had seen this day.

"Dammit, Paul! Look at me!"

The veins in my neck pounded with each pulse of blood.

"I know who you are. You offer your life as a sacrifice, as a beacon to show those of us who've experienced hurt and loss that it's okay—" John looked to the sky. He drew a deep breath. "I'd have given up if it weren't for you."

For years, it was he who had supported me. How could he possibly say this?

"I know exactly what you mean, John." Marc rested his hand on my shoulder. "Paul, I saw what you did that first night I met you. You walked outdoors and gave those two old men your jackets. You didn't think I saw you. But I did."

Blood rushed to my face.

"You're like the Psalms, '. . . such knowledge is too wonderful for me, too lofty for me to obtain.' My dad always said God works through us even when we think ourselves least worthy and when we least expect it."

"Yeah, pal. Like St. Paul, it's through our weaknesses that we find our strengths."

Could this be true? Were they correct?

"I could tell hundreds of stories about the good things you've done, but I don't think it would matter to you. I really don't think you get it. That's why I agreed to come here with you. I . . . ." John's voice faded. A young man lurking around us drew my attention away. His face and his gate were familiar. Had I seen him before? "Paul, are you listenin'?"

"What's that?"

"Just as I thought. I swear before I get you home we're gonna finish this discussion. Somebody's gotta get through that thick skull of yours." The wind whipped through the ravine just as John finished. Pulling his jacket collar up around his neck, he paused to survey the area.

The young man now loomed close by like a puppy circling its injured master. His wool pants and jacket were modern cuts, unlike the dress of the other locals. Even his backpack was an anomaly among the knapsacks, picnic baskets, and sheep's-skin bags of the pilgrims.

"I have home here." His accent was thick. "I vould please if you come and be zhere tonight."

John stood up and puffed his chest even though the young man towered over him.

"Please to share my home vit you." He smiled.

"Do we know you?"

"Da. I meet you church vit Father Andrei."

John snapped his finger. "You're the novice, the priest with Father Andrei from the Cathedral. I knew you looked familiar. I'm sorry for not recognizing you. Whacha doin' way out here?"

"Family home here and in Poland. I help sick. Bring medicine from city vhen find. Smuggle across border."

"Well, you are a sight for sore eyes. How far is your home?"

"Over four hills." He pointed to the northern corner of the meadow. "Ve go, da?"

"Da." John helped me to my feet.

We shadowed Oleksa across the meadow. Snow sloshed under my dragging feet. I stepped over a stone, almost stumbling. My foot hit the ground hard and I wrenched from the sharp pain in my side.

"Just a little farther, pal."

"Pascha, hurt? Come. I help. My home near." Oleksa wrapped his arms around me. "How zhis happen him?"

Marc shared some of the story. It made the journey go by quicker. We topped a hill, and then another. My legs grew weary from prodding through the thick grass and lifting over the occasional rock.

"Zhere, just over hill." As we climbed over the fourth hill, a cottage sat cloaked against the backdrop of the forest canopy. With twilight upon us, its gray logged exterior and white mud seams welcomed us.

Opening a wooden gate of a weathered picket fence, we walked along a stone path to the cottage. As we entered, a small fire glowed in the hearth. "You come. Sit by fire." Adding several logs, he stoked the flames. The wood crackled as heat rushed towards us.

Marc and John helped me into a chair beside the hearth. A wooden table, a few wooden chairs, and a bed filled the quaint one-room cottage. Compared to our recent accommodations, it was a luxury.

"I get food and drink. You please varm. Velcome my home."

"May we help?" Marc offered.

"Oleksa cook. You rest."

Oleksa scrambled fresh eggs adding cheese and sausage. As he prepared the feast, he set dried fruit and bread on the simple wooden table.

"Oleksa, did Father Andrei tell you anything about us?"

"Da. Father Andrei tell how Pasha fix Ivan statue. He happy for zhat." Hearing Oleksa say my name in Russian warmed me.

"Ivan. What of him? Do you know if he and his family are safe?"

"Net. Babo come to mass. Speak Father Andrei. Not sure vhat discuss." Silence enveloped the room." Ve pray for zheir safety, da?" We bowed our heads as Oleksa led us in prayer. "O kto Nykolaja ljubyt', o kto Nykolaju sluzhyt, tomu Svjatyj Nykolaj na vajakij chas pomahaj."

290

"That's beautiful, man. What did you say?"

"Pray Saint Nickolas Myra. Ask help time need. Please to eat, da."

We ate like starved men. Our appetites by most accounts would have been considered rude. "My food good for you. Da?" Our host appeared amused.

Marc patted his shoulder. "Da! Excellent. You're very kind to invite us here. Thank you for making us welcome."

"Oleksa, how far are we from the border?"

"You near Hrushiv. Poland twenty-five kilometer."

"Hrushiv. Do ya know Olga, the lady who's the friend of Ivan's grandmother?"

"Da."

"Maybe she can help."

"Ve not go willage. Better to go border."

"Easy to get across to Poland?"

"Net. Many troops. Passage fifty kilometers east. Must go to mountain passage. Wery narrow. Still wery dangerous now."

"How do you cross the mountains?"

"Train take us north willage Turka. Follow Dinister River. Zhen border little further. Border guard is Oleksa family. He allow cross and wisit family Poland. Ve . . ."

As John and Oleksa discussed government outposts and communication hubs, the dull throb of my side sharpened. I stood to walk it off, but I moaned in pain.

"Paul." Marc grabbed my arm. "Here, let's take a look."

"Put him bed." Oleksa rushed to a small double bed tucked in the corner.

"Sorry, guys."

Marc helped me down. "For what?"

"Being such a pain in the ass."

"No pain ass. Pain side, da?" Oleksa's smile broadened.

"You even got a priest making fun of you." John chuckled.

"It looks a little red and swollen." Marc probed it gently. "Probably from all the walking. Let's get it cleaned up and then you can rest. I'll give you the last of the painkiller I've got. That should let you rest without it bothering you tonight."

The medicine burned as before. With the bandages replaced, he taped the gauze to my side. Their voices faded. My eyes grew heavy. I felt myself drift off.

■

The crowds gathered as we neared the crevasse. The beauty of their smiles surrounded us on all sides. The smell of roses filled my senses. With the sun brightening the ravine, all seemed well.

"Ave, Ave, Ave Maria." We prayed and sang in anticipation of her arrival. The crowd pressed closer together.

A glow emanated from the crevasse above. The crowd kneeled. Her hands opened to greet them. The lady spoke, but I could not hear her words.

"I can't hear you. What is it that you want me to do?"

Shadows filled the crevasse. I looked up to a darkening sky. Thunder rumbled like the empty belly of a beast.

A woman dropped next to me. A pool of blood surrounded her body. Another man fell, then one more. Screams replaced the hymns of praise.

Gunfire crackled like lightning striking the ground. The crowd scattered, but there was no place to find shelter. Soldiers with rifles showered bullets on helpless victims. They were slaughtered before me, and there was nothing I could do for them.

Light reflected off my chest. I looked up at the whites of a soldier's eyes. He aimed his machine gun at his next victim.

"Paul." John rushed towards me.

"No!" I lunged to push him out of the way. More gunshots fired. A sharp sting, a numbing of sorts, rippled through my chest. I dropped to the ground. There in the ravine of "Our Lady," I lay dying, a pool of blood fanning around me. "Why? Why? Why?"

■

"Paul! Wake up, pal. You've had another nightmare." John stood over me with Marc and Oleksa nearby.

"Oh God, John," I caved into his arms, weeping. .

"Breathe, pal. I've got ya."

Marc grabbed my hand. Oleksa stroked my head to comfort me. But there was to be none. I had foreseen my death. But when?

"Paul, what happened?" John wanted me to speak. I could not. I would not.

Oleksa walked over to the hearth, adding wood to warm the cottage. I lifted up, but John stopped me. With their assistance, we left the bed and walked to the hearth. I stared at the floor.

"You wanna talk?"

I shook my head.

"Okay, then. Just rest."

Maybe by morning all of this would pass. Maybe I would awaken from the dream inside the dream. Anne would be there to greet me with her beautiful smile and warm laugh. This would prove the vision to be nothing more than a nightmare. No one, except me, would then need to know of its content.

Twenty-Two

December 13, 1986

Morning came. I reached for Anne, but she was not there. I woke as I had gone to sleep, in the hospitality of our newfound Ukrainian friend. Encircled by Marc and John, I was still in the place of my reverie. What I had hoped to be a dream seemed all too real.

Oleksa was already up. The aroma of hot bread filled the cottage. John rose from the bed. Dark circles encased his eyes. "Oleksa, can I give you a hand?"

"Breakfast ready. Let us eat." The wooden chairs surrounding the table rubbed the stone floor. Oleksa grabbed my hand and then John's. Marc joined us. "I pray English zhis morning. I apologize for vords not so good." He bowed his head. "Our Father, I ask you bless us. Food and drink, bread you give us good. For friends I ask safe trip today. For all you give I say zhanks. Purest wirgin mother Russian land, vit angels and saints ve magnify you. You ease suffering sinners vit hand. Do not let us perish. Keep us safe today. Amen."

Keep us safe today! We were nothing more than string-drawn puppets of a superior puppeteer. How could God manipulate and play us as ploys for Divine entertainment?

Oleksa served the bread and cheese. I ate even though my stomach churned.

John searched me with his eyes. I took a deep breath and then another. "You look a little pale. Are you okay?"

Maybe I wasn't being fair to him by hiding the content of the dream. But what if by sharing it I created the very outcome I hoped to avoid?

Throughout my life, religious authority told me not to hold onto life too tightly. Everything I learned on the plantation reflected that lesson. The crop came and went. Cattle and other farm animals were slaughtered for meat. Changes in the season signaled life and death cycles each year. In it, they all told me about the promise of life after death. But it seemed shallow when considering the price required for safe passage. The journey there was anything but safe. With that as a reference, who knew what actually awaited?

"More eat bread and cheese?"

"Thank you. It's quite good." Wishing not to offend him I forced a smile as I grabbed another small piece. With broadening eyes, he looked at me. Mim's eyes would enlarge that way any time she was concerned about me.

"This was another wonderful meal. Thanks, man." John cleared the dishes from the table. He cranked a hand pump several times, priming it until water flowed. At first it squeaked, but ceased with the first drip of water. The tub filled.

A couple of chickens cackled, joining the moo of a cow. Oleksa moved towards the window.

"Oleksa, ti v hati?" A young man's voice called from outdoors. It sounded as though he was speaking Ukrainian.

"Cousin come." Oleksa rushed to the door. A tall, gangly fellow greeted him. "Mischa, zahod. Zihriysa bila vohnu." Oleksa hugged him and then helped him with his topcoat. They walked together to the hearth and began warming themselves. From the side, he looked like my uncle.

"Hto voni?" Our guest nodded towards me.

"Moyi druzi z soboru, pro yakuy ya tobi rozpovidaw. Tu pamyataesh, Pascha?"

"Tak. Vin rozmovlaye Ukrainskoyu?"

"Ni, traha Rosiyskoyu." Oleksa faced us. "This is my cousin, Mischa. He guard border to Poland. He help us cross."

"Pleased to meet you, man. I'm John." He extended his hand.

"Good meet you, John. Oleksa tell me about you."

Oleksa showed them to the table. "Mischa, zhis Pascha."

"You fix statue of Wirgin Mary, da? Many people here know. You do good zhing." Mischa's charcoal eyes pierced through me. It was as if he knew something, beyond the repair of the statue.

I stood. "Gentlemen, if you would excuse me, I think I'll go for a short walk."

Marc moved to join me. "Actually that sounds like a good idea. John—"

"Y'all go ahead. I'll go over the plans with Oleksa and Mischa." John probed Mishca. "Are there many soldiers between here and the border?"

"Few in willages. Border still open. But ve get zhere before soldiers arrive, da?"

Thank God. They were talking about our escape. What a welcome reprieve from the path I had dreamed.

I could feel the warmth of the sunlight the moment we opened the door. Chickens scattered as Marc and I stepped into the gated farmyard. A weathered fence protected the rows of a naked and snow-covered small garden.

"You seem stronger, Paul."

"Feels that way."

"I bet you're ready to get home."

"More than you know, Marc." Puffy white clouds drifted from the south. A gentle breeze rustled the spotty grass of the meadow surrounding us, billowing through the canopy of conifers behind us. I was eager to return home. Anne's sweet scent seemed to fill the air. Her green eyes greeted me. Her brown hair flipped in the Gulf breeze. I wondered if the day was as bright and clear there as it was here. She loved days like this one.

Marc turned as the cottage door opened. John stepped out, toting our gear. "It's settled then. We'll meet you at the train. How do you say 'so long'?"

"Bud' zdorov."

John hugged Mischa. "Then, bud' zdorov. We'll see you soon."

"Nice meet you, Pascha." Mischa waved as he trekked towards the forest. "Soon you home." His silhouette quickly blended among the earthen colored bark of the trees.

"Well, boys, let's head home." John led us into the meadow. I lifted my eyes to the heavens. Maybe the thoughts that haunted me were nothing more than a hallucination no longer in control of us. We would forgo the ravine and head to Poland. I sighed in relief.

I peeked into the horizon for a brief moment. The puffy white clouds of earlier yielded to lower, flatter striations in the sky. Another front was building from the north. By day's end we were sure to see more turbulent weather, which made our choice to leave now all the wiser. With luck, we would safely cross the border by tomorrow night.

My eyes traced our steps along the ground. Rocks, and at times thick grass, forced me to pay attention to our path even though I paid little attention to where we were going. Poland was but a walk across the mountain, and then home.

■

"Vitayu." Pilgrims joined us at the entrance of the ravine.

I froze. "What's this? I thought we were heading to the border."

298

"We are. Oleksa thought it would be easier for us to slip out with the crowd after the apparition. Mischa agreed with him. Is there a problem?"

My breath was zapped away. Anxiety raced through my veins. In a flash, I realized that we were on the very path I hoped to avoid. Was God going to prey upon us by His very design?

"Paul, you look pale. What is it?" John startled me. "Let's rest before we continue."

We leaned against a boulder. Was I wrong for not telling them what I had dreamed? Maybe they held answers to my vision. Could it be possible that their involvement might assist in changing the vision given to me before something terrible actually happened?

"Paul, what did you see in that dream last night?"

Several pilgrims walked by us. "Dobry' ranok." An old man smiled.

An old woman grabbed my hand. "Yak vy nazyvayetesya?"

"Pascha." Oleksa answered for me.

She dug into her bag. Several other women surrounded me. They unzipped my jacket. I flinched as they removed it. The old woman placed a blue vest on me, then buttoned it. Beautifully stitched with richly colored needlework, an embroidered rose bud decorated the collar.

"It is bruslyk," Oleksa added.

"For me. Why?"

"Zhese good people. Zhey give much. You fix Ivan statue. Zhey know zhis."

"How do I say 'thank you very much'?"

"Duzhe dyakuyu."

As I peered into her blue eyes, her wrinkled face brightened. "Duzhe dyakuyu."

Her eyes twinkled. "Proshu. Slava Isusu Chrystu!"

"Oleksa, what did she say?"

"You velcome. Glory to Jesus Christ. It local greeting. Zhey bless each other zhis way. Response 'Slava na viky'! It means glory forever."

299

"Slava na viky!" She and the group of women turned. They nodded approvingly, waving farewell as they entered the ravine.

My heart pounded. I searched the ledge of the ravine, but the sun made it difficult for me to see anything. I had been down this path, just the night before, in my dreams—no, my nightmare.

I tripped over a rock and nearly fell.

John wrapped his arms around my waist. "What's wrong?"

My feet felt like cement blocks. I staggered even with John supporting me.

We reached the crevasse. I wiped the sweat from my upper lip. With a queasy stomach, I searched the ledge of the ravine above us. Nothing was there. But a glow permeating from the crevasse drew my attention. There the lady stood once more, her blue veil cascading to the ground. The black rosary beads intertwined in her hands turned to gold. Was I dreaming?

I squeezed my eyes shut. But as I reopened them, she greeted me with open arms.

"Find comfort in those you help, in those who help you." The lady spoke to me.

"How, where?"

"Look around you. They are here for you." She pointed to the masses.

"No. They're here for you."

"We are here for each other. All can be my hands and my arms. You can reach to them and touch them and they to you."

"But, there are so many of them."

"Many more even beyond these walls. You will find the way."

"I'm scared."

"I know. That is what makes you so brave."

"Brave? I'm such—"

"It is not those who are fearless that do brave things. It is those who weep and hurt, who fear and despair. It is those who reach out even when they feel least capable. You think yourself unworthy? You are blessed as they are blessed. None are less in the eyes of God. All are equal."

"But the hurt, the injury, the war?"

"These we will have as long as we possess need. Someday we will learn that there is no need, only each other. We can, Paul. You can."

"Miy sin, vin ruhaetsa." Shouts of joy from a woman interrupted our exchange. The boy with polio stood. His family wept even as they rejoiced. "Ya bachu." A man near me rubbed his eyes, pointing as if he had not seen where he was until then.

Pilgrims in different locations in the ravine stood singing. "Prechystaja divo Ruskoho kraju, S anhelamy y svjatymy tja velychaju, ty hrishnykov v tjazhkoj muki cherez tvoji spasajesh ruky, ne daj propasty!" Joy pealed from them. "Prechystaja—"

"What are they saying?" I looked to her, but again she was gone.

Oleksa drew closer. "They sing to honor purest Wirgin Mother."

My doubts waned as I witnessed Divine providence at work.

"Oh, my God. Soldiers!" John yelled. Gunfire echoed against the rocky walls. Bullets ripped through the crowds. Bodies dropped to the ground. The crowd scattered, screaming. They rushed for shelter that could not be found. More shots ended the beginnings found in this very ravine, the victims selected at random, yet not.

A bullet hit the dirt next to me. I searched for Marc and John. They rushed over to grab me. "No!" I screamed with all my might. If the bead of a rifle was on them, they might be hit by the bullet destined for me.

A woman grabbed my arm. "Dopomozhit meni, dopomozhit. Miy sin, vnyogo silno teche krow." Her son collapsed at her feet. I dropped to my knees. I placed my hands over the bullet hole that punctured his chest.

Shots continued to ring through the ravine. Bullets ricocheting off the stone walls dropped victims not even in the line of fire. Screams and shouts filled the place with chaos.

"Paul, come on!" Marc screamed.

John attempted to lift me. "I'm not leavin' without you."

"Leave me! I'm not finished! I've got to do this. Go. I'll catch up." I applied pressure to the young man's chest. Blood covered my hand.

John lifted the young man to safety. "Let's go!"

"I can't. There are too many of them."

Marc grabbed me. "Paul!" I resisted. "You can't save them all." He pulled me through a sea of bleeding bodies, felled by the bullets of the soldiers above.

"Here!" Oleksa shouted. He slid behind a large boulder. "Please to help!" He yanked dry brush and dirt away from the rocky wall. John and Marc clawed through the loose dirt.

Shots continued to rain down on the crowd in the crevasse. Blood curdling screams echoed against the rocky walls. I started back towards the rock that masked our escape.

"No, Paul! There's nothin' you can do." John's words pierced through me, just like the words of my father when Andre died. I couldn't save him then, and for all I had seen, for all I had experienced, I could not save these people now.

"Ve go!" A final rock tumbled near my feet, opening the entrance to a cave.

"Come on, pal." John helped me through the small opening. Yet the images of the first shots ringing out in the ravine remained like a frozen frame of a movie. Over and over, the words of the prophet Jeremiah echoed in my ears, "A cry was heard at Ramah, sobbing and loud lamentation: Rachel bewailing her children; no comfort for her, since they are no more."

I had failed once more. How could I? Without the courage to do as the lady instructed, I fled my post. My weakness had not become my strength. I didn't speak of what I knew.

"Hurry. Ve move here. You vatch head please." Oleksa led us deeper into the cave. Our eyes slowly adjusted to the darkness. He stopped.

"Danger here. Valk careful. Roof wery low. Rocks sharp." We slowed our pace.

"Damn. I just hit my head. Marc, can you watch Paul for a second?"

"Got him. Here, grab a flashlight from my bag." Marc tossed his bag to John.

The light reflected off of a low hanging, jagged edge hanging from the ceiling of the cave. John wiped away a little blood from his forehead.

Marc moved closer to him. "Do you need me to take a look at that?"

"No. It's just a bump. It was pretty stupid." John chuckled. "I saw it, turned for a moment, and walked right into it. Hold up."

With nothing more than a flashlight shining through the darkness, we stepped across ragged stones lining the floor. Our hands slid along rocky walls. We crouched low as the ceiling dropped.

A cool stench of stale air permeated the narrowing space.

"Damn! If it gets any smaller I won't fit through. Oleksa, how much farther?"

"Another hour ve see light."

Deep breathing replaced conversation. John struggled to get through the spaces.

Even as we walked, I could not get the images of the lady and then bodies dropping one after another to gunshots from above. Her words repeated, "Find comfort in those you help, in those who help you." What of the old lady who gave me the vest or the old man who offered us tea? What of the lady whose son was shot before my very eyes, now bleeding, maybe dead? What of all those unknown faces, screaming in desperation for help?

I lacked the presence to serve. My testament to the lady was my leaving those in need behind, just as I had left Andre. Her shrine would be built on her poor choice of me. This would be my legacy.

Finally, we reached several streaks of light streaming in through a small hole at the end of the tunnel. Fresh air seeped through the opening.

"Ve here. Dig out, da?"

"Good. Marc, get Paul situated. We'll rest for a few minutes."

Marc cleared a place for me to sit and carefully helped me down. We were all breathing heavily. He handed a canteen to me. I sipped and then handed it to John.

I closed my eyes, but immediately reopened them. The faces of those I had seen fallen ensorcelled me. Why had this happened? Why? If the lady wanted me to heal her people, why hadn't she given me the resources to do so? What was wrong with me? Every step I took in this journey seemed cursed. Why? God, please answer me!

The words of St. John resounded in my head:

> "On a dark night,
> Kindled in love with yearnings
> —oh, happy chance!
> I went forth without being observed,
> My house now being at rest.
>
> In darkness and secure,
> By the secret ladder, disguised
> —oh, happy chance!
> In darkness and in concealment,
> My house being now at rest.
>
> In the happy night,
> In secret, when none saw me,
> Nor I beheld aught,
> Without light or guide,
> Save that which burned in my heart."

What did it mean? How could my house ever be at rest, especially with what I had seen?

"Let's get with it." John was the first to stand. Dust and dirt streamed in as they cleared the rocks and shrubs blocking our exit. The small streaks of light expanded with the removal of each chunk.

"Are we making any progress?" Marc wiped sweat from his blackened forehead.

"I think we'll get this rock outta the way and have it cleared. Oleksa, give me a hand on the other side. On the count of three, we'll push." They moved into position. "One, two, three."

They grunted loudly. The stone slipped from its perch and rolled away. Dust filled the air. Rocks tumbled over one another as sunlight and fresh air broke through. Marc and John high-fived each other.

"Oleksa, lift your hand." John high-fived him.

Oleksa looked puzzled. "Vhat zhis hand slap?"

"A high five. It's a good thing. We got through the cave and moved the rock. This is how we celebrate in America."

"Da. Zhis good." He lifted John's hand and then slapped it. "I look out. If all safe, I get you." Loose gravel and dirt slid into the cave as Oleksa squeezed through the opening. "All clear. You come out now." His voice echoed in the chamber where we sat.

"Marc, why don't you go first? I'll help Paul up and you can help him out."

As Marc crawled out of the small opening, John turned to me. "Paul, let us do the work." John gave me a leg up. Marc reached down for me. We struggled for a few more minutes, but finally I was up and out.

The cave opened to a secluded forest, surrounded by boulders and covered with thick undergrowth. Encased by stone walls on all four sides, it could have easily served as someone's private courtyard.

To my left were scattered smooth blocked stones of similar sizes, looking like each had been hewn for some purpose. I walked over to examine them. The edifice of the rocky wall suggested that a structure of some sort once stood there.

"Oleksa, what is this place?" My voice bounced back at me.

"Shrine here many years. Cossacks destroy it. Merchant dedicate Mary. His vife buried here."

"Where?"

"What's up, Paul?" Dust puffed into the air as John pounded his pants.

"The legend. The statue. Father Barrios told me of the merchant, Pablo Pedro. This is the place where he built the shrine. This is where the first icon was placed, the one like Ivan's statue. Oleksa, show me her grave."

He walked to an alcove tucked into the mountain, just to the right of where I had been standing. Nestled in the side of it, an entrance to the tomb marked with the Star of David and the Cross of Christ greeted us with the inscription, "Marguerite Babin Guidry, le femme Pierre Paul Guidry, 1632."

My knees buckled. John rushed to my side. "Okay, pal. Let's take a deep breath." As we sat, I composed myself. Sipping on water from a canteen handed to me by Oleksa, I looked at the entrance to the tomb. I wondered if this was a dream. I breathed deeply. He firmly grasped my shoulder. Oleksa and Marc drew closer.

"When I was a small boy, my father took me fishing. When we returned to Oak Grove, I went upstairs to clean up for dinner. A section of the beaded wall opened. I peeked in, finding a passageway leading to a room. No one had ever told me about it. There was a trunk in the middle of the floor. It was open, filled with a bunch of stuff.

"I found a book, a leather one with a buckle. It told of my grandmother's family, the side we rarely spoke of. As I read it, I found the name Pablo Pedro Guidry, Pierre Paul Guidry, my great-grandfather eight generations back."

The wind whistled into our newest sanctuary. Dried leaves blew about as the skies darkened. Clouds covered the once blue firmament. Marc walked towards the stony tomb. He pressed his hands against the tablet blocking its entrance.

"What is it, Marc?" John joined him.

"Marguerite Babin. When I returned from Brody, I mentioned her to you guys. What I didn't say was that she was related."

The words of a Psalmist, "How weighty are thy designs oh God, how vast the sum of them," bellowed in my head. Now I could see in Marc my grandmother's eyes, my eyes. It was like looking into a mirror. I laid my hands on the earthen crypt. Reaching for Marc's hand, I found it reaching back to me. The warmth from it permeated my body.

John and Oleksa cradled us from behind. "Beautiful vitness zhis. Blessed God. Blessed zhose who suffer. Blessed zhose who heal. Blessed zhose who forgive zhose who hurt zhem."

Marc released my hand. I closed my eyes. When I opened them, Marc stood near me with four stones in his hands. He handed the first one to me and then the others to John and Oleksa. "Place it at the tomb." He placed a yarmulke on his head. With bended knee, he laid the rock at the base of the marker. "Join me. Please." He stood. We lined up with him. He took a deep breath and then released it. "Sherma, Israel, Adonai—"

Chills seized me. Anger coursed through my veins. I bolted from the tomb. There was no place to run. "I can't do this. Not after today." I searched the walls for an escape.

"Paul?" John lunged towards me.

"No! Leave me alone. Just leave me."

The wind howled. Leaves whipped. Branches cracked. Pine cones blown from their perch smacked the ground. A chill permeated the dampening air.

I climbed the steep walls to the ledge above, and looked back to the fallen rocks. Only ruins remained where once a legacy had built a shrine. Father had told me many times that to whom much was entrusted, much was expected. To receive what I had received, and then fail at achieving what was asked of me, was unconscionable. I wondered if the lady would ever show herself to me again. What did it matter anyway?

"Paul, stop!" John pursued me into the darkening night. Thick underbrush and tall trees slowed me. Danger seemed far removed for now. Of God, this might be true, and then maybe not. Yet of mortal man, it was anything but.

"Stop." He wrapped his arms around me. I caved into his arms. "Just let it out, pal." John lifted his head to the sound of feet crunching the snow.

Marc gasped for breath. "Is he okay?"

"Yeah. He's gonna be just fine."

"I want to check his side." Mark lifted my bandages. I flinched to his cold hands touching my tender skin.

"How's it lookin', Marc?"

"Red and swollen. Grab some snow so I can ice it."

I clinched my jaw.

"Just breathe through it, pal."

I closed my eyes, but immediately reopened them. The images were too horrific to view.

"Ve must go. Mischa vait. Get vord to other cousin at border." Oleksa's hand warmed the top of my head.

"Let's go, pal." John helped me up, tucked my shirt in, and then zipped my jacket.

Oleksa and Marc used the compass to guide us westward. Snowflakes drifted, except when the wind blew them about.

The sound of rushing water filled the air. "Dnister River. Ve follow into mountain. Vill lead to pass." Oleksa whispered as we paused to catch our breath. "Soon ve come Sambir willage. Ve go wery careful. Vatch soldiers. Zhen get deeper to mountains ve rest." Oleska turned off the flashlight. We marched on, gradually ascending the mountain through the rolling terrain. We hovered close to river's edge. As we followed the river around a bend to the left, faint lighting flickered in the distance. Oleksa stopped. "Railroad tracks cross river. May be guarded."

"Are we gonna cross the river?"

"Net. Just railroad track. I go first to check." We nestled close together at river's edge as Oleksa faded into a silhouette. He waved to us to join him.

John looked behind us. "Let's go, fellas." We moved towards Oleksa. With the village now just to our right, I hoped we might find lodging for the night. But we crossed the tracks and moved up the mountain without even pausing. I looked back several times. We turned with another bend in the river and the lights faded. "Just lean into me and let me carry some of your weight." It was a relief to be able to do so. My legs ached, as did my side. The thinning air labored my breathing.

Occasionally the canopy thinned. Clearing clouds exposed the myriad of stars in the heavens. Added with the moon, the light reflected off the ripples of the water to our left. The constellations floated across the sky. Hours passed. Would we ever rest?

"I hear that brain of yours workin' overtime," John whispered. We stepped over a fallen log. I was far too winded to say anything.

Oleksa stopped on a perch. "Rapids. Make camp here, da?" Stepping behind several large boulders bundled together, we shielded ourselves from the wind. The sound of rushing water reverberated against the rocks.

"Pal, I'm gonna get our beddin' together." John, with the help of Marc and Oleksa, quickly joined our sleeping bags. Snow blew about in the gusty wind. "Here ya go, pal. Let's get warmed up." I crawled in. John wrapped his arms around me. I shivered and my teeth chattered. He pulled me closer. "Rough day, huh?"

Silence filled the campsite. My heart pounded. It ached. A meteor streaked across the clear sky followed by another, then another in a shower of light.

"Why?"

"What's that, pal?"

"Those soldiers shattered it. Why did God let that happen?"

The wind gusted through the trees. The sleeping bags rustled as John sat up. Marc and Oleksa followed him.

"Free vill? Ve choose such things. Man shrink God to our level."

"What!"

"Easy, pal."

"Oh, that argument. We get to choose, but if we choose wrong He zaps us. And, if we happen to be in the path of that wrong, oh well, I guess shit happens. No offense, but right now that seems like a lame ass argument. People are dead. For what? Praying? If God is that much of a son of a bitch, then I don't know if I can go on believing. Enough already! Enough!"

Twenty-Three

"Hey, pal, wake up. We've gotta get goin'."

"What time is it?" My legs wobbled as I stood. I felt disoriented.

"It's early or late? Depends if you got sleep. Here, lean on me." He wrapped his arms around my waist. "Marc, if ya pack our gear I'll help Paul." The bags rustled as Marc stowed our belongings. Large snowflakes whitened the darkness of the early morning. Water rushed from the rapids just to the left of our campsite.

Oleksa lifted his backpack. Marc joined him as we renewed our ascent through the pass. The snow crunched under our feet. We walked and then walked some more. A ghostly sound churned the pine tree canopy above. Pine cones, snapped from their perch, pelted the earth. John heaved for each breath as he helped me over several large boulders.

Oleksa shined the flashlight at a stone tablet on the right edge of the path. Engraved with a cross and writing, the marker looked to be hewed from a larger rock into a flattened pillar. "Marker to right show pass through mountain. Here many years. Ve reach top in zhree hour."

"Hear that, pal? This trip is about to go downhill. We'll be home sippin' Mint Juleps before you can say 'Amen.'"

We turned a bend. Several fallen trees blocked our path. We climbed over one, then the second. Reaching the third, we paused to rest. "So much for the trip goin' downhill."

"We haven't reached the top yet."

"Okay, wise-ass." John handed me a canteen. "Here, have a drink." The water was ice cold, but felt really good as it went down my throat.

"Ve go." Oleksa's feet sank into thickening snow as we renewed our ascent. The higher we climbed, the bigger the flakes grew. Cascading to the earth in the absence of the wind, each seemed to gently land on the ground in an appointed spot. We walked and then walked some more.

Our ascent steepened. The sound of rushing water amplified. The current flowed swiftly, but not enough to create the sound I heard. Marc slipped to the ground. Water splashed.

"Marc!" John rushed to him.

He leaped up from an icy brook. "Burrrrr! That's cold." Standing under a waterfall pouring from the mountainside, Marc started to shiver.

John offered him a hand. "That was graceful."

"And you called Paul a wise-ass."

"River end soon. Soon ve rest and get food willage. Dry and warm."

"What village?" John looked into the darkened mountain path.

"My home. I send vord to my family ve come. Not to vorry." Oleksa led us forward. As the tree line thinned, the river narrowed into a rivulet.

In the distance lights dotted the horizon. We drew closer. Lanterns hanging on wooden poles marked our path. Smoke from chimneys lifted from several dozen cottages nestled in a small alpine valley. "Ve go here." The red logs of a small cottage contrasted the gray logs of the other buildings. A weathered picket fence enclosed a snow-covered vegetable garden. The smell of fresh baked bread wafted from inside. Oleksa knocked on the door.

An old woman opened it. She wrapped her arms around Oleksa through a smile that consumed her whole face. "Yak mayetes'." With the soft glow of crackling wood in the hearth, she welcomed us inside.

"Maty." Oleksa kissed her on the cheek. "Paul, John, Marc, zhis my mozher, Nadezhda. Please to call her Nadya."

She patted my cheeks. Her soft warm hand reminded me of Mim. Even the apron around her waist had laced embroidery stitched around its edges. "Pryyemno z vamy zapiznatysya."

"She says nice meet you."

"Tobi holodno. Zaydit, zihriytesa bila vohnu." She grabbed my hand and pulled me to the fire. She wrapped a blanket around me, and then did the same to Marc and John.

"She vants you to sit and varm yourselves."

Returning to the stove, she lifted warm bread from the oven into a basket. Oleksa arranged it on a tray while she poured five cups of tea. The cups rattled on the tray as he lifted it. "Yizhte. Tse vas zihriye."

"She vants you to eat." Oleksa placed the tray on a small stool near us. He removed the linen covering the bread, and then tore the first loaf into four pieces. Steam lifted, permeating the air with the smell of sourdough.

"Dyakuyu." I smiled at her.

She turned to Oleksa. "Proshu. Pascha rozmovlaye Ukrainskoyu?"

"Tak. Troshki."

"What did she ask?" Wanting not to insult her, I bit into the bread.

"My mother vant to know if you speak Ukrainian. I told her little."

John stood from the wooden chair. "More like six words. Won't she join us?"

Nadya circled John. "Ni. Ni. Sidyate. Yizhte!"

"John, she fuss. Sit. Eat. Make her happy."

As we ate, Nadya refilled our cups, keeping our tea warm. I searched the walls of the small cottage. The windows were barren, covered only by wooden shutters. Yet, in the middle of the far wall, purple satin draped an area about three feet wide and five feet long.

John pinched another piece from the loaf. "This is the best bread I've ever eaten."

"It's awesome." Marc smacked his lips. "Paul, you're not eating very much."

"Just not real hungry, that's all."

Nadya patted my shoulder. "Pascha, you see lady, tak? Heart heavy. Here. Follow." I walked hand in hand with her to the draped area on the wall. She pulled it back, revealing an iconoclast identical to the statue of the Virgin. Next to it hung a painting of a gentlemen dressed in fifteenth, maybe sixteenth century European clothing.

"Who is he?" I turned to Oleksa.

"Pablo Pedro, my grandfazher seven generation back." Oleksa patted his chest.

The room spun. Marc bolted towards me. "Pablo Pedro is your grandfather?" His voice quivered. "Why didn't you say anything back at—"

"Much confused story you tell. Pascha trouble bad. Not vant hurt him more."

I fixated on the iconoclast, then the painting of Pablo Pedro. I shivered. John rested his hand on my shoulder. Our eyes connected. It was as though my hurt oozed from me. "The ruins. Tell me more about the ruins."

"Cossacks destroy shrine, but not tomb. My family hide statue cave near willage. Ve take care many years."

"The original?" I moved towards Oleksa. "Can we see it?" As I reached for my jacket, Oleksa grabbed my arm.

"Ve dress for journey." Oleksa looked to Nadya. She handed shirts, pants, vests, hats, and even jackets to him. "Go room behind curtain and change." He led us to a small doorway covered by a rust colored woolen blanket.

"Paul. Marc. Hand me your passports, wallets, watches, rings, anything that looks American. I'll hide them in my backpack."

"Net. Use zhis." Oleksa handed him a sheepskin bag with straps.

We emerged from the room in Lemko dress; our pants tucked in boots called chboty. I had the vest given to me by the woman at the ravine. John and Marc sported a blue lejbyk, a vest richly decorated in needlework. Black coarse wool jackets and black hats with short rims bent upward completed our disguise.

I walked to Nadya. "Duzhe dyakuyu, Nadya." She opened her arms. I hugged her, sighing as I wrapped my arms around her.

"Slava Isusu Chrystu, Pascha." She released me from her motherly hug and turned to Oleksa. "Vatch soldiers."

"Tak, Mamma. I careful." Oleksa peered out of the door. "Ve go."

With the village still fast asleep, we followed train tracks until our path separated from it. The whiteout conditions did not slow Oleksa as we trudged upward. My feet sank into thickening powder. Heavy breathing spewed steam from my mouth.

∎

We broke through the snow into a clearing. Oleksa stopped. Just to our right another tablet marked our path. The alpine forest had given way to rocky pediments. "Follow." Oleksa stepped off the side. A ledge hidden from view stood just below.

John climbed over. "Damn this is narrow. Paul, hold on to me." Protrusions, seemingly hewn from the mountain, served as handles to guide us along the descending ledge. Rocks trickled as we teetered on the three-foot-wide path. I looked up and could no longer see the cliff. I held on to the ragged wall as we inched sideways.

The smell of burning wax filled the air. The wall opened to the entrance of a cave. We walked inside to a faint glow that brightened as we ventured deeper. With a left turn through the orifice and around a rock pillar, racks of candles surrounded the icon.

Nearly six feet tall, it almost touched the roof. Her stunning blue eyes pierced from her pear shaped face. The blue veil draped her head. It looked real enough to blow in a breeze. Her slender fingers grasped a rosary. She stood in a bed of roses. The aura surrounding her head blazed in gold inlay. She was the lady of my dream.

315

My hands rubbed the pediment where she stood. Inscribed were the words spoken to me by Father Barrios. "La Madre de Dios calma el huracán con Su mano."

John knelt by me. "The Mother of God calms the evil winds with her hand. It's identical to Ivan's statue."

Ivan, what of him? I feared for his safety. Everything remotely associated with this statue was destined to agonize in some sort of hurt. I turned away, moving to the entrance of the cave.

"Paul?" John's voiced echoed against the stone walls.

"Leave me!"

"Why? This is what we've been searchin' for."

"Leave me before something happens to you."

"Nothing's gonna happen to me." He clutched my arm.

"I'm cursed! Can't you see it? If you stay, you might die. Leave me!" I pulled away.

"That's nonsense and you know it."

"Nonsense? Andre, Father, Xavier, Kevin, Meg, those people in the ravine. What about them?" I thought of jumping from the ledge. No more. I could take no more. This obsession, this statue, all of it, every bit of it was hogwash.

John spun me around. As he hugged me, his tears dripped on my jacket. "I love you. Don't you understand? You're my best friend. You're all I've got left." My arms tightened around him. An eagle shrieked from outside the cave. I didn't want to let him go. I just wanted to stop hurting so bad.

I looked into the haunting eyes of the statue. Fear coursed through me. Her life was filled with torment. Was she asking the same of me?

"Ve must go to make border."

"What about the statue?" John approached the base.

"Ve protect. Many people vatch. No harm come to it."

John reluctantly turned away. "Let's go, pal." He spoke softly. We exited the cave to the eagle soaring towards the heavens. It welcomed the dawn as we followed the narrow ledge back to the pinnacle.

Oleksa's first step down the other side of the mountain sent wild sheep scurrying through the rocky tree line. Mountains jutted to the right as the path wound through them. Clear skies greeted us. We turned back to the east for just a moment. Rays, the fingers of God, streaked through broken clouds as the sun raced to catch us.

Our feet shuffled across the rocky ground. The fifty or so feet of clearing through the underbrush and forest opened into a small valley, maybe three or four hundred feet wide. We topped another small hill and then another as the valley rolled down the mountain. We hovered close to the tree line. As the sun rose, the temperature slowly warmed.

Marc pointed to the valley beneath us. "Is that fog?"

"Net. Vater from river. Valk up river. Ve cross train—" Oleksa froze. Voices filled the valley. "Take cover!" We dove into the underbrush.

"Kovo mi zdes' ischchem? Mi nikovo ne videli krome koz za dvadt-sat' kilometrov!"

"Zatknis' Kolya. Ti stonesh kak stariy osel." Two Russian soldiers chuckled as they walked by. We hid until their voices faded.

John peeked out. "That was close." The pulse pounding in my head slowed. Oleksa and Marc emerged from their hiding place. I joined them.

Marc panted. "Did you guys hear what they were saying?"

"Yes. They haven't seen anything for twenty kilometers. And, one of them told the other that he whined like an old mule."

"Russian wery good, Pascha. Vhere learn speak?"

"Studied it in college and then conducted a number of seminars in Moscow."

"Know Russia, da?"

"Enough to know to stay out of the way of the soldiers, police, and the KGB."

"Da. Ve go voods now." Oleksa led us through thick underbrush. As we followed the river, his pace slowed. He pointed to a wooden tower on the opposite side of the river.

"Looks empty," John whispered.

"Da. It vorry me. Vatch soldiers."

We snuck deeper into the woods. With John and Oleksa now on point, Marc helped me navigate through the thatch anchored into the rocky floor. Sweat beaded from my forehead even though a chill remained to the air. We labored to breathe.

Oleksa perched low to the ground. John followed his lead. Marc and I waited fifty or so feet behind until they waved us to join them.

The forest thinned, opening into a rolling valley lined with white fence posts. Railroad tracks coiled away from us, crossing the river on a steep bridge supported by bricked archways. To the right, a white hut served as a guard outpost. Across the river, a farmhouse, nestled in the curve of the track, sat on the riverbank.

"Zhat patrol ve cross probably guard. I go first to check out." Oleksa sauntered out of the forest and into the meadow. Stopping to gaze at the trees, it looked as though he was a local out for a casual stroll. As he neared the guardhouse, someone approached him.

"Who's that with him?" Marc whispered to John.

"I don't know, but it looks like a guard."

"Think he's in trouble?"

"No. Just bein' coy. Look. He's wavin' to us. I'll go first. Help Paul, okay?" John stepped into the meadow. Marc and I followed. Oleksa continued to wave us in.

"Bud laska." Mischa's voice echoed across the valley.

John wrapped him in a bear hug. "Man, are we glad to see you."

A train whistle blared from the mountain. Twin trails of mixed black smoke and steam whisped through the air as it drew closer. Pulling green cars, engines churned to control the train's descent, the red wheels grinding as it braked to a stop. Steam puffed as the engines steadily cycled.

"Stay. Ve handle, da." Oleksa and Mischa joined the conductor as he stepped off the train. Laughter ensued as they swatted each other on the back.

Oleksa rejoined us with Mischa only a few steps behind. "Board rear car." Leading us past a coal car, a second engine, and then a series of passenger cars, we walked to the caboose.

"Oleksa. Yak mayetes'?" A young man called to him.

"Dobre." They exchanged a hug. "Zhis my cousin, Vasya. He vork train."

Oleksa's head bobbed forward from John slapping him on the back. "Oleksa, you're like Paul—related to everybody." As I climbed into the caboose, my side tugged. The wooden seats of the car were a welcome reprieve. The whistle blew. The aroma of burning coal floated through the open windows as the train pulled forward. "What a relief. Better than walkin', huh, pal?" The train clattered against the tracks.

My feet throbbed, as did my side. We crossed the small river. The sun undulated in and out of the trees. The click-clack of the train joined the swaying rhythm of the rocking car. My eyes closed to haunting scenes. Sleeping didn't seem that appealing.

My eyes popped open. Oleksa and Marc reclined on the seats in front of me. I looked back. Sunrays blanketed John's face, then faded as the train turned. He stared out the window in a blinkless gaze. I joined him in his seat. He remained statue still.

"Reminds you of a street car, doesn't it?"

He nodded. I leaned my body against his. His hand squeezed my knee. Our eyes locked. I knew of nothing to say to comfort him.

The fading sun flipped from side to side as we wound down the valley. The wheels ground as the winding track led us to safety. "I'm ready to go home."

"Yeah, so am I."

Suddenly, the trained braked. Oleksa jumped up. Stress lines marked his face. "Stay. I look." He snuck to the front exit to the car ahead of us.

"Get your stuff together." John grabbed the backpacks. Marc joined him.

Oleksa burst through the door. "Ve go! Hurry! Russian patrol block track."

The train slowed to a crawl. Hot, wet air rushed from the steam relief valves. Oleksa jumped first followed by Marc.

"Okay, pal. We're gonna take this easy." The train stopped. John braced me. I jumped to Oleksa and Marc. My side burned. I moaned. The seeping vapor masked our escape as we bolted along the track.

"Go! Go! Go!" John pushed me into the underbrush. We shielded our faces from low hanging branches. We ran until the sounds of the train began to fade.

Oleksa froze. He signed to us to duck.

"Kuda vi edete?" The Russian guard asked the other soldier where he was going.

He approached the tree line. "Mne nuzhno powssat'!" We crouched lower. The soldier unzipped his fly and then urinated on the tree only twenty feet from us.

We waited until their voices faded. "I think safe. Ve go." Oleksa led our escape. We crossed several hills, pushing our way through dense underbrush. We climbed to the top of a ridge. Oleksa hid behind a tree. We joined him. "Border crossing." He pointed to the narrow passage beneath us. "Ve cross small bridge." High bluffs on either side made this the sole passage.

Four armed guards walked the barricade. "There. Look. More guards." John pointed to six heavily armed soldiers walking from a hut near the border crossing. Oleksa signaled for us to follow him. "Are we gonna backtrack?"

"Da. Ve go road. Valk edge like ve come willage. Guard think ve pass patrol. Mischa vait for us to cross border. He near hut." John followed Oleksa's pointing hand. Mischa stood just outside a small guardhouse. "I get dress priest." The black robe slipped over his head. The white collar tightened around his neck.

"Okay, gents. Let's do a final check. Nothin' glarin'ly American on ya, right?" John looked us over.

"I valk vith Pascha. Marc, John follow close." Oleksa pointed to a brown box in his knapsack. "Hand package, please."

"What's in it, man?"

"Food, medicine, cigarette for guards."

"It's like Louisiana. You've gotta provide inducements to get somethin' done. What's that?"

"Papers. Allow to cross border. I talk. You say nothing, da? If ask question, I answer. If must speak, say Russian. Ready?"

Oleksa led us down the ridge. We backtracked across two hills, searching for a safe place to enter. "Here." Oleksa pointed to a boulder sitting almost on the road. "I go first vit Pascha. You and Marc follow close behind."

We began walking as though we had been strolling along, uninterrupted by troops who had passed us by. A stream rushed just to the left of us as we crept along the winding road. To our right, the rocky, earthen wall of the bluff jutted upward with a sparse tree line. The wind churned through the narrowing pass. My eyes watered. I lowered my head to my feet crunching along the snow-covered road. We came to the narrow curve we had observed from top of the bluff earlier.

"Dobroe utro." Oleksa greeted the first guard.

My heart pounded like never before. I thought my head was going to explode. I shivered. Certainly the cold wind wasn't helping.

"Kak dela?" Three more Russian soldiers passed by us, with one asking Oleksa where we came from.

"Horosho."

We neared the border crossing. Guards paced back and forth on both sides. It looked as if a medical team waited just over and to the right of the narrow wooden bridge.

"Oleksa. Kak dela?" Mischa called to Oleksa. He smiled.

"Horosho." Oleksa handed our papers to him. Another guard approached.

"Moi tovarichtch upal kogda pahmagal Krasnomu Krestu. Ya vezu ego k doktoram cherez granitsu." Oleksa pointed to the medical team as he explained that I was injured in a fall. My wound was finally serving some useful purpose.

"Prokhodite." The guard waved us through.

Oleksa helped me across the wooden slats. Freedom was a stone's throw away.

"Kak vashe imya?" Another guard stopped Marc.

Oleksa froze. "Paul, cross border. I get zhem. Go!" He gently pushed me forward, then turned. John moved a few steps ahead, but stopped as well.

I had left my post once already. This time I would not leave, not without Marc and John.

"Kuda vy edete?" Marc's inquisitor yelled. "Chto eto takoye? U vas est pa—"

Unable to answer the barrage of questions being directed to him, Marc continued walking. Oleksa started back to him. "On glukhoi. Ego bumagi u menya," Oleksa shouted to the guard.

The guard reached for his side arm. Others soldiers rushed towards Marc. Again Oleksa shouted out to them, " Ego bumagi u menya! On glukhoi."

"Marc, run!" John dashed towards him.

Marc bolted towards the border just yards away. Shots rang out. A bullet tore through his body. Marc smacked the ground and rolled.

"No!" John's scream echoed in the valley.

I lunged back, but Oleksa pushed me across the border. Guards grabbed hold of me. Sharp pains raced through my body as I fell. "Let go dammit," I screamed in horror as John fell next. A bullet ripped through Oleksa's chest as he raced to help. I watched him fall as well.

Someone grabbed me. "I'm an American medic. You're badly hurt!"

I shoved him away. "Leave me alone. I've got to get to them."

"There's nothing you can do for them. Stop or you're going to die. Just lay still!"

"Those sons of bitches shot my friends. Let go—" I coughed up blood.

"I need help here!"

I grabbed my side. Blood dampened my hand.

"Lay still!" He held me down. "Someone get over here and help me!" The medic shouted. Several of his colleagues rushed over as shots continued to ring out. I fought him with what little strength I had left. "Hurry, sedate him before he kills himself."

"Let's get him out of the gunfire."

"No. He's fighting me. Inject him."

The sedation stung as it entered my body. I screamed "No!" and struggled to get free. Their voices clamored above the chaos surrounding us.

"He's not going to make it if we don't get this bleeding stopped!"

"Hold him down while I apply pressure!"

"We're losing him!"

"Hurry, get an IV hooked up!"

"Let's move him on three. One, two—"

My world began to spin. Everything around me blurred. My voice slurred and the sounds around me garbled. The medication raced through my veins.

The night made it difficult to see. I took a deep breath and sighed. Drifting out of my body, I was certain that like John, Marc, and Oleksa, I too was dying. I let go.

I drifted into darkness. Weightlessness encased me. Cold and alone, I was frightened, yet not. A distant voice spoke to me.

■

I floated towards a light. It grew in size and intensity. A white door materialized. The walls surrounding it were blacker than coal. I struggled to lift my heavy hand to the gold doorknob sparkling before me.

As I touched the warm knob, it turned by itself, and the door opened. Bright light blinded me. I shielded my eyes. Something guided me in. I could not resist. I attempted to call for help. With my throat parched and dry, I felt like I was waking from a bad hangover. Moving my hands and my feet was like moving two blocks of cement.

I rested on the ground, or whatever it was beneath me. Exhaustion consumed me. Keeping my eyes open became difficult. I was too weary to fight it and drifted off to sleep, or rest, maybe my final one.

Again, I floated. Soft, white clouds surrounded me. I appeared to be the only person in this place, alone, yet not. A woman's voice spoke to me, this time louder. I felt as though the source drew nearer. "Paul, listen to me." She whispered and touched my hand.

I breathed deeply.

"Follow me." She led me to a room. A high altar encased a throne of gold. Light undulated against crystal walls. Warmth filled me. I breathed easy. "Come. Rest." The light from her face no longer blinded me. Her sapphire-blue eyes warmed me. She spoke to me once more.

> *"On a dark night,*
> *Kindled in love with yearnings*
> *—oh, happy chance!*
> *I went forth without being observed,*
> *My house now being at rest.*
>
> *In darkness and secure,*
> *By the secret ladder, disguised*
> *—oh, happy chance!*
> *In darkness and in concealment,*
> *My house being now at rest.*

In the happy night,
In secret, when none saw me,
Nor I beheld aught,
Without light or guide,
Save that which burned in my heart.

This light guided me
More surely than the light of noonday
To the place where he
(Well I knew who!) was awaiting me
A place where none appeared.

Oh, night that guided me,
Oh, night more loved than the dawn,
Oh, night that joined
Beloved with lover,
Lover transformed in the Beloved!

Upon my flowery breast,
Kept wholly for himself alone,
There he stayed sleeping,
and I caressed him,
And the fanning of the cedars made a breeze.

The breeze blew from the turret
As I parted his locks;
With his gentle hand he wounded my neck
And caused all my senses to be suspended."

"I love you." The words floated off my lips. Our eyes fixed on each other. She wrapped me in her gentle and loving grasp. She cared for me as I lay in her arms. Her hands stroked my hair.

If this was heaven, it wasn't bad. At least I was in a peaceful place where I could rest. Wherever I was, it felt like home. I wanted to remain here forever. But something pulled me from her arms. I resisted.

"Let go. Trust. All is well." Her voice caressed me like a gentle breeze. "I will, to will, Thy will" reverberated once more.

I let go, drifting downward like a sinking stone, hoping, and trusting that all would be well.

Twenty-Four

"Mr. de la Moret, would you enlighten us with a quote from Mr. Henry Wadsworth Longfellow's "Evangeline?" Father Cavender sat behind his white oak desk, peering into a leather bound version of the work.

A lump lodged into my throat. I stood to a silenced classroom. The wall clock ticked away the seconds, which felt like hours.

"Mr. de la Moret, I'm sure we can get to this before the turn of the next century."

Clearing my throat, I spoke:

> "Within her heart was his image,
> Clothed in the beauty of love and youth
> as last she beheld him,
> Only more beautiful made by his death-
> like silence and absence.
> Into her thoughts of him, time entered
> not, for it was not.
>
> Over him years had no power; he was
> not changed, but transfigured."

The death-like body of Evangeline's love lifted from the cot where he lay. Ghostly figures of those near him rose to join him. A death stench permeated the air. Yet, Evangeline's loving eyes focused on the frail frame of the man she once knew.

■

My eyes fluttered. Bright light blinded me. A blurred image hovered above.

"Welcome back. You've been asleep for quite some time now." A woman spoke to me. "I'll lower the blinds. That'll help." The room darkened as the sound of metal clanged. "Now there. That should be better."

I tried to speak, but something blocked my throat. I couldn't swallow either. My arms and legs were like lead. They wouldn't move. Even my jaw ached.

"How's he doing?"

"Well, we're trying to wake up. His vitals are strong."

"Good morning. I'm Greg Hansen, the attending physician. Let's get this tube out of your throat." He tugged on it.

My throat felt dry and scratchy, and my tongue twice its size. I moved my lips.

"Just relax. The tube irritated your larynx. In a day or so the swelling will be down and you'll be able to talk." Something entered my arm, burning up towards my shoulder. "I'll check on you this evening." He patted my hand. "Hope, keep a close watch on his vitals."

"Yes, doctor." She leaned over me. Her brown hair was pulled back behind her ears. The white uniform made her complexion look dark. "Don't worry. You're safe now." Her touch comforted me. "Woozy aren't you? Close your eyes." She hummed a soft tune. It faded as my head started to spin. Maybe I was dreaming, possibly having a dream within a dream. Nothing about this place seemed familiar.

The world wildly swirled around me. I felt dizzy. My eyes closed. Where was the door? I searched. It was so dark. I was lost. I wanted the lady to return. Perhaps she could tell me where I was and what was happening to me.

■

"Well, well, Mr. de la Moret, you even recite with a hint of the Acadian intonation. I think I would like to hear more." Father Cavender lowered the book from viewing level, something he rarely did. Yet, he did not smile. Rather, he stared at me stoned-face, as usual.

I searched through my memory of the poem hoping to recollect others segments I knew well. An image of a church triggered a thought.

> *"Thus, at peace with God and the world,*
> *the farmer of Grand-Pre*
> *Lived on his sunny farm,*
> *and Evangeline governed his household.*
> *Many a youth, as he knelt in the church*
> *and opened his missal,*
> *Fixed his eyes upon her,*
> *as the saint of his deepest devotion;*
> *Happy was he who might touch her hand*
> *or the hem of her garment!*
> *Many a suitor came to her door*
> *by the darkness befriended,*
> *And as he knocked and waited to hear*
> *the sound of her footsteps,*
> *Knew not which beat louder,*
> *his heart or the knocker of iron;*
> *Or at the joyous feast of the Patron saint*
> *of the village,*
> *Bolder grew, and pressed her hand in the dance*
> *as he whispered*
> *Hurried words of love,*
> *that seemed a part of the music."*

The murmur of several voices drew me to a dim light. As I neared it, my side started hurting. I reached to find something to hold onto. But my arms moved uncontrollably.

■

"Hey there." The room was darker. Her foggy smile greeted me. Something tugged on my side. I flinched. "It's okay. We're just taking a quick look. You're doing great. You're probably still pretty groggy, but you should start feeling less so tomorrow."

I wanted to talk, but still couldn't. Was I ever going to speak again?

The doctor placed the end of his stethoscope to my chest. "Looking real good. Can you take a deep breath for me?" Air flowed in with no pain. "Good. Hope, let's get him cleaned up and re-bandaged."

"Right away, doctor."

"I'll check on you tomorrow morning." His image blurred as he turned away.

She taped the new bandage to my side. "Are you hungry yet?"

I shook my head.

"Well, that'll change. You've come a long way in the last week." She draped the gown over me and then walked to the end of the bed. "I'm going to do a little exercise for you. We don't want those muscles shrinking to nothing." She lifted my right leg and bent it towards me. "Just relax and let me do the work. Now let's do the left one. Soon . . ."

What happened to me? Where was I? Nothing about this placed seemed familiar.

The needle stung as Hope moved it. "I'm sorry. Judging by that grimace, your IV's pretty sensitive. As soon as you can swallow, we'll get fluids down you and yank this out." She tucked my blanket around me. "You rest now. The medicine will wear off by morning and you won't feel so woozy." She hummed the lullaby again. Her soft hands warmed my face as she stroked my head.

I closed my eyes. Maybe the lady brought me here to help me get better before she took me to whatever was next. I could only imagine seeing her again, her blue veil draped over her head. If only to hear her words— so soft, so loving. My heart ached from her absence. But neither a single sound, nor an image greeted me. Nothing but darkness filled my view. I concentrated on her. *Hail Mary. Hail Mary,* I repeated the words in my mind. Still she did not come.

■

Father Cavender gave an approving nod to my recitation of Longfellow. "Well, Mr. de la Moret, that was quite nice. Would you care to share more with us?"

The image of an Acadian cottage snapped into view. Oak Grove, my home, it was my home!

> *"Firmly builded with rafters of oak,*
> *the house of the farmer*
> *Stood on the side of a hill,*
> *commanding the sea, and a shady*
> *Sycamore grew by the door,*
> *with a woodvine wreathing around it.*
> *Rudley carved was the porch,*
> *with seats beneath; and a footpath*
> *Led through an orchard wide,*
> *and disappeared in the meadow.*
> *Under the sycamore-tree were hives*
> *overhung by a penthouse,*
> *Such as the traveler sees in regions remote*
> *by the road-side,*
> *Built o'er a box of the poor,*
> *or the blessed image of Mary."*

"I'm sure your classmates would agree with me in saying, 'job well done.'
Now, if you will be kind enough to take your seat, we will learn if others join-
ing us today have prepared equally as well."

I sat back down at my desk, but my body lifted into the air. I hovered
above the classroom. I reached for John, but could not grasp him. I floated
away from his shrinking image.

My body turned over. Now facing the heavens, I sailed towards a clear
blue sky dotted only by sparse puffy white clouds.

Soon I soared above the earth. A hurricane peacefully spun in the ocean.
From a distance, it looked so tranquil.

With another roll of my body, I faced sparkling stars nestled against the
darkened backdrop of the heavens. I seemed to find my place among them.

Bright light blinded me. I neared it. Voices carried from the distance. I
felt as though I was waking.

■

"Hope. Hope." My eyes fluttered to the brightened room. Even
though my throat was raspy and my voice weak, words came out.

"I'm right here." Her hands squeezed my own.

"Where am I?"

"You're in a Red Cross hospital just inside Poland, near Slovakia.
We're relief workers helping with refugees. Do you know who you are?"

"Paul."

"Well, Paul. I'm pleased to meet you."

The doctor approached. He pulled his stethoscope from his white
jacket.

"Paul, I'm Greg. Its good to meet you at last. Let's take a listen." The
cold knob pressed against my side. "Take a deep breath. Good. Now, say
your name."

"Paul de la Moret."

"Well Paul de la Moret, your lung sounds great." His blue eyes sparkled. His long blond hair and his slender face made him look like a kid.

"What happened to me?"

"Do you remember anything?"

"Yes, I mean no, I mean—"

Greg continued with his examination. "You punctured your lung crossing the border. Do you remember?"

My stomach tightened.

"Are you okay, Paul?"

"My friends, what of my friends?"

The room filled with a deafening silence. Hope's hand gently touched me. "I'm sorry, Paul. We couldn't get to them."

Tears welled in my eyes. I looked away. Waking to this fate was worse than death. "Paul, I'm going to give you something to help you rest." The medicine burned as it entered my body. Maybe I wouldn't wake from it—a merciful ending for me. Lacking courage, I fled my post, and then deserted my friends. Now I knew why the lady abandoned me.

My eyes closed to the crackle of gunfire echoing against the walls of the passage. First Marc and Oleksa, then John, their faces contorting as bullets pierced their bodies. They fell one at a time as I was pushed to safety. Guards rushed to them, even when I did not. I just lay there, cared for as they died.

I felt sick to my stomach. How could I bare the loss of another? Why? What was the point? How could I live with the horror of my actions? Living was such a fitting punishment.

"Can't sleep? You need something for the pain?"

I shook my head.

"Let's do this. We've not gotten any information on you. Why don't we take care of that, and if you get tired, you can tell me and we'll stop? Okay?"

I nodded.

"What happened to your identification?"

I thought about it for a moment. "My friend, John, has my wallet and passport."

"Oh, I see. Where do you live?"

"Oak Grove Plantation, Thibodaux, Louisiana. My wife . . ."

"You have a wife. Good. Who is she?"

"Anne. Her name is Anne."

"We're going to get word to her—"

"When?"

"As soon as possible. It may take a day or so."

I smiled at Hope even though I felt disappointed. I yearned to be in Anne's arms again, walking hand in hand with her under the oaks to the sound of a locust chanting its hymn. I could almost smell the Nina Ricci perfume she gently patted on her arms and neck.

"So what happened to me?"

"A broken rib severed an artery. A medic saved your life."

"Is he still here? I—" Two nurses rolled another patient into my room. As they positioned the bed next to me, I got a glimpse of him. Blood surged to my head. I sank into my bed with a sick feeling in my gut.

"Doctor, quick." Hope quickly drew the curtain and separated us from view. It was he, the one who had shot them. I remembered all of it. How dare they place that murderer in a bed next to me! The doctor checked my injury while Hope checked my pulse. "Paul, sweetie, what is it?"

I looked away. No words could describe the rage within.

"How's his pulse?" Greg placed his stethoscope to my chest.

"Elevated. So is his respiration."

The pain pulsed in rhythm with my heart until the medication burned in my arm. The sedation numbed the anger coursing through my veins. I wanted to hurt him as he had hurt me. I wanted him dead and I wanted him to feel it as I had. He had taken so much from me. His presence near me smacked of injustice. So many had lost their lives at the hands of men like him. How could they treat him as they were?

I wanted to cry, but I couldn't. I wanted to scream, but it would not help. Why would God do this? Where was his sense of fair play? And the lady, where was the lady? When I needed her most, she abandoned me once more.

■

"Paul, you've been staring at that patient for hours now. What is it?"
"What's wrong with him?"
"He's blind and can't move. If something's bothering you—"
Blind! If I could only get out of bed. I could wait until Hope was gone and then reach to him and strangle him. But even his death would not bring John, Marc, and Oleksa back. At least in his injury there was some justice assigned to his actions. He would spend his years, and I hoped they would be many, in darkness. What a welcomed tribute to the fate he had assigned my friends.

"Why don't you try to get some rest? I'll be right here if you need me."

I rolled over, but twisted and turned, at least to the extent I could twist and turn. Surviving the loss of loved ones was difficult enough. But doing so while resting next to the one who had killed them was unbearable. I hated him.

The hours near my murderous chum slowed to an agonizing pace. Sedation provided the only refuge, letting me doze off only to awaken where I had left off.

My mind obsessed with feelings of hate undulating through me. I imagined dropping to my knees. The tubes and clamps entrapping my body prevented me from doing so. It seemed that God had become silent one more time. His timing sucked!

"Pomogite! Kto nibud'." The young man spoke. "Pomogite mne! Kto nibud' menya slishit?" He called again, and then again. I squeezed my eyes shut, not wanting to hear him. But with his plea, the words spoken by Father Barrios at Manresa sounded in my head.

"To you who hear me, I say: Love your enemies, do good to those who hate you: bless those who curse you and pray for those who maltreat you. When someone slaps you on one cheek, turn and give him the other; when someone takes your coat, let him have your shirt as well. Give to all who beg from you. When a man takes what is yours, do not demand it back. Do to others what you would have them do to you. If you love those who love you, what credit is that to you? Even thieves love those who love them. If you do good to those who do good to you, how can you claim any credit? Sinners do as much. If you lend to those from whom you expect repayment, what merit is there in it for you? Even sinners lend to sinners, expecting to be repaid in full.

"Love your enemy and do good; lend without expecting repayment. Then will your recompense be great. You will rightly be called sons of the Most High, since He Himself is good to the ungrateful and the wicked.

"Be compassionate, as our Father is compassionate. Do not judge, and you will not be judged. Do not condemn, and you will not be condemned. Pardon, and you shall be pardoned. Give, and it shall be given to you. Good measure pressed down, shaken together, running over, will they pour into the fold of your garment. For the measure you measure with will be measured back to you."

But how? He was a murderer.

"Paul—" It sounded like Maria. I searched the room. But only barren concrete walls painted white stood there. "Paul, heal my people. Reach to him." Chills rushed down my spine in hearing the lady's voice. The words "reach to him" sounded over and over in my ears. How could she expect me to do it? I resisted, but the words still haunted me.

"Paul, who do you say that I am?" I heard a man's voice.

"I must be dreaming."

"No. You are awake. Who do you say that I am?"

"The Messiah?"

"Then do as my mother asks. Touch him."

I pinched myself. The room was in color, not black and white. I was awake just as he said.

"Reach."

With tubes and clamps, the pain insisting that I lay still, I lifted out of the bed and to his side. The young man's hand was there before me, close to my reach.

"Pomogite mne!" He called through his darkness. He was saying, "Please help me." I could hear his anguish. I stretched my arms, reaching to his hand. With that, I touched him, and he touched back. He turned his head, not knowing who I was, yet pleading through his bandaged eyes. His hands were coarse and his frame thin. He couldn't have been twenty years old. His face was pale. He trembled. He grabbed me tightly. "Pomogi mne! Gde ya?" He cried for help.

A tray crashed to the floor. "Paul. What—" Hope stood in the doorway.

"Paul—" I heard the lady's voice again. I thought I was hallucinating. Maybe my memory of it tricked me.

"Look, can you see it?" My room filled with people. They pressed towards me like the pilgrims in the ravine near the crevasse. The smell of roses permeated the air. Angelic voices singing praise resounded through the room.

"Paul." Mary's aura glowed in bright light. "You do as I ask. You bless me in doing so."

"I bless you?"

"Yes, Paul. Hail Mary, full of grace. The Lord is with thee. Blessed are you among women. Yes, Paul. You bless me."

"But, I don't understand. I've been so weak."

"No, Paul. Not weak. Brave. It is not the lack of fear and anger that makes us brave. It is living goodness in those feelings that make us so. He in need that gives of himself to another blesses me, and my Son."

"Mother, I'm frightened."

"Yes. I know well of your fear. When all was revealed to me, I carried fear deep in my heart. I knew the day would come when all would manifest and I feared the day."

"How did you do it? How do I—"

"Know this. As I have been sent only as a messenger, there is One whose love endures all things. He is with you always." I peered deeply into her eyes. She gazed into mine. "If you are to heal, then surrender, not to anger, but to the love that radiates from that part of you that is of God. Suspend your cares. Fall prey to His will."

"Just as you did as a young girl?"

"Yes. I will, to will, Thy will. His will is one of love, capable of conquering all things. His love is timeless, filled with the power to suspend even natural forces when harnessed and given freely. It is the cornerstone of miracles provided through heavenly beings that surround you daily, even in the midst of chaos and tragedy. When we are at our worst, when the worst is being done unto us, it is then that we are being provided the opportunity to be most Godly.

"From an earthly perspective this may make little sense. Like all our brothers and sisters, we are linked to the earth by our physical bodies. But our bodies are flesh, made of elements, made of matter, containing energy. A split of any one of our atoms can cause cataclysmic things to happen or Divine will to unfold. This energy is that of our spirit, and that is what we truly are. When our bodies pass away, our spirits remain in tact. Before we are even born, we are that way and we remain that way in the hereafter. We must choose the path.

"Fulfill the quest. Be as John, the disciple my Son so loved. Be as St. John of the Cross. Rapture your soul by reaching out beyond yourself. Allow God to lift you to His level rather than diminishing Him to your own. This day greet your enemy as your friend. Turn the other cheek, and in doing so, witness to the capability of God's Kingdom being firmly established upon the earth.

"Find a world of peace, filled with peaceful people, a world in which creation is expressed in the birth, life, death, and resurrection of these people, a world filled with possibility and wonder. Believe in the faithfulness of a benevolent and loving God. Emulate His will. Through your faith, impact the natural order of things, disasters, limitations, fears, shortcomings, and so much more. Suspend your inability to see God's goodness in yourself and in others.

"Be blind no longer. Accept the Divine gift presented in those who cross your path. Focus not on that which is difficult and tragic so to manifest it in your life. See rather that which is sent by the Divine, missing no longer that which makes it Divine. Blame the Divine no more for its absence. Allow its good to permeate through the armor created by that focus.

"He is loving and benevolent, especially when you feel least disposed to being loved. See in your enemy the light reflected by a universal conscientiousness of the Christ present in him. Although difficult to see in him at first appearance, it is there nevertheless, and in the whole of creation. Find it in your enemy. This will free you.

"Allow grace to free you from those things that divide us and separated our connection to each other and the Divine. Take his wound. Allow it to be your own. Heal yourself through it in witness to Divine providence, recipient of a miraculous occurrence. Remember, I am with you always, even to the ends of time. I love you. I love you. I love—" Her image paled as did her voice. I turned to find the room filled with people, kneeling and praying.

I reached to him, the one who was once my enemy, and cradled him as John had once cradled me. I helped him see even in his blindness. Even in his unknowing, he healed me. Even through our differences we communed, the language of the heart serving as our communion.

Hope touched my shoulder. "You have a phone call. We've gotten through to your wife."

My heart leaped, my breath all but taken away. Finally, I would speak to Anne, telling her of all that I had been through, the loss that I felt, and the love I had for her. For all those unspoken words, I would now be able to say to her those things that really mattered.

"Ya ne nadolg." I released the soldier's hand. Hope positioned a wheelchair under me. She wheeled me to the phone.

"Anne? Anne, is that you?"

"Yes, Paul. Are you okay?"

"Yes, sweetheart. Oh, my God, Anne, I miss you."

"I'm on my way. I'm coming there tomorrow." Her voice drifted in static.

"Anne—"

"I know. They told me."

"Anne, I miss him."

"Yes, I know."

"He—"

"Shh, we'll talk about it when I get there. They say you need to just focus on getting better."

"Yes, I—" More static filled the line. Before I finished, the connection was lost.

"Paul." Hope touched my shoulder. "Are—" A hum of those gathered filled the room. With my victim's victim in the bed before me, I found my humanity. In it all, through it all, I was still alive. Although I knew that I would deal with the loss of John, Marc, and Oleksa for many years, I would find the strength to go on. If for no other reason, I would live to the ideals of love in honor of my friends.

For Andre, I would look at those I met through the eyes of boyhood innocence. For my father, I would search for virtue in them. For Xavier, I would be reminded that every one deserves a second chance. For Oleksa and Marc, I would look to those I met as though they were my family, for they might well be. And for John, I would work as he to help those I met fulfill their quest. This would stand in tribute to their memory. Their sacrifice would live on through me. Their deaths would not be in vain. My life would be their monument.

Twenty-Five

February 1987

The plane jolted. My eyes popped open. "Ladies and gentlemen, the captain has turned on the 'Fasten Seat Belt' sign. We ask . . ." I peered out the porthole at the big orange moon rising into the clear winter night's sky.

Lightening flickered through thunderheads below us. Darkness undulated to light and then back to darkness again. Momentary flashes penetrated the vapory billows casting shadows across the sky.

"Sweetheart?"

I jumped.

"I'm sorry. The flight attendant wants to know if your seat belt is buckled." Anne patted my hand. Her green eyes twinkled. I searched for reassurance that all would be well. Even for all that I had experienced, I could find no solace.

Our inquiries delivered no news of John. I wasn't sure if his body was recovered. At the very least, he deserved a decent burial and a final resting place befitting him. And what of Marc and Oleksa? Didn't they deserve the same courtesy?

I searched the seat back pocket for something to read. With luck, I found a book.

"What's that, sweetie?"

The book slipped through my fingers to the floor. "St. John of the Cross. *Dark Night of the Soul.* I found it in the seat back." The words resounded in my head. "On a dark night, Kindled in love with yearnings—oh, happy chance!"

"More wine?" The flight attendant's sweet voice startled me.

"Yes, please." Maybe another glass would help still my mind.

"Okay?" Anne stroked my hand. The warmth of her touch calmed me. "Why don't you try to rest?"

I reclined my seat and closed my eyes to the hum of the jet engines. With my encounter with the lady now so far removed, my ability to speak about it seemed to remain behind in a distant land. I yearned to share with Anne those thoughts that once clearly resonated in my head and my heart. Yet, the words evaded me.

■

"Sweetheart," Anne whispered. "We're preparing to land."

"What time is it?"

"Four o'clock." Anne peered out of the plane window. "Paul, the river. It's so beautiful." Sunrays rippled off the murky waters as the Mississippi snaked east and west. Shadows formed on it as clouds hid the sun. Towards the west, filtered light cast the sky ablaze in red, orange, pink, and gray. Levees zigzagged with each bend and turn. Even in winter's grasp, the oaks lining the banks sported a dull green coat of leaves. I could all but smell Mim's roux wafting through the grove.

"Ladies and gentlemen, we're on our final approach into New Orleans. Flight attendants . . ." A flight attendant reached over to pickup Anne's coffee cup. "We'll be landing in just a moment." We lifted our seats. Anne grabbed my hand.

A lone egret floated beneath us as the cypress swamps emerged on our final approach. The lime green of floating duckweed once covering the water had vanished into a dried bog. Only clumps of Spanish moss and clutters of palmetto leaves dotted the rust-colored barks of the barren cypress trees.

The wheels of the plane pounced the pavement. Tears streamed from my eyes. "John!"

"Oh, sweetheart, are you okay?"

"I'm so empty." My throat tightened.

"Ladies and gentlemen, we want to be the first to welcome you . . ." The engines purred to a mild hum. The plane slowed to a taxi. I couldn't say anything more.

We reached the gate. The seat belt sign binged off. Overhead bins once closed sprang open. Folks scurried about, quickly gathering their belongings. As they deplaned, Anne and I waited to be escorted off the plane.

"You ready?"

I nodded. My heart hammered. Anne helped me into the wheelchair. As the flight attendant wheeled me down the jetway, Anne walked by my side. She rested her hand gently on my shoulder. I placed my hand on top of hers.

"I've been searching for the ass I've been riding on."

"What's that, sweetheart?"

"Just talking to myself." But this Chinese proverb was true. Everything that I ever really wanted had always been there right beside me. Anne loved me as had John. Why wasn't that enough? Why couldn't I find the words to tell her, to speak of what I had experienced? When? When would I find the strength?

My heart swelled at the sound of Mim's voice. "Suga, dere dey come." Mim stood by Mother. Goose bumps rose from my arms, and my hair stood on the back of my head. Tears streamed down my face as I saw

Mother, Dad, and other family and friends waving to me at the end of the jetway.

We reached the terminal to cheers as they held up a big sign saying, "Welcome Home Paul." I was dizzy from the excitement and overwhelmed by the welcome.

"Thank God you're safe." Mother hugged me.

"Welcome home, son." Dad stroked my head. They stood there for a few minutes just looking at me. Tears filled everyone's eyes.

"Sho' is good—" Big John stepped forward.

"Move out ma way so I can git a look at 'im." Big John moved aside as Mim pushed forward. "I gonna tell ya one thing, I'm gonna fatten ya up. Come here and give me a hug, child." Her bosoms almost smothered me. "I'm tellin' ya naw, don't put another foolish notion about leavin' again. Ya hear me!"

"Yes, ma'am."

"Aren't ya gonna say hello?" In the midst of the excitement, I heard a voice. I turned and looked through the crowd.

Mim beamed. "We've gotta a surprise for ya." So much energy poured through me I felt delirious. Mom, Dad, all of them grew silent.

Anne looked at me. Tears started pouring from her eyes. I searched in hope of finding him, yet knowing it couldn't be possible. I had left him behind, having seen him fall. Yet, I heard it again. This time it was louder. "Man, ya can't even find me when I'm right there by ya. How the hell did we make it through all that shit with your inability to see the obvious?"

"John?".

His arms reached around me as he pulled Anne to us.

"How?"

"I just arrived this mornin' on a military transport."

"The bullet?"

"Only a flesh wound. I pretended to be hurt. Oleksa's cousin hid me until I could get out."

"Tell me. Oleksa—"

"Recovering, but okay."

"And Marc?"

John looked away. "Let's grab a seat."

Anne led the family. "Everyone, let's give them a few minutes."

John wheeled me to a remote section of the terminal. "I was with Marc when he died. He told me that if anything happened to him, he wanted you to have somethin'." John placed a neatly wrapped package in my hand. I untied the string and peeled the brown paper open.

"I—" Blood rushed to my head.

"It belonged to his grandfather."

I placed the yarmulke carefully on my head. Lifting my hands to my face, I pressed my fingers to my forehead. With my eyes closed and head bowed, I took a slow deep breath. As I released the air, I recited the words that Jesus himself spoke. "Sherma, Israel, Adonai, Elohainu, Adonai, Echod." I looked at John. He returned the stare. "Just let this be real." I prayed in earnest.

"What's that, pal?"

"If this is a dream and I wake up and you're not here—"

"It's real and I'm alive. Let's go home." The wheelchair squeaked as John turned it. I lifted my hand back over my shoulder. His hand gripped mine.

Laughter and celebration echoed from the terminal as we moved towards Anne and the family. Dad nudged John. "So, tell me. Did Paul behave for you overseas?"

I stared John down. "Don't you dare."

"And resist an entrée like this. Just sit your scrawny little butt in that chair." A devilish grin swept across John's face. "Y'all gotta know Paul slept with another man."

"What?" Anne reacted in surprise.

"He was naked and everything. I tell ya, that boy can shuck clothes off faster—"

"You pulled my clothes off because I was soaking wet and we were freezing."

"Who are y'all gonna believe? Me, or mighty mouth here?" Everyone roared with laughter. John survived probably to tell that story. This story once paralyzed me with fear, but not now.

Francis greeted us at the curbside. "I got de bags. Dey in da car."

Mother directed everyone to the rides. "Anne, Paul, John, Mim, y'all ride with us. The rest will follow in two other cars." The car door slammed. The green dome of the main terminal faded as we joined the line of cars along Airline Highway.

"Mother, where are Grandmother and Grandfather?"

"They're waiting at home. We've got quite a few folks waiting to see you."

Anne lowered her sunglasses. "Miss Renee, that's a beautiful dress."

"This old thing. Suga, we've got to go shopping . . ."

I looked towards John. Even with Marc's loss, I was happy for God's gift in bringing John back safely. Maybe happy endings did happen.

We crossed the Mississippi, and then made our way to U.S. Highway 90. The cypress trees were barren. The low water levels exposed their knees.

"Whacha thinkin' about?" John whispered.

"Ever notice how cypress knees look like people?"

"Yeah. All the time."

I searched for one that looked like Marc, even as they zipped by.

We crossed the Des Allemands bridge. Wild ducks and poldeau, coot as they were called elsewhere, floated on the waters of the bayou. The skies above the marshlands surrounding the highway teemed with egrets, duck, red-winged blackbirds, and more. The marsh grass swayed in the wind as clear blue skies greeted us.

The car turned onto Highway 308. We wound north along the banks of Bayou Lafourche, greeted once more by oak trees and Spanish moss. The white billows of above ground tombs peered from the graveyard across the bayou as we drove past St. Mary's Nativity Church. There, members of my family rested.

Sugarcane fields lay barren from the harvest. The milky white soil of the rows, melted by rainfall, looked crusted over. Only the oaks lining the small plantations along the way stood covered in green.

We drove under the railroad bridge of Lafourche Crossing. Oak Grove awaited us just a little farther north. My heart started beating faster. Dad nudged me. "Excited to be home?"

"Yes, sir."

"I gonna tell ya right naw, he's gonna put some meat on dem bones of his. Ya here me, child?"

"Yes, ma'am."

Francis turned into the white gates surrounding the house. We steered through the oaks. He slowed the car. There Oak Grove stood, draped in her Mardi Gras regalia, the purple, green, and gold flags sporting the crown of Mardi Gras royalty.

The words of Longfellow rang out in my ears:

Near to the banks of the river, o'ershadowed by oaks
from whose branches
Garlands of Spanish moss and mystic mistletoe flaunted,
Such as the Druids cut down with golden hatchets at Yuletide,
Stood, secluded and still, the house of the herdsman. A garden
Girded it round about with a belt of luxuriant blossoms,
Filling the air with fragrance. The house itself was of timbers
Hewn from the cypress-tree, and carefully fitted together.
Large and low was the roof; and on slender columns supported,
Rose-wreathed, vine-encircled, a broad and spacious veranda,
Haunt of the humming-bird and the bee, extended around it.

Cars lined the entrance. We drove around to the porte cochere. It looked like a hundred people waited with signs. "Welcome home." I hugged Grandmother and then Grandfather amidst shots and well wishing. The plantation bell rang. All grew silent as Grandmother led us in the Angelus. "The angel of the Lord declared unto Mary—" Three times the bell sounded as we recited the Hail Mary. I was home. At last, I was home.

The party raged until late. Friends and family departed. Oak Grove grew quiet.

Anne placed a couple of extra logs on the fire, stoking the flames for a late night conversation. "Good night." She brought a snifter of our favorite brandy to John and me.

"Where are you going?"

"Up to bed."

"You complete me." I kissed her. Anne caressed my neck then quietly slipped from the room, leaving John and me alone.

"So what now?"

"Oh, John. I can't think past tomorrow right now."

"Yeah. I'll give that a week."

John and I sat quietly until the fire waned. With the embers slowly burning down, he turned to me. I looked into his eyes. He reached over and hugged me. I returned the sentiment. There we sat, safe at last, free from that which we yearned. Our journey was complete.

"I was noticin' the quilt in your bedroom, the embroidery. It kinda reminds me of—"

I sprang up. "Follow me."

"Take it easy. The last thing I need is to have to get ya to a hospital tonight."

"Look, we're not in the Ukraine anymore, so go easy with the orders."

"That'll be the day."

"Just shut up and come with me." With everyone fast asleep we slipped up the staircase. Searching the walls of the upstairs hallway, I ran my hands against the boards where once I had discovered the passageway to the hidden room.

"What are ya doin'?"

"Shh. Watch." My fingers detected the slightest ridge. Pushing on the wall, I tried to open it, but it did not move. I stepped back five feet to gather a better look. The dimly lit hallway made it difficult to see.

"What are you lookin' for?"

"A secret passageway."

"What? Are you still doped up?"

"No. Be quiet so we don't wake anyone." A knot in the baseboard caught my attention. I tipped-toed to it. I pressed on it. The wall popped out.

"I'll be damned!"

"Shh." The hinges creaked as we opened the door. I rubbed my hand against the wall to guide us up the narrow staircase. Waving my hands in the air, I grabbed the string to the overhead light. With a pull it clicked on. The lone trunk stood in the middle of the floor.

"I'll be damned."

"Go close the door." While John snuck down, I opened the trunk. I froze. There on top of the embroidered-edged quilt lay the statue.

"Where the hell did that come from?"

I lifted the icon. Beneath it, the leather bound book I had once read sat in the right corner.

John loosened the cover straps. "St. John of the Cross. It looks like his original writings." The letter I had once started to read fell to the floor. "What's that?"

"Here. Read it."

"It's in French."

"I'll translate."

"I love my family and always will. But, to the Virgin I have consecrated my life. Even though they choose to leave France, I will not follow. Rather, I with my wife will travel to Spain. There I will reside faithful to the vow once made. Pierre Paul Guidry, 11 November 1611."

"Are there any more?"

"I don't know. I was never able to get back up here." We flipped the pages to the rear. There another letter lay, the ink bleeding through the parchment. The single page crinkled as I opened it.

"My dearest family:

I can only hope this letter reaches you. I am an old man, soon to die. I have many regrets in my life, but none more than that I never saw you again. Through it all, I hope that you know that my life has not been in vain. For of man I may have failed. But, of God I hope to have been His faithful servant.

In my journeys I have encountered much. On my last pilgrimage I met a man who calls himself, John of the Cross, and a woman, Teresa of Avila. Their writings have possessed me, just as the Lady of my prayers. As with John, I have lived many a dark night, none more beautiful than that night in which the Lady appeared to me and my men. It is through this that I have dedicated my life. I have done so in reparation for my many sins.

I have in the past days peacefully defended a shrine dedicated to Our Lady, hewed in the mountains of the Carpathians. My wife, Marguerite lies entombed there. Soon I will join her, as in laying down my arms I received wounds that are serious. I pray for those who have harmed me as I ask for forgiveness for all I have hurt in my life.

I have attached with this letter fabric embroidered by my beloved Marguerite. My hope is that this reaches you so together we create color and texture, weaving intricate threads of goodness and kindness to those in need. This will have us live through you forever.

This holy man, who calls himself John of the Cross, tells me we are all wounded. He, through his prayer and devotion, has shown me that we must reach to others through our woundedness. In this, we find the courage to reach in love rather than hate, to rejoice in hope rather than despair, to live in grace rather than guilt. It is he who has guided me to surrender my armament and defend the faith in hope and in charity.

Remember, in death we only find life, cradled in the care of the One who loves us. May you have the faith to be at peace, filled with prosperity, surrounded by abundance, living in joy, and sharing harmony with all of God's creation. You will find me as part of that creation in the leaves of the trees or a gentle breeze that blows by you. Until we meet, I shall watch over you from the stars. Pablo."

I stored the letter back into the book. The leather binding whined as I closed it. There painted on its cover was the family crest with the motto inscribed, "Je mourrai pour quex j'aime." I looked at John. "I guess you are my brother."

"What?"

"I would die for those who I love. That's what you did. You would have died for me."

"And you for me."

The room filled with the aroma of roses. A light glowed. The image of the lady filled the corner.

"Hail Mary—"

The End